I dedicate this boo[k]  that could never be repla[ced;] love and influence contin[ues to inspire my] dreams: Josephine Rebec[ca ....,] [you had my] heart and because of you, I am still searching for other people like you. Becky, I love and miss you, but always know that you have my back and are watching over me. Michael Bowens; we weren't the best of friends, but as a young man, I watched your style and swag at hair school. You were an inspiration to me as a young gay man. For that, I thank you. Gone but never forgotten; thanks to my young cousins and young friend Danitzia Pasillas, Jaclyn Pasillas, Alejandro Pasillas, Dominic Valdez and Todd Francis. Your spirits continue to motivate me...Special thanks to: Keisha Simmons and Patrice Basanta-Henry, for taking the time to be supportive and for reading my book...To mom and dad; thank you for your support through all of my endeavors. To Shamus William Smith; thanks for being an encouraging little brother! Love ya! And a special big thanks to my baby and other half JJ...I Love you!!!

J. Martinez

Chapter 1: The Beginning

My name is Gustavo Huerta. I'm 37. I'm gay and I am HIV Negative. To say the least, this life has been a roller coaster. I say that because as I sit here, thoughts begin to roll around in my head just like the twists and turns on a carnival ride. On this day, the ride takes me back to when me and my twin brother Hector were nine years old. I'm thinking about the happier times before our lives became a nightmare. I don't like to think about nightmares. But we lived through one. It happened and it was a part of my childhood. We were growing up in Sacramento, California back then. Waking up, there were some good days and bad days. But this morning in particular promised to be good just because it was the first day of school and the beginning of what I expected to be a great fourth grade year at Caleb Greenwood Elementary School. It was close to our house in Oak Park. I wondered if anyone from my third grade class was gonna be there. I woke up, pushed Hector on his forehead and said, "Wake up! We're going to school." He said, "Shut up, bitch!" I didn't pay him no attention. I took a shower, jumped out and ran to my closet to pull out my All Stars that my Tia Loose bought us. I had a green and red pair, but I wanted to wear one of each like Punky Brewster. I love the way she dressed. I put on my Miller's Outpost jeans and Mervyns T shirt. I ran downstairs so excited! I loved having upstairs and downstairs. It made me feel rich like Arnold and Willis on Diff'rent Strokes. I just loved that show. Our family was the only one in the neighborhood whose house had two stories. I went downstairs to see if my mom maybe cooked for us. She used to cook all the time but lately, we've been eating Church's Chicken and Lil' Caesar's pizza. I ran back upstairs and stood in front of her door. I knew it was locked, so I knocked. No answer. I only knocked once then went back downstairs and fixed me and Hector a bowl of Lucky Charms. He came downstairs and turned on the TV to watch He-Man. Trying to control my temper, I hissed, "Hector, eat your food or we're gonna be late!" He said, "Shut the fuck up!" in a whisper, but I heard him. We walked up the street and caught the bus and headed to school-me and my brother Hector. As my stomach slowly returned to normal, I found myself telling no one in particular, "I love him so much even though he said I'm a fag like Boy George. He thinks he's being mean but I think Boy George is beautiful and I would love to look like him." After school, we both jumped off the bus and ran home. My mom was up and said, "Hi, Mijitos. Sorry I missed sending you off to school today, but I had a headache." I thought to myself, *She always has a headache.* "How was school, Gustavo?" mom asked. "It was fun," I said. Hector blurted out, "All he did was talk in class and hang around those girls Lorena and Lupita." My mom responded, "I don't like you talking to Lupita. She's *cochina.* What types of girls call a boy all time of the night and she's only nine?" I said, "Mom, she's my best friend!" My mom said, "Well you better not be doing anything nasty with her, Mijito because I don't trust *putas* like that." "*Putas like that,"* I thought to myself. "*Yuck! I don't even like girls*." But I loved Lupita and Lorena. They were my best friends. "Go upstairs and do your homework," my mom said. "Dinner will be ready in a minute and your dad has something exciting to tell you." My stomach turned when she said the word Dad. Sometimes, I wished he were dead. I said it out loud once to Hector and he got mad at me. He punched me in my stomach. It hurt really bad. Hector's strong, but I'm strong too. One time, he threw my Barbie away that my Tia Loose bought me. I picked him up and slammed him like Andre the Giant slammed Big John Stud on the Friday Night Main Event. He cried. My mom got mad at me but she also winked. I think she was finally happy to see I was fighting Hector back. She always hated to see me cry when Hector or my dad were mean to me or hit me. "What's Dad have to tell, Mom?" Hector shouted. "Mijo, he will tell us when he gets home," she answered. "Are we going to Disneyland?" I asked. "Mijo, what did I just tell you and Hector? Now go upstairs." Hector asked, "Can I ride my bike?" "For 30 minutes. And then take your shower and get ready for dinner," she said. She always made Hector take a shower before he ate because he would fall asleep as soon as he finished eating. I said, "Mom, can I talk on the phone for 30 minutes?" I asked. She said, "Yes, Mijo." Back then, I loved when mom called me Mijo because I felt like she was happy and she loved me. I ran upstairs and dialed Lupita.

The phone rings and I scream our secret made up greeting, "Hi, *pinche calaweta*!!" I hear, "Who is this? Is this Gustavo?" the voice says. I hang up. I think it's Lupita's grandma. She scares me a little. Usually, Lupita answers the phone. Me and her are the only people I know who have three-way calling. I love to call her because we always prank call people. My mom got three-way when my tio was in prison. My dad hates my Tio Julian. He says Julian is Mexican trash. My dad doesn't know we have three-way. He would be pissed at my mom. But my mom got it so Julian can call his girlfriends. One time I heard him say to this lady on the phone, "I want to lick that white pussy and cum in your mouth." I thought to myself, *"What is cum?"* I was kinda grossed out after hearing the way he was talking to her, so I don't pick up the phone when my mom calls his girlfriend for him on three-way. He doesn't call that much anyway because my mom has to be careful my dad doesn't find out. Yeah, my dad hates Julian, but I love him. He is nice to me and I love my cousins Julian, Jr. and his brother Mario. Hector and I love going to their house. Their mama's name is Gina. She's so classy and pretty. She looks like Diana Ross-a Mexican Diana Ross. My cousins can rap, dance, fight-they can do it all! Hector and me love them. We always want to go over there but they're in high school and are busy. I want to be just like them when I grow up. I looked at the phone and dialed again. This time, I was calling Lorena. "Hello?" the voice said. "Hi, may I speak to Lorena?" The man on the other end was Victor, Lorena's dad. "Hi, Gustavo," he said. "No, you can't. She's doing her homework. Can I give her a message?" I said, "Can you tell her to call me back?" "Not tonight," he said. "But you can talk to her in school tomorrow." "Ok." After a short pause he said, "Shouldn't you be doing your homework?" "Yes." Another brief silence... "Good, Gustavo. Have a nice night." "Bye," I said and hung up. I loved Lorena's dad. Every time he came for parent's day at our old school, he would sit down and it looked like he had a piñata in his pants. I always wanted to kiss him. He was fine. He was tall with curly black hair. I wanted a curly perm just like his. I gazed at the phone again and decided to call Lupita again. The phone rang and she picked up. "Hello?" I screamed again, "Hi, *pinche calaweta*!!!!" Lupita spoke back in a hushed voice. "What's wrong, Lupita?" "My mom died." "I'm sorry, Lupita." Then she quickly said, "I gotta go," and hung up. I felt bad. I went to the TV because I didn't feel like doing homework. Our real teacher, Miss Nava wasn't even at school. Her substitute was some woman-I did know that much. She said Ms. Nava wouldn't return the next day either because she was still under the weather. I turned the TV on in our room. It was black and white. We had a color TV in the living room and in our parent's room. But I liked the black and white TV in our room. I feel safe when I'm in our room. "What's Happening!!" is on. I love this show. I wish I were Dee. She's cute and funny. I guess I fell asleep because the next thing I hear is my mom say, "Come downstairs, Gustavo." I run downstairs. "Wash your hands-both of you!" Hector was sitting at the table and jumped up out of his seat to race me to the bathroom. My mom screamed for us to stop running. As I was washing my hands, I heard my dad's car pull up. I got this strange feeling. Hector and I both walked back to the kitchen and sat at the table. When we were little we ate at breakfast, lunch and dinner at the table. But lately, it was only breakfast and dinner sometimes. My mom has so many headaches she lets us eat wherever, even in our rooms. My father worked nights but sometimes we didn't see him for weeks. My mom looked happy to see him when he walked in. She went up to him and kissed him on the lips, but he turned his face. He didn't look happy. "Mijitos, your dad has a surprise for you," she said. I screamed out, "Is it Disneyland or Hollywood so we can see Madonna and Prince?" My dad looked at me and said, "Shut the fuck up, you *pinche hotto.*" I immediately started crying. My mom came over to hug me. Thomas-that's what I call my dad when he acts crazy-he just stood there in disgust. As my mom hugged me, he screamed, "You're a fuckin' nasty *puta*, Belinda you fuckin' lazy bitch! You don't do shit all day and then you try to fuckin' embarrass me in front of my fuckin' sons you fuckin' nasty whore!" My mom walked towards the bathroom. I stopped crying but was shaking. Hector was looking at the tortillas that were sitting in the middle of the table. Thomas went to the fridge, grabbed some vodka from the freezer and then poured it into a drinking glass. I heard my mom walking back into the kitchen. She calmly said, "Thomas, are you ready to eat?" she said with a straight face. Thomas looked at my mom and said mean tone, "Belinda, do you know how hard it is to be a Mexican-American man?" Silence. "Do you, bitch?!" His thundering voice shook the walls. "I've worked at the fuckin' prison for 10 years-day and night-as a correctional officer and can't be promoted because I'm Mexican. Bitch, do you know what that feels like, *puta?!*" Silence. "I'm talking to you!" Thomas screamed again. My mom calmly said, "No Thomas, I don't and I'm sorry." Before I knew it I zoned out. My stomach was sinking to my feet. "Think...just think," I repeat to myself. My thoughts return to getting on the bus and seeing Kevin, Hector's best friend. I'm so happy that he is going to Caleb Greenwood with us. Hector told me he might be going to another school so when I see him, my ears feel red and my knees are weak. I've liked him ever since first grade. We kissed in the bathroom in second grade and I fell in love with him. We haven't kissed since then. He always has girls liking him. I think even Lupita likes him. I told her we kissed. I even told her and Lorena I was gay. They are my best friends because they never told anybody and they always stick up for me when Hector's not around too. As soon as happy thoughts consumed my mind, Thomas grabbed my mom by her hair and started punching her in her face. Hector immediately jumped up and started landing his own blows on my dad's back. He always dove in when Thomas beat her. I just stood there. Before I knew it, Hector was thrown across the kitchen by Thomas who then turned his attention to dragging my mom towards the stairs. I ran at them screaming, "Stop! Stop! Stop!" Usually, fear gripped me not allowing my feet to move when Thomas beat her. But this time was different. I ran to the phone and screamed, "I'm going to call the police!" As I tried to dial 911, I was slapped so hard Thomas put me to sleep. When I woke up, my head was hurting. The house was so quiet. I couldn't hear a sound. My back was sore and it hurt when I walked. But I went to look in the kitchen to see what happened. I wasn't sure if I was dreaming until I saw the broken vodka bottle on the floor. I then went to the window to see if Thomas' car was outside. It was gone and I was happy. I stepped over the glass and walked towards the stairs hoping he would never come back. Thomas was so mean.

Chapter 2: Daydreamin'

I walked up the stairs and looked in our room. Nothing. I went up the hall and walked up to my mom's door to see Hector rubbing her back. As I walked in, I could hear her crying. But it was such a low and quiet cry. Hector looked at me and put his finger to his face to silence me. I walked around the side of the bed so I could say something nice to my mom but as I walked over, I saw her face. She looked... almost Chinese because her eyes were closed but I think they were open. Just as she looked at me, the low cry turned into a loud scream. I jumped back because it scared me. "Mijito, look at your face!" She sat up to get a closer look but let out another scream as she tried to crawl towards me in the bed. She said, "Mijito, I'm so sorry!" holding her hands out to me. So, I went over to hug her gently because I didn't want to hurt her. "Mommy, it's Ok." I then looked over at Hector. He looked like he was frozen. But just like that, my mom said, "Boys, go clean up and get ready for bed. If you're hungry, eat some cereal or make a sandwich or some tacitos with the frijoles and papas I made."
She then got up, looking more like my *ouilita*, and walked towards the bedroom door. "Come on Mijitos. Do what I told you." We both walked out the room and Hector looked back.
When I turned around she said, "Boys I love you very much. Always remember that." As she was closing the door, I saw fresh tears seep from her swollen eyes. I heard her turn the lock. I looked at Hector and he put his arms around me. We went into our room and took our showers, ate some papa tacos and went to sleep. The next morning, I woke up excited to go to school. I didn't have to wake Hector up because I could hear the TV downstairs. I knew it was him so I went down to see if Thomas was home. I ran to the kitchen window to see if his car was there. It wasn't. I walked into the living room and saw Hector was already dressed and watching *Bewitched*. He turned to me with a blank stare and said, "You can't go to school today." I loudly said, "Yes, I can!" "No you can't. Dad called and said if

there was a mark on your face you couldn't go and I'm looking at your face and it looks kinda purple." As soon as Hector said that I ran to the restroom and looked in the mirror and thought I looked like how my mom sometimes looks. Thomas never really hit me a lot. He would just say mean things to me like hotto, fag and dick sucker. But sometimes I would rather he beat us then beat our mom. I went back into the living room to watch TV with Hector but he got up and said I gotta go to school. He came up to me and gave me a hug and kiss on my cheek. He was always super nice to me when something bad happened. I just loved my brother. Hector left so I just watched TV until noon. *All My Children* was over and the news was coming on. That meant I had an hour to eat and take a shower before O*ne Life to Live* and *General Hospital* came on. I just loved Tina on O*ne Life to Live*. Her long, red hair and bangs were perfect. I just loved her evil ways-how she was mean and sexy. I went to the kitchen to eat before my shower when I heard a knock at the door. I walked over to the kitchen window so I could see if I recognized the car. It was a green Pinto that I had never seen before. I got on my tippy toes and looked out the peephole but all I could see was a white beard. "Who is it," I said. "It's Warren. I'm a friend of your dad's." I rolled my eyes and opened the door. I jumped back a little because he looked like Hulk Hogan. He had long, white hair and a beard. He had muscles and he also smelled like cigarettes. I just stood there and looked at him. He kneeled down and got right in my face and said, "You must be Gustavo!" I tried to plug my nose because his breath smelled like caca. But just as I went to put my hands to my nose, he grabbed my face and put his big hands on my chin and said, "Yeah, you must be Gustavo! Look at your pretty face and your eyes. You look so good, I could eat you up!" I just looked at him. He said, "Give this to your mother. She's been waiting for it." I looked down and it was a Hello Kitty plastic bag. I love Hello Kitty. Lupita has everything Hello Kitty. Her grandma buys her it all the time. He stood up and walked away backwards just staring at me. As the smell went away I looked at him. He was cute and I never seen muscles that big.

My cousins have muscles but not like his. They were much bigger. He gave me a girl wave and so I gave him one back and said, "Bye, Warren." Then he winked his eye. I looked in the Hello Kitty bag to see what was in it. It was a paper bag with tape around it. I ran upstairs to knock on my mom's bedroom door. But I didn't think she was going to answer because when my dad hit her or she had a headache, we wouldn't see her for a while. I knocked real hard three times and then headed back downstairs to watch TV. I looked at the clock. It was almost 12:30 and I hadn't taken a shower. I love taking showers and then using the blow dryer. It always makes me happy. I ran back downstairs to catch up with Tina and *One Life to Live* when the phone rang. "Hello," "Hi, Mijito. What you doing home for school?" my Aunt Loose asked. I told her I didn't feel well. "Oh really?" she said. "Well, I was going to take you and Hector to the 29 cent hamburger stand after school. Did you want to go?" "Yes!" I screamed. I loved the 29-cent hamburger stand. It looked just like McDonalds but with a black and white sign. Hector came home around 4 p.m. I yelled, "What happened at school?" Hector ignored my question and just said, "Miss Nava is fine!" "Who's Miss Nava?" I asked absently. "Our teacher, queer," Hector said. I walked up to Hector and gave him a Benny Hill. A Benny Hill is a slap on the forehead. My cousin Julian, Jr. did it to us every time we were around. I hated getting a Benny Hill but loved my cousin Julian, Jr. As soon as I hit Hector, he punched me in the face and it hurt from where Thomas had slapped me. The pain raced in all directions throughout my body. It hurt so bad and made me so angry that I picked Hector up and slammed him on the ground. He landed with a thud and started kicking but I still jumped on him and we were fighting. "Stop it!" I heard, but I didn't stop and neither did Hector. Before I knew it, my Tia Loose had me by my ear and hair and said, "What's wrong with you two?" "You're brothers! You and are not supposed to be fighting like that. You guys looked like you were going to kill each other." Hector got off the ground and my tia looked at me. "Gustavo, what happened to your face? Did Hector do that?" "Yes!" I lied. She looked at Hector. He said nothing. I didn't want to tell her Thomas did it because my tia didn't like anyone hitting on us-especially not Thomas. My tia was sassy. She was sassy and she was sexy. And she had the best curly perm I ever saw. Even the banana clip in her hair was hot. She kinda looked like Lisa Lisa. I just saw that video, *I Wonder if I Take You Home*. Lisa Lisa was beautiful and so was my tia except my tia was dark like me and Hector. We were brown like my dad. My mom was light. She almost looked white and she had green eyes like me. People have told me how cute I was ever since I could remember. They would say it wherever we went-the grocery store, department store-wherever. Gustavo and Hector were the cutest twins they'd ever seen. Suddenly, my aunt said, "Look, there's glass here. Who broke it?" Hector and me looked at each other and didn't say a word. "Get a broom and pick it up," she said. "I'm going to fix my make up then put some ice on your eye and then we can go eat." I picked up the glass and my tia said, "Mijito, this looks bad." She put some peroxide and ice on it and said, "Ok, it looks like the swelling is going down. Let's go eat and then we'll work on it some more when we get to Grandma's house." We walked out of the house and headed to her candy red Mustang. I thought, When I grow up I want a candy red Mustang. It was beautiful. We got our food at the 29-cent hamburger stand and sat down. I had cheeseburgers and fries. Hector had three hamburgers, two orders of fries and a Coke. He said he didn't like the spaghetti they had for lunch at school. My tia looked at us and said, "Mijitos, you know I love you both very much! So, I have to tell you something but you have to keep it a secret, ok?" she asked in a serious voice. "Ok," we both said. She paused before blurting out, "I'm moving to L.A. to start my acting career!" She was looking at us as if she wanted us to be excited. "Me and Chris are going." My heart sank down to my stomach. I didn't want her to go. When I wasn't outside playing or on the phone having fun, I wanted to be with my tia. She loved us so much. She was my favorite relative next to my mom. I begged her not to go. "I have to Mijitos. Chris and me need a change and he has family in L.A. I can't do movies and TV living in Sacramento," she complained. "Besides, Latina actresses are in demand in L.A. Look at Maria Conchita Alonzo and Charro…Well, Chris told me I'm wasting my looks here so I'm going to listen to him and we're going to go this weekend," she said as if her mind was made up. "I'm not telling anyone. Chris said it would be best. But soon as I get situated, you guys can come down and we will have some fun!" I said I wanted to meet Appolonia and Vanity. "See there, another Latina," my tia said. "Appolonia! I forgot about her. If her *chee chees* could be in a movie then my *nalgas* can be on TV too." She got up and started dancing like Charro. Hector and me started laughing. We went back to my Grandma's house. When we pulled up, there was a fancy car in the driveway. Chris got out the passenger side and gave my tia a kiss. I love my tia but wished it could be me. Chris was tall and skinny with pretty, light brown hair. He kinda looked white but he talked like a *vato*. Thomas hates *vatos*. He says they're trash. Chris said, "*Oadale,* homies!" Hector said *oadale* back and I said hi. "We're ready to go," he told my tia. "Come back around 10," she said. "I want to spend some time with the boys." Then he looked at me and said, "*Vato*, what happened to your face?" I didn't say anything. I just kept quiet. "They were fighting," my tia informed him. Chris looked at Hector and said, "It looks like you can throw down! You two pretty *vatos* don't need to be fighters. You need to be lovers." My tia said, "Be quiet! They're too young. They need to concentrate on school." Chris looked back at her and said, "Ok, I'll be back at 10." She gave him a kiss and said ok. We all got out the car and headed towards my Grandma's door. As me and Hector went up the driveway, my tia walked Chris to the car. He got in and she said to the driver, "Hey, Smiley. I'll see you two later," "Ok, Loose," Smiley said. I looked at Smiley. He looked like a Mexican Jabba the Hut. He was fat and looked mean but he seemed nice. They left and we walked into the house. It was cold in my grandma's house and always super clean. She and my mom were the same. She was always in her room. My mom said she got headaches a lot but Thomas said she was a drunk bitch. When we saw her, she was nice but that wasn't often. It was almost like my tia lived there by herself. My tia was perfect. She could clean, cook, dance and would sock a girl up in a minute. I saw her fight. She even almost fought our dad one time when he hit my mom. My mom said her sister could handle herself because when she was little, my uncle Julian would beat her ass if she didn't cook or clean up my grandma's house. He was mean to her, so she doesn't like him just like my dad doesn't. My tia said, "Let's put some ice on your eye. Then we will watch Cujo." I said, "What's that?" She said it was a movie about a killer dog Chris had bought for her when he bought her a VCR. I thought to myself, I can't wait until we get a VCR. I'm going to love it and watch movies all the time. It was 10:30 and my heart was racing. And Hector looked like he was scared to walk outside to my tia's car. We had just finished watching Cujo. "Come on boys," Tia Loose said. "I need to take you home. It's late and you have school tomorrow." I already knew I wasn't going because my face looked bad. We got in her car and she was playing this song I never heard before called, *Look out Weekend.* I said, "tia, who sings that?" she said Debbie Deb. I told my tia I liked her but had never seen her on Friday Night Videos. I felt sad because before we left my grandma's house, I saw my tia's suitcase in the driveway. She must have put them out there while we were watching Cujo. We pulled up to our house and it was pitch dark. Thomas' car wasn't there. I was glad. We walked in, closed the door and turned on the lights. My tia started calling out, "Belinda! Belinda! Belinda!" She walked up stairs and knocked on my mom's bedroom door. "Belinda, I need to talk to you." She stood there for a minute and then said, "Are you ok, Belinda?" Not a sound came from my mom's room. "Ok, Belinda. If you don't answer this door, I'm going to call the police." Just then, my mom yelled, "I have a headache, Loose! I will call you *manana.*" Tia said, "I'm going to be busy tomorrow. I have a letter I want you to read. Gustavo! Bring me my purse." I wondered why she always asked me and never Hector to bring her purse. I grabbed her bag from the kitchen table and ran upstairs to give it to her. "Thanks, Mijo," she said. "Belinda, I'm going to put it under your door. I love you, Belinda...I love you!"

As my tia turned from the door, she really started crying. I'd never seen my tia cry like that before. It made me sad. "Tia, are you ok?" I asked. "Yes, Mijito," she said before turning to walk me downstairs. "Hector. Come here." She sat on a chair and looked at us. Even through her tears-which by now were melting her makeup-she was striking. Her face was just as pretty as Vanity from the group Vanity Six. My tia then said, "I love you boys very much and I want you to know that. You boys are good looking and smart and can do or be anything you want to be when you grow up. I'm going to L.A. and Hollywood to become famous and as soon as we get our place, I will send for you. I love you guys and I will call you in a week with our new phone number." I started crying a little. Then we both hugged and kissed her goodbye. I thought to myself, pretty soon we will be in Los Angeles with her. Yay, I said in my head. A week went by. We hadn't gotten a call from tia and Thomas had not been home. I was ready for school though because my face was better. I couldn't wait to go and see Lupita and Lorena. But I really wanted to see Kevin. I didn't get to see him much the first day of school because we weren't in the same fourth grade class. He had Mr. Norton, a chubby little white man who looked like a real life Fred Flintstone. Kevin and Hector always sit next to each other on the bus with their other friends. Every day, Hector and me walk to the bus stop together. We get on the bus and Hector sits with his friends. Every single time. I sit with Stephanie, a beautiful coffee-colored black girl. She's my friend. We've known each other since pre-school. I like her a lot. I love when she plays foursquare or tether ball because her beads and braids swing all over the place. My dad always said her family was trash because her mother stays in and out of jail and her dad is locked up in the prison where my dad works. She used to have a phone and we all talked on three-way for a while, but I think her phone was cut off. Lupita and Lorena like Stephanie too. She's funny and has an angelic voice. She's always singing church songs. "What's been up, Stephanie?" "Nothing, child. Miss Nava is giving a lot of homework but I do it as soon as I get home. "Did you finish yours?" she asked, twisting her neck and narrowing her eyes with a knowing look. "Yes. Hector brought it home," I said. "It was hard but we figured it out." Stephanie shot back, "Why didn't you ask your mama?" I didn't want to talk about that so I changed the subject. "Do you think Miss Nava is pretty? I asked. "She just look like a light skin bitch," Stephanie said. We both started laughing. "Her shoes were nice though. She had on high heels I've never seen before. My mama used to wear high heels two years ago but every time she goes to jail somebody steals them from my grandma's house." "Who steals them?" I asked.

"Probably my uncles. They're trifling." "What's trifling?" I quizzed her. She said, "It means it don't make any sense." Then we started laughing again. Every time I'm with Stephanie, I get a great feeling. She's so funny. We pulled up to the front of the school and get off the bus. As we were walking I stopped suddenly. I had left my bag on the bus, so I told Stephanie I would catch up. I waited for some kids to move so that I could get back on the bus. Just then, Hector and Kevin were getting off. "I forgot my back pack," I told my brother. He did a head nod like a vato to let me know it was cool. He's so protective of me. My mom loves that about him. He can be so mean to me but no one else can. I went to my seat, which was second to the front because I have liked to sit in the front since first grade because some kids stink and fart and I don't want to throw up. I walked off the bus and headed to the cafeteria. Some kids get free breakfast. We don't because are dad makes too much money. Plus, that food is nasty. But Kevin always ate it even when we were in first, second and third grade.

Chapter 3: Me and Kevin

I walk towards the cafeteria when I here, "Psst! Psst!" I look over and it's Kevin standing in the boys' bathroom telling me to come over. My heart started beating fast and my ears felt like they were on fire. I was so nervous. I didn't know what he was going to say. I walked in the bathroom. He locked the door and said, "I miss your green eyes." Then he kissed me. But this time with his tongue. He told me to open my mouth. So I did. He grabbed my hand and put it on his penis. I had never felt a real penis. I had thought about it but never touched one. We kept kissing until we heard the bell ring. We had 10 minutes before class started. He took my hands out of his pants and put his whole mouth on my ear and said, "I love you." I felt like I was going to faint. He was so gorgeous...smooth, brown skin like mine and a thick Jherri curl. He smelled like baby lotion. After he stopped sucking on my ear, he kissed me again on the lips and said, "Talk to you later." He unlocked the door and was gone. I stood there so confused.

I'd never kissed anyone like that-or held a dick. *I love him!* I thought to myself. I went to pee then headed to my classroom. I walked in and took a seat. I felt weird. Like I was going to be sick. What did I just do? What did he just do to me? Do I have AIDS? That disease that gay men get on the news? Overwhelmed, I just started crying. Hector looked at me from his chair. "Gustavo, what's wrong?" Before I could answer, Miss Nava-with her black, curly hair and flawless skin-walked up to me and said, "It looks like you could use a moment. Do you want to go outside for a minute?" I told her yes while wiping my tears. She put her hand out for me to grab it. I wanted to but I didn't because I didn't want to give her AIDS, so I started crying again. She put her hands on my shoulders and said, "Walk with me handsome." We walked outside and she sat me on the bench and then kneeled in front of me. "What's wrong Gustavo?" I said nothing. Hector walked out and stood beside me. Miss Nava asked, "Hector are you ok?" Hector said, "Yes, Miss Nava." "Ok, good," she said in control of the situation. "Do me a favor and pass out the sheets I have on my desk. We're having a math quiz on last week's lesson and were going to get started in a minute." Hector said ok and looked at me and gave me the vato head nod to let me know everything would be ok. As Hector walked back to the classroom, Miss Nava looked to me and said, "Gustavo, I cry when I'm happy or sad…or sometimes even mad…which one would you say you are?" I looked down at my red left shoe and said, "I'm happy and sad." "Ok, well tell me why you're happy? I said, "I'm in love." She looked at me with puzzled look on her face. "You're in love?" Ok…that can be a good thing. Are you in love with a puppy or maybe a cat?" I quickly dismissed her confusion and said, "No, I'm in love with…I paused in that instant realizing I was about to tell an adult that I loved a boy. Suddenly I screamed, "No one!" "No one?" she repeated-half asking a question and half make sure she'd heard me correctly. "Ok…well, tell me why you're sad? I started crying again and said, "I might have AIDS!" She relaxed her kneeling position, sat down beside me and said, "Gustavo, do you know what AIDS is?" I said, "Yes-when gay men kiss or love each other." "Well, that's part of it," she said. "Tell me what makes you think you have it? Did someone do something to you that they shouldn't have?" I shrugged my shoulders. "Gustavo, maybe we should go talk to the nurse," she said with worry in her voice. "No! Please, Ms. Nava...no please!" I was scared to death. "Well, Gustavo, you have me a little concerned that maybe an adult has either been bothering you or doing inappropriate things to you," she stated. "It wasn't an adult, Ms. Nava." "Well, who was it?" she gently pressed. I needed a name-any name other than Kevin. "Stephanie!" I spat. "Stephanie Smith?" she asked. "Yes." She looked puzzled. "What did Stephanie do to you?" I lied and told her Stephanie kissed me. She looked me in my green eyes and asked, "Is that all she did?" I nodded my head. She giggled a little and said, "Gustavo, I think you're going to be ok. I'm going to give you a hall pass. Go and blow your nose and maybe get a sip from the water fountain," she said. "Ok," I said. Then I looked at her and asked, "Ms. Nava, are you wearing Charlie?" She replied, "No, it's White Diamonds. Why do you ask?" I smiled and said, "Because my tia wears Charlie and it smells good like you." She smiled and said, "I'll be right back with the hall pass. As she stood up, she said, "If anyone ever touches you or does something to you that don't make you feel good, always tell someone...An adult. If you don't have the courage to tell anyone you can always tell me, comprende?" I said ok. I was sleepy when I came back to the classroom. All I wanted was for school to be over for the day so I could go home and sleep. When the final bell rang me and Stephanie walked to the bus together. "Where's Lupita and Lorena today? She asked. I let out a scream and Stephanie cocked her head to the side and asked, "What's up with you, *pinche calaweta?*" Then I said, "Lupita's mom died and I haven't talked to her in a week!" Stephanie said, "Well, Where's Lorena?" I told her I didn't know but would call her when I got home. Stephanie and me sat in our usual spot close to the bus drive-a red headed white lady who popped her gum. I loved listening to her pop her Wrigley's. I'd been trying to pop mine but could never get the hang of it. Kevin, Hector and the rest of their crew got on the bus. Kevin walked right by me like I wasn't even there but I caught him staring at me when I was swinging back and forth on the monkey bars. He looked as though he'd never seen anyone as strong as me. The conversation between Stephanie and me had ended. We were both exhausted from school-or at least I was. The bus pulled up to our stop and me and Hector jumped off and walked to our house. Thomas wasn't home. I was glad and wished he never came home. I wished he'd stay gone forever. We both walked in the house and noticed my mom was sitting in the living room watching Phil Donahue. She loved that show. I ran up to her and said, "Hi, mom." She looked sad and tired but gave me a hug and said, "Hi, mijo," in a very low voice. Hector came from behind me and hugged us both. I said, I asked her if I could get on the phone. She said yes. Hector asked to go outside and she said he could for about an hour. I ran upstairs and called Lorena first. "Hello?" she said. "Hi, Lorena, why didn't you come to school?" I wanted to know. "I have chickenpox, she said sadly. "Ohhh, I'm sorry," I stressed to let her know I felt bad for her. "Does it hurt?" She said no. It just really itches. "Where's your dad?" I asked. "He went to the pharmacy to pick up the cream I need to make them better," Lorena said. I asked her if she had spoken to Lupita but she said no. "But my dad went to her mom's funeral a couple days ago and he said she was crying a lot," Lorena offered. I wondered what happened to her. "Someone killed her," she reported. "But they don't know who. She was on drugs real bad and I heard my dad talking to his brother on the phone saying it probably was a drug dealer or her pimp." I was floored. "Her pimp?" I asked. I didn't know she was a *puta*. "I think she was," Lorena before adding, "My dad just pulled up so I better get off this phone. Talk to you later." I told her to feel better before she hung up the phone. I looked at the receiver for a few seconds before deciding to dial Lupita. As I dialed, I realized I hadn't heard from her and we've been talked non-stop on the phone since third grade. It rang three times before I heard Lupita's voice. "Hello?" she said. "Hi, pinche calaweta!" She immediately started laughing and said hi. "What are you doing?" I asked. "Eating Lucky Charms she said between a mouthful. "I just love that cereal," I said and she said, "Me too." Not really knowing what else to say, I asked her if she was sad. She said, "Of course, I'm sad. But I'm ready to go back to school." I asked her when she planned to return but she wasn't sure. She said her dad wanted her to come live with him so he wouldn't have to pay her grandma child support anymore for taking care of her. I was crushed because that would mean one of my best friends would be leaving to go live in Fresno. Neither Lupita nor her grandma wanted her to leave either. "How's Lorena and Stephanie," she asked trying to catch up on the latest. "Lorena has chickenpox," I said. "I just went back to school today myself. Stephanie kept singing that Lionel Richie song-*All Night Long*-at recess. "I love that song," Lupita said. We talked and laughed for about an hour and then just casually told her me about me and Kevin's kiss. Silence. I looked at my phone. "Lupita, are you there? " I asked. "Yeah. I'm here," she answered. "Did you hear what I just said? What do you think?" I really wanted her to say she was cool with it. "That's nice," she said flatly. I went further and said, "I love him." I was about to give details when she interrupted and said, "Gustavo, my grandma's calling me. I gotta go." Then she hung up. I felt bad for telling her. She was my best friend and wasn't freaked out when I told her I was gay in second grade and she's never told anyone. But when I talk about certain guys I have a crush on or Kevin, the love of my life, she gets quiet. Oh well, let me eat so I can be ready for *Who's the Boss* and *The Cosby Show*. My brother and me love watching those shows. Hector *loves* Denise Huxtable. And he's crazy about Samantha Micelli from *Who's the Boss*. But I love Theo and Samantha's dad, Tony. Sometimes I imagine kissing them both. Now that I've touched a penis for the first time I would touch theirs, I thought.

Chapter 4: The Long Ride

"Come downstairs and eat," my brother yelled. "Mom made us papas frijoles and eggs for dinner." We ate, took showers, watched TV and then we both went to our room. As I began to doze off, I was thinking about Kevin the sound of Thomas' voice shredded my peaceful dreams. "Get up!" he shouted. "Get up, mijos, get up!" When he clicked on the light, Hector and me jumped up and out of our beds. Thomas got on his knees and said, "Mijos, I need you both to get dressed. You're going to LA to visit your tia. I want you to pack a bag quick with some shoes and clothes then meet me downstairs in five minutes." I looked at the clock on our wall. It was 3:45 a.m. and he wanted me to be ready in five minutes. I just stood there until the clock read 3:47 a.m. Then, Hector came out of the bathroom and gave me the hardest Benny Hill I'd ever had. I fell hard on the bed. "Get up and get your shit together now," he said. "We don't want to make dad mad, so hurry up." Well, I hurried but before I knew it was 3:50. I was running towards the stairs when I thought, Wait a minute. I need my sticker book and Cabbage Patch cards so I can buy more in Hollywood to add to my collection. I went back in my room, stuffed them in my bag then headed back towards the stairs. I could hear Thomas talking as I walked down the hall. As I got closer, I heard him say, "Lift your head up." Standing in my mom's doorway, I could see that Thomas was putting, what looked like flour that you make tortillas with, in her nose. I backed up and just listened. "The boys are going to stay with Loose for a while so you can get yourself together," he said. "No, Thomas. She can't afford the boys right now," my mom said. "Belinda, I've gotten the sergeant position," my dad announced. "They thought about it and now I'm sergeant, so I'll have money to pay Loose to take care of the kids while you get better." He said it as if he had it all planned out. I peeked back into the room and saw Thomas tying a string around my mom's leg and pulling it tight before putting a needle in it. I felt the tears fall thinking my mom must really be sick. Thomas heard me crying and looked over and said, "Gustavo, get your faggot ass downstairs now!" As I walked away I heard my mom say, Thomas, don't call him that." SLAP! I heard the loud noise and ran back to the room. I wanted to kill him! My mom was lying on the bed and she looked like she was dead. I tried to jump on the bed with her but Thomas grabbed me by my neck and slammed me on the floor. He looked at me with a crazed look and said, "When I tell you to fuckin' do something, you listen! Do you hear me!?" I said, "Yes!" as my tears streamed. He picked me up and told me to get downstairs. Still crying, I looked back at my mom once more. She was motionless. I slowly walked downstairs to look for Hector. He was waiting outside by the car. He saw me crying, as I walked towards him, and asked, "What's wrong?" I said, "Mom's really sick." Why do you say that?" he asked. "Because she has needles going into her," I said. I was about to tell him what happened when Thomas came outside and unlocked the door. Hector and me just sat there quietly. I didn't want him going crazy on us. The clock in the car read 4:30 a.m. When we pulled off the Stockton, California exit, it was 5:02 a.m. From the exit, we pulled into a school parking lot. The sign said, Thomas Jefferson Elementary School. We pulled into the parking lot next to a very large van. Thomas said, "I'll be right back." He got out of the car, walked over to the van as a big white man was getting out. "That's Warren!" I yelled. "He came over one day and gave me a Hello Kitty bag to give to mommy," I said. Hector took one look and before he could get the words out, we both said, "He looks like Hulk Hogan. We both laughed. Thomas came to the car told us to get out. So we did. Warren stood in the back of the van and watched us as we walked over. "Hi, Warren," I said. "Call me uncle," he replied. "Hi, uncle," I flirted. Just then, Hector pinched me hard. "Owwwww!! I yelled. Then Uncle Warren said, "Why don't you boys get in? I'm going to talk to your dad." We both got into a smelly van that smelled just like a thousand cigarettes. The windows were tinted so dark, I could barely see what Thomas and Uncle Warren were doing. I looked on the trashy van floor and picked up a couple of magazines. The first one was *Lusty Ladies.* The other was *Playgirl* magazine. They were kind of like the magazines Thomas had in the bathroom, except his was called Playboy. Hector grabbed the one that said Playgirl and looked shocked at what he saw. It was picture after picture of naked men! He handed it to me and snatched *Lusty Ladies* out of my hands. We both sat there and just stared at the magazines. I had never seen so many dicks in my life. My heart was racing and I loved looking at them, but I still thought about Kevin's dick. I mean, I was just holding it a little while ago. We kept looking at the sticky pages when we heard Thomas' car start. We put our faces to the window to see him as he was driving off. "Shit!" Hector said. He was about to say something else when Uncle Warren jumped in the driver's seat. "Hector, you come up here and sit with Uncle in the front seat." Hector screamed, "No!" Then I said, "I will Uncle Warren." In an instant, he just flipped out and said, "Listen, senorita. I didn't tell you to sit up here, did I?" Hector and I were both quiet until Hector said, "Why the fuck you want me to come sit up front? You some kinda fuckin' fag?" My brother was not afraid. "Who the fuck are you talking to, bitch?!" Uncle Warren yelled. "You, motherfucker!" Hector shot back. He then tried to open the door but Uncle Warren reached back, grabbed his arm and said look, "It's my job to take you to Los Angeles, so sit the fuck down so we can go." But Hector screamed, "I don't want to go to Los Angeles! I want to go home!" "I want to go to Los Angeles," I heard myself say. Hector told me to shut up as he was twisting trying to get at least one of his arms loose. By now, Uncle Warren was hanging over the driver's seat holding both of Hector's arms with one hand. "Just sit back and be quiet and I'll take you to your aunt, damnit." We got quiet and Uncle Warren let my brother go. Hector was still angry a few miles later when Uncle Warren said he had to get some gas. He looked back at Hector and said, "Then, I will take you to back to Sacramento." I screamed, "I don't want to go back to Sacramento! I want to go with my Aunt Loose." Just as the words came out of my mouth, Hector punched me so hard, I could taste the blood. "Shut the fuck up, Gustavo!" he screamed at me. I started crying again when I saw blood all over my hands. All I remember from there is the car starting and Hector looking just like Thomas. He got angry the same way. We pulled up to a gas station and Uncle Warren, who all of a sudden started being nice, told me he would get some peroxide for my lip. When he'd walked off I asked, "Hector, why did you punch me?" He just stared out the window and said, "Because I just want to go home." Hector looked out the back window to see if Uncle Warren was still in the store. He then unlocked the driver side and dashed to the pay phone. I just sat there wishing I was at school or anywhere but where we were. I saw Uncle Warren coming back with a bag of stuff. Just as he was a few steps from the van, he dropped the bag, turned and started running towards Hector and the payphone. He reached in the small sliding door and began choking my brother. I rolled down the window and started screaming for help. No one heard me so I ran up to Uncle Warren with my fists swinging. I was punching him with all my might. He picked us both up, carried us back to the van and threw us in. After making sure the door was locked, he got back behind the wheel and slammed his own door shut. I screamed, "Take us home!" followed by Hector yelling, "I called the police!" In a blur, Uncle Warren pulled out a cold, blue steel gun, turned around in his seat and warned, "If you don't shut the fuck up, I'm going to kill you both!" With that said, we both got quiet. Satisfied with our silence, Uncle Warren placed the gun beside his right thigh before taking off leaving a cloud of dust behind us. Once we were a few miles back on the interstate, Uncle Warren made an announcement. "Look boys and girls, I've been real fuckin' nice...real fuckin' nice and now I'm pissed. I was waiting for him to say something else but he just drove for what seemed like forever. After a while, I couldn't see any lights at all outside. I didn't know if it was of the tinted windows or the dark. Finally, he stopped the car and got out. He pulled out a beer and went around to the back of the van. We just looked at each other and remained quiet. Uncle Warren opened the side of the van and said, "Look, I'm sorry boys for getting so mad. Let's have a beer and then I will take you to Los Angeles or home to Sacramento...where ever you wanna go.". He pulled out three dirty cups from under the van seat then said, "Here, let's toast." Hector was still shaking. He couldn't even grab his cup so, I grabbed both of them. Uncle Warren said, "Soon as you finish that, we will be on our way." I handed it to Hector. "Please drink it so we can go," I begged. As I drank the last gulp, I could feel myself growing very sleepy.

Chapter 5: A Friend in Need

I don't know how much time passed and I don't know where we were, but wherever it was, it was dark. I couldn't even see my hands in front of my face. It was just pitch black, very hot and smelled a lot like old piss. As I tried to get used to the darkness, I noticed my brother was not next to me. Hector was calling my name from the other side of the room. "Hector, where are we?" I asked. He didn't have an answer. I looked around for a sign of anything and all I could think about was getting some cold water and turning on a light so I could sit next to my brother. We felt through the darkness until I felt his hand touch mine. We sat down and I tried to turn over onto my belly, but hit my head on something hard. Then I heard a little girl's voice say, "Who are you?" I jumped and said, "Who are you?" It was too much for Hector who started screaming, "Where the fuck are we at!?" to anyone that would listen. I felt in the dark for my brother's body. "Hector, I'm right here," as I pulled my body close to his. I could feel his arms and tears as we hugged in the dark. I could still feel him shaking. "It's going to be ok, Hector." Again he screamed, "Where the fuck are we?!" My brother was freaking out. Out of the darkness, the voice said, "I think we're in Texas." I was still holding my brother, but his shakes were getting worse. It was at the same time I felt the warm stream of water next to my leg that I realized Hector was peeing and it was getting on me. I didn't say anything because I was just as scared. Still, I'd never seen him so terrified in my life. "I'm thirsty," I heard the little girl say, her voice tearing my attention away from Hector. "Who are you?" I asked. "Angelo." I thought it was odd that a girl would have a boy's name. "Angelo-that's a boy's name," I said. "I *am* a boy," Angelo said with a very low and sad tone. "Oh," I apologized. "You sound like a girl to me." Angelo was quiet. I hugged Hector harder and could tell he wasn't shaking as much. "Are we at your house, Angelo?" "I don't know," he replied. Then I asked him if he was from Sacramento. What's that?" Angelo asked. "It's the capital of California." "Ohhh," Angelo said. "Are we in California?" I guess he had no idea where we were either. "Yes, I think." "I've never been here before," Angelo said. "Well, where are you from?" I asked. "Houston," he replied. "Houston, Texas." "Well, why are you in Sacramento?" I asked just as confused as he was. "I don't know!" the cold and hungry boy said. "All I know is I was at my tia's house and she said I was getting on a bus because she couldn't afford to take care of me and she was sending to live with my mama and papa," Angelo said. "Where are your parents? I asked. "I don't know," he

replied again. "I've never met them before. I cried when she put me on the bus because this tia was nice to me. She fed me and didn't hit me a lot." I was totally interested in Angelo's story and went on to ask, "So what happened to you when you got off the bus?" Angelo was silent for a few seconds and then said, "I got off the bus in Texas. Then, this man holding a sign that said Angelo Perez, was there waiting for me. He took me to McDonald's-bought me somethin' to eat...and that's all I remember." I was thinking about what Angelo had just told me when I noticed Hector snoring. He never snores unless he's real sleepy. I was starting to get sleepy too when I heard Angelo's voice sing: My baby he don't talk sweet/ he ain't got much to say/ But he loves me, loves me, loves me/ I know that he loves me anyway. I screamed, "Angelo, that's Deniece Williams' song! I love it! You sound so good!" I could tell he was blushing when he said thanks. "I just saw her on Soul Train...and I saw the movie Flashdance," Angelo said. "My tia, that I just lived with, said people like me watch that show. I watch that show... and I watch American Bandstand, Friday Night Videos and MTV sometimes." Angelo said he loved Whitney Houston. "Have you heard of her?" he asked. I told him I had. "My tia bought me her album and put me in the basement to listen to it," he went on. "I'd be down there for hours listening to it. It made me happy." I asked Angelo if he missed his tia. "Kinda," he said. "She fed me more and didn't whip me with a belt like my other tias and tios did." Then I asked him how many tios and tias he had. "Well, I've lived with five tias and four tios." he answered. "You've lived in nine places?" I asked. "No. Five places. The last tia didn't have a husband," Angelo explained. I wondered if all Angelo's tias liked each other. "Umm, I don't think so," Angelo said. "But they don't know each other well." Then I wondered, "If they don't know each other, then how can they be sisters?" Just as he was about to answer, his words turned to screams.
"Ahhhhhhhh...Ahhhh...Ahhhhhhhhh!!" So I started screaming, "Ahhhhhhhhhhhh!!!" Hector joined in. "I think something just bit Angelo!" I screamed Angelo was crying and yelling, "It hurts! It hurts!" I could hear something scratching the floor. It kind of sounded like a lot of Chihuahuas running around. "Somebody

help me, amigo!" Angelo screamed. We all screamed and yelled but nobody heard us and nobody came. We ended up crying ourselves to sleep. A few hours later, Hector woke up and said, "I can't take this anymore, Gustavo." I told him everything would be ok. "Someone will find us." Then Angelo said, "Hey Hector, do you like Tina Turner?" Hector said no, but I said I did. All this time, my whole body was aching but I didn't want to let my brother go. We were holding on to each other tight. "You want me to sing "Private Dancer?" I told him I did. Hector didn't say anything. Angelo jumped right into the song. *"I wanna make a million dollars/ I wanna live out by the sea/ have a husband and some children/ Yes I guess I want a family,"* Angelo sang the whole damn song. We were amazed. "Angelo, you can really sing," I kept telling him. He said thanks and we were all quiet again. Then Hector said, *"Amigo*, why did you pick that song?" Angelo immediately said, "Because I like it." "But you're a boy aren't you?" "Don't be mean!" I interrupted. "I'm not being mean," Hector said. He was just being curious. But I had already realized Angelo was just like me-different. He also liked boys. We were quiet again until Angelo asked Hector if he liked rap. "I fuckin' love rap," my brother replied. "Ok, do you know who the Real Roxanne is?" Angelo asked. Me and Hector both shouted, "Yes!" "Well, I know her rap," Angelo said proudly. "You want to hear it?" We listened and were amazed that Angelo could really rap. "How do you know all these songs by heart?" I asked. "I told you, I always watch *Soul Train,"* he said. "I've been watching since I was little. Most of my tias would let me watch it." "Oh," I said. We talked for a while longer before Angelo said he was hungry. I was too and so was my brother. We looked around but there was no food in sight. Plus, the longer we sat in there, the worse it began to smell. We kept talking to keep our minds off the hunger pains and smell and fear that covered us. "I wish I had a brother or sister," Angelo said. "I just have my cousins." I asked him if he liked his cousins. "Kinda...well I love my cousin Jaime," Angelo said. "He's my Tia Connie's son. He's really my brother, kinda. He was adopted at the first foster home I went to from when I was born until I was seven. Connie was mean to me but nice to Jaime. But Jaime was always sweet to me. He cried when she hit me or was mean to me. I talked to him on the phone when I went to my new house with my other tia. He's so funny...He's the only person I love. Everyone else is mean." The room was quiet. We couldn't even hear the Chihuahuas running around anymore. All of a sudden Angelo asked the question we were all thinking, "Are we gonna die?" I thought about all that had taken place since I saw Thomas hit my mom. I thought about when Uncle Warren pulled the gun on us. Fresh tears begin to roll down my face. That made Hector start crying again. We held each other tight and told each other everything would be alright. But, then he started shaking again. I tried not to think about being hungry and Angelo just started singing another song. This time it was *Silent Night* in Spanish. It was beautiful. He sounded like an angel. "Why did you pick that song, Angelo?" "I like it," was his reply. He then asked us if we liked it. We both said yes. "All my tias said people like me eventually die, so that's why I wondered if we are going to die," Angelo said. "What are people like you?" I asked. "Because I like boys," he said. "I like boys and Jaime likes boys too, but my tia only said people like me...So I guess people like me means because I like boys." I felt connected to him when he talked because what he was saying made me feel a little better and a little stronger. I wanted to tell him I felt the same way about Kevin and I loved a boy too but Hector would have heard. So instead I asked, "So, why is she so nice to Jaime?" He said his Tia Connie was nicer to Jaime because he was very smart. "He knows all of his math and spelling and history," Angelo said. "The State of Texas even gave her a lot of money for being a great foster mom. She was in the paper too. Angelo went on and on. "Her husband is nice to him too. But her husband was mean too me." I was nosey so I asked, "What would he do to you?" "Lots of things, but I don't want to talk about it" Angelo said. "Well, why did you leave Tia Connie's house?" I pressed on. "I'm not sure. She just said I didn't fit in with the family. So, when they adopted Jaime, I went to stay with three more tias before I moved in with Tia Sally." We laughed. We'd never heard of a tia named Sally before. It kind of sounded like a white girl's name, we thought. "She is white," Angelo said. "She's a *wetta*. I never lived with a *wetta* before.

But she was nice." All she dated was Negros. She had them in and out the house all day long. She put a TV and record player in the room so I wouldn't get in the way." He went on to say his tia really just wanted to see what being a parent was like. That was her reason for fostering him. "She had a nice house with rich parents, but her mama and papa didn't like the fact she had so many Negros in her house," Angelo said. He said they were nice to him though. He said they even bought him two Cabbage Patch dolls. "A white one and a black one," Angelo said. "A white one and a black one," I repeated. "And Tia Sally bought me Barbies," he added. "She was pretty nice except for one time this guy came over. He was so cute. He looked like Michael Jackson. Hector broke in—"Was it Michael Jackson?" "No, his name was Joe" Angelo said. "Was he big?" I asked. "Hmm. Kinda," Angelo replied." He always looked at me on the way downstairs to the basement whenever he would come over. Then, one time, he spent the night and came into my room and woke me up." My heart was racing. I squealed, "Then what happened?" "He told me to sit up...and then... he started kissing me. He would do it every time he'd come over after that. Then one day, I saw Tia Sally peek in the door while he was on top of me." I was stunned. Hector was shocked. "Did she beat his ass or shoot him?" he asked in a very protective voice. "No, she didn't do anything," Angelo said plainly. "He finished and then I went to sleep. The next morning, she bought me some more Barbies and a little refrigerator for the basement and told me when company was there, I needed to sleep there." I think I would have been scared to sleep in the basement. But Angelo said the basement was beautiful. "It was like my own house," he said. I didn't have to ask him if he missed it. We all wanted to go home. Instead Hector asked if Joe ever bothered him again. "Yeah," Angelo said. "The day before my Tia Sally put me on the bus, he met me at the bus stop and told me to get in the car," Angelo told. We wanted to know what happened next. "He took me to his house and had sex with me. Then he started hitting with a belt," Angelo said. "What do you mean he had *sex* with you?" I asked. The room was very quiet. The Angelo said, "He put his *velga* in my *nalgas.*" My heart was beating so fast. I started to feel sad.

Hector said, "He's a fuckin' faggot!" "Don't say that! Don't say that!" Angelo screamed. "That's not nice! That's not nice! That's not nice!" I tried to change the subject and asked Hector if he wanted to talk about wrestling. "I want Cyndi Lauper to be Randy the Macho Man's trainer, not Elizabeth," I said. "Who cares about that?" Hector shot back. "I want Andre the Giant to fight Kamala and Big John Stud at the same time. I was listening to my brother but could still hear Angelo sobbing in the background. I didn't know what he looked like or what he was wearing but I believed him and wanted to hug him. After talking about wrestling with Hector I asked Angelo if he was ok. He said nothing. I asked again just in case he hadn't heard me the first time. "No," he finally said. "I don't feel too good. I'm hungry and thirsty. His voice was very light and weak-sounding. A few minutes later, Hector asked, "Angelo, are you awake?" I could barely hear him say yes but it was a little happier. "Do you feel better?" Hector asked. "No, not really," Angelo replied. We continued to sit quietly in the dark. Suddenly, we heard a loud noise-and it wasn't the Chihuahuas scraping their nails on the floor either. It sounded like a car or truck. "Yayyy!" I screamed. "They found us!" I was the only one screaming yay. Hector and Angelo were silent. When the first sunrays came through that door, we all started screaming as the sun blinded us. I kept trying to get my eyes used to the light, but I couldn't. I could hear either a woman and a man or two men talking in Spanish. Then, one of the voices started talking to us. "They said they're here to give us a great life if we listen to directions," Angelo interpreted for us. Then the man spoke more Spanish and Angelo told us to get up because we were leaving. We got up as our eyes finally adjusted. Someone turned on a light in the room. That's when we saw the Chihuahua-rats and started screaming even louder. My eyes were still blurry but Hector grabbed my hand and pulled me up as we ran towards the door. There was a fat lady with red hair standing outside. "Hola, Mijitos!" she said. "Come here, I am Rosalinda." My eyes were still blurry. I let go of Hector's hand and took a good look at her. Rosalinda's red hair, red dress and red hat made her look like someone from *Alice in Wonderland.* I looked over at Hector who was still rubbing his eyes. Then I sensed someone behind us. I turned and saw a Mexican man. Then I turned to get my first look at Angelo, even though I had forgotten about him for a quick minute. He looked like a girl. He had dirt and blood on his shirt. But when he smiled, I could see he had beautiful dimples. He also had gorgeous curly black hair. I just stared at him and he just kept smiling. In that instant, I felt like we were going to be best friends. I never saw the slap coming. But the man slapped me so hard, I fell to the ground. I looked up to see Hector punching the man, but his fists were slow. He was too tired. Rosalinda just got in a truck and drove off. I looked up at the sky and all around me and noticed trees everywhere. I'd never seen so many trees. As I turned to my brother, I saw Angelo take a rock and throw it at the man. I tried to turn onto my side to see my brother on the ground balled up in pain. "Hector, are you Ok?" I asked. I tried to reach for him, but as soon as I did, the man punched me in the stomach. After that, all I remember is him taking his pants down and his caca falling in my face.

Chapter 6: October 1992 Atlanta, Georgia

I'm on the Marta south bound headed back to Lakewood Station. My brother and me will be 18 on November 13. Life is good. We just got our G.E.Ds and on top of all that, we'd only been in Atlanta a week and Angel already had us a pad! Damn, I love that girl. I've never met a person so happy about life no matter what life hands her. That's my sister. Oh shit! This is my stop. I always get confused with the Lakewood and College Park stations. I guess I need to cut back on the weed. It's only been a week since I moved to Atlanta, but I promised to always know where the fuck I am at all times. I guess that's because I didn't know for a while where I was when I was younger. Ok, let me change this CD because right now I fuckin' hate thinking about the past. I just left the West End Mall with my brand new Mary J. Blige CD. Hector and I already have her *"What's the 411"* album, but I want my own Mary CD in the ATL. This shit is the junk! Ok, I don't feel like waiting for this bus anymore, so let me walk my ass on this freeway. Damn, I would never do this shit in Cali.

Never. But who gives a fuck. Nobody knows me here in Atlanta. But then again, shit...no one really knew me in Oakland or L.A. either, I laughed to myself. I'm walking and thinking about if me and Hector never went back to Sacramento. It would be ok with me...Crack head mom. Dad in prison. I do have much respect for Victor and Ms. Nava. They fuckin' saved our lives. Plus, Lupita and Lorena can move here or come visit me now. Damn, I'm happy! I'm about to go home, smoke a joint and then lift some weights. I'm almost home so I cross the street to get to the apartment when this girl pulls up beside me. "Hey shawty! What you is, Chinese?" I stopped in my tracks. "What?! Chinese? Hell no, I'm Mexican," I said. She shot right back, "I don't care what you are. You're fine as fuck!" I told her thanks and kept walking. This chick just bust a U-turn and rolled up and says, "Look, shawty. I have some fire head. I know you want your dick sucked!" she said. Even though I wanted it sucked, I sure wasn't going to let no bitch suck it. Even though people in Cali heard I might be gay, pussy has never been something I've had trouble with. Bitches throw it at me in Sacramento. White...black and most definitely *cholitas*. I laughed to myself. All that pussy I could get and I never even touched or tasted it. I was still daydreaming when I realized this chic was still following me. "Ohhh, shawty...you is fine but you must be crazy," she said. I just smiled, stuck out my tongue and started Crip walking and telling her, "I'm crazy! I'm crazy!" She pulled off quick. I walked up the hill past a bunch of guys in an old school Cutlass that looked like it was straight from Cal. They were bumpin' Dr. Dre's *The Chronic.* That shit sounded nice. As I walked past them, they were like, "What up, folk?" I gave them a nod. "What's up?" I replied. It was so different here in the ATL. Even though we've been here a week, nobody has tried to fuck with us. Shit, me and Hector fought everywhere in Sac. If it wasn't some of the Franklin boys trying to run up, it was Delpaso Heights slobs trying to run up. We were from Oak Park, but we still had Bloods from other sets trying us. We weren't officially Bloods, but we represented where we were from: Oak Park!! I laughed to myself and kept walking. I noticed one of the guys starring at me. He was dark skinned and short with gold teeth in his mouth. He was hot! I continued to our apartment, opened the door and Mary J. Blige was blasting from the stereo. I love this song, *Changes.* It reminds me of times I spent with Kevin. Damn, I can't wait to let him know I'm in Atlanta. He's in college down here but he don't know I moved down here too. The last time I saw him was a month before he moved to the A and that was in early May. I love him even though he tried to be with his chick. I know he still cares about me. I came out of my daze in time to notice the music was still blasting We had a tight ass stereo system that Angel brought over for us. My sis was down for her brothers. She's been in L.A. making big things happen. I turned down the music and heard screaming. "FUCK ME!! FUCK ME!! FUCK ME!!" Damn, I didn't know Hector had company. I walked to the refrigerator and pulled out some fried chicken we cooked the night before and some tortillas. I looked on the counter to see if there were any roaches. There were none, so I turned the stove on to warm up the chicken. I thought to myself, "Soon as I make some *dinero,* I'm buying a microwave." I put the chicken in the oven and started the "What's the 411?" CD from the beginning. Then I sat down and rolled me a joint. Damn, I'm down to my last two papers. I should have stopped at the gas station before I got home. Maybe, I'll page Angel and see if she can pick some up when she comes over. That girl has a rental car. My Angel don't play. I rolled the joint and just sat there. Boy was I high. It was almost the last of my Cali green bud and I wasn't too happy about having to get some Georgia weed. I heard the weed in Georgia is straight dirt. I smoked my joint all the way down to a roach...well probably less than a roach because you couldn't see it in between my fingers. I laid back and closed my eyes. Then my pager went off. It was my new pager with a Georgia number and the only person who had it was Angel because she bought it for me. I walked to the kitchen to grab the cordless phone and sat back on the floor. Damn, it sucked not having any furniture. And I was wondering how whoever was getting fucked by my bro was ok with getting dicked down on the floor. I giggled because I knew Lorena would take it any way she could get it from Hector. He told me he fucked Lorena in every hole but her ears. I knew that if Victor found out he would try to have him locked up. Man, why does my bro have to fuck my friends and then they come crying to me? I looked at the phone totally forgetting that I was getting ready to call this number back on my pager. "Hello," Angel said in a voice that was half California Valley Girl and half Shanaenae, from *Martin*. "What's up, *pinche calaweta*!" I yelled. "What's up, *pinche calaweta*!" she replied. "What you doing?" I told her that I had just gotten home from the mall and had just smoked a joint. "You know that shits bad for you, Miss G." Angel loved to call me Miss G. She said it's because I'm a fightin' muthafucka with a 10 inch dick and a body like Robocop. She said I have these bitches and fools thinking I'm a hard muthafucka but I'll jump on that dick faster than a freak can pull his money out. Freak is the word we use for men that are not our boyfriends or husbands.. "Are you there?" Angel asked. "Yeah, "I'm here," I responded. "Well, I'm on my way over," she continued. I'm at the pay phone at Lennox Mall and I just bought me a pair of Manolo Bhlaniks." I had no idea what she was talking about. "Shoes*, bendeho,"* she said. "Oh. I never heard of those," I replied. She said she hadn't either until her tio bought her some. "These shoes were muthafuckin' $650 dollars!" she said. I screamed. "You spent $650 dollars on shoes? Are you crazy?!" I asked. "No, I'm good. This man followed me in the parking lot when I was trying to find a parking space." She explained. "I was trying to go to Wild Pair to get me some cute boots for this weekend. Then, I noticed this Lexus truck following me so I parked the car and put my gun in my purse because I wasn't sure who it was. Then he parked and got out of his car and followed me as I walked into the mall. As soon as I opened the door this fool ran up behind me! I turned around I told him, Listen fool, I will blow your fuckin' brains out. Don't fuck with me. He jumped back a little bit then he said, Whoa, I'm not trying to hurt you, beautiful! I just wanted to see if maybe you wanted to grab some lunch." After deciding he was cool I agreed to go to eat with him. Then we walked to a restaurant called Prime. It was a steak place. "He kept telling me I was so beautiful," she added. I asked her what he looked like. She said, "Miss G, he made my pussy throb...he was sooo damn fine! He looked like Michael Jordan, but a little thicker like he lifts weights. So let me finish telling you, *bendeho*, what happened." I was all ears. "We were eating our food and he said what nationality are you, if you don't mind me asking? I said, "Guess." Then he said, "Well I would say Puerto Rican." I said, "No I'm half Mexican and half black. "What's your last name?" he asked. "You're asking my last name and you don't know my first?" I asked. "I'm sorry," he said. "I guess we just skipped all that. What's your name?" I told him my name was Angel and he told me I was gorgeous. He said, "There are a lot of beautiful women like you, but you just have me mesmerized, Angel. Can I get you a glass of wine?" I told him I didn't drink. "Well, would you like to order?" he asked. I said yes and looked over to the couple eating next to us and said I'll have that-a steak and baked potato." I asked her if it was good. She said "G, it was so good...But not as good as his dick!" she screamed. "You fucked him!?" I asked. "Yes," she giggled. "In his truck-but let me finish telling you the story. So then he asked my age and when I said 18, he looked like he wanted to eat me right there. So then he asked me what it would take for him to get with a woman like me. I said a fat fuckin' bank account." I asked her what he said next. "He said, 'I have that!' Then I said, Well, I guess you just met the mother of your children." "Shut the fuck up," I laughed. Angel's tale seemed to bring me out of my high. That bitch was no fuckin' joke. But she continued and I just listened. "So we finished our food and he asked me where I would like to go first. I was going to say Macy's, but I really wanted these boots from Wild Pair, so I asked if we could go look there. He said, "Wild Pair? Let's walk this way." So as we walked the other way through the mall. It seemed like we were fuckin' in San Francisco. Every fuckin' guy I passed would stare at me like they just seen Janet Jackson-but the Latina Janet-then they looked at him." I asked Angel what her friend's name was. She said he told her to call him D and continued her story. "So, anyways, all I saw was fine ass black men. I mean fuckin' gorgeous ass men and they didn't look like *cholos, vatos* or any gang banger in Cali. They were tall, good looking men that looked like they had money. But damn, you know I think I'm that bitch and I'm in competition with D. Those fagots were looking at him like his dick was dragging. Anyways, he took me to this store in Neiman Marcus and all these old ass white bitches looked at him first and then looked me up and down. I'm like, shit must be dikes!" I screamed, Angel you're so fuckin' funny you make my stomach hurt!" She just went on with her story. "G, let me finish! Stop interrupting me!" she commanded. "So then we went to the shoe part of Neiman Marcus...I have never seen shoes so beautiful! I picked up these pink pointed toe slides with a skinny heel on them and when I tied them on, he got hard. And Gustavo, he had on a suit and his dick was hanging down the side of his slacks. I couldn't believe it. I couldn't even focus on my shoes. So then he asked if I liked them and I said yes. He said we should get them sounding like he was President Reagan or somebody. But he sure don't fuckin' look like him. The lady that handed me the shoes to try on came to me and put the shoes in the box and asked me for my American Express. I looked at that Mrs. Roper-from-*Three's Company*-looking bitch like she was crazy. Then he was like, "Mam, why are you asking her for the card? Don't you know a gentleman always pays?" The bitch just looked at him, grabbed his card and walked off mumbling something out the side of her mouth. You know my ghetto ass was like, "What, *puta!*?"and D was telling me to chill out because he had it all under control. Then the lady brought back his receipt to pay and she said, "It's going to be $677 with tax." My heart stopped, Gustavo. I just knew that old bitch did not say $677 with tax. So I looked at the box and read Manolo Bhlaniks. The price on the box said $650. G, I felt so good. I was thinking, "Damn, I'm a bad *cholita* spending this fool's money and ain't even fucked him yet. So then we walked out the mall, but on our way to the car, some more fine fags were starring his ass up and down. Then we get to his car and he told me to come with him but I told him no. He kept trying though. I told him I would follow him but I wasn't going to ride with him. He said Ok and then he kissed me on the lips. G, his fuckin' lips felt so big and strong against my lips. He had me so horny! So, then I followed him down Lennox Road and guess what I saw? I said, "What, more fags?" She laughed. "No*, bendeho*! I seen *mejicanos viva la Mexico*! There's lots of *mejicanos* down the Buford Highway. Then we drove down another street and he pulled into the Waffle House parking lot. I pulled up next to him. He held his door open and told me to come sit with him. So I did. We sat there for a minute and he asked me if I'd mind if we took a drive around the corner. I told him to go ahead. I don't think he realized I really had a Glock in my purse fresh from East L.A. We drove around the corner and parked. He pulled his dick out and G-I know I'm crazy but I started sucking it. It was beautiful. It was big and circumcised. And you know I love my *vato's* dick with some skin, but his dick was so big I couldn't fit my mouth over the head. I was so into it. Before I knew it, he had his hands on my ass and I realized he was about to reach too far and feel my tuck. I jumped up and said, "Take me back!" He was like, "What's wrong, baby?" I said, "I need to go to my brother's house." he said, "I'll give you money baby, please finish sucking my dick!" I told him ok, but that he couldn't' do anything because I was on my period, so please don't touch me down there." Soon as I said that, he looked at me with a strange expression. I grabbed my purse and put my hands in it. I felt my fingers squeeze my gun when he said, "You're so beautiful, I want to fuck you on your period. I felt so scared but at the same time, I knew his ass wanted me bad. I told him I would suck but no touching my pussy. Then he just asked me if I had a dick. "Why the fuck would you say that?" I asked. He said, "Because your voice changed earlier today when I came up behind you... and now it just did it again." G, I was so nervous! It was so quiet in the car. He grabbed for his wallet and pulled out $500 and said, "If I give you this...can I fuck you?" "It depends," I said. "I've never fucked a woman with a face as pretty as yours," he said. "It's cool. I don't care. I just want to fuck you," he said. So, I pulled a condom from my purse, put it on his dick and he said, "I've never done no shit like this before." All of a sudden, he didn't sound so much like Ronald Reagan anymore. I pushed the condom all the way down his big dick and said, "You're not going to go crazy are you?" "No" he said. "I'll try anything once." He pushed his seat back and I took my pants down and untucked my dick. He just watched and started sucking my titties. I got on him and rode him for maybe five minutes until he came. After he came, he lifted me up and put his mouth on my like clit." I said,

"Bitch, he sucked your dick?" "She said, "No, bitch. He just kissed it a little." We started laughing. She said after that, D took her back to her car. "He wrote down my pager number and I grabbed the money and took my ass back to Lennox and bought my boots from Wild Pair!" she said. We continued laughing and joking until a lady came on the phone and told us to please deposit 25 cents. Me and Angel screamed, "SHUT THE FUCK UP, BITCH!!" at the recording. Then Angel screamed, "I'm on the way over."

Chapter 7: ATL Love

I hung up the phone and remembered I had started the oven but never put the chicken in to warm it up. But I was so hungry, I just put some hot sauce on it and sat on the living room floor to eat. It was quiet now. No CD and no noise. I heard the bedroom door unlock and out came an angel. I took my chicken and bit watching as the angel came over to me and said, "Hi, I'm going to use your restroom, if that's ok." As she walked into the bathroom, Hector came out of the bedroom. "What the fuck you looking at me like that for?" he said. "Hector, that bitch is beautiful!" He said, he knows and then whispered, "I've never tasted pussy like hers before." I wondered what he meant and he said it tasted like some sherbet or something sweet that you just couldn't get enough of. I was like, "Whatever." Then the Barbie doll/angel comes up to me and shakes my hand. "Hi, I'm Star and you must be Gustavo." She giggled and said, "You look just like your brother except for your beautiful green eyes." I told her thanks. "So how do you like Atlanta so far?" she asked. I told her I liked it. Everyone speaks and seems to be very friendly. "Good! I'm glad you're getting some southern hospitality," she said. Hector came up behind her and put his hands on her little bitty waist and kissed her on her neck. I just watched in amazement, Usually, Hector fucks them and sends them on their way. But he was so affectionate with Star. She looked to be about 5'6 with big titties, an impossibly small waist and hella hips and ass...and that wasn't even the part that had me mesmerized. Her skin was as dark as a fresh black olive and her face was the most perfect I have ever seen. Deep dimples set in smooth, dark skin with almond shaped eyes and hair that grew just a little past her shoulders. I just kept staring until I heard her tell me goodbye. I jumped up and said bye and she gave me a tight hug. She smelled like fresh clothes tossed in Downey before coming out of the dryer. Then she said, "I'll see you both a little later." Hector walked her to the car. I wasn't really high anymore. Now I was horny. My brother having sex and Angel telling me about sex made me ready to get some dick. I washed my face, threw on my Adidas shower shoes and headed down to the store. Star was pulling off and asked if I needed a ride but I told her I was ok and continued walking. "Alright, cutie," she said before she drove off. I walked down the hill and noticed that it was quiet. No one was really out or around then I crossed the street and headed towards the gas station on Stanton Road. As I walked up, I saw the guy with the gold teeth in his mouth. He was coming out of the store but and he wasn't in the car he was standing by earlier with his homies. He was walking to a green Suzuki motorcycle. Damn, that shit was hella tight. I was about to walk into the store and saw him quickly turn around as I was going in. I was looking back to see if he was looking at me but he wasn't. He put on his helmet and drove off. I already thought he was fine, but looking at him on that motorcycle made me really want to fuck him. I bought my rolling papers and headed back out the store when I saw Gold Teeth steer his bike back into the station parking lot head over by the air and vacuum pump. He took off his hat and picked up the air tube and started putting air in his tire. I was almost ready to pass him up. I wanted to say something but as soon as I walked by he said, "What up, red?" I turned around and said, what's up but kept walking. "Red. Come back," he said. So I turned around to see if anyone was looking. I was kind of nervous because this fool turned me on. "What yo name is?" he said in a thick Georgia accent. "It's Gustavo but you can call me G," I said. "What's' your name?" He said, "Chad," with a deep, country accent. "Chad," I repeated. "I like that." Then he stammered, "What you mean you like that?" with attitude in his voice. "Aw man no disrespect," I said. "I just haven't heard that name much. That's all amigo" Then he said, "What if I told you I like the fact you likes my name?" I just stood there and said, "Then I guess it's all good." Chad started laughing and asked, "Where you from, Red?" "I'm from Sacra," I said. "Sacra? What's that, G?" I told him Sacra was short for Sacramento, "You know, the capital of California?" Chad just nodded his head and said, "Got ya." So, you speak Spanish?" he asked. "A little," I said. I know the things I need to know to get by. I mean I know what to say when the time is right." When I looked at Chad, he dropped the air tube and put his hand on his dick. Then he looked around and said, "You ever been on a bike before?" I said, "Yeah, with my cousins back in the day." "Hop on," Chad said. "You could wear my helmet. I got one at the house." I liked his aggressiveness and his pretty lips. And I was really feeling his fuckin' country ass accent. I thought about how it would feel kissing him with all those gold teeth. I jumped on his bike and we hit the freeway headed down 75 South. I was kind of nervous but I held on tight. But I realized the tighter I held on, the faster he went. We drove for a minute until we pulled off onto Cobb Parkway. We made some lefts and a few rights and I was kind of dizzy but was trying to keep up with where the fuck I was at. We pulled into these nice apartments-at least I think they were apartments-and parked. I'd never even seen no nice shit like this in Sac-well maybe in Green Haven. We parked his bike walked up three flights of stairs to his apartment. His fuckin' place was beautiful with black, leather couches, a big ass TV and a bar with a family table in it. I was wondering what the fuck this dude did for a living. He said, "Can I get you something to drank?" I answered back, "Yeah, what you got?" He said, "Hennessey, wine...some beer." I asked him if he had some gin. "You know gin makes you sin," he said showing his gold tooth smile. "I don't ever sin," I said. "Ain't shit about me no sin." I stood up and I could feel my muscles flex. He turned around and said, "Calm down, shawty! What I say?" I caught my breath and told him it was nothing. I don't like being judged by nobody. He then walked over to me and put his lips on mine. They felt so good and he smelled just like Joop cologne. He kissed me and I kissed him back. He grabbed my hand and walked me to the bedroom. It was beautiful with a nice, big bed. He sat me on the bed and said, "I'll be right back. I sat there and listened as he went to the stereo and started playing Heavy D's *Is it Good To You?* mixed with Mary J Bilge's *Real Love.* Damn, that was a good CD. By the time he got back, the stereo was playing *Honey Love* by R. Kelly and Public Announcement. He held a cigar and a glass of wine in his hand. He handed me the wine and said, "You a pretty muthafucka and I want you to drink this wine because pretty boys drink wine." I took the wine and drank it like it was a shot of tequila. He lit up the cigar and said smoke this. I said, "I don't smoke cigarettes or cigars- only weed." Chad said, "I know you smoke weed. I seen you put those rolling papers in your pocket. But this here is a blunt." I was confused. He laughed. "A blunt is weed wrapped in cigar paper." I said ok. He lit the blunt and took a puff. Then he gave it to me and said, "Have fun. I'm bout to jump in the shower." I smoked almost half that blunt and was high as fuck. I went to the bathroom to take a piss. When I walked into the bathroom, he opened the shower curtain and I couldn't believe what I saw. That fool's body was perfect. I thought my body was hella ripped but his ass had python arms and he had a big chest with a small waist. His dick was huge and uncircumcised. It was hella dark- darker then Kevin's. I walked over and said, "I got to take a piss." As soon as I finished pissing, I dropped my pants and took off my shirt and jumped in the shower. I left the curtain open. I don't know if I did it on purpose or because I was so high. I turned around and he was just standing outside the shower looking at me. He asked me if he could get in and I said yes. He took the soap and rubbed it in his hands and before I knew it he had two fingers in my ass. I couldn't believe it. I had only fucked Kevin and this *cholo* when I got to L.A., so it's been a minute since I'd let anyone play with my ass. I was so high that his body looked like it was in 3D. I realized I was taller than he was. I'm 5'10 and he had to be about 5'7. I looked at his arm and noticed a keloid on his arm. It looked like a couple of homies from Oak Park that have the same scars on their ears. But his keloid was shaped like a letter or something. I looked down at his big feet in the shower. They weren't that pretty but before I knew it, I was on my knees in the shower. I opened my mouth and started sucking his penis without using my hands. I then put my hands on his calves and couldn't stop. He was saying, "Damn baby... damn baby... damn baby." He pulled me up and started kissing me. His tongue was so strong and big. And his saliva tasted great. While we were kissing I was wondering if Chad was really that good or I was really that horny. He turned off the shower and picked me up. I was in shock. He carried me to the bed and turned me over on my stomach and asked if he could taste me. I said yes and he worked his tongue in my ass. Kevin ate my ass before but never like this. Chad's tongue was so deep in me I was ready to squirt. I tried to pull myself together because I didn't want this fool to think I'd never had good sex before. I paid attention to the music. New Edition's *Candy Girl* was playing with to the beat of *Rumpshaker* by Wreckx-N-Effect. "Life is good," I said to myself. I felt pre-cum bubbling out of my dick and onto his sheets. He pulled up from my ass and got on the bed on his back. He told me to put my ass on his face but for my face to face his feet in a 69 position. I grabbed for my dick, which was hard as fuck but he grabbed my hands. I looked down and saw his gorgeous, 12- inch dick standing straight up. So, I got on my knees and sucked his dick while he ate my ass. I felt like we stayed in that position for hours. Then he grabbed something from the drawer and tore it open. I knew it was a condom and I was glad he had one. I let him start to put it on then I finished it and made sure it was on good and tight. He threw me on my back and I let him. I felt comfortable with him. He leaned down and kissed me and said, "Just chill, baby" He rubbed some oil in my ass and then pushed his dick all the way in me. I screamed and I couldn't stop screaming. He asked me if I liked his dick and I said yes. We fucked and fucked and fucked. We used three condoms in two hours. I looked at the clock and it said 8:30. Oh shit! I jumped up he looked at me and said, "What's wrong?" I ran over to grab my pants and my pagers. Both of them showed my home phone number followed by 911. I asked Chad if I could use his phone and he tossed me his cordless. I called my phone and Angel answered, "Hellaaaa?" in that ghetto valley girl voice. When she heard my voice she shouted, "*Chingow,* you muthafucker! Are you ok?" I told her I was ok. Then Hector grabbed the phone. "Where the fuck you at? Don't you fuckin' know you left to go to the store and you knew Angel was fuckin' coming over and your ass didn't even fuckin' call?" Not wanting to get into a full-blown argument, I interrupted with a loud voice, "Look! I'm ok. I'm on my way home. I love you and I will be there in a minute." When I hung up the phone, Chad was staring at me. "Was that your man?" he asked. "No." He raised one eyebrow and said, "Your girl?" I could tell he was concerned so I said, "That was my brother" Then he repeated with relief, "Your brother?" I told him about my twin and how he looks just like me except for the green eyes. Then Chad sat on the bed and asked me how old I was. He jumped off the mattress when I told him I was 17. "But in just a couple of weeks, I'll be 18," I said. "Your ass look like a grown man!" he said. I looked him directly in the eye and said, "I am a man." He said, "I know...a beautiful man. I'm 23." "You're not that much older," I stated. "Man, I've been out of college two years and yo' ass just getting out of pre-school." We started laughing then got back on the bike and headed for the freeway. I thought, "I really like Chad. He looks straight, but he's a gay man. Well...I think he's just gay." We drove up to my apartment and I was kind of surprised that he didn't want to drive me back to the store in case his homies were outside. "Oh well," I thought. He asked if he could come in and use the restroom and of course, I said yes. I unlocked the door and soon as I walked in, I saw Angel on the floor holding the phone. I heard water running so I figured Hector was in the shower. I introduced Angel to Chad. Angel said, "Chad's your name? *Que weno.*" Chad responded, "Thanks," Surprised, Angel said, "Oh, you know Spanish?" "A little somethin'" Chad said. Hector walked out of the bathroom wearing a white wife beater and grey sweat pants and said, "*Bendeho!* Get ready. We have to take Star to work." Then he looked over to Chad and said, "What up, bro." Chad spoke then looked at me and said, "I'm 'bout to piss my pants." As he went to the bathroom Angel said, "*Iiiiii que chula.* I said, "I know!" Hector told me again to hurry up and get ready because Star was going to pick us up. "Where does she work?" I asked. He said it was The Gentleman's Club, a popular

ATL strip club. "Shit! That's where I want to go!" We laughed. "I asked her if we could go in, but she said they don't play with fake IDs. She said she going to work it out so I could come one day." Chad walked out of the bathroom and said, "Gustavo, can I talk to you outside for a minute?" we walked outside and I was wondering what Chad was going to say to me? I heard your brother say Star was coming to pick y'all up? Chad asked. I said yeah thinking she might have been his girl or something. "Do you know her?" I asked. "Yeah...that's my cousin," he said. "Oh really? She's beautiful," I said. Chad said, "Yeah, she's beautiful. Look here, shawty. I'd appreciate it if she didn't know about me and you." I looked at him thinking to myself, "Why the fuck would I bring your name up?" Then I said, "It's cool, *vato.*" Chad repeated, *"Vato?"* Then he looked around to see if anyone was outside with us then said, "Look, let me get your pager number." "Why?" I asked with just a little attitude. "Shawty, what's up with you?" I brushed it off. "Nothing, man...nothing." I gave him my pager number and he left. When I walked in the apartment Angel said, "Alright, G you betta' work, *muchacho!!* You know that's a fine man! I stopped her in her tracks and said, "Now look! We only been here a week so don't be getting me all up in a relationship! If it ain't Kevin, it won't be going down." Hector walked out and said, "I still can't believe you and Kevin fucked around. That fuckin' gives me the creeps." I asked why it would give him the creeps. "Cuz that was my homie," you fuckin' slut." Angel and me started busting up before she announced that she needed to go to Jaime's house to get dressed. "That fool be having his shady ass friends over there," she said. "Those fags think they're all that." She went on. "I love my cousin, but damn I want my own place. By the time his bitch-ass mom Connie comes in town we need some money and some money fast or my ass is going to be over here with both you *cholitos!*" Angel said. She gave me a hug and kiss and told Hector goodbye. She told me she'd page me when she was dressed. I took a shower then put on some black Dickies with a black T-shirt and some Jordans. Hector had on a Girbaud outfit that Lorena bought for him. Star pulled up and blew the horn. It was 11 p.m. She walked to the door and said, "You two ready?" After we locked the door and headed to her car I noticed she smelled so good and looked even better. She had on high heels, red leather pants and a black top. She looked great walking to the passenger side. It wasn't cold at all outside. Like, it was fall but it felt like summer. Atlanta's weather reminded me of life back in Sac. We got in the car and she was bumpin' music I'd never heard. "Star, who is that playing?" I asked. "Kilo," she said. Kilo was one of Atlanta's earliest rap stars. "That shit's nice," I said. We jumped on the freeway and before I knew it we were downtown Atlanta. We pulled up to The Gentleman's Club and Star kissed Hector on the lips. "I'll page you 911 and that means come get me," she said. Then she jumped out the passenger side and ran to the door. I was wishing I could go in there with her and see all those fine guys. "I don't see any women," I remarked. "I think she's a dancer." "Stripper," I said. Just as he asked me where we were going, my pager went off. I told Hector to pull up to the payphone the next street up from the club. I got out of the car and called the number back collect. The phone rang and the operator said, "Do you accept a collect call from Gustavo Huerta?" The voice told the operator yes. The voice on the other end called my name and said, "It's me...Victor!" I told him it was good to hear his voice. It was hard to believe that I was once attracted to him. I get grossed out thinking about it. But still, I love him so much. He was so good with helping me and Hector out by giving us a place to stay and always making sure we were ok. Lorena was lucky to have a dad like him. Lost in my thoughts, I snapped back when I heard Victor say, "Gustavo, are you there?" "Yeah, I'm here, Victor," I said. "How are you boys doing?" he asked. "You have food to eat?" "Yeah, we have food to eat." "Well, where are you guys living?" Victor asked in his thick *vato* accent. His accent always came out when he was worried about us. I told him we had our own apartment. "How?" he asked. "You have no job!" I told him Angel found this apartment for us. "There's no furniture but we have a stereo, phone and some pillows," I said trying to convince him we were good. He said, "Listen, *muchacho,* you and your brother don't have to run from California. You both are good boys and can stay with us. Please don't sell no drugs or take any drugs." "We won't," I promised. "Where's your brother?" he asked. "He's in the car," I said as Hector sat in Star's car waiting on me. "In the car!?" Victor screamed. What car? Whose car is in? And who is driving?" I got quiet and then said, "Hector's friend Star is driving." Victor calmed down some then said, "Look, *mijo.*" I cringed when I heard that word *mijo.* I couldn't stand being called *mijito* or *mijo.* And when we were staying at Victor's house, I could never tell him I hated being called that. All he did was try to support us. He would always say things like, "You boys have come too far to be messing up your futures. I watched you and Hector study-day and night-here at my house-for your G.E.D. I know you have it in you to be successful. I will not allow you to ruin your lives, so if you need to come home don't hesitate. I love you. And remember...God loves you." I would try to hold back my tears but I couldn't. I knew he loved me and Hector. I knew he wanted what was best for us but I didn't know what best was for me. All I know is I prayed that God would lead me in the right direction. After he said what he had to say, Victor said, "Alright, *mijo* Sonya wants to talk to you." I wiped my face then looked back at the car and saw my brother staring at me. Sometimes he looked so sad. But he never would cry or want to talk about a lot of stuff in our past. "Hello, Gustavo," Sonya said. Her voice was still as beautiful as it was when she was our fourth grade teacher. Even though we weren't at that school but a couple weeks, I just loved her. She was beautiful. It's funny that Ms. Nava and Victor ended up together even though she also taught his daughter. "Gustavo, are you there?" she asked. "How are you boys doing? Well I guess I can't call you boys anymore because you're almost 18, which makes you young men. Look, I don't want to keep you. Lorena is over here looking like she wants to chew my head off. She can't wait to talk to you." Before she passed Lorena the phone, Ms. Nava said, "If you're serious about staying in Atlanta, let me know. I'm going to do some research and see what opportunities Atlanta colleges have for Hispanic men. I'll give you a call on your house phone in a couple days and we can talk more about what you and Hector might want to do in your future. I just want to tell you both how proud I am of you two and remember, if you or Hector ever need to talk about anything, call me at any time." I could tell Lorena was grabbing for the phone as I heard Ms. Nava say, "Alright, alright. Ok, talk to you later Gustavo! Tell your brother we send our love." The next thing I heard was, "*Hiii, pinche calaweta*!" "Oh, Lorena I miss you!" I said. "I miss you too," she replied. "We have got to talk. What's Atlanta like? Are there a lot of Mexicans there? Have you partied? She had so many questions. I guess Hector could tell by my excitement that I was talking to Lorena. He honked the horn and said, "You and Lorena hurry up and finish talking!" Lorena asked, "What he say?" "Nothing," I said. "Don't lie, Gustavo!" "I'm not, Lorena!" "Yes, you fuckin' are!" "Where's Lupita?" I asked trying to change the subject. Lorena wasn't having it. "Oh, so you're not going to tell me? Then I won't tell you what I heard about Lupita and Kevin. My heart dropped. "What?" I asked. "Wouldn't you like to know?" she shot back then laughed. "Oh my God, that's hella cold blooded, Lorena!" I would never, ever sell my brother out…ever! But something about Kevin made me weak! "Go first," I said. Lorena dove right in and said, "I heard she fucked him when she went to Millers Park with her home girls. "She fucked at the park?" "No, she hooked up at the park and took him back to her house and fucked him in the basement," Lorena said. "How do you know? You know that bitch is a slut!" I was hot. "I don't know why you still fuckin' hang around that *menteosa!*" I shouted. Just then, Hector screamed, "Hurry up!" "What he say?" Lorena asked again. Then I said, "He said hurry up both times." "He's a fuckin' asshole!" Lorena said. "Where's your parents? Can they hear you cursing?" I asked. "You mean my dad and his wife," Lorena said. "Why are you so hard on her, Lorena? She's so cool." "Gustavo, shut the fuck up and tell me why your brother's mad at me," Lorena said. Then I blurted out, "You know why, Lorena?" She cut me off. "Why…because I had an abortion?" she whispered. My fuckin' dad would've killed me and your brother!" "Lorena, please don't say that!" I said. "Gustavo, you fuckin' know my dad loves you and Hector. But he would have been hella mad if he knew we were having sex." "I know," I said. "But I don't like the word killed and my *pinche* brother's name in the same sentence," I said. "Come on Gustavo, you know I have your fuckin' back," she said. "And I didn't want to get rid of the baby, but I did it and I still fuckin' love your brother." I heard her voice start to squeal like she was going to cry and that's not like Lorena. She was a strong, beautiful girl. The bitch would fight at a drop of a dime. She was 5'10 with a flat ass and big ass titties. She always kept her hair long and curled cute. She could hang around *cholas*, white girls or black girls, but she hated a two-faced bitch. Hector said she had good pussy and she would suck his dick like it was the last tamale in the house. But he also said her feet were as big as his and her flat ass made him never want to fuck her doggy style. She was brought up with a good dad, so she was street smart and book smart. I really loved my friend. She and Angel were my sisters in my heart. I also loved Lupita. Lupita was short with big titties too but with a black girl's ass. She could almost have any *vato* or brother she wanted. She lived with her grandma because her mom died and her dad didn't want to be bothered with her. Her grandparents raised her in a nice house but they both were hella old. She had a basement where she would party or invite people over and fuck them because she was kind of a hoe. At least that's what the word was. Her grandparents never came down to the basement because they could barely walk in their walkers. By the time I was 9, I told Lupita and Lorena I was gay. I told them all that they were the only ones who knew and to this day, I don't know if they ever shared that information. I only told Lupita and Lorena about that time in the 4th grade bathroom with Kevin and us hooking up from the time I was 14 to this year. I never told Stephanie. Not because I didn't trust her. But I always knew she had a crush on him. She also liked my brother and damn if my brother didn't fuck all three of my friends. "Hello? Hello?! Gustavo, are you listening to me?" Lorena asked. "Yes, I'm listening," I lied. "How's Angel?" she asked. "She's good," I said. "Look, Lorena, please tell me everything you know?" "All I know is Kevin's family was having a cookout for him at Williamland Park for his going to college in Atlanta party. "It was big. I heard his family, friends, and all the football team- everyone was there. But they decided to cruise at Millers Park when it got dark so they could go drink because you know Kevin's family would die if they knew he drank." I asked, "So he had the party when me and Hector were in L.A. with Angel?" "Right," Lorena said. Just then, the car horn honked. Hector was about to lose it. I put my hand up and told him I needed just five more minutes. He had to read my lips because he was playing DJ Quick's old shit loud as fuck. I said, "I have so much to tell you, Lorena about Atlanta so far, but please call Lupita on three-way." "Ok," she said. "But I'm telling you that you better stop fucking with that bitch. She trouble," Lorena said. I missed the day when all four of us were close: me, Stephanie, Lupita and Lorena. "Please call her quick," I begged. "I won't tell her you're on the phone." Lorena said ok and called Lupita. "Hello?" Lupita answered on the first ring. "Hey, bitch" I said. "*Hiii, pinche calaweta!*" Lupita screamed. "Where have you been?" she asked. "Last I heard you were in L.A." "I'm in Atlanta," I said. "I've been here for about a week." "Oh really?" she asked in her baby voice. "Yeah, I've been here a week," I said. "Is your brother there with you?" She asked. "Yep," I said. "I'm down here with him and Angel. "I heard she's a man," she said flatly. "Who fuckin' said that?" I demanded in my annoyed voice." "Gustavo, word gets around. People talk. They also say your brother's gay like you. I tell them you're not gay and neither is your brother. But a lot of people be talking shit. And some of the Franklin Boys said they're gonna fuck you up when they see you and Hector. I've been wanting to tell you but I lost your pager number and I haven't run into anyone who knew it. I was gonna call Stephanie, but I heard she's in Atlanta too. She going to some all girls' college." I was feeling kind of mad and upset talking to Lupita and just as I was going to tell her goodbye she asked, "Did you move down there because Kevin's down there?" "I didn't know Kevin was down here," I responded. "Yeah, he's in Atlanta going to an all men's college." She giggled as she said it. "What's so funny?" I asked. "Well, if the stories you told me about Kevin are true, then maybe that's why he went to an all boys college," she said. I was so pissed I could spit on that bitch. But I couldn't say anything. My brother shut off the music and screamed, "Let's fucking go!" "Look, Lupita...I have to go'" I said. Then she said, "Wait a minute! I have something to tell you." "*Whaat?!*" I said in an irritated voice. "I'm pregnant," she said.

47

"By who?" I asked. "You don't know him." "Who is he?" "This guy from Del Paso Heights," she said. "I have to go...my lines clicking," Lupita said. I said bye and hung up. I walked to the car and got in. Hector asked, " You Ok?" "Yeah," I said trying to forget about the conversation I just had. " Fuckin' talked 30 fuckin' minutes," Hector said. "Somebody's phone bill is going to be fuckin' high as hell. You better be glad Star has all these fuckin' tight as CDs in here. That girl has good pussy, ass and titties...let's me drive her car with no license *and s*ucks my dick just how I like it-like a vacuum. Damn, I'm loving Atlanta! If all the bitches are like Star, I'm never leaving." I tried to get my mind off of the telephone conversation I just had so I thought about what Hector just said about Star. "Yeah, she is beautiful. Shit, she's gorgeous!" If I can find me a guy version of Star... maybe Atlanta will be home."

Chapter 8: Shining Star

"Hey, Star," the bouncer said when I walked in the door. "Hi, handsome," I said back to him. I love my job! These men treat me like I'm Janet Jackson. I walked straight into the dressing room, taking a quick peak to see if my regulars were there. Even though I had only been dancing six months, I had quite a following. It was easy for me to take $700 to $2,000 a night. These females hate me in here. I tried to be nice but I gave up. They're not going to like me and that's that. Most of these bitches don't seem like they even finished the eighth grade. I laughed silently. I really know how to entertain myself. My mom always told me I was a good child and I always knew how to fill my time when I was little. No matter how hard I tried, I couldn't get girls to be my friend in school. My school was predominately white and the white girls couldn't stand me because all of their boyfriends wanted me and sent flowers to my classroom for every Valentine's Day and birthday. I think I was the only girl in that school to get roses from numerous guys at least once a semester. Then the black girls hated me because I was the darkest girl in the school and they couldn't believe a dark girl could get so much attention and not fuck. They tried to make up rumors about me but they didn't realize one thing: my mom raised a strong black woman. I miss my mom very much. She would kill me if she knew I was stripping for a living. She left me a house and about $100,000 that I can get when I turn 21. I guess she didn't think she would die before I had my 21st birthday. Well, I have a lot of bills that come along with the house, but my plan is to work six more months, save some more money and sell the house so I can get the fuck out of Atlanta. I ran into the mutherfucker who killed my mom the other day and boy did I want to pay someone to kill him. As I walked in the dressing room I felt tears running down my eyes. I quickly wiped them because the last thing I wanted was to let these bitches think I was weak. There are some pretty girls who work here, but if they're not eating pussy, they're snorting coke or just so dumb they sell their pussy for a dime. Not me. I'll sell some pussy, but I'm going to need more than a dime. I've only really fucked one guy for money in six months and boy, if I asked him for a million he would probably give it to me. He's a redheaded Irish baseball player with a professional team up north. I never asked him the team because I didn't want him to get a big head. All the bouncers told me who he was the first time he came in here. Now he just sends for me to come to his room. And I don't mind. He's 25 and he's 6'4 with a fat, pink dick and red pubic hair. I must say if he stopped paying I might even consider still fucking him. Ok, let me stop daydreaming and go make some money. I open my locker trying to figure out which outfit to wear tonight, I have two new ones in my locker and I just bought two. People think being a stripper easy. But it's expensive because you have to buy clothes to wear in the club, tip the bouncers, tip the waitress, tip the DJ, tip the bartender and then pay some fucking money for a license from the State so I can take off my clothes and show my jewels. I loved when my mom told me about the birds and the bees. She always said nobody gets your jewels until you're married I told myself, that's not going to be anytime soon. I want to go to medical school eventually and become a doctor. Shit, I'm smart enough for it. I just need a little break from school to get my finances and my mind right. I can see it now: Dr. Star Angel

Sparrow. I like the sound of that. My mom always said go after your dreams. I finished putting on my clothes and closed my locker. Then I hear, "Bitch I swear-you come with me to some of these private parties and your black ass won't be having to shake your pussy and those titties but once a month," Royalty said. She was a dancer at the club. She was 30 and from L.A. but sounded like a southern drunk lady. I couldn't believe how country her ass sounded when I thought of California. I never had a voice like hers in mind. It was like her look didn't match her voice. She was tall, light skinned with beautiful long, straight hair like the Asian lady that be dancing on *Soul Train*. She said she was black and Hawaiian, but if you ask me, she didn't look black at all. She looked like a hula dancer with a black girl's ass. She almost had an ass like mine except she had some stretch marks on her. The rumor was that she had lots of kids. She told me she didn't but you never know with these bitches. They lie so much around here. I thought to myself, Girl you keep talking about these parties and all this money but never follow up with the amount. "Look girl, I need to know if you're down because I don't need everybody knowing our business around here and I really don't know if I can trust your young ass yet," Royalty said. "That's why you can't tell me how much?" I asked. "I mean, you're just giving me a price so I can decide if I want to be a part of your private parties," I said with a stern voice. Royalty walked up to me and looked in my face and said, "You're a pretty, young bitch that motherfuckers would pay top dollar for, so if you're serious then call me. Here's my pager number." She wrote her number down on a $100 bill and handed it to me. I thought, damn this girl just gave me $100 bill with her number on it. She must know I can make some money. I got up to walk to the mirror to put some lipstick and one of the bouncers screamed in the dressing room: "Star! We need you out in V.I.P. pronto! A gentleman just paid in advance for an hour with you. "Ok, I'm coming," I said. I put on some lipstick and some hoop earrings and was ready for show time. Boy I never thought I would enjoy stripping. But some nights, I really do. I guess always knowing the affect I had on guys made me go through with the decision to dance once my mom passed. Plus, I spent enough time with my cousins in

Bankhead to know how to shake better then a Luke dancer, I laughed to myself. My mom always acted like she didn't want me to dance-*ghetto*-as she would call it, but I think secretly she liked the fact that I went to almost an all white school but could still fit in with my family in Bankhead. I guess you could say I'm Buckhead with a drop of Bankhead in me. I walked towards the door and was feeling ready for the night. I mean who ever thought I would have been fucking a big dick Mexican that looked like a fucking model? I mean that boy fucked me and ate my pussy just as good as Rich. I walked into the main floor and headed towards V.I.P. when I saw a beautiful, dark skinned man in a Tommy Hilfiger shirt, jeans and some Jordan sneakers. Boy, he was fine! As I walked by, I looked at him and he kinda looked at me but then turned his face. I thought, no the fuck he didn't... I was like, that's different. There's not a guy in this place that doesn't look at me like I'm the last cookie in the cookie jar. I walk up the steps wondering which customer of mine requested an hour of my time. I walked towards the back of V.I.P. and saw this trashy hoe giving a blow job, but her customer was giving me the signal to come join them. I looked at him and rolled my eyes. I kept walking to the last V.I.P. room, which was in the very back. My mouth dropped when I saw Rich. He looked so damn good! His tall ass had a red goatee and he was wearing a suit. I ran up to him and jumped in his arms. He held me up and we started kissing. I didn't want to let him go and damn his breathe tasted like peppermint and whatever cologne he was wearing made me want to fuck him right there. He laid me on the couch and started eating me out. I was so horny that all I wanted was to feel him inside of me. He stood up with his tie and jacket on and I gave him head. I loved sucking his white, pink dick. Boy, it tasted so good. He pulled me off of it, laid me on my back and put his dick inside me. I was so caught up I didn't know if he had put on a condom. He started fucking me. I screamed, "Rich! Rich! Did you put a condom on?" "No, baby I love you. I want to spend my life with you. Please let me feel you without one," Rich said. My eyes opened up wide and I said, "No!" I tried to push him off of me as I did, I could feel him cumming in me. I felt dizzy and nervous. It was the first time I had ever let a guy fuck me without a condom. Though it felt good, I couldn't get over the fact that no one had ever cum in me before. He sat up and pulled me close and said, "Star, I love you. All I do is think about you day and night. Before every game...when I eat...when I sleep...I want you in Boston with me." I was shocked. He went on, "I want to spend every hour of the day with you." I was so happy! A million things were going through my head. I kissed him and before I knew it, we were making love again. We finished and got up. He put his pants on. I helped him fix his tie just like my grandpa showed me when I was little. "Star, we have a big game coming up so, I'm going to send you a plane ticket. I'll have my assistant bring it to you next week. I would love for you to come stay with me for a couple of weeks while I'm in Boston. How's that sound?" he asked. I looked at him and told him that it sounded great. I gave him a kiss and he walked towards the door of the V.I.P. room. I sat there for a minute just thinking about what had just happened. I mean, my mom always told me to give up my jewels to my husband. And I was thinking *maybe* Rich was my husband. And then I was thinking about all the good colleges in Boston. I could go to school, get married-maybe even have some kids. I never thought of my life going in that direction. But maybe that's what God had planned for me. I was so excited I wanted to get dressed, get in my car and go home. Then I realized I didn't even have my car. I had let Hector and his brother take it. "Hector," I thought. "What was I going to do about Hector? Would I have to give him up? Oh well let me run in this V.I.P. room and clean up. I got myself together enough to walk back to the regular dressing room where I paged Hector. But just as I was walking through the room, *Comforter* came on. Shai is one of my favorite groups. I loved that song! Even though I really wanted to dance, I also knew I needed some lipstick. But just like a strip club DJ, the DJ said, "Can we please have Star on stage?" I knew he was going to do that because he knew I did some great pole work to that song. I didn't hesitate either. I got on that pole and made loved to it. I was feeling so high off of life. I think I might have even been in love with Rich. I finished dancing two more songs and realized I was thirsty. I walked off stage and saw the fine dark skinned brother I had seen earlier when I was on my way to the V.I.P. But this time he was staring and staring hard. I walked past him and boy he was fine. Before I made my second step past him, I heard him say, "Excuse me Star...can I have a word with you?" "You can have whatever you want," I was thinking to myself. "I must say you're a beautiful woman," the gentleman said. I thanked him for the compliment and he asked me if he could buy me a drink. "I only drink champagne," I said. "Is that right?" he said. "Well, Ms. Star, champagne it is," he said sounding like Bill Cosby. Not missing a beat, I blurted out, "I like Moet as he placed the order with the waitress. He looked at me and said, "How about we make it Cristal?" "That sounds even better," I said. Then the waitress said, "She can't drink!" I looked at her because she was the one I tipped the most. I couldn't believe she was giving me trouble. None of the other waitresses cared as long as I gave them a big tip. I always tipped her big but it seemed like when she knew the customer had money, she would give me problems. He just looked at her and handed her some money and said, "Just pretend I'm the only one drinking." He winked at her and she smiled and took her raggedy butt to the bar to get our bottle. Soon, I was almost finished with the bottle and feeling pretty tipsy. I guess I was so thirsty from making love twice and dancing on the pole that the champagne tasted more like sweet tea. And the more I looked at him, the more I wanted to see his dick. I mean it had to be small because this man was fine! Beautiful teeth...pretty dark skin...tall...dressed nice. I was impressed. I asked him why he was so quiet. He replied that he just enjoyed watching me drink that champagne. I played along and said, "Really? And what else would you enjoy doing?" He responded with, "It depends on what the offer is?" I looked at him and asked how much he was willing to spend. Then I stood up and started dancing for him. First, I took off my top and bounced my titties in his face. I didn't know if it was because I was drunk...but it seemed that he was really interested. Then my song *Daisy Dukes* came on and my bottoms came off. I had my pussy all in his face. He took out some cash and placed it on the table. I looked. It was what looked like $300. I finished dancing and sat back down. He ordered another bottle and I felt so good.

I knew I was going to be fucked up but I didn't care.

Chapter 9: Clubs, Cars and Corners

So I jumped back into the car with Hector and had a sick feeling. I mean, I loved talking to Tio Vic but, Lupita and the way she said Kevin's name made me feel like throwing up. It's probably just me so let me get over it. "Mijito doesn't live here...Mijito doesn't live here!" I said to myself until Hector whacked my chest. "Where to?" he asked again. "How the fuck do I know?" I asked back. My pager went off. "Turn back around," I told Hector. "I think its Angel." I walked back up to the pay phone and dialed the number. Angel answered, "Hi, *muchacho!*" she screamed. "Meet me at Fat Tuesdays in the Underground! I'm going to be with Naomi-this chick from New York that my cousin hooked me up with to hang out with. She don't know my "T," so don't say shit." I responded, *"Puta,* give me a fuckin' break. I've never said anything crazy," I said. "I know, but I don't want her to know D is fuckin' with a bitch like me. She might trip even though she seems cool." I hung up the phone and we headed down to Underground Atlanta. We parked and I was getting stares from some guys who looked straight but the looks they were throwing me weren't straight. Hector was getting the looks too and was not feeling them at all. As we were trying to find the elevator, this guy was getting on with us and he was tall, brown and fine! He was looking at me like he'd never seen a Mexican before. It wasn't rude and it wasn't strange...I kinda liked it. Hector and I got off the elevator and headed to the neon light that said Fat Tuesdays. I wasn't sure what it was. It kind of looked like a club but there were tons of people outside and inside. The outside looked live and there were hella fine guys everywhere. Inside I was feeling so horny. I needed some dick bad. We walked in and saw Angel and her friend Naomi at the bar. As we walked over, Hector grabbed me and said, "That's a man." I said, "No, it's not," but in the back of my mind I thought the same thing. Man or not those bitches had guys on them like they were made of 14 karat gold. We scooted towards them-well

I did. Hector got stopped by one of the girls working there. "Hi, *pinche calaweta!*" Angel screamed. "Fool, I'm tipsy off these slushies. They are hella good! I'll get you one." Angel ordered my drink and I introduced myself to her friend. She said, "Hey *papi!*" in a Spanish accent. She was outstanding with jet-black hair that made her look like Halle Berry. Angel shoved the drink in my hand and said, "Here, brother. Drink." And as I took a sip all I could hear was Angel going on about how gorgeous Naomi was. I had to agree. She was very pretty. Angel said, "I'm taking her back to Los Angeles to let bitches have it. They thought I was over being the baddest bitch, but wait 'til they see Naomi!" I asked Naomi how old she was. She told me she was 19 with an accent I'd only heard on TV but didn't sound Mexican. So I asked, "What are you?" She replied, "My mother is Venezuelan and my *papi* is *Dominicano.*" "Wow," I said. "You *really* look like Halle Berry." She looked me dead in the eye and asked, "Who is that?" I looked at her a bit surprised but told Naomi that Halle Berry was one of the prettiest women in the world and stars in the movie *Boomerang* with Eddie Murphy. I had just gone to the movies to see it. "Ohhh...Ok," she said and continued to sip her drink. I was still nursing my own drink when my head started hurting. I drank too much too quick but as soon as it went away, I finished and asked Angel what was in my slushy. Laughing, she said, "Fool, its 190 Octane and its good!" I agreed with Angel as the buzz began to take over. I looked around to see that all eyes were on us even though it was packed. Everyone was staring. I loved it because it felt like there was no one looking crazy wanting to start some shit. I looked around for Hector to see he was still posted up with the girl. But by this time, they had made it to the corner of the bar. She looked pretty but I really couldn't get a good look because the place was so packed. I mean it was so crowded that I didn't realize Naomi was wearing a sheer turtleneck with her titties sticking straight out and some black leather Daisy Dukes. She was looking great. It was the first time in a while where there was a bitch with style like Angel. I started working on my third drink and realized how much I loved Angel. She was a beautiful friend with major style and game. She did not play. You either came to her correct or you didn't come at all.

Angel slid up to me and said in my ear, "Do you know Naomi's a boy?" I nodded that I did. "No you didn't!" she said. By that time, Naomi was talking to this fine, tall guy who looked like LL Cool J. Me and Angel continued talking when Naomi asked what we were talking about. Angel immediately responded, "You, bitch!" And I looked at Naomi's face thinking, "I don't think she liked being called a bitch." But Naomi laughed and said, "Girl, you crazy!" in that accent that was sexy, funny, and classy to me at the same time. Finally, Angel said, "I'm buzzed. Let's go dance." The guy Naomi was talking to said hi to me and Angel. "I'm Tre and Naomi was telling me that y'all are new to Atlanta," he said in his country voice. But boy was he fine. As he talked, all I wanted to do was stare at his lips. I felt a little too tipsy, so I said, "Can you guys excuse me? I have to go to the restroom." Then I quickly introduced myself to Tre before asking him where the men's room was. Tre pointed me in the direction. As I headed to the bathroom, I was thinking to myself that there are all these straight guys in here and half of them are looking at me like I'm what they want. I shake my head and think surely it's just my imagination. I almost made it to the bathroom when I looked outside of the large window where I could see people mingling outside the bar. I was about to turn from the window when I noticed the same guy that Hector and me had gotten on the elevator with. He was on a bench drinking and staring at me. My heart stopped. And then he motioned his finger for me to come and talk to him. I threw up my finger to let him know I would be there in one minute. I ran into the bathroom and pissed for three minutes. I was so excited as I thought, "Damn, Atlanta has all these fine black men! I'm here with my brother and Angel and just realized that we had definitely made the right move by coming to Atlanta. I splashed some water on my face and looked in the mirror. "God, I'm good looking!" I said into the mirror. My hair was shiny and black. My complexion was a beautiful bronze color like Apollonia from the movie *Purple Rain*. Everything was so good and right at that point. I took a breath and said, "Mijito doesn't live here anymore." It was something I said when things were going good so I would be reminded to not go back to my old life. It always made me feel better... almost like a prayer. I walked out of the men's room towards the crowd and out the door. I made sure I didn't look out the window but I saw him from the corner of my eye. Walking through the crowd, my eyes met Angel's and I motioned to let her know I was going to be right back. I glanced out the corner of my eye again to make sure he was still on the bench. As I approached him, he stood up... and he was tall. He shook my hand with a tight grip. I gripped him back just as tight. "What's good folk?" he asked. "Just kicking back and having some drinks with my homies," I replied. "Where you from, folk?" he asked in what that deep, deep country voice that I was beginning to get used to hearing in Atlanta. I told him I was from Sacramento. "I was in Los Angeles just last week," he said. "Really?" I asked. "How did you like it?" He said. Oh, it was straight. So how long you going to be in town?" "I live her now," I said. "Really?" He looked excited. "So, what you do?" he asked. "Nothing yet," I answered. We've just been here a week, so I will be looking for work next week." "Who's we?" he asked. "Me my brother and my sister," I replied. "What's with all the questions homey?" I was starting to get a little irritated. He was fine but I was buzzed and this fool was starting to get annoying real quick. I backed up a little in case he was about to swing. I was not enjoying all the questions. Noticing my body language, he said, "Look folk...I don't mean no harm I was just curious. Let's start over again. My name is Sex Machine." I immediately started laughing and I couldn't stop. He started laughing too. After we finished laughing like we were both kids, he said, "No, for real though, I'm Rico-also known as Sex Machine." I just repeated his name...Sex Machine. "What's up with that?" I asked. He replied, "It's my stage name." I was lost. "Stage name?" I asked. Rico shot back, "So, now you have all the questions?" I just smiled and said, "I'm sorry man, and I've heard hella nicknames before like El Soldier Boy, Mexiblood, Insane but never Sex Machine." Rico said, "It's good, folk! I'm part of a male review and I'm one of the headliners. Last couple of months, they been flying me out to New York and California. I'm off tonight because my girl wanted to spend some time with me. But that bitch was getting on my nerves, so I jumped on the Marta and came downtown." Now I was the curious one. "So, you're from Atlanta?" I asked. "Nah, I'm from Miami," Rico said. He asked me if I'd ever been there. I told him no but would love to go and meet the 2 Live Crew. "What you know about 2 Live Crew? Rico joked. "Shit," I replied. "I love Luke and 2 Live Crew! They only play their music at certain clubs in Sac, but I love the videos! Shit they be getting down on those videos." He smiled so big and put his hand out and said, Folk, I think I just found you some work. "What?" I asked. "Can you walk with me up the street for a minute?" Rico asked without answering my question. "Why?" I asked. I wasn't about to be led off somewhere to get robbed. But he reassured me that it was nothing like that. "I just want you to see what you'll be doing so you can buy you a nice ride and a new house," he said. My heart started beating fast with curiosity and I said, "Ok, but let me go tell my family." Rico said, Cool, I'll be right here." I walked back into Fat Tuesdays thinking about how fine Sex Machine or Rico was. I was just a little concerned because he looked like someone tried to cut him on the neck judging by the big scar on his neck. I walked up to Angel and then looked over at the corner where Hector was. He was sitting with a waitress when I waved for him to come over. Hector walked up as I was telling Angel that I was going to take a walk with Sex Machine. "Where you going?" Hector asked. "I'm not sure, "I replied. Then Angel said, "Well, Tre said he would take us and Naomi to a club called 112 He said he knew the bouncer and he could get us in, didn't you Tre?" He was like, "Yeah, let's go!" I said, "Well, let me see what this fool is talking about first. He said he could get me a job, so if he can do that, then I'm down." Hector said, "I'm coming too. I'm getting a job with you. He was slurring his words a little. "How many drinks have you had?" I asked. "Shiiiiiit, only one but I had four shots of tequila," Hector said. "Damn, Hector I want four shots too!" Angel said. I was buzzed but I noticed how Naomi stared at Hector and Angel. It was kind of a strange stare. When she noticed me watching her, she started laughing for no reason saying, " *Yos mios.* You two are soooo funny!" I looked back over at Tre. He was looking towards the bartender but he was listening to our whole conversation. "Look I'll be right back," I said. Then Angel said, "We're all coming." It was fine with me.

"But let me pee first," Angel said. "Cool," I replied. "Meet us outside." But Naomi asked, "Hey, what about 112?" "We're coming right back," I assured her. When I looked over at Tre, he was staring down at Naomi's titties. I couldn't believe what she was wearing! The shit was hot though! She looked like a goddess. Then I grabbed my brother and we headed out the door. I saw that Rico, aka Sex Machine, had been watching me the whole time I was talking to Angel and Hector...but then again, it seemed like everyone was staring. We got outside and I introduced Hector to Rico. "I thought I was seeing two of you walking out here but then I said to myself, "Hell nah, I can't be that lucky in one night," Rico said. Hector's eyes lit up. "What you mean by that, homey?" Rico replied, "I mean today is yours and my lucky day, folk cuz we all going to be some rich men!" Angel said, "I love rich men," looking up at Rico as if he were 10 feet tall. "Damn baby! God knew what he was doing when he made you...if he made you!" Rico said Angel smiled and said, "Thanks, *me amor.* That's so sweet!" Rico went on and said, "So all y'all Cuban or Puerto Rican?" Angel quickly said, "*Eses e mejicano and mejicano*." "So you're Mexican?" Rico asked. "Yes." Angel said with her round the way girl attitude. "Is that a problem?" Rico cracked a smile and said, "Nahh shorty. You just don't look like the Mexicans I see on Buford Highway." Angel shot back, "Well you don't look like the Africans I see on TV needing money for food." Even though Angel was half black and half Mexican, she was proud of her heritage. We all screamed in laughter at Angel's African clowning. Finally, Rico stopped laughing and said, "Come on and let's go see about this money." We followed him through Underground Atlanta and could see most of the shops were closed but, there were lots of people walking around. We took the escalator upstairs and were now outside on Peachtree Street. We walked about a block up and saw a line about a mile long with just men. Men were parking at the pay lot across the street from the club and all I saw was Range Rovers, Mercedes, BMWs...so many nice cars with fine men all in line. All the men in line were black. I saw a couple of white guys but the majority were black. I was wondering if all these fine men were gay. We walked up to the front of the line and the bouncer opened up the velvet rope. We walked straight in. I looked at Angel and she looked at me and said, "Goddamn, these men are fine!" Then I looked at Hector. He looked liked he'd seen a ghost. Rico let all three of us go before him, so we all started walking up the steps. When we made it to the top, the cashier lady said that it would cost $20 to enter. Then the lady looked at Rico and he told her we were with him. The lady smiled and told us to enjoy ourselves. We walked in the club and damn it was jumping! The music was blasting Poison Clan's *Shake What Your Mama Gave Ya.* My body tingled all over. This shit was live as fuck! I looked at Hector. He looked like he wasn't feeling good. "Are you ok, Hector?" I asked. Then Rico asked him if he was alright. "Look man...if it makes you feel better-I'm straight!" Hector looked at him and just said, "I'm cool dude. I'm cool." We all walked over towards the other side of the club just in time to see a muscular, fine ass stripper on the pole. He jumped off the pole, took off his underwear and was dancing like I've never seen before. The club's energy was jumping. There were fine men everywhere and they were going crazy for the male stripper. After the dancer finished, Rico told me to walk to the bar with him. We all walked to the bar and Angel was getting a lot of attention. They were screaming out, "Work, bitch!" "Fierce!" and "Alright, *mamacita*!" Angel was eating it up. Guys were kinda checking me and Hector out but were really trying to figure out who we were and why we were with Rico. As we got close to the bar, guys were screaming: "We want see you dance, Sex Machine!" I looked over at Rico and asked, "Are you a dancer?" He said, "You betta know it, shawty!! That's what I wanted to talk to you fellas about." Hector looked like he'd quickly sobered up and said bluntly, "I ain't stripping," I thought about what Rico had just said. Stripping. Money. Men and fame! I wanted it. Gustavo!!!" Angel screamed. "*Pinche calaweta,* I know what you're thinking. I looked back at her and laughed because of all my friends and even my brother, Angel knows me inside and out. I was thinking about how much money we could make when Rico said, "Let's order these drinks and head back to my office and talk. Rico ordered us a drink and a shot each. We downed the shot and headed to his office. We walked into the first room, which was the dressing room for the strippers...and some were naked! They had big dicks-bigger than mine. I mean dicks down to their knees. I tried not to look but I was so horny. We finally walked into a room with a computer and some chairs. On the walls were pictures of different nude male models. We all sat down and I looked to check on Hector again. Suddenly, he said, "I feel sick before he threw up all over the floor. "Daammnn!!" Rico screamed and Hector just kept throwing up. Angel screamed, "Where's the restroom?!" Rico nervously responded, "Outside those doors." Angel directed me to go to the restroom to get some wet and dry paper towels pronto. I ran and grabbed what she told me to get. Angel quickly started cleaning vomit from the floor and chair. It was a mess. I asked Hector again if he was ok and he said he was. I spotted vomit on his shirt and looked over at Rico-this big, six-foot-something man with a fuckin' nice body and a fine face was starring like someone just died. "Rico, are you ok?" I asked. "Yeah," he said. I'm good, shawty. Angel cleaned everything up and I walked Hector to the bathroom. He said he was beginning to feel better before asking me for the time. My pager read 1:15 a.m. He said, "Let me check my pager to see if Star called." He took off his shirt and we cleaned it in the sink. He had on a wife beater underneath, but we had to clean that too. We walked back into the room where Angel and Rico were waiting. They looked like they were talking about something serious. Rico turned and looked me and Hector over and his eyes got real big. "Goddamn, boy. You got a twelve pack on you!" Hector said, "Thanks, amigo." Then I asked Rico, "Do you happen to have a T-shirt or something he can wear? We left our coats in the car." He said, "Sure thing. Won't y'all walk with me?" So we followed him out the door and back into the club. As Hector walked out, the gay guys were like "Damn, baby! How much for a lap dance? I mean the guys were going crazy! I even heard, "Damn, y'all are some pretty motherfuckers. We walked through the club into what seemed to be like a closet. Rico gave my brother a shirt and said, "Do you see how much attention you boys got? Do you know how much damn money you could make? Rico was excited and we all looked at him then. Angel looked at us then looked back at Rico and asked, "How much?" "A whole damn lot!" Rico said. "Look, Hector...I strip for women and for men, so you just tell me when you ready. We'll see how y'all dance and go from there. To show you how serious I am, meet me here at noon on Monday. Y'all take your clothes off and dance a lil' and I'll pay you $300 out of my pocket." Angel was in shock. "Just for that? You'll give them $300 just to see how they can shake their rump shakers?" "Yes, *seniorita*", Rico said. "I want to strip too!" Angel said. Rico replied, "You get done what we was talking about in the room and you'll be a millionaire in a year as fine as your ass is." I wondered what in the hell Rico was talking about with Angel. Then I thought about the $300 on Monday! We could pay our rent for next month. Money was kind of running low and Angel had been treating us to eat for the last month. The money sounded good to me. "We'll be here on Monday," I said. Hector said, "Yeah man, that sounds cool but I don't want no funny business." Rico replied, "Man look...it's an interview. And if y'all boys want to make some money... sometimes you gotta show a lil' honey. Then Angel said, "OK, well we better go because we're supposed to go to 112 with Naomi and Tre. "Cool," Rico said. "I'm coming with y'all if that's cool with you?" We walked out the club and headed back to Fat Tuesdays. But when we got there, there was no sign of Naomi or Tre. I asked Angel if Naomi had her pager number. "Yeah, she has it," Angel said. "But that bitch is probably letting Tre fuck the shit out of her and I don't blame her. That man was fine," Angel said in her sista voice. I always loved Angel because she was a *cholita*, sista, Valley Girl and even Texas country sometimes. I laughed to myself. We all got to the parking lot and jumped in the car. "Whose car is this?" Rico asked. "It's my girl's car," Hector said with a jealous voice. "Nice ride. Would you like me to drive since I know where it's at?" Rico asked. "Yeah, I think you probably should since you seem to not be that tilted," I said. Hector looked at me and said, "I can't let him drive her car! She don't even know him." And I said, "She don't even know you." Hector shook his head and handed Rico the keys. I jumped in the passenger side and Angel and Hector got in the back seat. We drove down Peachtree Road until we hit Piedmont. Then we took a left and pulled into this parking lot that was packed like Black

Family Day or Mexican Day at the Sacramento State Fair. We drove around just looking out the window. There were fine guys everywhere: outside the car...in line...walking, I mean this shit looked live! There were two clubs-Club Rupert's and 112. And I mean fine guys everywhere. I looked back at Angel to see if she was looking and she was. "Look let me off right here in the front while you *muchachos* look for a parking space," Angel said. She got out of the car and fools were going crazy! That bitch was walking and twisting and the men were losing it. We parked hella far away and eventually made it to the front. She was surrounded by so many guys it was unbelievable. I mean, I could believe it but we never really kicked it at a straight club before. When I would go to L.A., we would go to Circus and Arena. And when she came to Sac, she always had a man or was on business. We walked closer up to her and all these guys. Angel looked at me and Hector and said, "Hi, cousins!" I looked at Hector and he whispered in my ear, "Is some shit going to go down if they find out she's a man? Because this is a lot of muthafuckin' dudes to fight!" Hector said. "She's ok," I reassured him. "I mean, how would they know? She looks just like a girl." I looked over at Rico. He was talking to the bouncers in front of 112. Then I looked over at the main guy that Angel was talking to and he looked so familiar. I know I'd seen him before. Then he made his way over to me and HectorHector and me and said "What up?" in an Oakland voice. "Y'all's cousin is beautiful." Me and Hector both looked at each other. It was a famous Bay area rapper. Hector seemed more excited than me. My brother and me both loved rap, but I loved Miami bass and some gangsta rap. Hector loved straight gangsta rap. We both shook his hand and Hector told him that he had his newest CD. He smiled and said, "Why don't you guys come to VIP with me?" We all started walking in with him and his entourage and Rico-the dancing machine-followed us. Everyone at the door and inside the club seemed to know Rico. We went into this section with the rapper's whole crew and the music was bumping! There were all kinds of fine dudes and pretty ladies and it seemed like there was no fighting. Everyone was just having a good time. Hector told me he was hungry as fuck and I told Rico. We ordered wings and fries and sat down on the velvet couches and just grubbed. Angel was drinking and flirting with the rapper's friends. They let some more females come to VIP with us and every female was pretty with a small waist and big ass. I looked over at the bar and saw a guy staring at me. I couldn't get a good look and wasn't even sure if he was staring at me, but then I looked again and it was Chad. He looked like he was with a group of friends and he looked so damn good! He didn't have his hat on. He was wearing an all white Nike jogging suit that looked so beautiful on his skin. We stayed for about another hour and then Hector got the 911 page from Star. I called Angel over to tell her we had to leave so she said ok and wrote her number down on some napkins and gave them to a couple of the guys in VIP. She looked over were the rapper was but he had so many chicks around him she just walked over to us and said let's go. We looked for Rico and saw him talking to some white guys in the club. We told him we were about to leave. He looked over at me and put up his finger for me to wait. I looked over at the bar to see if Chad was still looking and he wasn't. He was talking to some white chick that was all up in his face. I really couldn't see if he looked that interested because he was so short and it seemed like all the guys he was with were tall. We walked closer to the door and Angel and Hector went outside. And soon as they did they were both macking with someone. I looked over and saw Rico headed my way. I noticed a lot of women smiling and staring at him as he walked by. He walked up to me and said, "I have some business I need to take care of so, I'll page y'all tomorrow and we can see what's good." I gave him a handshake and he pulled me close and said, "You're a pretty muthafucker. And when you start making that cheese remember...I want mine for free." I was shocked. I had totally forgotten I was even feeling him like that and then when he said he was straight and flirted with Angel, it just went out of my head. But my heart started beating and I wanted to kiss him right there. He looked me in my eyes and said, "See you later, shawty." I was shocked and happy at the same time. I smiled and turned around to head out the door but did a quick glance over at Chad and the white girl was still all on him. But he was looking at me. I couldn't tell if he was happy or mad but he was staring me dead in my face. I walked out the door and we tried to make it to the car but between guys mackin' with Angel and Hector mackin' with the ladies, it seemed like it took forever. I was daydreaming all the way to the car thinking how I always saw me and Kevin being together forever. He's the love of my life and I'll be down for him forever. Then I thought I would wait to page him and let him know I was in Atlanta because I wanted to make some money first and get some new clothes. I jumped in the car and we headed back down Peachtree Street headed downtown to pick up Star. We drove and were all good with directions but we turned down West Peachtree Street and realized cars were coming towards us. Angel screamed, "It's a one-way, Hector!!" Hector quickly made a right on another street and me and Angel stopped screaming. We drove up the street praying it was a two-way when we all yelled, "One Time!" at the same damn time. The only one with license was Angel and she wasn't even driving. The cop walked up to the car and Angel said, *"Hi, papi,"* as soon as he looked in the car. He looked at Angel and said, *"Hola."* The cop was obviously Hispanic. He was fine older man with beautiful lips and salt and pepper hair. Then Angel said, *"Que chulo."* The cop asked, "Can I see your license and registration please?" Hector looked and said, "I left my wallet at home." Then the cop asked, "Does anyone have a driver's license?" I quickly said, "Angel does! Show him your license, Angel." She gave me an evil eye and she never gives me that. The car was silent and the cop said, "Alright, everyone out the car!" in an irritated voice. We all got out and all you could here was all three of our pagers vibrating. The cop looked at us and said, "You must be a popular group of kids! I don't pull over many Hispanic teenagers. If someone doesn't give me an ID or license, you're all going to jail. He was getting angrier. Then Angel said, "Ok. It's in my purse. Can I go get it? The cop shot back, "I'll get it." Angel quickly screamed, "No I can get it!" "Stand right there!" the angry cop said. He grabbed the purse and opened it and said, "So what do we have here...a Glock?" he asked. "Were you planning on shooting someone?" he asked. "No, *papi*," Angel said in a baby voice. I forgot Angel always had her gun on her and that's why she gave me a crazy look! The cop put the gun on top of the car and then dumped everything out on top of Star's car. "I see someone was doing some fucking tonight," the cop said. As he picked up a roll of condoms and dangled them in the air. The cop was going through all her stuff and then a call came in on his walkie talkie asking if he needed some assistance. He grabbed Angel's driver's license and said into the walkie talkie, "No back up. I'm fine." The cop then looked over at Angel and said, "This says Angelo Perez. Is that you?" he asked Angel. She looked at him and told him it was. The cop then walked over to her and said, "You boys get in the car. I will be right back." I looked at Hector confused by the whole scene and said to the police officer, "Excuse me, sir?" He repeated, "Get in the car. She'll be right back." We both got in the car and Angel got in the back seat of the cop car. Then they pulled into a parking lot up the street. We could still see them pretty good. I could see him and her getting out the car and walking in back of a building. I was so scared. I didn't want him to hurt her. I looked over at Hector and said, "What should we do?" He looked at me and said, "Nothing, fool! That's the po-po." I though t about what Hector said and thought, "That's fucked up. He might try to kill her or something." Hector looked at me and said, "Stop fuckin' trippin'! He's not going to kill her. He's going to fuck her!" I was quiet and thought Hector was probably right. About 15 minutes later, Angel came walking back to the car with a smile on her face. She jumped in the back seat and said, "Let's roll." Hector said, "Shiiit, I'm scared to drive this bitch!" Angel said, "Well get out and I'll drive." She got in the driver seat and we took off. "What the fuck happened, Angel?" I asked. "That *hotto* took me behind that building and pulled my panties down and sucked my dick, Angel said. "That's fucking nasty!" Hector said. "Why's it fucking nasty when we hear about you eating out *putas* like it's going out of style?" Angel said. "What the fuck ever!" Hector said. "Come on stop it you two," I said. "I'm just glad we didn't go to jail. So he sucked your dick and let you go?" "G, you're so nosey!" Angel said laughing. "He sucked my dick for a minute then put one of my condoms on and bent me over and fucked the shit out of me!" she said. "Was it good?" I asked excitedly. "Hell yeah!" she said. "I wanted to suck his too. It was so big and pretty but soon as his nasty ass sucked mine, he was rock hard and couldn't get that condom on fast enough. Oh my God! I was so scared at first and then I realized he was *so* horny. And his horniness made me horny to fuck!" Then Angel screamed. "What, bitch?!" I said alarmed. "That muthafucker got my gun!" she said. "Who gives a fuck?" Hector said. "I do!" she shot back. "That shit took care of me in L.A. when those crazy hoes on Santa Monica were tripping. And when I didn't want a pimp I could protect myself. And even though Atlanta has been cool, you never know when a bitch might start tripping." "Well, we will get you another one!" I said. "Turn here," Hector said. "We pulled up in front of The Gentleman's Club and when Angel saw all the men and no bitches outside, she perked up and seemed not to be so upset about the cop keeping her gun. We pulled up in the front and Hector jumped out and walked up to the club. We parked in a parking lot across the street and waited for him and Star to come out. We waited about five minutes and we seen star being carried out by my brother and being escorted by a big guy who looked like he could be a bouncer. They walked up and Hector put her in the back seat. As soon as he did, Star opened her mouth and looked at Angel like she wanted to say, "Who the fuck are you?" Then she passed back out. We headed back to our apartment and decided we would wake up and take Angel to get her rental the next morning.

<u>Chapter 10: Hector and Star</u>

The next morning, we both woke up at the same time to loud screaming. I mean this bitch was screaming like someone was killing her. Me and Angel sat up from sleeping on the floor and started laughing. I turned Mary's CD on. *What's the 411 was* my favorite CD. Angel got up and took a shower. I looked at Angel after she got out the shower and put on her clothes. She had no makeup on and her hair was slicked back into a curly ponytail. I thought to myself, "God made a mistake by making her a boy, because nothing was boy but her penis." I jumped in and out the shower and then got dressed. By the time we were ready, I think my brother and Star had finally finished fucking. Star walked out and said, "Morning, everyone!" "*Hola,*" I said. This is my cousin/sister Angel." Star looked at Angel and said, "Hi, girl. I vaguely remember you from last night. I had a couple bottles of Dom Perignon...Cristal? I can't remember but all I know I was good and tipsy!" "You were fine girl!" Angel said. "You sure are pretty," Angel said. You're pretty yourself," Star said back. I never knew any Mexicans before I met Hector. I've seen some on Buford Highway, but they didn't seem to look like you three," Star said. "What's that mean?" Angel asked in a firm voice. "I mean...you kinda look black and I guess I just never seen a Spanish guy as fine as Hector, except for the big brother on the movie *La Bamba"* Star said. Right then, me and Angel walked over to her to give her a high five. But she hit Angel's hand and hit mine too but acted like she didn't really want to. I looked at Angel and realized she was trying to figure out why Star was being a little shady with me. But just then, my pager went off again. My shit's been going off all night. Angel said her had too. Hector walked out of the room. Star turned and looked at him and said, "You ready?" Hector said, "Yeah, just let me jump in the shower real quick." "No!" Star said with a giggle. You can take one at my house. I'm so thirsty I can't wait to drink some Gatorade." "Cool," Hector said. He looked at Angel and me and said, "What you guys about to do?" Angel said, "Well, I need to pick up my rental car from Underground Atlanta parking lot or my cousin Jaime will kill me and then we're heading over to his house so Gustavo can meet him." "What's he do in Atlanta?" Hector asked. Angel responded, "He's a hairstylist at the Buford Highway Flea Market and he makes hella coins!" "Coins?" Star asked. "My gay cousin uses that term a lot!" She stared at Angel real hard. "Well, look girl; if you're gonna stare, could you at least drop us off to pick up my car?" Angel said in a smart but sweet way. "Sure!" Star said. We all jumped in her car and it was quiet almost all the way there. I looked and saw Hector's hand on Star's lap and I also saw Star look over at him and wink. I had never seen Hector this much into any girl before. He always fucked them, got their money-not because he asked, but because they just gave it to him- then it was on to the next. We got to parking lot and I told Hector to page me later. We walked to Rent-A-Car and there was something on the back tire and the front. I attempted to tear it off but just as I started Angel told me to stop because a cop was coming. Well, it was no cop. It was actually a rent-a-cop otherwise known as security. The security guard told us that boots had been placed on the car and it would be $100 to remove them from the front and back tires. Angel looked in her purse and I checked my wallet. Together we had $10 dollars and some change. I looked at her and said, "Looks like you better get busy." She said, "Fuck no!" in a really loud voice. We both started laughing and asked the security guard to point us to a pay phone. As we walked to the pay phone, Angel said that's one dick I wouldn't suck for a million dollars. We couldn't stop laughing. We laughed all the way to the phone. "OK, let me call this number," I said. The phone rang and a guy picked up and spoke a deep, country "Hellooo" into the phone. "Did someone page G?" I asked. "Yeah...I did, shawty...last night and you just now calling me?" I knew it was Chad but I asked if it was him anyway as if I wasn't sure. "Yeah, it's Chad," the voice responded. "You said you only been here a week. How many muthafuckas have your number?" He was joking but I could tell he was serious too. "No one!" I lied. Chad repeated, "No one? Then you should've known who was calling you from a 404 area code. I ignored him and he said, "So, what's up with ya?" "We just go dropped off at the Underground and there's a boot on Angel's rental car. "How much is it to take it off?" he asked. "It costs $100, but we only have $10," I said. Chad busted out laughing and repeated, "$10?! So why you calling me?" Chad asked. "Look dude," I said in an irritated voice. "I was just calling the number back and..." Before I could even finish my sentence, Chad said, "Who you using that tone with?! Look, I'm asking you a question. You said you only have $10 and you need $100, so if you want me to give it to you, then you gonna have to ask me nice...then give me some of that good ass today!" I was quiet. Normally, the only guy I ever let talk to me crazy was Kevin, but I looked over at Angel and she saw me smiling. So I turned on the charm and said, "Can you come pay for the boot...pleeeassse?"Chad was enjoying the power play.

"Say...please daddy," he commanded. "I started laughing and then did as I was told. "Please, daddy?!" My begging was not lost on Angel who looked at me and started laughing her ass off. "Who's that?" Daddy Chad asked. "Y'all is funny! Ok, I'm on my way!" I thanked him and hung up the phone. Angel just looked at me and said, "Alright, girl! Daddy got you in check!" We both laughed. Then Angel said, "Shit, let me call my daddy!" She picked up the pay phone and dialed the number from her pager. "Hi, this is Angel. Somebody called me from this number all night and this morning, so when you get some free time, just call me back." "Who did you call?" I asked. Angel responded, "I think it's D. I know it wasn't any guys from 112 because they were paging when I first got to Fat Tuesdays. And I was trying to get some money together before you came. The tricks I did meet, I just took their numbers." Tricks were the guys that would pay Angel for her time. Fucking them was strictly business. "You betta work!" I said in my Ru Paul voice. "I'm so happy you're here Gustavo," Angel said. "You know you are my closest friend, brother, sister and *pinche hotto*." She was trying to be playful but she was serious. "I know," I assured her. "I really love you Angel. Sometimes I hate thinking about what happened to us in Mexico. But then again, I'm glad it"... "Stop!" I shouted not letting her finish. "What, Gustavo?" Angel looked worried. I said, "Please change the subject...please change the subject." I looked at Angel. She was quiet. Then I saw a tear drop before she could wipe it off. We were both silent. I walked off from the pay phone trying to pull myself together. A few minutes later, I walked back to Angel. She looked sad as if I had hurt her feelings. Then I said in a calm voice, "Angel, thank you for suggesting that me and Hector come live in Atlanta. I love it here, so from this day forward, I never want to talk about Mexico again. It makes me sick to my stomach." "Mine too," Angel said. I wanted to talk about anything except Mexico, so I asked, ""What made Jaime move to Atlanta from Texas?" "Well, he started clubbing at the gay spots in Texas then met some white man one night and moved down here with him," Angel said in a quiet voice. "Are they still together?" I asked. "Hell nah" she replied. "He probably realized how dirty and nasty that fool was and kicked him out!"

Angel said laughing. "*Nasty*," I repeated. "I thought he was like tight and all his shit was together?" "He has hella clients," Angel continued. "He makes these *Mejicanas* look like they have big, beautiful Texas hair. He works all the time. That's how I met Naomi. He does her hair. He cuts and styles it." "He does a great job because Naomi is hella pretty!" I said. "That bitch is beautiful!" Angel added on, "I know, right? And when I take her to L.A. with me, we're going to turn it out!" Then I said, "Shiittt, y'all are coming with me to Oakland and Sac!" "I'm ready," Angel said. "So how long has Naomi lived here?" I asked. "She's just been here a month, but she said she's going back to New York soon," Angel said. "That's where I want to go," I said. "Me too," Angel said. As we were talking, I heard a motorcycle in the garage, so we headed back to the car. When we'd gotten closer to the car, I could see Chad. He had on his helmet. Boy, I wanted to suck his dick bad. He pulled up, handed me some money and took off his helmet and said, "Hey, Pretties!" Chad said to Angel and me. "Look, I got to go take care of some business, so what time should I pick you up?" "Just page me," I said. Chad said, "Cool," revved up the motorcycle's engine and zoomed off. "Damn...no kiss...no hug...no nothing," I thought. Then I looked over at Angel. "What's wrong?" she asked. "Nothing," I replied. She didn't believe me and said, "Yes it is...so what is it?" "Nothing, bitch!" I said. "I just wanted to kiss him." Angel cocked her head and said, "Well, he's not going to kiss your ass out in public." "Why not?" I asked. "Gustavo, your ass be confusing me," Angel said. "You love masculine men...no you love thugs and you act like they're going to act like Richard Gere in a love story, she said laughing. "How much did he give you?" "$200 dollars," I said. "What!?" Angel screamed. "Fuck the romance! That fool gave you some money! Now, let's pay this man and get the fuck out of here." We paid the man and hit the freeway headed to Jaime's apartment on Shallowford Road. "You like him, don't you?" Angel asked. "Yeah," I admitted it. "I kinda do." "Well get over it. Just get the money because Kevin is living here and that's your true love!" I looked at her and said, "You know me so well." "I do," she agreed. "I've been hearing about Kevin for years and you going to be with him because God put us in

Atlanta for just that reason." I looked over at Angel and asked, "You believe in God?" "Of course I do!" She said it as if she was shocked by my question. "Don't you?" I answered, "I don't know. He never seems to answer my prayers and fuckin' Victor and Sonya would read me scriptures in the Bible talking about homosexuality was a sin. They tried that shit with Hector one day and he was close to whipping Victor's ass." "Well, how did you feel when he said it to you?" Angel asked. "I wanted to punch him, but Vic and Sonya did so much for us that I couldn't," I said. "And I really love them. They look out for us and make sure we're ok. Thinking back, I can't believe I used to look at his dick and want to suck it when I was little." "Ewww *cochino*!" Angel said. I responded, "Shiiiiit, the fool is fine still. But I see him kinda like a dad." "A dad you would fuck," Angel said laughing. "Nah, I couldn't do that to his new wife," I insisted. "Because if he got a piece of this ass, he wouldn't want anything else!" I said. Then we both started laughing. "G, your manly ass be fucking these fools up!" Angel said. "You don't look or act gay unless you're with me." "But I can pull a gold toothed wearing, fine ass motorcycle rider," I said. "And give them your bussy (boy pussy) and have them paying you!" she shot back. "When we go meet Sex Machine on Monday, you better dance like Oaktown's 357 singing *Juicy Gotcha Crazy*. Except you'll be singing, Bussy gotcha crazy. Bussy is what we call boy pussy. "I know!" I said thinking about Monday. "Can you still dance? Angel asked. "Well, last year, I went to this club that Kevin took me to in Oakland called Cables," I explained. "It was on Telegraph Boulevard. I used to watch those Oakland boys dance their ass off to Luke Skywalker. Between watching them and studying music videos, I would practice in the bathroom, so maybe I can. Well, I hope I can." "Well if not, you'll be hoeing with me," Angel joked. "Hey, why not?" I asked. "Good ass and a big dick? I'll be rich off that!" "Miss Thang, do you use your dick?" Angel asked. "Hell nah," I said. "But men love for me to jack it while I'm getting fucked." "Well, just how many men have you had? Angel said with curiosity in her voice." I tried to play it off but it was no use and I said, "Kevin, ok? Kevin likes me to play with my dick when he fucks me." "Does he suck it?" she asked. I was starting to get a little heated but laughed and said, "OK, bitch. Do they suck yours? Angel didn't hesitate to respond. "Hey, if the money's right, they sure do. But not for too much longer because Jaime said Naomi is going to take me to the Dominican Republic and we're going to get our pussies done there." I was in awe. "Bitch, you're going to be able to have any man you want," Angel said. "Shiiittt, I can do that now. Men never turn me down-even if I tell them!" I was inspired and said, "Work, bitch! You're fierce, *mamita*!" We arrived at Jaime's house, or apartment I should say, on Shallowford Road. I was excited to see some Mexican people because everywhere we went in Atlanta was either black or white. We pulled up and got out of the car and I followed Angel up the stairs to Jaime's apartment. We could hear music coming out of several different apartments but the closer we got to Jaime's the louder the music got. We knocked several times before Naomi answered the door. She looked absolutely incredible. She had on Daisy Dukes and a white V-neck T-shirt. She gave us a hug and told us to come in. I was amazed to see all of the Mexican queens- and I do mean *queens*. They had on cowboy boots, tight shirts…the fat ones *and* the skinny ones. And they were all sitting at a table with a plate and lines of coke or crank. I'm not sure which one. I just know they were passing that plate around. I looked at Angel and she told me to come to her room. I said ok but was kinda anxious to meet Jaime. We went into her room. I looked around. There was nothing but clothes-lots of clothes everywhere. There was no bed or TV, but it was still a beautiful room just because it was Angel's. I really loved her with all my heart. I was getting ready to sit on her bedroom floor when in walked a Mexican midget. I think they prefer to be called little people. But anyway, the little guy wore a tight ass shirt that looked like he needed a bra under it. And right behind him was every last queen in the house. "Hi, I'm Jaime," he said in a Hee-haw voice. He had snot running down his nose. He wiped it on his hand and tried to shake mine. "Look *cholo*," I said in an annoyed voice. "You need to wash your hands." He looked me up and down when I said it before he walked out of the room. Every last queen that was in the house stayed in Angel's room just staring at me. "I'm so thirsty," I said to no one in particular. "Do you want something to drink? Angel asked me. "Yes, please," I answered. "And where's the restroom?" "Down the hall, Angel said. It was a pretty big apartment-actually it was hella big. I walked into the bathroom and Jaime was washing his hands. He turned and looked at me and said, "You can come in." So I did since it was a pretty big bathroom. I walked over to the toilet and realized this fool was drying his hands and looking down at my crotch. I waited to pull out my dick because I wanted him to get his Tattoo from Fantasy Island looking self out of the fucking bathroom. "Ummm, Jaime, I'm about to use the bathroom," I said in a kind voice. Instead of leaving, he said, "Angel told me you were beautiful, but I didn't realize how beautiful you were. Oh my gosh! I could just work all day for you and give you my check," he gushed. "I mean you're so sexy. Can I suck your dick...please!?" His was the countriest Mexican voice I'd ever heard. "Dude, what's up with you?" I screamed. I must have been loud because Angel came running in. "What's going on?" she asked. We were both quiet. So I said," I have to use the restroom, please." Jaime looked confused and walked out of the restroom almost knocking Angel down as he walked out. I told her to close the door and she moved backwards closing the door behind her. "No," I said. "Come in here, Angel." I started pissing and said, "What the fuck is going on in this house Angel? Everyone is acting like a tweeker. Are they druggies?" I asked as I finished peeing. "No, no," Angel said. "They're just having fun. It's Jaime's start to his weekend. You know hair stylists like to party hard." "What are you fucking talking about?" I asked in a serious tone even though I was laughing at the same time. "He's just chilling with his friends and enjoying the ATL like we are, except they do a little white girl. White girl is a slang term for coke. "And," she continued, "We fuck with fine dudes." "Whatever!" I said. "Can we go please?" "Yeah, let me just change and put on some makeup," she said. "I'm staying in the bathroom with you," I told her. "Nooo, G," Angel insisted. "They're going to think we're being shady. I've told him so much about you and I always brag about you. Just go chill in the living room with them." I wasn't moving. "No. That Ewok-looking fool asked if he could suck my dick, so I'm going outside." Angel pleaded, "No! Please, please, please! Jaime lent me the money to put down on your apartment until I could trick the rest." I finally said Ok and walked into the living room. The Mexican music was still blasting and they were all sitting around the table snorting white girl. But I noticed there were two new guys and one was kinda hot. It was weird though because they both seemed to be mean-mugging me. I sat on the couch and waited for Angel to finish. I wanted her to hurry the fuck up. I turned my head and looked over at Naomi. She was doing a line of drugs and then she grabbed the cute Hispanic guy and they went to the back of the apartment. He was mean-mugging me the whole time, so I just turned because I didn't want to disrespect Angel. She finally came out of the bathroom and said, "Ok, I'm ready." She looked terrific as usual. "Angel darling," Jaime said. "This for you, *mijita*. Can you please take care of him?" "What?" Angel asked in a confused voice. "My friends darrrrling...from Texas... that's been so kind to me and you-need a lil' favor. So, can you please go in the room and help him?" Then Jaime did another line. Angel looked over at the guy and said, "I'm sorry *mi amor* but I have to go." The guy headed towards Angel and I jumped up and said, "Let's go." Jaime ran over to me and said, "Look, sexy...you can hang out with us until they're finished. This is important business." Angel whispered something to Jaime, but I couldn't hear. All I saw was Jaime's snot running down his face and landing on his titties. The look on the guy's face seemed to grow angrier and angrier. He started walking towards Angel like he was going to attack her. Without thinking, I knocked the shit out of that fool and then got on top of him. I was fucking him up! I couldn't stop punching him. All I heard was Angel screaming, "Enough, Gustavo! That's enough!" As soon as I let up, the other dude came running out with no pants on. I kicked him in his dick and then knocked the shit out of him too. He landed onto the kitchen table and everything that was on the table went flying off. All the queens scattered and started running. Angel said, "Come on. Let's go." Jaime followed us outside screaming, "Bitch! All that I've done for you, *puta* and this is how you disrespect my house!?" Angel jumped in the driver's seat and I headed back up the stairs to kick Jaime's ass when he started screaming, "You tell that bitch to give me that rental car that I got for her!" But as soon as I got to the second floor and moving closer to the third, he ran and closed the door. I turned around and Angel was pulling me and telling me she wasn't fucking playing and that I needed to come on. She was pushing me with all her might, so I headed to the car. Suddenly, I heard gunshots. Angel started the car and we mashed the fuck out of there. A bullet came through the window and glass went everywhere. I was pissed and scared at the same time. We both got to the main road in one piece and turned on Buford Highway. Immediately, we saw cops passing us in the opposite direction headed toward the apartments. After making sure each other were Ok, we just lost it. Angel started shouting, "Fuck!! What just happened?! Gustavo, what the fuck just happened!?" "That mutherfucker was going to rape your ass!" I said. "That's what the fuck just happened!" We pulled into the parking lot of a Kmart, found a parking space and jumped out of the car. I had to catch my breath and Angel looked crazy. We looked at each other and just started laughing. We couldn't stop. Finally I said still laughing, "When you used to tell me stories about Jaime, you forgot to leave out that he was a crack head midget!" "He's not a crack head, G!" Angel said. "Look bitch." I shot back. You're always real with me, so I'm going to have to be real with you. He's fucking doing drugs with a house full of reject fags and is trying to pimp you out with a fucking lowlife. Now you're telling me he's not a crackhead, basehead, tweeker or whatever you want to call him?! He's not cool and if I see him again, I'm fucking him up! Angel was shaking her head, "No, G! We got to let it go. He's well connected!" "I don't give a fuck, blood!" I insisted. "This is Oak Park, blood!" She started laughing and then started crying-and Angel rarely cries. "What's wrong Angel?" I asked. "We didn't get shot and those muthafuckers tried to kill us." "I know," she said. "But now, shit is all fucked up! My clothes are there and I can't go back no time soon. And look at this fuckin' rental car. It's got bullet holes in it, G!" All I wanted to know was who the hell those guys were anyway. Angel said, "I didn't realize it, but I think those are the guys that bring the dope from the border of Texas and Mexico to Jaime." I was confused. "He sells drugs? I thought he was a beautician?" "He is and a good one but, he started selling coke in Texas, then he moved here because he heard there was a market for it in Atlanta," she answered. "But he's fucked with both the guys that run the shit down here, so I sure in the fuck am not going to fuck with any of his tricks! He's my brother but he's nasty!" "Your brother my ass!" I said. "I'm your fucking brother! He's a lame...ass...faggot... ass...bitch! Does he know where we stay?" "No," she said. "He just gave me the money of the deposit. The receipt is at your apartment." "Good," let's clean out this glass and get the fuck out of here," I said. We cleaned up the glass without a scratch or cut anywhere and headed back to our apartment. When we got there, Angel said, "I'm going to have to live here with you two." "Good, I want you to!" I said. "I'm so glad I decided to wear my Manolo Blahniks" Angel said. "I was going to wear my boots!" "You think they're going to fuck up your clothes?" I asked. "Who knows?" she said. Just then, both of our pagers went off. "You want to use the phone first?" I asked Angel. "No," she said. "I don't feel like talking to anybody." I looked at my pager and it was Chad. As I was going to call him, my other pager went off. It was a 213 area code. Another page came right after with Lorena's number followed by 911. I started to call Lorena, but something made me dial the 213 area code. I told Angel I had no idea where the 213 area code was located. In her *chola voice, she said,* "It's L.A. Gustavo. Don't you remember? You're from California-and you don't know that?" Then she grabbed a pillow and lay close to my leg. I dialed and heard a voice say, "Hello?" It was a voice I remembered and could never forget. "Tia Loose?" I asked. "Yes, *mijo!*" she said. "It's me. Tia Loose!" It felt like my heart sank to my stomach. I hung up the phone and ran to the bathroom and started throwing up. I looked at my hands and saw where my knuckles were slightly bleeding from knocking those assholes out. I finished throwing up and heard Angel say, "It's Ok, Gustavo. It's going to be Ok." Just like she used to say when we were living in Mexico. I fell to my knees crying. I was trying so hard to think of something happy in my life. But I couldn't. I screamed for Angel to please put on my Mary CD. She put it on *Changes.* She knew I loved that song. I had told her that was how I felt about me and

Kevin's relationship. My mind started thinking about Kevin and how we were going to be together and raise a family. I jumped up and splashed water on my face holding back the tears. I was fighting them back just as much as I could. I looked in the mirror and said, "*Mijito* doesn't live here anymore! *Mijito* doesn't live here anymore!" I just kept repeating it to myself until it started to sound ridiculous. I shut the water off, put down the toilet lid and just sat there dazed. I could hear the phone ringing nonstop. I got up and opened the door. Angel was just sitting there with a puzzled look on her face. "Unplug the phone, please!" I said. She said Ok. Then I said, "Let's go, Angel." We walked out the door and headed down the hill to the package store. We got to the store and Angel asked this fine older man could he buy her some beer. And he did it. I bought a blunt and we headed back to the apartment with several guys blowing their horns at Angel. We got wasted that night. We drank and smoked ourselves to sleep.

<u>Chapter 11: Changes</u>

"Wake up! Wake up!" Hector screamed. "Did you two have a party?" Star asked. Me and Angel both sat up. Star was dressed up in a grey dress and as usual, she looked beautiful. "You look so pretty," Angel said. "Where you going?" I asked. "To church," she answered. Would you like to come with me?" "Not today," I said. "What time is it?" Hector said it was 8 a.m. in a very cheerful voice. "Why you so happy?" I wanted to know. "Duhhhhh," Star said pointing to herself. "Well, I gotta go," she added. She told Hector she would page him later. They both kissed each other like they were going to fuck! I jumped up, brushed my teeth and then came back to the living room. Angel asked me for a toothbrush. "I have an extra one," I said. Just then, the door opened up so fast it sounded like it was going to break. "What the fuck happened to Angel's car? Hector screamed. Star was standing right behind him looking worried. "What happened?!" He demanded. It kinda gave me the creeps. He sounded like Thomas. After a brief silence I said, "Where do we begin?" and we told them both the whole story. When I was finished, Hector was so pissed that you could see the veins popping from his arms and neck. He walked outside and the rest of us just sat there quiet. "So...let me get this right," Star said to Angel. "He wanted to have sex with you and your friend-excuse me-I you're your brother was Ok with it?" Then she looked at Angel real good and said, "Can I ask you a personal question and you won't be mad at me?" Without waiting for an answer, she asked, "Are you a he-she?" Angel looked shocked but had a smile on her face too. And if I know Angel, she was excited that Star had no idea until now. "Yes!" she said proudly. "I'm in the process of having gender reassignment." "A sex change?" she asked. "Yes, if you prefer that," Angel said with an annoyed tone. Can I ask you why did you ask?" Angel asked. "Well the whole time you were telling the story, you two said fag a thousand times," Star offered. "And there was fags all in the house. So then, why would a straight woman want to fuck a fag knowing they could get AIDS?" "Excuse me?" Angel said with an attitude. "I think what you were trying to ask is that if everyone in the house was gay; wouldn't it be weird if they were fucking a woman?" "Because why would a straight woman be fucking a gay dude, right?" I added. "Yeah," Star said her voice cracking. "Except gay men do fuck straight women. And their faggot asses kill women too." Then she turned and walked out the door. She went straight to Hector's room. "Are you a homosexual, Hector?" she asked him. "What the fuck you just say to me?" Hector asked. "Why didn't you tell me Angel was a man? Are you fucking her?" "Are you crazy?" Hector asked. "You know what... don't call me again," Star said. "I have no room for any queers in my life." Then she ran to her car. We looked out the window and saw Hector just standing there. Finally, he turned and headed back to the apartment and slammed the door. "What did you two tell her?" he demanded. I told him that Star asked Angel if she was a he-she and we told her yes! As those words came out of my mouth, Angel and me started rolling. I mean we laughed so hard that tears came out my eyes and Angel snorkeled like a pig. Hector just watched us laugh and soon as we finished he said, "So you two think that's funny!" He was not laughing. "Hector calm down!" Angel said. "It's ok...I am a man!" Then we started laughing again. "Yeah, yeah," Hector said. It's so funny that now she fucking thinks I'm homo and that bitch told me not to call her anymore. Man, we been fucking nonstop. She can't keep my dick out of her mouth! I don't get it! I mean her body's the most beautiful thing I've ever seen and her pussy feels so good on my dick!" I stopped laughing and said, "You really like her, don't you Hec?" "I like fucking her!" Hector said sarcastically. "Why the fuck is the phone unplugged?" He looked confused. I looked over at Angel and she was staring at me wanting to know why too. We both had drank and smoked the night before and just talked about men. I never told her about my Tia Loose calling. Hector plugged in the phone then grabbed the cordless and put it on the charger. I wanted to tell him about Tia Loose calling, but for some reason I couldn't bring myself to tell him. I started to ask Angel if it was just a dream. Did I really talk to someone on the phone and then run into the bathroom and throw up? But instead I lay down and wanted to go back to sleep. Just like before, my pager started vibrating and so did Angel's. I looked down at the number and realized it was Chad. Shit! We were supposed to do something last night...or at least I was supposed to give him something. I laughed to myself before I called his number. He answered and said in a serious voice, "Look, shawty. I hope you're not trying to play me!" I tried to reassure him that I wasn't. "No, no... why you say that?" I said like I didn't have a clue. "You for real, shawty?" He was mad. I walked outside with the cordless hoping it wouldn't hang up. When I got outside I told him, "Chad, you wouldn't believe the shit we've been through the last couple of nights. It's been hella crazy!" "Is that right?" he said sounding convinced. Then I said, "I want to see you! I'm starving. You want to get something to eat?" "Yeah, that's cool!" he said. "You think my brother and sister could come too?" I asked. "I mean I really want to see you, but it's Sunday and I would kinda like to be with my family." I used my sincere voice. "Well, shit if that's the case, y'all just come over here and I'll grill something," he said. Hell, it is a nice day, so we might as well take advantage of it." I was cool with that but asked, "Umm...you think we would get stopped by one time if we're driving without a back window?" "What?" he asked. "What happened to y'alls back window? Better yet, tell me when I pick y'all up. I'm going to jump in the shower and then we could all go to the grocery store together." We hung up and I told Hector and Angel that we were going to cook out at Chad's and he was coming with us. Hector said Ok but his whole attitude changed from when he got home with Star. He must have really liked her because he usually fucked and let the bitches be sad about him. We all got dressed. Soon Chad pulled up in a big Lexus. Boy was it tight! I didn't know he had that kind of car or any car at all. I just knew he had a motorcycle. Angel looked at me and smiled. I let Angel sit in the front seat. "I love your car," she told Chad. We pulled up in the Winn Dixie parking lot. As we walked into the store, I noticed that it was mostly white people in the parking lot and it was packed. As we walked in, this fine ass guy, that looked like he was seven feet tall, spotted Angel. He was gorgeous. As he walked out, he motioned for Angel to come outside. Chad started laughing saying, "That dude plays for the Atlanta Hawks." Chad grabbed a cart and Hector told us he was about to go look at the magazines. Chad pushed the cart and asked, "What would you like to grill?" Hmmm, I thought...Steak, hotdogs, hamburgers - whatever. I was just wondering if he was going to make me use the remainder of the money he gave me yesterday. We grabbed meat, chips, soda, cake-all kinds of stuff. We were in the very back of the store when Chad pointed to the restroom sign. I wasn't sure what he was talking about, but he held his finger to his lips and whispered, "Shhhh." And then we walked into the men's restroom. There were three stalls and no one in any of them. Chad locked the door. Then, he touched my face with his big hands. Instinctively, I squatted and took his dick out of his pants. My heart was racing. I was nervous but I was really feeling Chad. I sucked and sucked. He was so hard! I had my eyes closed but could hear him tearing something. His hands left the back of my head. I looked up and he had opened a condom. I thought to myself, "I'm moist, but not moist enough for his big dick." He reached into his pocket and pulled out some K-Y Jelly. He turned me around and I put my hands on the sink. He said, "Don't worry green eyes. I'm going to go slow. When he said that, I thought of Kevin and it turned me on so much I backed all the way into his dick. He was fucking the shit out of me and I was backing my ass as far as I could on his dick. We kept fucking until there was a knock at the door. I know they could hear me moaning. I was getting louder and louder. It felt so good! "Do you love this dick, baby?" He whispered. "Do you love this dick baby?" I screamed, "Yes! Yes! Yes, baby. I love it!" He said, "I'm about to cum in a minute." I spit in my hand and started jacking my dick. Suddenly, I heard him say, "I'm cummmmmmmmmming!!" Hearing him say that made me cum all over the bathroom floor. He pulled out. I stood up then. He came over and put his tongue in my mouth. We kissed and kissed. Then the knocking got louder. We hurriedly cleaned ourselves up and Chad unlocked the door. Then we both walked out while two older white men stood at the restroom door trying to figure out what had just happened. We walked over and grabbed our cart. It was still at the same place we'd left it. Chad paid for the groceries and we told Hector we were leaving. He put down the National Geographic magazine he was reading. Hector reads the strangest things, I thought. We headed to the car and I looked around for Angel. Chad popped the trunk and he and Hector started loading the groceries in the trunk. I was still looking for Angel even though I was still dizzy from fucking in the restroom. My heart was still beating fast. As we were getting into Chad's car, Angel pulled up in a car I had never seen before. It was beautiful. "Hey, cuties!" she said to us as she jumped out of the car and told the driver she would page him later. The guy threw up a wave and kept going. "What kind of car was that?" I asked out loud. "A Rolls Royce!" Chad said sounding a little annoyed. After we were all in Chad's car, Angel said, "That guy was so fine! He wants to take me out! I told him not tonight but maybe this week. I think he's rich." "Super rich," Chad said. "Oh, you know him Chad?" Angel asked. "Yeah...dude plays for the Atlanta Hawks," Chad said. "What's that?" Angel said in her goofy but serious voice. "Get the fuck out of here, homey...for real? Hector joined the conversation. "Yeah, for real," Chad said. "I've never seen a basketball player in person," Hector said. "I thought about that shit for a minute when he was looking at Angel, but that shit was for real." "Yup, man lotta folks with money live out this way," Chad said. "I want to have his baby!" Angel said. Me and her started laughing but we were the only two who did. Hector and Chad acted like they didn't hear it. We pulled up to his nice apartment and went upstairs. Angel and me prepared the meat and started getting the sides ready for dinner. Chad looked at us like he was shocked. I guess he didn't know we could cook. He turned his big screen TV on and set up the Nintendo for my brother. Then he said he was going downstairs to start the grill. "Bitch, I like him!" Angel said. "I mean I really like him for you!" I looked at Angel and said, "I like him too, but what about Kevin?" Angel was quiet like she wanted to say something about Kevin. But she didn't. I looked and said, "What about Kevin?" "You're right. Kevin is the love of your life," she said in a weird tone. "Where's the restroom?" Hector asked. I only knew of the one in his bedroom. But Chad's apartment was so big, I knew for sure he had two if that nasty queen Jaime had two restrooms in his project apartment. Man, the more I thought about Jaime, the more I couldn't wait to see him because I was going to fuck him up. Again Hector yelled, "Where's the bathroom! I have to piss!" I looked down the opposite side of the hallway and opened the door. It was a bathroom. Hector ran in and I walked back to finish talking to Angel about Kevin when I heard Hector say, "What the fuck!?" Angel and me looked at each other in the kitchen and wondered, what now? We both walked to the bathroom where Hector was. I knocked and asked, "Hector, are you Ok?" He unlocked the door and was holding a picture in his hand. There were several pictures spread on his bathroom sink. Is this Star?" he asked. Angel looked and said, "It looks like her." Then I just came clean and told him it was her. "Chad and Star are cousins," I said. Hector was mad. "Why didn't you tell me?" I answered, "Because he don't want her knowing his business." Just then, Chad yelled, "Where's everyone at?" We all walked back into the living room. "We were in the restroom," Angel said giggling. "Ummm, why?" Chad asked in his thick, country accent. "We were looking at the pictures," she answered. "Ohhh, ok," he said. "Hector saw a picture of Star and wasn't sure if it was her and I told him it was," I said. "So you hadn't told him?" he asked. "Nope," I said. "I really didn't even think about it." Hector gave me a crazy look and then said, "How's she your cousin too?" he asked Chad. "Our moms are sisters-well were sisters," he said with a sad look. "Come on y'all." We all headed back into the kitchen. Hector sat on a bar stool and me and Angel continued to prepare the food. "Who wants a beer?" Chad asked. "I do," Hector replied. Angel asked Chad if he had any margaritas. "No, I have some wine and vodka," Chad said. "And I do have some tequila." Angel made me a vodka and Coke and poured her a glass of wine. Chad turned off the Nintendo and turned the TV to the news but had the volume low. "Yeah, Hector," Chad confessed. "Me and Star are first cousins. She younger than me...and she's a good girl. She's just had to deal with a lot at a young age." "A lot like what? Hector asked. Chad guzzled his beer then said, "Her mama died from AIDS while Star was a senior in high school. She had been sick for a while but no one really knew what was wrong. She was a workaholic trying to make sure Star had the best of everything that her and my mom and my aunts and uncles didn't have." "How did she get AIDS?" Hector asked. "No one really knows for sure, but word on the street says it was this guy she was dating. He still alive. He looks like something wrong with him to me but no one can prove it. My uncles said they were going to kill him, but my mom begged and pleaded with them to just let it be. Star is very smart-a straight A student-and was accepted to a couple of Ivy League colleges. But after her mom died, she started dancing. I asked her if it was money she needed. She knows I would help her out. But she told me not to worry about her and that she was Ok and going to be Ok. I really love my lil' cousin but she has a strong mind. I told Gustavo not to say anything about me because I want to keep my personal life as private as I can." "That's cool," Hector said. "I won't say a word." We were all standing in the kitchen when Angel screamed, "Look! Look! That's Jaime's apartment!" She ran and we all followed her into the living room. "Turn it up!" she screamed. As Chad pressed the remote, we all heard the newscaster say, "A total of nine men have been arrested and charged with possession with intent to distribute thanks to the handiwork of the Atlanta DEA. Agents confiscated 10 kilos of cocaine. No bond was granted for either of the suspects. More on this story at 11:00." Angel was horrified. "Oh my fucking God!" she screamed. "Jaime's going to kill me!" I said, "Fuck that punk bitch, Angel! That dude ain't no family of yours. He's a fucking slime ball, bitch ass midget!" I screamed. Angel just shook her head and said, "My clothes, shoes, makeup- everything I owned was over there." Chad looked up and said, "Wait, is that where you said your rental car got shot at?" "Yeah, that's where the funk went down at," I said. "Boy-oh-boy," Hector said. "You betta be glad I wasn't there because I would have been fucking fools up left and right." "What happened?" Chad asked. So I told him: "I'd been hearing about Jaime for years from Angel always juicing stories about him. But even so, I wanted to be cool with him. But this fool was a crack head muthafucka who was trying to force Angel into fucking with his dope dealer runners who he had already had sex with. I mean, my gut didn't feel right the minute we pulled up to his apartment." I looked down at Angel and she looked sad. "Look, Angel," I said, "He never seemed like a cool dude from the stories you always told me and I hope you never have to see him again." Angel cut in and confessed, "Gustavo, he's my brother." "Your brother?" Chad asked. "Yes, my brother," she repeated. Then I said, "Family is not fucked up! Family don't do fucked up shit. Family-real family-has your back and looks out and not try to hurt you!" "Calm down, G!" my brother said. "It's obvious she loves him, so chill out!" I knew he was right. In the back of my mind, I couldn't believe my Tia Loose had called last night. I mean I haven't heard her voice since I was nine. She didn't come get us from that hellhole when we were in Mexico or even come around when we were moving from foster home to foster home. I was so worked up, I just walked into Chad's bedroom and repeated: "Mijito doesn't live here," and tried to think of something positive. But all I could see was fat, redheaded pale-faced Rosalinda in my mind with that ugly green housedress she wore. Then I thought about her making me smell her nasty pussy! I couldn't think of any good thoughts of all the memories I had of Rosalinda and Tito. Thoughts of them hurting us and making us have sex in Mexico were rolling faster and faster in my brain. I fell to my knees. I couldn't breathe. I started kicking my legs as hard as I could. I just remember waking up with Hector and Angel holding me. I looked at Chad and could see him looking back at me with a worried face. "It's Ok," Hector and Angel both said while putting a cold rag on my face. I thought about what had just happened. I was starting to feel so embarrassed. Then I sat up and said, I'm sorry, but I think I need to go home." "You're alright man!" Chad said with a nervous voice. "We need to eat first. We're all hungry and we're all together, so that's all that matters," Angel said "Amen to that!" Chad said. "Hector, come with me to put this food on the grill, if you don't mind." Angel told Hector that she would take care of me while he was gone. Then they both left the bathroom. "What happened, G?" Angel asked. "I don't know," I answered. "I just started thinking about all this stuff from the past and couldn't shake it. I mean, I tried and tried but I couldn't." Angel looked me in the eye and said, "Look, we're in Atlanta and I know a lot of shit's popped off already, but it's a new life for us all...And I need your little butt to be thinking about auditioning for Sex Machine tomorrow," she said trying to cheer me up. "Plus, I need a whole new wardrobe and as your manager, I can't be looking raggedy!" "Girl, who taught you to always know what to say?" I asked. "I'm just a smart, classy good pussy bitch," she said. We both laughed. "I need some weed now," I said. "I'm going to have to be high to be around Chad because that fool probably thinks I'm like that bitch from the movie Carrie!" We laughed again and then we jumped up, finished the sides, ate and watched a movie. Angel and Hector fell asleep on the couch and Chad got me high out of my mind. Then he fucked me in the shower so good that I slept on his bed with him like we were a married couple. The next day, me, Angel and Hector took the train to Five Points. We were headed to the audition to see if Rico aka Sex Machine could really make me a moneymaking dancer. We ditched the rental car in a grocery store parking lot because we didn't want anything to do with Jaime or going to jail. We knocked on the door of the same nightclub we were just at a couple of days before. I loved that club. Rico told me that's where we were going to be dancing for him. A guy answered the door and boy was he fine! His beautiful, brown skin and smile was making me feel good about doing this audition. He introduced himself and we all followed him upstairs. When we made it up there, I saw about 10 dudes with nice bodies and good looking faces. The guys were standing around talking. Then Rico came out of his office. "Hey, pretty boys and girl," he said as he kissed Angel's hand. "So this is my team of dancers and we dance from L.A. to Detroit to New York to Miami. Wherever the money is at, that's where we are." Then he looked at me and said, "When I saw you at Fat Tuesdays the other night, my money antenna went off... and then when I saw your brother, my money antenna went off again. So, I'm going to have one of my dancers show you some moves and I'm going to see if you can catch on. Also, I need you two to also show us what you got. If we like you both, you get the money and we sign you on. And if we don't, you get the money and y'all will be free to leave." I looked at Angel and she was smiling. Then I looked at Hector. He was biting his nails and looking down at the ground. Angel saw that Hector was nervous too, so she walked closer to Rico and whispered, "Can all of us and you go in your office?" "Yes, baby... anything for you," he told her. I saw how he flirted with Angel and I felt a little jealous. I mean he was just trying to run game on me at 112. We all walked back in the office and Rico said, "So what is it fellas? Y'all down?" I was quick to say I was down. Then we all looked at Hector and he said, "Look, I didn't know I was auditioning, so let me see what my brother does first...then I'll make my decision." So, Rico showed me what to put on and gave me some oil and some boots that looked kind of like girl boots but not really. I got ready and then all four of us walked out to where the other dancers were. Rico told me to stand over where Mocha One was and to follow his moves. So I did and they turned on the music. It was Shake What Your Mama Gave You by Poison Clan. Mocha was dancing so good you could see every muscle in his body and I wanted to have him on top of me like he was fucking the pole and ground. I mean it was amazing. "Green Eyes, why don't you and your bro do some stretching," Rico suggested. So Hector and me stretched while we kept our eyes on Mocha and his dancing. My heart was beating fast because I was so nervous. And when the song *Freaking You* by Jodeci came on, I started getting even more nervous. Mocha moved and danced like I'd never seen before. He was an outstanding dancer. I looked over at Rico and motioned for him to come over to me. "What's up, Green Eyes?" he asked. "I'm feeling it," I said. "I mean, really feeling it. But I think if I smoke some weed, it would take the edge off." We walked back in the room. Rico already had a blunt rolled. He lit it up and I smoked half of it and was ready. When I walked back out to where everyone was, I heard Rico say into the mic, "NOW TO THE STAGE...THE LATIN LOVER...GREEN EYES!!" The next sound I heard was MC Shy D's song *Shake It* and I let loose. I was dancing my ass off. Mocha was on the middle of the floor just sitting there. Then Rico said into the mic, "Give the man a lap dance!" So I walked over to Mocha and was shaking my ass and my dick all over him. Then they played my jam by Keith Sweat- *Make it Last*. It was an oldie but a goodie. "I need you to take your costume off, please," Rico said. So I did. I had my ass and dick out. I was feeling it so much I almost forgot Hector and Angel were there. When the song went off, I heard hands clapping. I mean, they were screaming, giving me hugs and going crazy! I was so happy. I finally felt like I was a part of something that was big and was going to make me a star. I guess those little boy dreams of Hollywood were going to come true. Hector walked over to me and said, "I'm going to dance... but tell Rico I'm not showing my dick to these dudes." Angel walked over and said, "You did good, you *pinche calaweta*! I started laughing. Then I asked Angel with a smile on my face, "Could you get Rico? We need to talk to him...manager." Rico came over and the music started blasting again with the song *Daisy Dukes* as the other dancers started practicing for their shows. We walked back into Rico's office. As we walked in, Hector blurted out, "I want to dance, but on one condition...only for women...not men. Can that happen?" He was serious. "Of course," Rico said. "Look man, we dance for men and women but the men is where our money is. Not nan one of us is a fag. We all like pussy!" My heart dropped when he said fag. I wanted to say something but I didn't. I looked over at Angel and she just rolled her eyes and twisted her fingers back and forth to let me know this was all about the money. I mean he did hit on me at 112. So

I'm sure he likes men...right? I mean...he does know I'm gay. All these things were going through my mind when Angel walked over to me and whispered, "He's being *machismo*." It's just a word. I calmed myself down when she said that to me. She always knows what to say. Rico told Hector, "Look, I'll only call you for ladies night, but in order for me to sign you; you're going to have to dance and show us your penis. The other guys are part of the Midnight Express...and y'all ain't black. All of Midnight Express is, so you're going to have to be better or just as good...you feel me?" Hector nodded, "Yea, I feel you. So what do I put on?" Everyone left the room except me and Hector. "I'm proud of you bro for doing this," I said. "Look, I need money and pussy," he said in his Oak Park Mexicano voice. "That's all I want in life. So if pussy can make me some money and money can bring me some pussy, then I will be one happy *cholo*!" I helped Hector get ready. I oiled his back and he put on his boots. "Damn," I said. "Your body looks better than mine." He joked back, "That's because I don't smoke no fuckin' weed and get the munchies." He started boxing in the air. We could still hear music bumping in the other room. We walked out of the room and heard Rico say, "NOW, WELCOME TO THE STAGE...THE HISPANIC PANIC!!" They were playing *Black Pussy* by DJ Quik with a booty shake sound. I was surprised. Hector could dance! There was a woman, that looked 70 years old, sitting on a chair and Hector was giving it to her. Boy, I wanted to laugh but the shock from Hector knowing how to dance and how to dance good was a shock. My bro was working it. The music went off and that old woman looked like she was about to have a heart attack from seeing Hector's big dick. Everyone cheered us on and gave us high fives. "Listen up," Rico said. "You are our official non- black, Latino Midnight Express exotic dancers. You will now have to meet here five days a week to get your pole work together. You will also be doing as many sit ups, day and night, six days a week. And we will have y'all making us and you some money in no time at all! Congratulations to Mr. Green Eyes and the amazing Hispanic Panic!" Rico screamed into the mic. We went into the room to change and Rico gave us $300 a piece. I was so excited. "The faster you learn that pole the faster you'll be ready to make this paper," Rico said. We both signed a contract without even reading it. Our birthdays were just weeks away and we were going to be paid and rich before we turned 18, I thought to myself.

Chapter 12: Hector or Rich?

It's been three weeks since I've seen Hector! I've been flying back and forth to see Rich! I love him...at least I think I do. I still wonder what Hector is doing. But I can't be down with no fag shit. I don't have a problem with gay people as long as they don't bring that shit my way. I turned on my TV and looked out my hotel window. Boston was beautiful but snowing. I feel like I'm kind of gaining weight. All I do is shop and then we order room service a lot and have sex. Rich is always busy with baseball and baseball practice. It's like damn; he never seems to get a break. But I love him. I'm ready to go ring shopping. He promised I would have it before Valentine's Day. Let's see...I think I want three karats...pear shaped. And I don't want gold because that's for ghetto bitches-not classy girls like me. Flying back and forth, I haven't even really been at the club too much. All I do is sit in luxurious hotels, sip fine champagne and watch Ricki Lake and Maury Povich and occasionally Oprah. Today's my mother's birthday. She would have been 40 years old. I miss her so much. I would do anything to have her back. I just hate AIDS! Why did the gays have to infect straight women? I just don't get it! I don't understand! It makes me so sad every time I think about her. The phone rang. I picked up in my Joan Collins voice from the show *Dynasty*. "Hello?" I said into the receiver. "Hey baby. I miss you!" Rich said. "I miss you too!" I answered like a baby. "Look, I need to take a flight with some of my teammates to Colorado for some publicity stuff for the team. I'm about to fly out in about an hour." "What about me?" I asked in my baby voice again. "Stay relaxed today," he said. "I'll have a ticket for you to fly out tomorrow in the a.m. So just rest and be ready for me in Colorado. If you need to go shopping for some clothes or whatever, you need to just charge it to the room. The concierge already knows. Ok, baby...miss you, love you!" "I love you too!" I said. I hung up the phone so happy. I decided to take off my teddy that I was wearing for Rich and put on some clothes to go shopping. I got dressed, hit up Gucci, Saks Fifth Avenue and Neiman Marcus. I was getting so many looks from women and men I started to feel like I was in the movie *Pretty Woman*. They didn't realize my mom had been taking me to all the high-end stores at Lennox Mall and Phipps Plaza since I was little. I never shopped at Contempo or Merry-Go-Round, Sears or JC Penny like those other white girls did at my high school. Their parents had money but no class. I laughed to myself. I finally got back to my room and threw my bags by my suitcase. I was going to watch a little TV and then pack when I heard my pager going off. It's probably someone from work wondering when I'm coming back to make them rich, I laughed. I looked at the number and realized it was Hector. He's paged me once a week for the last three weeks and I haven't called him back. I miss him even though I haven't known him that long. But the time we talked and had sex, I felt like I really knew him. I felt safe with him like I could just be me. He's almost perfect except for he's young and broke. But he has a six-pack to die for and some pretty feet. I still have to get used to Rich's ugly feet. Thank God I only see them when we're in the shower. I thought about calling him, but I don't want no gay or bisexual man-even though he seemed straight. I'm not taking no chances. I checked my pager again and saw a number I hadn't seen before. It was a 911 page. Hmmm, I thought. I wonder who that is. I turned on the TV and before long I dozed off. I woke up to my pager going off again. And this time it was the same person that sent me the last page. I decided to call the number wondering who it was. "Hello?" a deep voice said. "Hi, did someone page Star?" I asked. "I most certainly did," the voice said. I tried to place the voice but I couldn't. "May I ask whom I speaking with?" I asked. "Yes. This is D," the voice said. The bell in my head was still not ringing. "D who, may I ask?" I said in a polite voice. "Duane... the guy who bought you two bottles of Dom Perignon," the voice responded. "But then again, I'm sure you're used to that." Suddenly, I knew who he was. This was the guy I got drunk with at the club and passed out on. "Ahhh, hi!" I said. "I'm not disturbing you am I?" he asked. "No, no...I'm fine," I said. I'm just a little embarrassed," I said in my baby voice. "Why?" he asked. "Oh no reason," I said. "I'm sorry if I startled you, but I misplaced your number and I've been out of town, so I went to the club to see you and you weren't there. But a nice young lady was gave it to me." "Who gave it to you?" I asked. Not that it mattered because he was fine! "A young lady named Royalty," he responded. "But please don't get mad at her because I had to beg and plead with her. She drives a very hard bargain." I bet she did, I thought to myself. "It's fine," I said. "So how have you been?" he went on. "I've been good...and busy just taking care of business," I said. "You don't say?" D asked. "Well I couldn't get you off of my mind and would love to take you to dinner sometime. Would you like that?" I said, "Yes I would like that!" "Well, I wanted to call and touch bases with you, so just let me know when you're ready to see me," he said. "I will," I said. "Good," he said back. "Hope to hear from you soon." I hung up the phone and my heart was beating. D was soooo sexy and dark skinned! It wasn't usually what I was attracted to, but I'm glad he called. Then I thought, once I'm married, I'm going to have to be with one man for the rest of my life! Oh no! Can I do that? Then I looked at my bags of clothes; the room I was staying in at the Ritz Carlton and all the money I got from Rich just doing nothing but having sex with him and I enjoyed that and I decided that I love him. Yes, I love him! I'm going to make him so proud of me. I'm going to be the best wife ever that is if he really proposes to me. But why would he lie about it. Finally, I got up, packed my things, took a nice bath and ordered a bottle of Cristal to drink with my dinner steak and vegetables. You know a girl has to keep it tight and with all the drinking I've been doing, I think I picked up two or three pounds. The next morning, I had the bellboy take my bags downstairs. I gave him a $50 tip for being so helpful. I caught a taxi to Logan International Airport, checked my bags and bought some coffee from the coffee shop. I went and found a seat to wait to board when I heard, "Yo, ma...if God had made anything better then you, he must have kept it for himself," The Big Daddy Kane lookalike said. "So, ma...what's your name?" "Gladys," I said. "Well that's a beautiful name. I was just wondering..." I stopped him in his tracks. "Look, brother man, I'm engaged so I don't want to waste your time, but thank you so much for the compliment." I kept it very honest and classy. "Where's your ring MA?" He asked with a thick Boston accent. "Oh, I'm waiting for him to give it to me... soon, very soon," I said so proudly. "How old are you?" he asked. "You're never supposed to ask a woman her age," I sounded annoyed. "You ain't from up north are you?" he pressed on. "No, I'm a southern bell." I said. He went on and said, "Ma, don't tell people you're engaged until you are. You're beautiful, real beautiful. And a sista like you needs a ring." I shot back, "Oh, I'm getting a ring! But thanks for the advice." The man shook his head and walked away. Thank God. I was glad he was gone. I started wondering what we were going to be doing in Colorado. I've never been to Colorado and was curious to see what Denver was like. I boarded the plane and looked around first class and I was the only black person in sight. Nothing but old white men that were looking at me like I was Jesus. The flight attendant was a pretty, black, older lady with salt and pepper hair. "May I get you a beverage?" she asked. "Yes," I answered. "What champagne do you have?" "Young lady, can I see your ID?" she asked. "May I ask why?" I asked back. "Because yes you are a beautiful woman, but I see a young lady in your eyes," she said knowingly. I pretended I didn't know where she was going with it so I just said, "I'll take some water and some coffee please." She walked away and the man next to me said, "Looks like it's going to be sunny in Colorado." "Really?" I responded. "That's nice." I looked over at him and he said, "Would you like me to order some champagne and give it to you?" He sounded like Mr. Furley from *Three's Company*. "That's so very kind of you sweetie, but I'm ok," I said in my sexy voice. I don't know why I said it like that but I did while laughing to myself. "Can I ask you a question?" he asked. "Well, it depends on what it is," I said playfully. "Are you a model?" Mr. Furley asked. "No, I'm not," I answered. " "Why do you ask?" "Well, I don't know the last time I've seen such beauty. Your skin is so radiant. You actually look like a living doll," he said very sweetly. "I said, "Thank you! That was very sweet of you to say." "It's true," he continued. "Have you ever been to Paris?" I said, "No, I haven't, but I plan to go soon with my fiancé. "Fiancé?" he asked. "Well, where's your ring?" I answered, "Hopefully, I'll be getting it in Colorado today or this weekend." "Lucky guy," Mr. Furley said. "What's he do for a living?" "He plays sports," I said. "What kind," he asked. Before I could answer, my coffee and his Bloody Mary came. I was glad! I wasn't going to be able to take this for four hours on this plane. And I realized the guy on the other seat was also going to start asking questions. I wondered what I was going to do. I wasn't in the mood and had forgotten my CD headphones in Atlanta. "I'm going have to buy some more in Denver," I told myself. Just then it hit me: I had my Bible in my purse. Every time my mom wanted alone time she would read her Bible and wouldn't say a word. She was reading it a lot in the last year of her life. If she wasn't working, she was reading her Bible. I opened my purse and there it was-my beautiful Bible. And before the man or any of the men in first class could say anything, I pulled it out. But I really didn't want to read it the whole trip. I looked in my Louis Vuitton purse and remembered I had a Jet Magazine that I had bought at the convenience store in Boston when I was shopping yesterday. I said a prayer to the Lord that he would forgive me for putting this Jet Magazine inside the Bible and pretending I was reading the scripture when I was really getting the latest celebrity gossip. And it worked! No one bothered me as soon as I raised the Bible. I finished reading the magazine and then I fell asleep. The coffee couldn't keep me up. It was just something about flying that made me sleepy. Finally, we landed. Thank God! I stretched and we started to exit the plane but before I could get up, I had three white men handing me their business cards all at the same time. I took them all and said, "Thank you." I got off the plane and followed the signs to baggage claim so I could pick up my luggage. Then I realized something: I didn't know where I should be going. Then it dawned on me that I needed a cell phone. I see more and more people with them-even some of those raggedy ass dancers have a cell phone. I walked towards the door to where the taxis were figuring Rich might have the limo out there waiting. Or maybe he's going to surprise me and just pop up and propose to me in the airport in front of everyone.

I walked outside and behind me I heard voices yelling, "Star! Star! Star!" I turned and it was three blondes coming my way. "Oh my God!" said one of the blondes. "We were looking everywhere for you! Wow, Rich told us you were black, but I didn't really know he meant *black.*" "That's rude, Summer!" the other white girl said. "What she meant to say is she thought you were mixed like Nichelle," the second white girl said. "I didn't know Nichelle was mixed, Megan," the third white girl said. "She looks Latina." I stood there confused and wondered why these girls were in front of me. "Where's Rich," I said impatiently. "Oh, he told us to pick you up," white girl number one said. "He's with our guys doing guy things, so he said since we're all going to be together, we should pick you up and do some bonding. We asked Nichelle to go but she went with the fellas and said she would bond later. I'm Meagan. This is Summer and she's Debbie." "The limo's down there," Summer said. "Come on, Star." We got into the limo and I was so confused. I had no idea what was going on. I sat quietly and just listened to them go on and on and on and on. I really wished they would just shut the fuck up. They reminded me of the hating ass white girls I went to private school with except these three were pretty. But I wasn't worried. They were pretty with big boobs but walking to the limo I got a glance of their flat butts. I laughed to myself. "We're here!" Summer said excitedly. "Star, we cooked a great dinner. We started it last night and the boys are going to love it!" "All we really have to do is make the salad and warm up the soup and dinner will be ready," Debbie said. I just smiled and tossed my hair like they did. We walked up to what looked like a cabin. It was beautiful. We walked in and they showed me to our room. "So...let me get this straight," I said. "We're all staying in this house?" I was even more confused. The girls looked at me and Summer asked, "Didn't Rich tell you? The boys have been friends for a while and they get together as often as they can and hang out and have fun!" "Woo hoooooo!" Debbie screamed. It seemed like I was talking to triplets because they all seemed to have the same personality, I thought to myself. "Well, here's your room," Summer said. "Get comfy... and oh yeah, we saved some breakfast for you if you're still hungry." "Thanks," I said. The room was breathtaking. And our view looked out over the beautiful mountains and down to what looked like the city. I wrapped my hair then took a nice, long bath in the beautiful Jacuzzi-style tub. I couldn't decide what to wear being that they blond triplets looked like Barbies that shop at Kmart. I put on some jeans that fit every curve just right and a white V-neck long sleeved shirt with some black Gucci pumps. Then I headed down stairs. I was anxious to see Rich and I was starting to get hungry. Even though I don't eat everyone's cooking, I was still willing to see what it looked like. "Hi ladies," I said all chipper and happy. "I feel so much better now. I didn't get any rest on the plane. Seriously, it was like every old white man on there must of thought I was Janet Jackson because they just wouldn't leave me alone," I joked with the girls. No one laughed. They just looked at me like I was talking in Chinese or something. "Ohhh, I get it" Summer said in her snobby white girl tone. Then they all started laughing. Ok, I'm going to need a drink, I thought to myself. "So, ladies...where's the bar?" I asked. "Over there!" Megan pointed. I turned around and there it was-a real bar at the corner of the kitchen with what looked like every alcoholic beverage you could think of. As I made my way to the alcohol, Summer said playfully, "Well, I am a bartender in Vegas. So I'll make you whatever you want... just as soon as you show me your ID I didn't say anything at first. Then I blurted out jokingly, "I know you're not going to make me walk upstairs in these Gucci pumps are you? I mean they're pretty but not the most comfortable for walking up and down the stairs." Silence. Damn! Not this shit again! They were stone cold quiet and looking at me as if I had spoken in Swahili this time. "How old are you?" Summer asked. I answered, "I just turned 19 on September 6." They all gasped. "19!?" Meagan sounded shocked. "You're so young!" Summer added. "Where in the world did Rich meet you...at the skating rink?" Debbie said sarcastically. Then they all laughed. I wasn't sure what to say. I sure wasn't going to let these dizzy bitches know I was a stripper. At that moment it dawned on me: I *was* a stripper. A sense of sadness came over me. It was the same feeling I got when my mom was in my bedroom telling me she has full blown AIDS. "I met him at Phipps

Plaza," I said suddenly. "What's that?" Megan asked. "It's a high end mall in Atlanta," I responded. "I was shopping at Saks Fifth Avenue and he was doing the same. With one glance, I knew he was the one. I led so proudly. "The one?" Summer asked. "What do you mean... *the one*?" I didn't know if I should open my mouth. I didn't know who these bitches really were. But I went on and said, "Well, we've talked about getting engaged. Of course nothing's set in stone. It's just something we talked about. I had to be careful what I said in case this was my surprise engagement party. "Ohhh...Ok," Debbie said. "Why don't you make Star one of your famous margaritas, Summer?" Meagan suggested. "Well, I really only drink champagne," I said. "Moet, Dom, Cristal...but you know what? Since I'm here-and it calls for a great weekend-why not? Margarita it is!" I said trying to be a team player. "I'm on it!" Summer said. Before I knew it, I was on my third margarita and second shot of tequila. I felt tipsy but I felt good. I was still hungry but the breakfast they left for me looked like shit. We all talked and they told me their ages, what they did and how much they loved being with their men. "We're hoooooome!" a voice boomed as the door opened. It sounded like a brutha's voice. And sure enough, it wasn't just one, but four of them...four beautiful, black men with my fine, red head right next to them along with a gorgeous, tall, wavy-headed girl. I jumped out my chair and ran towards Rich and jumped into his arms. We kissed and kissed and kissed. Then I heard, "Hiii! I'm Nichelle," she said in a voice that sounded like it could have come from a female Mark Twain. Rich put me down with me still holding on to him. I looked at the female talking to me. She had a model's smile and she was a lot taller than me. "You're so pretty," I said to Nichelle. "Well, thank you!" she said back. "I was about to say the same thing about you." With that, she reached over and we embraced as if we'd known each other forever. I've never been one to hang around females, except for my Bankhead cousins, whom I love, but haven't seen much lately. We let go of each other and I said, "I'm Star." Then one of the bruthas said, "I thought you two were about to start eating each other." "You wish!" Nichelle shot back. "Damn Rich!" another brutha said. "When you said you were dating a sista, I didn't realize you meant literally. "Oh my God, Tyrone!" Summer said. "That's what I said. I thought she was going to be mixed." "Excuse me Summer?" Nichelle asked. "But you're not black are you?" "No, of course not," Summer said. "I'm white." "Well, why in the hell are you talking about a black subject? Didn't you see the movie *Jungle Fever*? Everyone but the three blondes was laughing. "Well, what do you mean?" Summer asked. She was clueless. "Oh sweetie, I'll let you read one of my Ebony magazines so you can figure it out!" Nichelle said laughing in her deep, country voice. "Where you from, Nichelle?" I asked. "Girl, North Carolina in the mountains," she said. "Honeyyyy, I'm a country girl." We high fived. "Girl, where you from?" She asked me. "Atlanta," I said proudly. I was still holding on to Rich when Nichelle grabbed me and said, "We'll be back." She held my hand and we went over to the bar. "What you drinkin' cowgirl?" she asked. "Well, I was drinking one of Summer's famous margaritas," I answered. "Girl, I wouldn't let them make me any more drinks," Nichelle warned. "I don't trust white girls. Honey, that's all I grew up with. "Really?" I asked. "Me too!" I was liking my new friend. "So then you know what I'm talking about," Nichelle went on. They'll try to fuck your man and smile in your face." I looked at her confidently and said, "Well, up to this point, I haven't had one who could take a man from me yet!" "I like you, girl!" Nichelle said like a hillbilly. "This is something I never ask," I said feeling more comfortable with my bonding buddy. "But I guess I don't ask because I really don't hang with too many females, but what race are you? I mean you're very, very pretty!" Nichelle didn't think twice when she said, "Girl, I'm black like you. My daddy black and my mama black too." It wasn't until I started dancing that I saw mixed-looking girls. I hate to say it, but even that he-she-or whatever the fuck Angel was-was beautiful, I thought to myself. And then I met Nichelle and she was tall, bronzed with wavy, sandy hair and what looked like natural blonde streaks. Plus, she had an ass on her. It wasn't as big as mine, but she did have one. "Girl, why you staring at me like that?" she asked me. "Oh I'm sorry," I said. "I'm not gay, but I was just admiring your beauty." "Star, I wish I had skin like yours...and you have boobs and ass! Girl, you're naturally pretty," she said. "Me? I smoke and been drinking so much, I don't leave out the house without foundation." She made herself a Bloody Mary and changed the subject. "Ok, now you said you been drinking margaritas, so you probably want to stick with that. What do you normally drink?" I told her I preferred champagne. "Girl, I can't stand champagne!" she said. "All these ball players try to impress me with champagne but I let them know that that shit gives me a headache. I will take some whiskey and put the money in my bra for the champagne." We both laughed. "Girl, let me shut up before Quincy hears me," she said. "Come on. Here's your margarita. I want to go outside to smoke." I turned around and Rich was sitting at the island in the kitchen just staring. "I'll be right back," I said to him in a June Cleaver voice. Then I blew him a kiss and he caught it. Me and Nichelle walked outside. It was freezing. It was hard to believe Christmas was in three weeks. The air felt good and even though I don't smoke, it smelled good for some reason. "Ok, so how long have you been dating white guys?" Nichelle asked. "Honestly, I date all guys, but white has been mainly what I attract," I answered. "But bruthas like me too. I don't know. It's just something about Rich." Well, have you ever dated a brutha?" she asked. "Kinda, but not really," I said not wanting to tell her Rich was my first real boyfriend besides the white guys I had sniffing around me in high school. "I guess I haven't dated a black guy per se. But I've kissed one." Nichelle went on. "Girl, how old are you?" I told her I was 19. "Damn, girl!" she was surprised. "You look young, but I didn't know you were that young!" I asked her age since everyone wanted to know each other's ages. I'm 24," she said. "I'm an old bitch. She sounded sad. "You're not old!" I comforted her. "I feel old," she responded. "I've been fucking around with these dumb ass athletes for the last two years. I was with my high school sweetheart until he married a white girl. I loved him. He was my first. He took my virginity and he took care of me. But then he left and I was damn near homeless. I had to move back in with my mama. Then I started going to Charlotte and I couldn't keep bruthas off me-especially athletes. The ones I've met are fine but are disrespectful and don't know how to treat a bitch. Excuse my language. But flying from place to place to get with them is cool. They're generous sometimes but they also will make you beg for the money or want you to suck their dick 10 times a day. It's getting to be too much. I've thought about getting pregnant but I don't know if I could deal with an athlete my whole life. I like older men who know how to treat a lady. I'm tired of these young bruthas who just want to bang a bitch out and give half the rent money." She started laughing. "Wow, it's like that?" I asked. "It's not all bad," She assured me. "But Quincy has never held a door open; never pulled out my chair and that big bear-looking muthafucker eats like a pig eating slop." Her country accent was strong." How's Rich treat you?" I told her that Rich was the total opposite of everything she'd just described. He's a true gentleman. I meant that. "Wow," she said. "That's sweet. This is the first time I've ever met him." I asked, "How long you been with Quincy?" "Too long!" she laughed. "Let's see...it's the beginning of December... hmmm.... I guess since September, so about three months. He flies me everywhere and when I get tired of it, I have a couple other guys I mess with too. But I'll say he gives me the most money. Rich plays baseball, right?" "Yes," I said. "Well, Quincy and Tyrone play football," she said. "The other two bruthas are groupies, but fine groupies." "Well, who are Summer, Megan and Debbie with?" I asked. "Whoever will fuck them!" Nichelle answered. "Even though I think they only like black men, I would still watch them around Rich because he's tall and has money enough for them to try him." We continued our talk, but it was chilly and I was starting to miss my man. I thoroughly enjoyed Nichelle's conversation though. We walked back inside and Summer yelled, "Girls! Dinner should be ready in a minute, but you have to taste this nacho cheese dip we just made!" I looked at Nichelle and we both busted out laughing. We both had tears streaming from our eyes before we could stop. It felt so good to laugh like that. I really don't remember the last time I did. We walked over to the crock-pot and Nichelle grabbed a chip from the bowl Megan was holding. She dipped it into the nacho cheese dip and it seemed like the whole room went quiet. Then Nichelle gave her verdict: "This is delish!" When she said it, I started laughing hysterically. I just couldn't stop. Rich came over and picked me up like I was a baby doll. He looked over his shoulder and said, "Good night everyone, we'll see you guys in the morning." I was still laughing but trying to regain my composure as he carried me up the stairs. That is until I heard Nichelle yell, "Star! You're missing out on this cheese dip! It's so delish!" Again, I couldn't stop laughing. Fresh tears were falling. My face was laying on Rich's chest and when I looked up, he was smiling and staring deep into my eyes. It was at that moment that I knew this was the man who would be my husband. He laid me on the bed; took off his clothes and I just watched this tall, sexy white man kneel between my legs and go down on me! We hadn't used condoms since that night in VIP. Plus, I knew his ass wasn't no fag! He ate me out for what seemed like hours. Then we made love over and over and over again. The next morning, me and Nichelle cooked breakfast and dinner. We cooked fried chicken, collard greens, potato salad and cornbread. Me and my new sister threw down! The triplets were so jealous that they seemed distant for the remainder of our Colorado gathering. It was Ok with Nichelle and me because we were having fun. That day I realized I was with who I'm supposed to be with for the rest of my life. And now, I also have a new best friend. And that's big because me and bitches don't usually mesh. But this girl was beautiful just like me and had a personality that could run circles around Oprah.

Chapter 13: Hector's Life

I'm still tripping off becoming an exotic dancer. I mean, I always thought of it as fag shit. But when I saw MC Hammer's video, *Let's Get It Started,* I used to practice that shit in the bathroom. That was when I lived at that lousy ass foster house. Man...I hated that shit to an extent. Now look at me. I'm going to be 18 in a matter of days and rolling in some bread soon. I don't want to dance forever. I'm just going to save money so I can go to barbering school. I love cutting hair. Shit, once we were rescued from Mexico, I started cutting Gustavo's hair. Then, I started cutting mine. Even in the juvenile hall detention center, I was cutting hair. The other kids at the foster group home used to tell us that me and Gustavo should be boxers. I mean we fought a lot at school. *Vatos* were jealous that we made Dickies and Nikes look so good. Everyone thought we stayed in the gym at the group home, which we did. But shit, I think we owe our great bodies to genetics. My dad used to say we had bodies like his brother that used to box before he was shot by some gang bangers in LA. I really miss my dad. I still don't want to believe that he sold us to those animals in fuckin' Mexico. The therapist at the group home used to tell us that we needed to talk about it in order to let stuff go. I used to want to tell them, "*You* let it go and shut the fuck up!" Other times I did let it go. But sometimes, I'd just start swinging on fools. On those days, I wasn't talking about shit with no one. I mean, how can I tell someone what happened to me and my brother and expect them to fix it? What was done was done to us. But a muthafucker would never ever try to do that shit to me or my brother again. I won't even let them fuck with Angelo...I mean Angel. She always looked like a girl even when we were kidnapped in Mexico. But now, she really looks like a girl. It kind of weirds me out a little, but she's good people and always had our backs. The shit they did to her sometimes was just as bad as when they tortured us. I hate thinking of that time but it doesn't go away unless I'm fucking. But it was with Star, that for the first time in my life, she had me thinking about her maybe being my girlfriend. Me saying that might sound funny because I love pussy so much that it would be hard to only have one piece of pussy all my life. My homies say they don't eat pussy. But I can't think of anything better to eat. Don't get me wrong; I love Mexican food, but I'd give that up for pussy any day. Star is only the third black girl I ever fucked. The first chick was cool, but she screamed so loud at the group home, I would have to put my baseball cap on her face to shut her up. Then there was Stephanie. Everyone else was Mexican. I mean, I love Mexican pussy and I love Mexican girls with that thick, black hair around their lips. That shit turns me on. I haven't seen no Mexican girls down here except one on the train...and she was ugly. And white girls….white girls…damn, I think every white girl at the group home sucked my dick. I guess word got around. And before Victor took us in, they were paying to suck my dick. I guess most dudes must have small dicks. I never realized mine was big until bitches started sucking it and telling me. I guess I kind of miss Sacramento. But so many guys had static with us that fighting is all we did. It got to the point where we stopped going to Miller's Park because the dudes from Centro and the Franklin Boys would trip with us. And that didn't make sense because we were from Oak Park and the group home was on Franklin...ignorant people. I just laid there daydreaming. I could hear Gustavo and Angel running their mouths in the other room like they always do. I can't believe Chad's a homo. I mean dude looks straight. But a lot of the black guys at the club that night looked straight too. I wonder if there are a lot of guys in Sacramento that look straight but are actually gay. One time, I could of sworn Kevin was watching me piss, but soon as I realized it and looked at him, he turned his face. I don't have nothing against gay people. Hell, my brother used to act like a girl when we were little. And every bitch I fucked in Cali wanted to hook their sister or friend up with him. I wanted to say, "He's not interested," but I thought they should just see it like I did. But they didn't. Wow, I couldn't imagine having no man as a sexual partner...in the bed...Ewww... I can't even think it. But what I could imagine is Star riding this dick and looking at me while she feels all of it in her. Damn! I think I miss her! I put my hands on my dick and yelled for G to bring me the phone. He opened the door and threw it at me. I couldn't believe I knew this bitch's number by heart. I hesitated to call because I wasn't used to jocking no bitch. I definitely didn't think I would ever be jocking no black bitch! But I think she's one of the finest bitches I've ever seen-and I had some banging ass Mexican girls. I looked at the phone then put it down. I looked at it again and said, "Fuck it! I'm in Atlanta and she's the only bitch I've fucked with, so I'm calling. I put in my number and paged her. I lay there horny as hell! I looked at the clock for a whole hour. Nothing. No call or anything. I sat up and was kind of frustrated. Finally, I couldn't take it anymore. I closed my eyes and thought of me sucking her pretty titties. Then I stroked and stroked. I hated jacking off. It took me forever to cum. I needed to be in some pussy. About 30 minutes later, I nutted everywhere! That shit shot out like a waterfall. I grabbed the towel next to me on the floor and nodded off. That shit put me right to sleep. I could hear the phone ringing in my dream. I opened my eyes and smiled. Star was calling me back, I thought. I did a quick glance at the phone and didn't recognize the number. "Hey, what up?" I answered. I didn't hear a thing. "What up?" I repeated. Then I thought, "Shit, this must be one of my brother or Angel's gay men and hung up. Just as I did, Gustavo walked in and asked if the phone had rung. I looked at him and those high ass eyes. It looked like he had just smoked. And he smelled like weed. "Man, when you going to quit that shit?" I asked. "When I make some money!" he said back to me. "Me and Angel are bored. And we've paged the little bit of freaks we do have in Atlanta and now we just waiting to see who's buying dinner." He annoyed me with that neck-rolling, finger popping gay shit. He always did it more when Angel was around and even more when he was high and Angel was around. The phone rang again and Gustavo reached for it. But just because his ass got smart with me, I decided I was going to answer the phone and pretend I was him as I laughed to myself. "Hello?" I answered in a high-pitched voice. As I was looking at Gustavo, I could tell he was mad even though he was laughing at the same time. My brother is crazy, I thought. "Hector?" the voice asked. I immediately knew who it was. I sat up and said, "Tia?" "Yes, *mijo*. It's me...your Tia Loose." I looked at Gustavo and he shut the door. "Umm, are you still alive?" I asked not knowing what else to say. "Well, of course *mijo*! I'm on the phone with you," she said. "Wow!" I said. "How did you get this number?" She said, "My mom is not doing so well. And one of our distant cousins ran into me at the grocery store here in Los Angeles and told me she was very sick. I plan to go to Sacramento this week. I haven't been in a while." I was very curious so I asked, "What's a while?" She said, "Since I last saw you boys." The phone went quiet and so I finally said, "What's up?" She responded, "I would like to see you guys. I called my mom-your grandma-and she said she heard you were in Atlanta and gave me the number. Is your mom out there too or are you boys in college out there?" "My mom's a crack head," I said flatly. "*Mijo*, please don't say that about your mom," my tia responded. "Say what?" I asked even though I knew what she meant. "Don't say what you just said," she said. I was getting annoyed and said, "Say what? That she's a fucking tweeker or crack head?" Again, the phone went silent. Then I said, "Is this some type of joke? I mean, you do sound like my tia but I we thought you were dead. But since you're not dead, where you been?" Now I was frustrated. "It's a long story, *mijo,*" *she said.* I will have to tell you in person. I really want to see my nephews. So, if I buy your tickets to Sacramento...will you come?" I was not moved. "We just got jobs," I said. "I don't know. Look, is this your number?" "Yes it is!" She said. "Well, let me talk to my brother and either him or I will call you back," I said trying to talk as proper as I could. *"Mijo,* I love you and your brother very much," my tia said. "Please, please call me back anytime. I will be waiting for your call. She sounded like she was crying. "Ok, cool," I said. Then I hung up the phone and just sat there for a minute. Finally, I jumped up and opened the bedroom door. Angel was painting her toes and Gustavo was in the kitchen fixing a sandwich. "You'll never believe who the fuck that was," I said. "Loose," Gustavo said with an attitude. "How the fuck did you know that?" I asked. "Because that bitch called the other day," he answered. "What?" I was confused. "Why the fuck didn't you tell me?" "Tell you what?" he said back. "That we haven't seen the bitch in 10,11...however many fucking years and she calls." My brother could be a bitch when he felt like it. "Well, I'm your fucking brother!" I said. "And if anyone from our family calls, you should at least tell me." I was pissed. "Family?" Gustavo shot back. "What do you mean...family? Whose family? I mean are you talking about Victor or Sonya or Lupita and Lorena? Or are you talking about Kevin, Stephanie and Angel? Because they're the only people that give a fuck about us. Can you think of anyone else?" I understood his point but I was still mad. "I just don't like when your ass get high and you start fuckin' acting like Sheneneh Jenkins and shit. You look stupid!" Then I heard Angel laughing. "What the fuck you laughing at?" I demanded. "One minute you're a white girl and the next a sista. Then you fuckin' start talking like you're a fuckin' feather-in-your-derby-wearing old school *chola* from Franklin!" Then

Gustavo started laughing and Angel asked," "What the fuck is Franklin?" "Aw shit," I said. "I forget you're not from Sac. Then the phone rang again and Angel said, "I'll get it." she grabbed the phone and took it outside. I calmed down and told Gustavo what Tia Loose had said on the phone about wanting to see us. "She said if she bought us a ticket to Sac, would we go see her. I told her I would ask you and get back with her. So... what you think?" as I play boxed with him. "Why now?" G asked. "I mean...I don't get it. She just calls all of sudden?" "Yeah, I said. "She said she ran into some cousin who gave her grandma's number and grandma told her we were in Atlanta." Gustavo was quiet and just listened to me. I told him just how the conversation went three times so I made sure he knew what exactly was said. That way, he could decide if he wanted to see her or not. "Hey *muchachos!*" Angel yelled. "I got us some dinner tonight! That was my freak, D. He said he had been out of town and he missed me! I told him that I was almost raped and now all my clothes are gone and he said he would help me get my pretty self back together. He also said he would take me and my twin brothers out for dinner tonight. At first, he just wanted to see me alone but that's going to be after he gives me some money." "Is he a fuckin' weirdo?" I asked. "No, Hector," she responded. "Why do you say that?" "Because what type of man goes out on dates with their chic and her brothers?" I asked. "I told him all the shit that happened to me and Gustavo and he felt sorry for us, I guess," she said. I wanted to stay home. I had $300. But me and my brother were trying not to touch the money we got from signing with Midnight Express so we could pay the rent. We all got ready. It took about two hours. Then, our phone rang and I picked it up. "WHAT'S UPPPP!?" I said like Martin Lawrence. "Yes, may I speak to Angel please?" The man said sounded like Ronald Reagan. "Yeah, hold up," I said. Angel grabbed the phone and started talking to Ronald. I laughed to myself. Then I went into the bathroom to make sure my creases in my T-shirt and jeans were tight. I walked back into the living room and everyone was looking cool and ready to go. D told Angel that he was lost and for us to meet him at the gas station. We headed to the gas station and it was so nice outside. The sky was so bright and peaceful. We crossed the street and the people in the cars were blowing their horns. I hoped they were blowing for Angel. We reached the gas station and there were a lot of cars there. But only one stood out. It was a Mercedes-silver with black tinted windows. Man, that shit was the bomb! We walked into the store while Angel tried to figure where D was. I bought some gum and bought a Gatorade. We walked back outside and there was a tall, dark-skinned black man hugging Angel. She waved for us to come over. So we did. "D, these are the loves of my life…Gustavo and Hector. They're my brothers," Angel said. "I thought they were your cousins? D asked. Angel just brushed it off and said, "Same thing…we're family!" Then D said to Angel, "Can I talk to you for a minute?" As they talked I was thinking: This fuckin' dude looks straight. What the fuck is going on in Atlanta? Shit, I'm gonna be solo down here…no homies. They talked for about five minutes then headed our way. "You fellas ready?" Angel asked. I nodded yes and Gustavo said, "You know it!" We got into the car. Something about D made me think he was nervous or something. "Dude, I like your ride," I said just trying to break the ice. "This is my first time in an expensive car." Then my brother added, "Yeah, it's the bomb in here!" Angel looked at D and said, "See there? They're nice guys. We're all nice. D looked in the rear view mirror and said, "Listen guys, I'm not used to having dudes in my car…and when Angel said cousins, I don't know why I was thinking little cousins. I definitely wasn't thinking you would be grown men. You know, now days you have to be careful. Hell, Angel almost shot me the first time we met at the mall." I started laughing. "Yeah, I told Gustavo but I never told Hector," Angel said. "Damn, I miss my gun." "Well, where is it?" D asked. "Long story," she responded. "I'll tell you when I get a drink." D changed the subject and asked, "So fellas, how are you liking Atlanta?" "I like it a lot," Gustavo said. "It's cool," I said. "Good, good…love to hear that," D said. "In Atlanta, you can make your dreams come true." We pulled up to this restaurant named Houston's. "This place looks fancy," I said. "I don't think I can afford this." "Don't worry," D said. "This is my welcome to Atlanta dinner." "Cool," I said. Then D drove up to the front of the restaurant and valeted the car. I've never been anywhere where there was a need to see a valet. I was really feeling this shit! We walked in and the host seated us. "So, what are you ladies and gentlemen drinking?" D asked. We all looked at each other. Then Gustavo said, "I'm going to order what I always order in Oakland at the club," "What's that?" we all asked at the same time. "A Long Island Iced T!" he said. The waitress came and asked for our drink orders. D looked at Angel and asked in a corny-ass trying to be sexy voice, "What would you like?" She wanted a Long Island too and I ordered the same thing. "Ok...three Long Islands," D said. "And I will have a scotch on the rocks, please." The smiling waitress said, "Sure thing! My name is Sue. Can I please see all of you pretty peoples' ID?" D just looked at her and said, "Ummm, this should take care of that," as he handed her a $50 bill. I thought: Fuck! People must have money on this side of town. But where we live, they seem broke. Chad lived in a kind of nice place too. It kind of reminded me of Greenhaven in Sac, I thought to myself. We were on our second Long Islands and I was buzzed. I looked over at Angel and she was smiling and just running her mouth telling D about what's had been going on with us recently. Then she said, "I want to propose a toast...to Gustavo and Hector's new job!" Everyone toasted but me. I was kind of hot about that shit. I wanted to say, "Damn, bitch! I don't want everyone to know I'm going to be shaking my dick for money." But since dude was treating and being so cool I went ahead and toasted. "So fellas...what's your new job? D asked. Before I could interrupt, Gustavo blurted out, "We're going to be exotic male dancers! And after tonight, no more eating or drinking bad because we will be working out seven days a week." D raised an eyebrow and said, "Really? You don't say?" I just sipped on my drink and thought about how much I wanted to be fucking Star. Finally, our meals came and we ate. I had the barbeque ribs. Then Duane took us back to the apartment. As we pulled into our parking lot, I thanked him and told him how nice it was of him to treat us so well. I then jumped out of the Benz and started walking towards our door. I saw what I thought was a badass bitch on the steps. But when I got closer, I realized it was just that man-bitch that was with Angel down at Fat Tuesday. "What the fuck are you doing here?" I asked. "I'm looking for Angel," the chick said. Then Gustavo walked up and asked, "How the fuck do you know where we stay?" The chick responded, "Angel and I came over here to lease this apartment out for you." Again I asked, "What are you doing here?" Without answering my question, Naomi asked, "*Papi*...what's the matter? Did I do something to you?" I looked at my brother then said, "Look, I don't think you should be here. They told me how the shit went down. So you need to leave." I saw Angel get out the car and walk towards us as D pulled off. Angel walked up and said, "Hey girl. What's up?" and gave her a hug. As she did, Naomi started crying. I unlocked the door and looked back at all three of them and said, "I don't want any shit or there will be some problems." Then I went to piss. After washing my hands, I went straight into the bedroom to see if Star had called. Looking at the call log I saw there were no messages from Star, but Lorena had called twice. I was so horny I decided to call her back. The phone rang. "Hello?" Lorena answered on the first ring. "So... you finally call me back?" I said, "Yeah. What's up?" She wanted to be a smart ass and said, "Well, actually I called for Gustavo." So I just said, "Ok cool. Let me get him." "No wait!" she yelled. "I was just kidding. I mean, I did have to tell him something but I also want to talk to you." I already knew what she wanted to talk about but I played it off and asked, "Talk to me about what?" She immediately said, "I miss you!" I decided to play along and said, "So...if you miss me...then play with your pussy and tell me what you would do with my dick." Lorena talked nasty to me until I jacked off again. I don't even remember saying goodbye. I think I passed out right after I squirted. As I slept, I heard the phone ringing again. I also heard G, Angel and Naomi in the living room running their mouths. I picked up the phone not looking at the caller ID. I was hoping it was star. It wasn't "What's up, my brother from another mother?" the voice asked. "Who's this?" I asked back. "It's Kev, man!" the voice said. "What up bro?" I answered. "So, what the heck you doing in the ATL?" he asked. "Man, it's a long story!" I said. "Anyhow, I'm glad you're here," he said. "Where you staying?" I told him I was staying on Stanton Road in East Point. "So, you moved from one hood to another." Kev stated. "You got a ride?" "No...no not yet. But I hope to have one soon," I said. Then he asked, "Who you down here with?" I told him I was with my brother and Angel. "Your brother's here?" Kev asked. "Yeah, he's here!" I said. "Who told you I was down here?" I asked. "Well, a couple of the homies told me they heard you moved out of Sac, but they didn't know where," he said. "But I was on the phone with Lupita yesterday and she told me when I was talking about you. She acted like it was a secret." "You still talk to that bitch?!" I asked. "Yeah, I do man," Kevin said. "I got something to tell you. But we will talk when I see you. I have a heavy class load this week man so let's try to get up this weekend." "Cool, I said and I hung up the phone and went back to sleep.

Chapter 14: Work Out

We sat there and talked for hours and I was not convinced that Naomi could be trusted. But she cried and cried and cried and told us about her childhood and everything else about her life. I admit it was sad. But then again, who doesn't have a story. She left about midnight. Then me and Angel sat up talking about everything she said. Angel really likes her and I liked her too at first. I just didn't like the fact that she was being used by Jaime and she was a druggy. I don't trust drug addicts. But she's fucking beautiful. I mean she has almost a boy haircut and still looks just like a girl! The bitch is almost as pretty as Angel. We both were about to make a pallet on the floor when my pager went off. I hoped it was Chad because I hadn't heard from him. But nope. It was Lorena. I called her back. As the phone rang I was so hoping Victor or Sonya wouldn't answer because I wasn't in the mood for a lecture. "Hello?" Lorena answered. "Hi, *pinche calaweta*!" I screamed. Angel screamed it too. "Who's that in the background?" Lorena asked. "That's Angel," I said. "I can't wait to meet her!" Lorena squealed. "I feel like I kind of know her even though you haven't told me how you met." I told her how I knew Angel was not important. "But what is important is that we're all friends!" My words were kind of slurred. "Have you been drinking?" Lorena asked. "Yeah," I confessed. "Earlier. But my buzz is gone now. We went to this bomb ass restaurant with Angel's freak." Then she asked," Did Hector go?" I said, "Yep. He went and he was tore up too." Lorena said, "He sounded a little drunk when I called earlier. I have so much to tell you, girl! I mean, the men down here spend money and are fine," I said. "Mexican guys?" Lorena asked. "No," I said. "Just black men. That's all we really see besides white people and a little bit of Mexicans on this street called Buford." "You've always loved black guys, Gustavo," she said. "Not true," I laughed. "I love all men- especially ones with big, brown dicks!" "Well, speaking of black guys, I need to tell you a couple of things," Lorena said. She sounded serious. Have you talked to Lupita?" she asked. I told her that I hadn't. "Well, I was in old Sac last night club hopping and I saw that bitch cruisin' with her cousins and some other bitches. I heard her cousin yell something out the car. So when they parked, me and Yolanda, Anna and Bertha walked up to them. I got all up in Lupita's face and said, "Did you say something, bitch?" She said, "No, I didn't. And then she said she was pregnant with Kevin's baby. So I was like, Kevin who? And guess what the fuck she said?" My heart dropped. I really didn't want her to say it, so I said it before her. "Kevin Brown." "You got it!" Lorena said. "So then I took my hand and everyone started screaming, don't hit her! She's pregnant! But I said your stomach is pregnant...not your face. I socked the shit out of her! Then all my home girls grabbed me and we ran and jumped in our car and left before the police came." I just quietly held the phone. I didn't know if my feelings were hurt because that slut bitch Lupita betrayed me or because I thought I loved Kevin. I mean, he had been shady to me a little the last couple of years. Sometimes he was all about being with me and sometimes he wouldn't answer my page. And he would say how he wasn't gay. That shit was confusing. But I still loved him. "Hello?!" Lorena screamed into the phone. "I'm here," I said. Angel looked at me and knew something was wrong. Then Lorena said, "That shit made me so mad! I mean she backstabbed me by fucking your brother. But I never thought that nasty slut would betray you too." I just listened to her. "Well, I'm saving my money and I'll be down there to kick it with you!" she announced. "I don't think

I'll make your birthday, but maybe by Christmas or New Year's. Look, Gustavo...I know you love him. But you deserve the best in life. And if God doesn't want Kevin for you, then God knows what's best." Your dad would kill you if he heard you say that," I said. I knew how he felt about gays. "Look," she said. "I love my dad. But I've known you all my life and you were born gay just like you said...and God don't make mistakes." That was one of the most beautiful things I'd ever heard in my life. I felt a sense of peace come over me. "Well, look *pinche calaweta*," my friend said. "If that bitch calls you, tell her I'm fucking her up soon as she drops her baby." I said, "That bitch better not call me ever." Then she said, "Alright, G. I gotta go help Sonya-Miss Nava-pick up some *carnitas* and food from some place on Franklin for church tonight. I laughed at the way she said Sonya-Miss Nava and said Ok. "I love you, G," Lorena said. "I love you too." I said as I hung up. Me and Angel fell asleep. I woke up later to the phone ringing. None of us wanted to answer it. But it wouldn't stop. "Hello?" I answered half asleep. The voice on the other end said, "Pretty boy! Get yo ass up and meet me at the club, ASAP!" "Who is this?" I demanded. "It's Rico!" the voice said. "Damn! How many guys be calling you?" He said it in a flirty way. I laughed and said, "Not enough!" "Well," he said. That's all about to change because I have a job for you so, you need to meet me at the club-you and your bro so we can see how strong your upper body is. See you in an hour!" "An hour?" I repeated. Then I looked at my phone and realized it was 7:00 a.m. "Ok!" I said. "See you in a bit, sexy," Rico said. I sat up and thought how confusing Rico was to me. Is he straight or gay or bisexual? I wasn't sure but I was attracted to him. I walked into the bedroom and told Hector to get up. "Rico wants us downtown in an hour," I said. "Alright," my brother said. I was surprised but glad that he didn't give me any lip. We both took showers really fast, threw on some sweats and I packed us some extra shirts in my backpack. We ran to the bus and waited about five minutes before we decided to just walk on the freeway to the train station. We could hear the train coming as soon as we put our money in the turnstile. I looked at some of the females on the train and noticed that a lot of those females down here wore their hair like they do in Oakland. Soon, our stop came up at Five Points train station. I grabbed my pager and looked at it. The time was 7:55 a.m. So I told Hector to hurry and we ran up the stairs to the main road, which was Peachtree. From there, we could see the club. We ran over there and knocked on the door. "Well I'm glad to see y'all are punctual," Rico said. He closed the door and looked at us and said, "I know you young bucks ain't out of breath are you?" Neither one of us said anything. "So look," he said sounding like a southern Martin Lawrence. "I got us some passes to this gym up the street. We're going to jog up there and get our work out on!" We jogged about three to four long ass blocks until we got to this high rise. It was hard jogging on the sidewalk because it seemed like everyone on the street was in a hurry to get to their job. We walked into the high-rise and strolled right past the security desk. It was obvious that the security guard knew Rico because his eyes got big as if he'd just seen Denzel Washington. I laughed to myself. Rico pushed the button for the 14th floor. The door opened and we got off the elevator and boy was it a big, first-class gym! I looked at Hector and he said to Rico, "Hey, *vato,* this is nice!" Rico looked at him and said, "*Vato.* I like that! It sounds cool." We walked up to the front desk and filled out some paper work. I finished first, so I asked Rico to point me to the restroom. He showed me where it was and as I walked, I thought, damn this place is big! I finally made it to the men's dressing room. When I walked in, I saw fine men walking around naked. There were white men...black men...I mean, it was packed in that dressing room. I put my head down and tried not to look but, I was a little surprised. I guess this was my first fancy gym experience and maybe this was how they did it. My heart was racing so fast! I decided to be nosey and take a look around. I walked around and realized there was a steam room and sauna. As I walked past, it looked kind of crowded. I wasn't sure but, I thought I saw feet and lots of steam. Then I went past the sauna and couldn't believe what I saw next. I looked closer and a guy waved for me to come in. There was a muscled white guy sucking a black guy and a white guy's dick! I just stood there. My dick was so hard that the longer I watched, the dizzier I became. I mean, it was hot in there. The door opened and I turned around and to see a guy that looked to be about 7 feet tall. He was white and his dick was just hanging there soft. He put his hands on my waist and scooted me as if I was light as a feather. He sat down and looked over at the action going on at the side of the room and started playing with his dick. My head and heart felt like they were going to burst. I was so horny! Without thinking, I had my mouth on his dick and was sucking like I never sucked before. As I was blowing him I was thinking, what if Hector or Rico came in? But I couldn't stop. He just kept saying, "Yes, baby! Yes, baby!" He sounded Russian or something. His accent was thick. I was so into it. Then I felt a tap on my back and I was like, oh shit…who's that? I turned around and it was Rico with the door open standing there like he was my father. I got off my knees and took one more glance at this giant white man with a huge dick to match and walked out. Rico walked a couple of steps in front of me then turned around and said, "Your brother's on the treadmill warming up some more. Look man, I'm not sure what was going on in Cali but you can't trust every muthafucka in Atlanta. For one, it ain't safe. And two, if you're going to be sucking dick, then you need to be charging. This ain't the time for us to be talking about this, so I'll get with you later about it." I was quiet and embarrassed-and still quite horny. It took all the strength in me not to walk back and finish what I started in that room. But I knew there would be time for that later. I followed him out to the gym room floor and we stayed there for almost two hours. We lifted weights like they were going out of style. I could tell by the look on Rico's face that he had no idea how strong we were. If I had to guess, I would say he was happy about it. A couple of the other members of Midnight Express came in as we were leaving. If they were headed to the sauna, then I wanted to be in there too. We took the elevator down and walked back up the street towards the club. Peachtree Street was busy with bumper-to-bumper traffic. Plus, it was feeling kind of like winter just a little bit. We made it to the club, went inside and Rico told us that we were going to do some cardio. And the day after that, when we let are muscles heal, we would be practicing pole work. Then he also said if all went right, me and him were going to New York to dance up there. "New York?" I asked. "What about me?" Hector asked. "It's an all men's club" Rico responded. "I'm cool," my brother said. "I'll stay here." Then Rico told me we'd be gone November 13th and 14th. "That's our birthday," I said. "Really?" he asked in his country accent. "How old y'all gonna be again?" Me and Hector yelled, "18!" at the same time. "Damn!" Rico said. "Y'all boys are young! You know I'm going to have to take an extra fee in New York for pulling some strings to get your young ass in the club. I keep forgetting you two are tenderonis. No offense player-just being honest. Alright, y'all can go and I'll see you here at 8:00 in the murning. Rico sounded so country. We both laughed. "What's so funny?" Rico asked. "Aw nothing, man," Hector said. But when we walked outside and headed to the train station, we both laughed and said "See you in the murning!" As we laughed, we jumped on the train and made it back to the apartment. I could already hear the phone ringing as we walked inside. I looked at the caller ID. It was Rico and I was thinking he probably wanted to talk about what happened in the sauna. Ok, I thought. Let me get this talk over with. I answered the phone and he said, "Good news! I just bought us two round trip tickets to New York. So, from this point on, you and your brother drink plenty of water; as little alcohol as possible and eat lots of protein." I was so excited! "What days are we going to be there?" I asked. "I told you-the 13th and 14th. It's next weekend. And oh yeah, Green Eyes...once we get there, I'll need you to practice your head game on me just in case we have a big spender. You'll make me proud!" Then he hung up. I thought, there he goes again. Is he serious or just playing with me? I wasn't sure but it was making me want him more. I noticed that Angel was gone. Maybe she's with her freak, I thought. She did tell me he gave her $300, so maybe she's working for it today. I cooked some eggs and bacon for us and after we ate, me and Hector went to take a nap.

Chapter 15: Tricks and Dicks

"Oh my God! I can't believe how they treat *senoritas* down here!

I just love it. But I'll love it more when I buy some clothes. I'm walking in an almost $700 pair of shoes and the same damn clothes I've been wearing for almost four days. I'm so glad I told Naomi to meet me at the mall. She's going to shop with me and tell me how living with Tre is. She landed her a real straight man. He didn't know she was biologically a boy until the night he took her home from Club 112. She said he was kind of tripping at first like they always do, but he was into her. After the shit went down with Jaime, he just happened to text her and she ran to the nearest gas station when she heard the gunshots. She said she was so scared she was going to get shot that she didn't think about anyone else but herself. She said she feels bad but she had to do what she had to do. I arrived at Lennox and I told her to meet me at the food court. But when I got there, she was already there with Tre looking like a million dollars. I walked up and gave her a hug and then gave Tre a hug too. He held me so tight I could feel his dick press against me. I pulled away but tried not to make it obvious so Naomi wouldn't trip. One thing you don't want to do with a tranny is to fuck with her man! I had plenty bitches on the Santa Monica hoe stroll trying to kick my ass. They thought that because I was half black that I couldn't pull as many *vatos* as them. And they were wrong. But one of my regular tricks bought me a gun when I was 15 and showed me how to use it. And I did even though I don't like to think about it. And I would again if I had to, I thought to myself. After I pulled away from Tre, I sat down. Then I looked back up at Tre and he said, "Well, I'm about to go. I just wanted to make sure she was in good hands. They kissed goodbye and he told her to page him when she was ready to be picked up. Then he said, "Alright ladies...talk to you in a bit!" He walked off and I looked. I had forgotten how fine he was. I looked over at Naomi and said, "You did good, *senorita!* She smiled and said, "I think so too," in her thick accent. I really like having a pretty girlfriend that was like me and didn't hate because she could pull men just like I do. We had some Taco Bell then headed upstairs to go shopping. We went to Contempo and Macy's and spent money. Naomi actually bought more clothes than me. We both are tiny so we can fit the same everything-even shoes. I still can't believe all these gay men are in the mall. Everywhere we went, they were saying things like, "Work, fish!" and "Work, *senoritas!*" "You betta do it, *mamacitas!*" We were getting our props! We walked around with our bags, but I sure didn't want to get on the train with all my stuff. I don't have a gun and don't trust that a fool won't try to jack my shit. My pager went off so I told Naomi that we needed to head back to the food court area. That's where the payphones were. I dialed the number and the guy answered, "Yeah, what up?" And I asked, "Hi, did someone page Angel? I said it in my white girl voice. "Yeah, it's me," Wah said. The way the guy said it, I knew exactly who it was. But this was the type of *cholo* I was used to dealing with in L.A. He was full of *machismo* and had lots of money. I didn't tell Gustavo, but Wah was hella aggressive in his truck the day I met him at the grocery store on our way back to Chad's house. Once he had opened the door for me and I jumped in, he pulled out his dick and I guess he was expecting me to suck it. He was fine and I mean real fine! It seemed like his dick was as long as his arm. But one thing about me is this: I've been tricking long enough to know when a trick is trying to trick for free. Shiiittt...I've been fucking for free ever since I was a kid-and without me saying it was Ok. Nasty old men were raping me in Mexico! So I knew right off that I was going to have to make this fool become my trick and make him trick big! He got plenty of money playing basketball, so he's going to give me some if he wants this pussy! I laughed to myself. But I was so serious. From here on out, I was going to open up a bank account and save every last dime so I could buy myself a real pussy! I mean if I'm getting guys like this, imagine how they're going to go crazy for me when I have my pussy. No more tricking and maybe I could even get married, adopt some kids and treat them kind like human beings are supposed to! I always wondered why people were so mean to me growing up even during my teenage years. But as soon I started taking hormones and developing into the *cholita* I am, things changed and you're not going to fuck me for free unless I decide it's Ok, I thought to myself. "You there?" Wah asked. "Oh yeah." I said. "I'm here, *papi.*" "So what's up, lil mama? What you doing?" "Well, I'm shopping with the only money I have left that was supposed to be for my rent," I said. "Is that right, *mamacita?*" he asked. "What mall you at?" "I'm at Lennox!" I said. "Who you with?" "My *amiga!*" I said. "Oh ok...so y'all want me to scoop y'all up and maybe have some fun?" Wah asked. "How much you talking, *papi?*" I asked. "Baby, you must not know who I am," Wah stated. I played right along and said, "Yeah, I know you're a fine ass, tall, black man that I would love to show a good time to!" Then he said, "So then meet me out front with your girl and we will make it happen." I said Ok and started thinking about tricking with him by myself, but then I remembered I didn't have a gun. That might not be so safe. I'd never tricked two on one with Naomi before. I've did husband and wife or two straight guys but never me and another tranny. I hung up the phone and told Naomi what was up. "That was a trick and he wants me and you to come with him," I said. "He plays pro ball and has a lot of *dinero!*" I said. "What's up?" But Naomi said, "*Eyyy yos mios*, I can't take that long! Tre's going to be wondering where I'm at." So I said, "Ok, let's walk out to the front of the mall and see what's up with him then." As we were walking through the mall, Naomi looked at me and said, "I know a place in *Tijuana* where we can get are pussies for $5000 cash." "$5000?" I repeated. "Yes. We can get it done at the same time," she said. "Well, I need to start tricking to make that," I said. "But why is it so cheap?" Naomi rolled her eyes and said in her thick accent, "*Mami,* it's not like we're going to be in a hospital like in Beverly Hills. It's going to be much smaller. And everything is much cheaper in Mexico. Shit, the *gringos* are expensive in *Ammmerica.*" "I know," I said, "But Mexico? I'm not too sure about that!" "Why *mami*?" she asked. "You're Mexican!" I wasn't budging and said, "I just really don't want to go there." Naomi stopped and dropped her bags then said, "I've wanted a pussy ever since I was little. I couldn't think about anything else but coming to *Ammmerica* to get my surgery. Now I'm here and I can't afford it and I'm telling you its $5000 in Mexico. We can be complete! No more having to tell guys that we have a *velga* and you want to pass that up?!" She tried to say it in a whisper. "Well, it does sound good," I finally agreed. "But shit, it still will take some time to make $5000." Then she said, "I know a way we can make $10,000 fast and split it." We picked up our bags and kept walking. I looked at her after thinking about it and asked how we could make that much money. She leaned closer to me and said, "Before you came from L.A. I met this *wetto* that hangs around *Mexicanos* in Texas. His name is Popeye. He used to come with those *cholos* to bring the cocaine. He told me when I got serious to call him and he would make sure I would make some money." I thought about it for a minute then said, "Ok, let's do it. Who do we have to fuck?" Naomi smiled and said, "No one, *mami!* That's the good part. All we have to do is drive to Texas and he said he would make sure we get to Mexico." I sat and listened but still had no idea about what we would have to do. We walked outside and Naomi walked close to me and said, "Sit down. All we have to do is bring the car to them and it's going to have what they need in it." I figured it would be cocaine but she put her face close to mine and said, "No. Heroin." I looked at her and just said Ok. I knew at that moment, that if I did this, I would come back to Atlanta as a woman and get me a rich husband. "Good!" Naomi said. "I'll call Popeye tonight and make arrangements fast." I couldn't believe it! I was going to get my vagina sooner than I thought. I was shaking scared but I was also very happy. A few minutes later, a guy pulled up in a white Range Rover and whistled at me. It was Wah! I looked over at Naomi and her eyes looked like she had just seen the man of her dreams. I told her watch my things while I went over to the Range Rover. I walked over to the driver side. Wah was licking his lips as he watched me come toward him. *"Hola, papi,"* I said in my sexy *chola* voice. "What up, girl?" he said back. "You, *papi!* Only you!" I said. "Look what you did to me," he said as he grabbed me with his long arms from his window and pulled me closer to the door. I looked in and there was his big dick just sticking straight up. It looked good but I knew this had to be about money-and as much as I could get. I was going to have to be straight up with him and tell him my secret fast. "So, *papi,"* I said. I want to show you a good time..." But he interrupted me and said, "Damn, your home girl looks good! But not as fine as you!" I thanked him then got back to the business. *"Papi,* you know I'm young... and we don't have a lot of money. So how much could you give us both for sucking your dick?" I realized I was treating Wah like any other trick on Santa Monica. "Damn, baby!" He shot back. "Y'all some real life hoes!" But I corrected him and said, "*Papi*, I'm not a hoe. I'm just a special kind of girl that needs money to get what she needs." Wah looked me in the eye and said, "Look, baby...I'm not used to paying for pussy. I get pussy handed to me left and right so...$50 dollars apiece would be generous." I couldn't believe how cheap he was being. Hell, I could make $50 off a homeless trick in L.A., I thought to myself. I stood there for a minute then said, "It was nice meeting you." Then I walked away from the car like I would do any other trick on Santa Monica Boulevard when they were being cheap fuckers. I just walked off and didn't turn back. As I got closer to Naomi I said, "Let's go." She stood up and we walked. Once we got back into the mall, Naomi asked what happened. "That cheap fucker said he'd pay $50 a piece!" I said. "And he doesn't even know our fucking "T." He thinks we're female hoes that ain't worth any money, so fuck him!" I was irritated. But at the same time, I couldn't believe I just walked away from a tall, rich man with a big, fat dick. That's Ok, I thought. Once I get my pussy, I'll only be fucking with rich men. We called Tre and he took us out to eat and to get some drinks. Naomi told him we were getting our pussies and he seemed happy. I think he really likes her. I just knew I wasn't telling Gustavo, because there was no way he would let me think of going to Mexico- ever. But I'm not letting the past get in the way of my future and my dream of becoming all woman.

<u>Chapter 16: Getting' Money</u>

I can't believe I'm taking this trip to Philly with Royalty. I was going to say no, but the money she's offering and the club we're going to work at is legendary from what I've heard from the bouncers. Ok, I have to think of a lie to tell Rich this weekend in case he calls. I can't call him from a different area code because then he will know I'm out of town. Hmm...I know! I'll tell him that I'm going on a last minute church retreat to cleanse myself and that I'm giving up my exotic dancer career since I will soon be Mrs. O'Bryan. I liked the sound of that. I packed my clothes and asked my cousin Chad if he could take me to the airport. I missed hanging out with him, but ever since mother died, I've been in another space. But I'm coming back and ready to start seeing my family more often. I love all my family-especially my bigheaded cousin Chad. As I waited on Chad, I decided to call Rich. The phone rang three times before he picked up. "Hello?" he answered. "Hey baby!" I said. "Hey yourself!" he said. "What's my princess up to?" "Well, that's why I'm calling," I lied. "An old church member of mine called me last night and asked if I would like to go to an all women's retreat today until Sunday and I was thinking I would like to go. What do you think?" I asked. "I think that's amazing!" Rich said. I felt kind of guilty for lying to him, but until I got my ring, I was going to have to make this money-especially the kind of money Royalty was talking about, I thought to myself. He knows I'm a stripper. That's how he met me. "Babe...are you still there? Rich asked. "Yes, handsome. I'm here," I said. "So what's your plans for this weekend?" I asked. "Babe, I'm going to be pretty busy," he said. "That's about it." "So, are we still going to be together on New Year's?" I asked. "You know it!" he said. My line clicked. I was about to tell him to hold on, but he said, "Listen, doll...can I call you back tomorrow? I said, "I won't be able to talk at the church retreat, babe." "Ok, call me when you get home," he said. I hung up and the phone rang immediately. I forgot someone else was calling in. Still, I couldn't help but think that Rich had rushed me off the phone. "Hello?" the person on the phone said. I recognized the voice and asked, "Is this Nichelle?" "Yes girl," she said. "It's me...and guess were I'm headed?" I had no clue. "Where, girl?" "Atlanta!" Nichelle screamed. "Atlanta?" I repeated. "For how long?" "Until Tuesday!" she said. "I had to break away from Quincy's dumb ass," she said in her southern voice. "The boy's fine but dumb as a stack of hay. Anyway, girl I have some corporate bruthas lined up to wine and dine a bitch...you down?" "Oh my gosh, girl!" I said. "Why does that sound like so much fun? But I'm on my way to a church retreat." I could tell she was disappointed when she said, "A church retreat?" "Yeah," I said. But I assured her that I would be back early Sunday morning or late that afternoon. "Ok, girl," she said. "Well, call me when you get home. This is my new cell phone that Quincy just bought me. I'm actually driving and talking...imagine that!" Nichelle started laughing. "You lucky bitch!" I said. "I'm so jealous. That's it. Rich is buying me one ASAP!" "Well, girl let me let you go because holding this phone and driving is something I have to get use to," Nichelle said. "Ok, girl," I said. "Be safe and I will call you Sunday!" As I hung up, I realized how excited I was to have a girlfriend-and a pretty, funny girlfriend at that. Sooner or later I was going to tell her about my stripping days. I really don't feel like she would judge me. I ate some breakfast, took a shower, got dressed and just as I'd finished, I heard Chad blowing his horn. I was only taking a garment bag and a big purse for my heels. I wasn't going to take much because I was going to make my money and come back. I still couldn't believe how much I would be making-not including tips. And that bitch Royalty said no sex would be involved. Sounds like a win-win to me, I thought to myself. Chad popped the trunk. I threw my stuff in and was ready to go. When I looked into the car, I noticed that Chad's eyes were puffy. I opened the car door and sat in the passenger seat and asked if he was Ok. "Yeah," he said. "I'm fine, Black. He always called me Black when he was being playful with me. But this time I said, "I know you're not calling anyone black!?" I was thinking we would both start laughing. But nope. Silence. He didn't laugh or say anything. So I decided to see what's been new with him. "Are you still seeing Akilah?" I asked. Akilah was his college sweetheart. She was pretty and smart. She kind of looked like Nichelle but she was short, light skinned and had long straight hair. I thought she was white or Hispanic until I met her folks at Chad's graduation party. I was younger then both Chad and Akilah, but they both treated me like an adult even when I was just a teenager in middle school. Last I heard, their relationship was rocky. My cousin might be short, but he's quite the ladies man. "She's pregnant!" Chad announced. "Congratulations!" I screamed. I was so happy. But I looked at him and I just saw tears rolling down his eyes. I was confused. The only other time I saw him cry was when my aunty whipped his behind when he

was little. And then at my mother's funeral. When I thought about him crying at my mother's funeral, tears came rolling down my eyes too. We just drove and sniffled as the tears dropped. We were quiet most of the way to the airport before Chad said, "Star...I'm bi-sexual." Did I just hear him say what I think he said? I was quiet. Stunned. "Well, aren't you going to say something?" he screamed. I looked at him and said, "You just told me your girlfriend, whom I've known for years, is going to have your baby and you're gay within 10 minutes, Chad! I yelled back. "Does aunty know?" I asked. "No," he quickly said. "I can't tell anyone and I'm sick of it!" He cried even harder. "Sick of what, Chad?" I asked. I was really concerned. Then he said, "I'm sick of not being happy. I'm sick of having to live two lives. I'm sick of wanting to love and I can't!" By now, he was screaming and crying. I was so taken aback by my cousin's confession. "Happy?!" I asked. "Happy?! How can you be happy being a fag?" I shouldn't have said that because as the word fag left my mouth, he broke down even more. He started swerving as he drove the car while trying to wipe his tears. "Chad, it's a sin! You know it's a sin! The bible says it!" I screamed. I didn't want to hurt him, but I had to tell him the truth, I thought.
"Why...why...why are you judging me?" he asked weakly. "I have no one to talk to." He could barely get his words out. I held my ground and said, "Chad, you know a homo killed my mom. You know this!" Chad shot back, "It wasn't me! I'm a good man! I graduated high school and college. I make close to $60,000 a year! I treat people right! I treat my mama right! I'm always here for you! I've never, ever thrown your choice to be a stripper in your face!" I couldn't believe he was trying to compare what I did to what he was telling me now. "I'm dancing for men!" I screamed. "It's natural, Chad! It's natural!" My cousin just shook his head and said in a lowered voice, "I just want to be happy. We pulled up to the airport and I wiped my face. I jumped out of the car. I ran to the trunk and grabbed my garment bag and purse, then walked off without even looking back or saying goodbye. My heart was aching. It was aching for my mom. It was aching from seeing my favorite cousin hurting. It was aching from not knowing what to do or think. I checked in, caught the

train to my terminal, went to my gate and had a seat. I reached into my purse for some sunglasses, just hoping and praying I brought some. Whew, I did. I put them on, faced the window and just let my tears pour. I looked at my watch and realized I had cried for about 20 minutes. Then they started boarding to Philly. I thought maybe Royalty and me were on the same flight but, I guess I thought wrong because as I was boarding for first class, she was nowhere in sight. I walked on board and took my seat. I almost forgot where I was going for a quick minute. Then I thought about how I would love to be on my way to see Rich so I could hold him and feel better. Even though I've never told him anything really personal besides my mom dying. I looked over at a car magazine that this older white man, on the opposite side of me, pulled out. It said Low Rider Magazine. And when he opened it, there was a picture of a fine Mexican guy. Well, I think it was a fine Mexican guy standing by a car with rims. I thought of Hector and I missed him a little. Something about being with him made me feel safe. Just as I was about to daydream, I looked at the empty seat next to me and hoped it would stay empty. Then, all of a sudden, what do I hear but someone loud popping their gum and I knew it was ghetto ass Royalty. "Hey gurl," she said. I couldn't believe this bitch had on pajama bottoms, a fur coat with bunny slippers, and a headscarf. She looked like a Hawaiian version of Monie Love! I was mortified and thinking the people around us was too. I know they've never in their lives seen a ghetto bitch like this in first class, I thought to myself. "Gurl, sorry I'm late," she apologized. "My old man was tripping about me going, but I told him if he wanted to keep living in that high-rise and eating at Benihana every weekend, then he'd better shut up and take me to the airport to make this money!" I went from wanting to just lie down in my bed to now wanting to jump off the plane from embarrassment. Just when I thought things couldn't get worse, she pulls out some Church's Chicken and a biscuit. "You know they feed us on first class?" I said sarcastically. "I know, Miss Thang," she said. "That's the only way I fly! You betta ask somebody. She laughed out loud. I couldn't believe I was having such a crazy day. The only thing that was keeping me together was the $13,000 I was getting and

I already had $3000 of it. I was going to have the other $10,000 before tonight or early tomorrow morning-whenever I finished shaking my ass and titties, I thought to myself. "So, who are these clients that we're dancing for?" I asked. "To be honest," Royalty said, "I've never met them. I just know I got a call from some Italian guy and he said he'd put a down payment in my account. He also said that he needed a pitch black, pretty bitch. And that's you!" I sat thinking about what Chad had just told me and wondered why God was putting homosexuals in my life. I just didn't understand. My mom had gay friends growing up who were nice, but just like my mom, they too died from AIDS. I tried to change my thoughts so I closed my eyes and daydreamed about the new life I was going to have with Rich. "Gurl, can you open this bag for me?" Royalty asked. I opened my eyes and put my shades on top of my head to see if this bitch was really doing what I thought she was doing. And she was. She had me open a garbage bag while she was taking down her braids. She was literally taking out her weave and throwing it in the garbage bag. I was lost for words. Mortified doesn't begin to explain how I felt. Apparently, the white and black flight attendants were too. I put the glasses back on my head and pretended I was asleep until I actually fell asleep. We made it to the Philly airport, got our bags and had a limo waiting for us outside. We jumped into the limo and headed to our hotel. About 20 minutes later, we pulled up to the Four Seasons. It was one of my favorite hotels. Rich always stayed in the one in Atlanta and sometimes the one in Boston. We got out of the limo and checked our bags with the bellboy. Royalty looked like Daryl Hannah from the movie *Splash* with her long hair crimped from taking her braids out. I still couldn't understand why the hell she added weave to her long ass hair. We checked into our room, which was on the 10th floor. It had a gorgeous view of the Philadelphia skyline. I lay down on the bed with all my clothes on. The events of the day had completely drained me. But I was kind of looking forward to seeing some handsome men tonight. The telephone rang in our room and Royalty jumped up to grab it. After a few seconds she said, "This Royalty. Ok...Ok...got ya. See ya in a bit." Then she hung up the phone. "Who was that?" I asked. "Gurrl, one of the owners of the club!" she said excitedly. "He sending another limo to pick us up so we can see the club before tonight!" "Haven't you been to this club before?" I asked. "No, gurl," she responded. "But I can't wait to see it. It's the high-class club of Philly and very few black, Spanish or mixed bitches get to even step in this club. The white men love 'em blond with big titties." So I asked, "Well, why are we here then?" "Because of a special request from some millionaire who loves black dancers!" she said. I sat up and said, "He sounds like my kind of man! Money and class!" We both high fived. I went to the bathroom to put a little make up on my eyes because they were still a little puffy from crying. I was excited and anxious to dance, make this money and go home to kick it with Nichelle. We both sprayed on some perfume and headed out the door. We walked to the elevator and when we hit the first floor, we started out for the front of the Four Seasons. But walking out of the elevator, I heard someone say, "No way! You have to be lying. Ohhh my gosh!" The voice sounded so familiar. I turned back towards the elevator to see who it was. But by the time I was fully turned around, the elevator doors were closing. I knew I heard those voices before. Maybe it was someone I went to school with. I wasn't sure but it sounded like a white girl's voice that I knew. Outside the hotel, our limo was waiting and we jumped in. It was only about a two-minute ride, but there was a bottle of champagne with a card next to it that said, "For Royalty and Star. We buzzed the driver. He rolled his window down and said, "Yes, ladies?" Then Royalty said, "Do you mind circling the block while we have a drink?" "Sure," he replied. "Come on girl!" Royalty said. "We're not dancing til tomorrow. So let's have a toast." "Well, I won't argue with that," I said. We sat there and drank the whole bottle within 10 minutes and were laughing our butts off. I couldn't believe I was actually having fun with Royalty's ghetto ass. After sipping and laughing, we told the driver we were ready to go back to club. We pulled up in front and it didn't look like much of anything. But there was a big sign in the front that said Allegro Gentlemen's Club. I wondered if that was Italian for fast, I thought to myself. We walked in and it looked like it was very classy. And it was big. There were many poles. From where I was standing, I also counted four bars. We were greeted in the front by some fine Mexicans. Maybe they were Puerto Rican. I'm not sure what they were. But I knew they were Spanish and tall. They wore black suits and had pretty but masculine faces. Looking at them made me think about Hector's fine ass. I think I missed him. But it might have been just the champagne talking. The bouncers walked us to a room that turned out to be a nice office. A man named Harvey introduced himself and showed us around the club. He showed us the room where I would be dancing with Royalty and the private party that requested us. Boy oh boy was the room as big as the Fox Theatre in Atlanta. There were three poles and a stage with spotlights. Then, there were two bars in this one room. We talked to Harvey for a while. He told us what we would be dancing to and that the gentlemen were having a bachelor party for a good friend. I think he could tell that we were a little tipsy, so he asked us not to drink tomorrow or we would not be able to dance. He also said he had to pull some strings to get us in here with no stripper license so it was crucial to be on our best behavior. Then Royalty piped up and said, "We ain't no little girls! We work in an upscale club in Atlanta. We know the rules! Harvey didn't look like he gave a shit about me or Royalty. His fat ass was strictly about his business. We left the room we were going to be dancing in the next day and headed towards the main room. The crowd was beginning to grow. It was a little after lunch and they were doing good business. The white men in there all looked like they were on their lunch breaks from their executive jobs. We finished up with Harvey; got into the limo and headed back to the room. We ordered room service and I listened to Royalty's childhood stories. Later, we decided to down to the bar and the lobby to see who we could meet. We sat down there until about 1 a.m. drinking with some German guys that were in Philadelphia on business. I decided to head up to the room. But before I could, one of the guys asked if $1000 could get me to spend the night with him. I looked at him and said, "$2000 will get you a couple of hours." Royalty looked surprised when I said it. "We need the money now," she told the guy who was trying to solicit me. I stood up to walk to the bathroom. But I fell back in my chair and hit the ground. I was so embarrassed and so drunk, I asked

Royalty to walk me upstairs. She did but gave me a lecture telling me how I'm fucking up money getting this drunk and I was going to have a reputation for being a drunk bitch and clients weren't going to want me to dance for them. As soon as she unlocked the door I said, "Who gives a fuck?" Then I started crying. Royalty put me in my bed and turned off the lights.

I woke up with the sun shining in the room. For a minute, I forgot where I was at. It was 10 a.m. and I had the worst headache. On top of that, I was so damn thirsty. I looked around and realized Royalty's bed hadn't been slept in. I sat up and went to pee and then started to wonder where the hell she could be. I called room service and asked if they could bring eggs, bacon, toast, Sprite and a gallon of orange juice. I laughed to myself. The food came and I ate and drank all the orange juice I possibly could. I thought about how I was so drunk the night before and felt kind of embarrassed again. Then I realized I had just pigged out and was going to be dancing for millionaires later that night. I decided to just drink water for the rest of the day. I fell back asleep until I heard Royalty walk in the door screaming, "Bitch, you fucked up!" "Why do you say that?" I asked. "Bitch, the muthafucka offered your ass $2000 for a couple of hours in his room and you were falling down and shit and couldn't even recoup the money!" she said. I was pissed that I had missed my lick but I just said, "So?" "So?" Royalty repeated. "Well, don't you worry. I made $3000 for talking to all four of them in their penthouse suite." I was hot. "Girl, I know you did more than just talk." Royalty just smirked and said, "You damn skippy I did! I let each one of them take turns eating my pussy. And when I say those German men made me cum, I mean they made me cum." "Ok, that's enough," I said. Royalty looked at me with her head cocked to the side and said, "Gurl, why you acting like you don't sell pussy for money?" "Because I don't," I said. Ok, you don't." She was mocking me. "Last I remember you be face down ass up naked in the club dancing for some dollars just like me." I stood up and headed to the bathroom. I could taste and smell champagne for some reason and it made me sick. I ran into the bathroom and threw up in the toilet. "Girl, are you pregnant?" Royalty asked. "Of course not," I said. "I've only had unprotected sex with one person and only one person." "Yeah but how many times?" she asked. "I don't know!" I said in an irritated voice. "Maybe 15, 20, 30 times?" "Gurl, didn't you go to that smart private school?" she asked. "Because you sound dumb as shit now." She walked out of the room. I can't be pregnant, I thought to myself. I tried to remember back to when me and Rich first fucked without a condom. No, that's not enough time, I concluded. Me and Royalty decided to take a walk in cold Philadelphia so I could get some exercise before the night's activities. Philly was old and had lots of buildings and lots of Spanish guys trying to talk to us. We made it back to the room and I fell asleep again while Royalty was in the bathroom doing God knows what. I was so sleepy and really hungry. But there was no way I was not going to make this $10,000. I needed it as much as I wanted it. Soon, 9 p.m. came around and we started getting ready. We were told that we needed to be there by 10 p.m. and that we would be dancing from 10 p.m. until 1 or maybe 2 a.m. We were also told that we would be paid in traveler's checks. We made it to the club and walked inside. Boy, were we getting some dirty looks from the big hair white girls. We were shown to the dressing room and Royalty was mumbling, "Lord, I need this money. Please don't make me have to beat a bitch ass!" The tension was thick in the dressing room. Girls were looking at us like they'd never seen black girls before. We finished getting ready and sat around the dressing room waiting to be called. Harvey made it clear that we would not be on the main floor-only the VIP room with our party. I wasn't too thrilled about the music that was selected except for *I Wanna Sex You Up* from the *New Jack City* soundtrack. It was kind of old, but I was going to kill it. They announced us on the stage as The Two Southern Belles. The first song was a *Def Leopard* oldie that I kinda liked. We got on stage and I couldn't see the crowd-just the spotlight shining in my eyes. I decided to do some pole work to get adjusted to the lighting. When my eyes finally adjusted, I saw lots of black, white and Hispanic guys sitting there with money out. We started working the room. Then my song came on. But just as I began to gyrate to the music, the DJ made the announcement that the groom had just arrived. "So, I want all you guys to give him a big congratulations when he comes in!" he commanded. The music started playing again and in walks two black guys I recognized. I looked closer and then Rich walked in with everyone screaming congrats to him. The music got loud again and all the guys standing by the door were hugging and congratulating Rich. Did I miss something? I felt numb. I just stood there confused when the DJ said, "I think you ladies need to let the bachelor know what it feels like to be single for the last time!" Rich walked my way and then his eyes got big as saucers. It was as if he was expecting to see me. Then I realized it was Tyrone and Quincy with him and all the guys around Rich picked him up and sat him in a chair. The next thing I know Royalty was over there with her pussy in his face. I never imagined in a million years I would feel so bad and not know what to do. I picked up my top from the stage and ran into the dressing room. I ran into a bathroom stall and I couldn't cry. I just sat there. Then I heard a knock on the door. "Get out here now!" the voice shouted. It was Harvey standing with one of the bouncers. "If you don't get your ass out there in two minutes, you won't see a penny!" Royalty walked into the restroom and told Harvey, "We're coming right now. Just give us five minutes!" Harvey screamed, "Look, you have two minutes!" They walked out and Royalty bent over and said, "Gurl, he's a trick! They're all our trick ass clients. And at the end of the day, they want pussy!" I sat there shaking cold and a little hungry. Then Royalty said, "Stay right here." I sat on the toilet trying to think how the fuck I was going to get out of the club when Royalty came back. "Here," she said. "Try some of this. She had some white stuff on the end of a key. I didn't even hesitate. I just started snorting and snorting. I'd never did drugs and never thought I would. I stood up and felt strong. I felt invincible and Royalty told me to treat Rich like the trick he was. I followed her and felt like I was walking on a cloud. My mouth was dry but I felt like a princess. I went back into the VIP room. There were some white girls dancing for the men. Rich was sitting down with a cigar in his mouth and he looked drunk. The music was playing but I had no clue what song was on. I just felt good and I danced on him and took my top back off and whispered in his ear, "Is this you what you want?" "I love you, Star," he said. I said nothing. I danced and then asked him if I could go and still make the $10,000 I was promised. "Of course," he said. "I'll come over later." "No," I said. "I just want my money...now!" I looked over at Royalty and she was dancing for some of the guys but looking at me to see what I was doing. Rich looked over at Quincy and asked, "Are you going to pay her?" Quincy nodded and pulled out some hundreds and gave them to me. I counted the money and looked at Quincy and said, "Hey, this is only $2000." "I have the rest," he said. "Just give me a minute." "I'm leaving! Please leave my money at the front desk tonight," I said. I walked into the dressing room and grabbed my stuff. I ran out of there so fast I don't even remember seeing anyone. I jumped into a taxi and headed to our room. I paid the driver and began walking towards the elevator hoping one of the elevator doors would open soon. Well, one opened and out walks Meagan, Summer and Debbie! "Hi, girl! How are you?" they all screamed. "What are you doing here?" Meagan asked. "I know you're not coming to the wedding...are you?" Debbie asked. When she said wedding I threw up over all of them. But I think Summer got it the worst. They were screaming as I jumped into the elevator and pushed the button. The elevator door opened at the 10th floor and I ran to my room; opened the door; and jumped in the shower with my clothes on getting my hair wet. I just sat down and cried.

Chapter 17: Bright Lights, Big City

I couldn't believe it we were on our way to New York! I would have never thought in a million years I would be going to the Big Apple. We made it to the airport after one of the fine ass dancers dropped me and Rico off, and we were about to spend two days making money. We got on the plane and found our seats. I was by the window and Rico sat in the middle. Some old Asian lady sat on the aisle seat. I kinda felt sorry for Rico because his legs were so long. He looked uncomfortable. The plane took off and I asked him how long it was going to take. He said it would take about two and a half hours. "This is only my second time flying,"

I told him. "Oh yeah? So when was your first time?" he asked. "The first time was when I was coming to Atlanta," I said. "Really?" he asked. "And your young ass is barely 18. You doing big thangs, man!" This was the first time me and Rico were ever by ourselves. Well, I mean the first time we got to talk one on one without anyone interrupting. We were in the air when the flight attendant came over and Rico ordered two vodkas with seltzer water. The stewardess came back and gave him the drinks and me the Sprite I asked for. As soon as she walked away, he passed one of the drinks to me and said, "Here, mix this together. There's not a lot of calories in this and I want that pretty stomach nice and flat." I looked at the drink. It didn't look too tasty but I downed it like it was Olde English 800. We sat there and I was really buzzed off that one drink. I looked over at Rico and he asked me what Angel was doing for the weekend. "She said she was trying to get a flight to Los Angeles because she had a trick that was sending for her and the money was good," I said. "You don't say?" Rico replied. I couldn't believe I'd just blurted Angel's business out loud. What the fuck, I thought to myself. I was so light headed. Rico pressed the button for the stewardess to come. When she came, he ordered two more drinks and flirted with her. She didn't even charge him. She walked away and he handed me the second drink. I took it to the head again. This time I was really buzzed. I felt good. I felt so happy about life. I looked over and the Asian lady was snoring. Then I looked down at Rico's long legs that looked uncomfortable. And then I looked up his leg and saw his long dick. It was lying down the side of his jogging suit pants. I was so horny that my heart started beating fast. I couldn't take my eyes off his dick! He saw me looking and didn't say nothing. He pressed the stewardess button again and this time he told her that he was cold and could she please bring him a blanket. The stewardess came back with a blanket and a big smile. Rico unfolded the blanket and covered himself. Then he looked at me and asked, "You ain't cold?" "No, I'm not cold at all!" I said. I looked down and could see his hands down where his dick was and my heart was racing so fast. I looked at him and said, "Can I touch it?" "What you going to do for me?" Rico asked. "What do you want?" I asked. And he said, "Money...lots of money. Can you help me make that happen?" I quickly said, "Yes! Yes I can!" in a sexy voice. He lifted the blanket up slightly and my hand went straight to his dick. I couldn't believe how big he was! Where did it stop? It was so big. I mean really big! I wanted it so bad. He put his hand on top of mine and helped me rub it. It felt good, but then I had a flash back of a guy in Mexico forcing me to grab his dick when I was little. I was going to pull my hand away, but it felt so good and I realized it was Rico and not those fucking perverts Rosalinda sold us to. I don't know what happened but Rico removed my hand and looked at me and said, "What's wrong?" I replied, "Nothing...nothing's wrong." I was so horny, dizzy and light headed. I was ready for the plane ride to be over. "Are you sure you Ok, man?" Rico asked. "I'm Ok. I'm Ok," I blurted. I excused myself and headed to the restroom. I stood in line anxiously waiting until I made it in. I splashed water on my face and tried to think positive thoughts. I took my pants down because it felt like I had to shit but I couldn't. I sat there in that small ass bathroom and I felt like I was going to die. I didn't know if I had to throw up or shit. I felt dizzy and just wanted to lie down. I stood back up with my pants still down and tried to splash water on my face. Then the plane shook and I lost my balance and fell on the door. I was still standing but all my body weight was on the door. Then I heard a voice say, "Are you Ok?" "Yeah, I'm fine," I said. But I didn't sound fine at all. I told myself, *Mijito* doesn't live here... *Mijito* doesn't live here and tried to think about my mom when she was beautiful and loved us. But then I heard Rosalinda's voice saying, "*Mijo*, you do good job and you make your *mamita* very proud!" I couldn't shake it. Her voice just played over and over in my head. I woke up and there were three women standing over me. One of them was giving me mouth to mouth. I opened my eyes. The stewardess asked me if I knew where I was. I told her I did. I opened my eyes and realized that I had passed out. I couldn't believe this was happening, I thought to myself. "Do you have family on the plane?" the stewardess asked. "No. Just a friend," I said. "Well, what's your seat number?" she asked I sat up. Before the words could come out my mouth, Rico was staring in disbelief. I looked down and realized my boxers were still at my ankles and the three women were just standing there. One of them had her eyes on my dick. I stood up and headed to my seat. Rico was close behind. I sat down trying to figure out why I had just fainted. Then I looked up and all three stewardesses were handing me ginger ale, crackers and cookies telling me to feel better. They were so very nice. As they walked away, Rico started laughing so loud that the Asian lady next to him was staring like she wanted to say something. "What's so funny?" I asked "I guess they liked what they saw because these flight attendants were ready to give you anything you needed," Rico said and continued laughing. "I'll just take it as a good sign that you and your special friend is going to make me some money!" he said. I was assuming he was talking about my dick. But he didn't know I'd never stuck my dick in anything but my hand. I mean, it's big but I don't use it. And I don't think I want to use it. I like getting fucked, I thought to myself. We exited the plane, got our bags and flagged down a taxi. LaGuardia Airport was busy and dirty. It didn't look as nice as Atlanta's airport. I was just mesmerized as we rode in the New York taxi. All I could see was tall buildings and people everywhere. I couldn't believe I was here. We got out of our taxi somewhere in Manhattan. I couldn't remember the name of the street because there were so many. We found our way to our hotel and walked in. it was a Holiday Inn. It was really nice. I was so excited! Rico checked us in and we went up to our rooms, put our bags down and headed back outside. The air smelled like popcorn and gas. I was so happy to be in New York. We jumped back into another taxi and Rico told the driver to take us to 46th and something. I was trying to pay attention but was too interested in seeing what everyone else was doing. We finally made it to a tall building. Beside it was what looked like a supermarket with a sign right next to it that said Club Stella's. It looked like it was kind of little. And it was. But we walked in and there were a handful of white men-old white men. Then I saw the most beautiful man on Earth. He was talking to an old white man and his smile was perfect. We sat down and ordered a drink. The music was loud. I could feel the bass bouncing against my body. They were playing *"Every Little Thing You Do"* by Christopher

Williams. I had just heard that song on an Atlanta radio station and I loved it! We sipped our drinks and I turned around to see another fine guy in the club. I asked Rico, "Is this where we're going to be dancing?" "Yup!" he said. This club is New York's finest! The old, rich, white men in here have money-real money-loonnng money! They come here for the Dominican and Puerto Rican dancers. They love dark meat." I just listened and sipped my drink while taking it all in. Suddenly, I felt a hand on my back. "Well, hello boys!" the voice said. I turned around and it was an old, white, gay man who looked like he was half drag queen and half skeleton. He was really skinny with a big belly and was losing his blondish white hair. He wore a ring on every finger and had arched eyebrows. "Well, Rico," he said. "I'm glad you could make it and bring your new boy with you! I'm so glad to see you!" He sounded like Fran from the show *The Nanny."* I'm Kitty. What's your name?" I looked at him for a second then said, "I'm Gustavo. But people call me G." Kitty smiled and said, "Well, Rico and G, follow me back to my office." His voice was so annoying. We followed him but I couldn't keep my eyes of the fine guy I'd seen when I walked in. He looked like he was Mexican with a curly afro. I don't ever think I'd seen a pretty guy like that ever. "Stop daydreaming!" Rico said in my ear. "This is important." We walked back into Kitty's office and I noticed some coffee and a donut on his table with a roach running around it. I couldn't believe what I was seeing. Then I saw another roach and Kitty still picked that nasty ass donut up and ate it. "So, here's the deal, Gustavo," he said. "You dance tonight and tomorrow. If you can pull us in 10 VIP dances in two nights, you're hired. "Look, Kitty," Rico interrupted. "This is his first real time dancing for men or anybody. And to pull in 10 VIP dances might be asking a lot!" Kitty just smiled that crooked grin of his and said, "Rico, babyyyy! You know I would do anything for you. I would marry you if you asked me. But you're bringing me a Latino? I mean, *helllooo*? We're in New York! And yes, he is beautiful and brown with green eyes, but there's a lot of pretty Latin guys waiting in line to dance or escort here." "Yeah, I understand that," Rico said. "But he has a West Coast flavor and can dance like a black man...and did I mention his dick?" "Rico, I hear you,"

Kitty said. "But what Latino man do you know that doesn't have a big dick?" "Well, look at him naked." Rico said. "Take off your clothes, G." I jumped up and striped all the way down. I was scared that a roach might get on my clothes. I hate roaches! Whenever I saw one at the group home we stayed in, I made sure I would tell the janitor. "Well, well," Kitty said sizing me up. "You were telling the truth. It's pretty and uncircumcised like most. But it's nice. Ok...five VIP dances the next couple of days and you can come back." Rico jumped up and said, "That's my man!" as he shook Kitty's hand. I put my clothes back on and heard Rico and Kitty whispering to each other. I tried to listen but Rico asked if I could step outside, so I did. The music was loud and sounded so good. I was still trying to hear what Rico and Kitty were saying being that they left the door open. "You dance for free but I want half your VIP," Kitty said. "But G and I need some money for both nights and all his VIP!" Rico said. Then I heard Kitty say something to Rico about not trying to cut no side deals and fuck or let someone suck him at the hotel. "Because if I find out, you won't be able to come back!" Kitty warned. "Now, come on, Kitty!" Rico said. "I'm running a business in Atlanta. And I know you're the man in New York! I would never burn bridges. I listened and was confused as to why we were paying to work here. Finally, Rico walked out and we caught a taxi back to the room. I lay down as soon as we got to the room. I looked over at Rico and watched as he was taking off his clothes. His body was incredible. He was so tall and had long legs with a firm butt. He seemed like he was taking his time to turn around and let me see his penis. He walked right into the bathroom and closed the door. I was thinking maybe he would ask me to join him. But he didn't. He was in that restroom for an hour. I fell asleep until he opened the bathroom door and I looked at the clock. I sat up kind of disappointed because I was horny and I wanted him bad. I walked over to the window and looked at all the buildings and was trippin.' You could see people in the buildings next to us. I don't remember if I had ever been on the 15th floor of a building before. I mean except for the gym in Atlanta. I don't think there are many high rises in Sacramento. I turned around and Rico was putting on his shoes. Where are we going?" I asked. "I'm going to handle some business," he said. "I'll be back. You rest and then do some sit-ups and push-ups to be ready for tonight." I was disappointed and said, "Well, I kind of want to walk around and see New York." Rico looked at me and said, "Look, shawty...this is a two-day money making trip. When I get back, it will be time for you to show me what you got at Stella's and then we will rest and we have another event." I sat back on the bed thinking, that there's a whole world out there and I want to be in it. Rico left and I turned on the TV so I could fall back asleep. I turned the channel and *Leave It To Beaver* was on. I sure missed the days of watching shows in my room on my black and white TV while mom was cooking. Why did things have to change in my life every year? I was somewhere else. I went from being with my family to being a child prostitute in Mexico. Then I was living in two foster homes until they couldn't handle me and Hector. From there, we were living off and on again with Victor. I wish Victor would have been our dad. Lorena's a lucky girl. Why did we have a fucked up dad with a cracked out mom? Why, God? I just don't understand. God, I want to know you. I want you to come into my life and release me from the pain...please, please, please! I beg you. I fell asleep praying to God like I had never prayed before. I woke up to Rico yelling, "Yaaaaa, buddy! Wake up and take your shower!" As I woke up, I wondered why he was so happy. I got up and did what he asked, I mean, I hate being told what to do, but when Rico told me I knew it was to better myself and to make us both some money. I jumped in the shower and washed good. I stuck my finger as far up my asshole as I could to make sure I was good and clean. I always did that before I had sex. And even though I wasn't going to unless Rico wanted some, I felt like tonight was the start of my new life and I was doing it all in the big city of dreams. I jumped out of the shower and opened the bathroom door to let some of the steam out when in walks Rico. My heart started beating so fast again! I was ready. I mean I was so horny! He walked in and started washing his hands. He was scrubbing them with a washcloth and acted like I wasn't even in there. So I walked out and over to the bed-there was only one-and pulled my underwear from my bag. "Stop!" he commanded. "No underwear. We're going to put your dance gear on and you can slip your jeans on after. Then, we heading to the club. I turned around and said Ok. Then Rico sat on the edge of the bed and told me to come over. I still had my towel wrapped around me but I automatically got a hard on and was sticking straight up. I stood in front of him and he took the towel off and rubbed Vaseline and some cocoa butter in his hands and mixed them together like he was making tortillas. He rubbed it all over me from my neck on down to my feet. I put one foot at a time on his lap. He lotioned the first one and put it down then he grabbed the other foot and put it on his lap. After he was finished rubbing my foot he put it up to his mouth and kissed it. Then he turned me around with my ass facing him and rubbed it all over my ass while telling me my body was a work of art. He continued to rub me down. Then he opened up my butt cheeks and put his finger in my ass. I felt my dick rising and rising; higher and harder than it had ever been. He took his finger out my asshole and kissed both of my butt cheeks and said in a sexy voice, "I had to make sure you are good and shiny because tonight's your night." He stood up and told me he was jumping in the shower again. He finished his shower and I watched him rub himself down with the Vaseline and cocoa butter just like he had rubbed me. "Can I help you?" I asked. He dropped his towel and his dick was hard, long and beautiful. "No, Green Eyes," he said. "I'm good." I felt like I was going to explode. I was so horny. Rico finished oiling himself and put his clothes on. Then, he walked over to me with a lit blunt and said, "Smoke this so we can roll out." We smoked half a blunt and I was ready. I felt so good! I had energy and usually, weed makes me chill. We got into the elevator and took it down to the first floor before we headed to the street so we could catch a cab. I felt like I was Madonna or someone. I was high and felt good. No. I felt great. I was going to show them what a Cali boy was made of. We reached Stella's and I was excited and ready to dance! As we approached the door, we were getting looks from guys that were on line waiting to get into the club. We walked in and the bar was packed. There were two guys on different poles in the club and lots of guys standing on the pool tables. We walked through the club and headed to the dressing room. The club was small with music playing so loud that you could feel it in your soul. I was excited and ready. We took off our clothes, oiled up again and headed back out. The DJ said we have some down south fellas here from the ATL here tonight! I want you to welcome Sex Machine and Mr. Green Eyes, a Latin from the south that will make you want to put your money where his dick is-or ass-depending on which way you're flipping tonight!" I watched Rico jump on that pole and everyone sitting at the bar went crazy! I looked around and saw the same fine guy I saw earlier at the club, but he had changed his outfit. A dancer who was tall like Rico, but real light skinned came over and said, "*Oya* here *papi*. You're on this stage. I jumped on this little box they called a stage and went with the music. I saw a crowd where Rico was dancing, so I tried to imitate everything he was doing as much as I could without looking like I was following him. I danced three songs and started walking around. I ended up in VIP dancing in this private room that was kinda dark with other dancers in there dancing too. I wasn't sure what I was supposed to be doing, so I looked over at some of the other guys and they were grinding with their dicks. But the guy I was dancing for said, "Show me that ass!" So I turned around, bent over and he was blowing in my asshole. I was still horny, but this dude wasn't my type. Still, the fact that he wanted me so bad that he was willing to pay money to see me act nasty for him was ok with me. We stayed in there for 30 minutes. Then, another dancer in the room came over and whispered, "You're finished." The man handed me $70 dollars and said, "$20 for you." I thanked him and headed out to the main room. Rico asked me if I'd made any cash. "Yeah! I made $70!" I said. "Well, you did goood," he said. "It's $50 for 30 minutes; $80 for an hour. There's going to be guys that will ask you to blow them or will want to blow you. I always say $500 to suck my dick with a condom and $1000 without. So, go big and make that money! You can give me the $50." So I did. "What about the $20?" I asked. "That's your tip," he said. "Keep it and keep working. Walk around and talk to those men at the bar." So I did and this old white man gave me $50 dollars in ones just to sit and have a drink with him. He talked and talked and talked. I guess he saw me looking over at the guy I saw earlier today and asked, "Who are you looking at?" I quickly said, "No one." Then he said, "Look, young man. You don't have to lie to me. You can tell me if you see someone else you would like to talk to." "No, I want to talk to you and get to know you," I lied. I couldn't believe what was coming out of my mouth. But it worked. He was tipping me more and more and more the longer I sat and told him how I loved his conversation and how he had beautiful blue eyes. There are a lot of things about me that aren't perfect. But I loved the fact that I tried to tell the truth. That's one thing my Tia Loose and mom taught me that I've held on to. But, tonight I was lying. And I loved it. I was telling these men whatever they wanted to hear and letting them know I would appreciate a tip. I mean, what's better than this? Life is great! All I have to do is show my body, listen to good music and smoke some weed. Most of the night, I stayed close to the bar talking to different older white men. But I was still looking around at my surroundings. I realized that every stripper in there was Latino, but some looked black even though they talked with a Spanish accent. I saw one guy that was not a dancer, talking to the white men just as I was. I saw the guy get up and head towards the back of the club. I told the trick I was talking to that I was going to use the restroom and that I would be right back so he could watch me dance just for him. I felt like a pro. This was easy and fun. I had been holding my pee, so I really didn't feel like I was following this guy. I just had to use the restroom. I walked in and he was pissing in the stall. I pissed right next to him. He finished and went to wash his hands. Then I followed behind him to wash mine. As he was washing his hands he asked, "You alright, Sexy?" I just stood there and looked in the mirror. He was staring right at me. "I'm Ok," I said. He turned around and got right in my face and said, "Oh. It looked like you had a problem. But as the words came out of his mouth, I looked at his brown, full lips and perfect nose. He had long eyelashes and thick eyebrows with big, fat curls that almost made him look like he had an afro. "No problem," I said. "I just never saw such a beautiful man." He smiled and asked, "You think I'm beautiful? Well, I think you're beautiful!" We stood there for a second. Then, he kissed my lips and it felt just like the first kiss Kevin gave me in elementary school. "What's your name, *papi?*" he asked. I told him my name but that most people call me G. "You really from the south?" he asked. "No," I responded. I live there, but I'm originally from California. "Yeah, sun!" he said in his New York accent. "I knew it, cuz you sound like a white boy from Cali." "Is that bad?" I asked. "Nah, sun." he said. "It's bananas. You look Puerto Rican, but sound like a surfer kinda. "I'm actually Mexican," I said. "Word?! Well, you the prettiest fucking Mexican I've seen, sun. Look, I have to go attend to some business. Can I get your number?" he asked. "Yeah, fo' sho'" I said. He smiled and said with his hands on my waist, "So now you wanna get gangsta on me." He took his hands off and all I could smell was him. His scent smelled so good. I mean, I guess it was so strong because the bathroom smelled like straight piss. He pulled out some matches and wrote his number on the back of the matches. Then he wrote mine on another pack of matches. "Green Eyes, I got your number," he said. "I'll page you tomorrow. Name's Johnny by the way." He kissed me again on the lips and said as he walked away, "Green Eyes, you know how to shake that ass, kid. Me and Rico stayed at the club until about 3 a.m. Then, the club started clearing out so Rico went into Kitty's office and took care of business while I went and changed clothes. I got dressed and waited for him to come and get dressed. He put his clothes on and told me how proud he was of me. Then, we left and caught a taxi back to the room. We got out and were both so hungry. We ordered some hella good pizza and ate it in this little pizza shop. From there, we walked back to our room and passed out on the bed. I woke up and felt hands playing in my ass. I looked at the clock. It was six a.m. I was so tired that I had to think where I was. I heard Rico whisper, "I'm going to be gentle. And he was. He put his whole dick in me and I was screaming. I was screaming because it hurt but also because it felt good. He was on the side of me holding my leg up and fucking me. "You like daddy's dick! You like daddy's dick!" he kept saying. "Yes...yes...yes," I moaned. "Tell me you love daddy's dick," he commanded. "Tell me my dick is important and you cherish it." "I love your dick; cherish your dick...it's so, so important." I was screaming. Rico fucked me from for about 30 minutes and asked, "Do you want to cum with me?" "Yes," I said. "Let me fucking know it!" he said. "Grab that dick and cum for me while I cum in you! Say cum daddy cum! I did as I was told and before I knew it, he was holding me and had his long legs wrapped around me so tight. And then he started saying, "Shaba shinga la high ya...shaba shinga la hiya!" He just screamed that over and over until he wore himself out. I was about to cum too but hearing him screaming whatever he was saying threw me off. His dick was still hard inside me, so I jacked my dick and squirted everywhere. He was still in me. And I was pretty sure he used a condom. But, then again, I wasn't sure and I started getting nervous. "I'm going to clean you up," I said. He pulled out and I turned to look fast. He laughed and asked, "You alright?" I looked down at the condom that looked like a water balloon with a little Hershey' Kiss on top. I was so embarrassed. I gently took the condom off of him and went to grab a towel to clean him off. Then, I jumped in the shower. When I finished cleaning myself, I got out and we both fell asleep. The next time I woke up it was 2:30 p.m. "Let's go again," Rico said. This time, my ass was sore. But I took it. And he fucked me until three o'clock. This time, I was on my back and he was fucking me in the buck. I screamed and screamed and screamed until he was finished. Then, he laid on me and we kissed for the first time using tongues. We got up but didn't take showers. We caught a taxi to Times Square, had some lunch and just people watched. There were people everywhere. There were also hookers everywhere. It was a busy place and I loved it. I thought about moving here myself. We finished up and got back to the room around 7:30 that evening. We took showers and oiled each other up. I hadn't looked at my pagers since I'd been in New York. Both of them had several messages. My Atlanta pager had a call from Chad. But my California pager had Lorena and Victor's job number. Lupita had paged too. There were also two numbers with Atlanta area codes. I didn't have time to call all of them, so I just called the house phone. "What up," Hector answered. "What you doing, bro?" I asked. "I'm getting ready to dance tonight," Hector said. "Where at?" I asked. "At some 50th birthday party out in Kennesaw. I'm going with Mocha One and some of the other dancers." I told him to be safe and that I loved him. "Love you too, bro," he said. Me and Rico headed back to Stella's for our second and last night in New York. Walking in, I noticed that this time, it was twice as crowded and Kitty was at the bar good and drunk and hugging on all these fine men. I looked around to see if I could see the fine guy from the night before, but I didn't see him. We took off our clothes and went back out and made lots and lots of money.

<u>Chapter 18: Hector's Debut</u>

 I shaved my under arms and legs just like Mocha One told me to do over the phone. He said we were dancing for a white woman who loves black men. I asked him why was I going and he said I was brown enough and I had what they wanted-dark meat. So after I shaved, I jumped in the shower. It was 8:30 p.m. and the fellas were coming to scoop me up around 9. They said it would take about an hour to get to Kennesaw. They also said we would be finished by midnight and I might have to go sit at the gay club with them because they would be rushing on the way back. I was thinking about just catching a taxi back. I mean, I love my gay brother and I love Angel too. But hanging out in a gay club does not sound fun at all. I put on my boots and what I was supposed to wear under my sweats. I have to admit, I was kind of nervous. But Rico said this would be a starting point to get the hang of dancing with women for money. He also said some of the older women like being fucked at these private parties depending on how drunk they got and if they were swingers. I had to ask Rico what swingers were because I had never heard of that shit before. I was in the living room stretching when I heard my pager go off. And it didn't stop. I went to see who it was. I looked and it was either Victor or Lorena's number. I wasn't sure which one, but I decided to call back. "Hello?" Victor answered. "Hello," I answered politely. "How are you doing, big guy?" he asked. I told him I was good and he asked about G. I told him that my brother was good also. "Look, *mijo*," he said. "I know we've had our ups and downs but I see great potential for you boys. I know in my heart of hearts you're going to be something great!" Even though Victor could give me a hard time, it really feels good when he says shit like that because I know he means it. "*Mijo,* you there?" he asked. "I'm here," I said. "Well, listen. There are a couple of reasons I need to talk to you. And if you don't want to discuss it, then that's fine with me. But I have to start off by letting you know your grandma is in the hospital and she's not really doing that well. She might not make it, *mijo.* So, do you think I need to send for you guys to come to Sacramento?" I thought about it for a second and then said, "Umm, look. I haven't seen my grandma in years. And even when we did see her, she was mean and drunk." "Yes, yes I understand," Victor said. "Well, I've been talking to your Tia Loose almost every day and she told me that she had a conversation with you but Gustavo hung up on her. She will be in Sacramento on Monday and I will be meeting with her for lunch. She told me some of the reasons she had not kept in touch with you boys and I told her you boys thought she was probably dead." To be honest, I did think she was dead and for her to call out the blue creeped the shit out of me, I told Victor in a firm voice. "I understand...I understand," he said. "Well, listen *Mijo,* I'm going to keep you posted. I was going to send you money last week. But since this came up, I'm going to hold out to buy you guys some plane tickets. Hector, please be safe and tell your brother that I love him and I will be calling your house phone or pager tomorrow or definitely on Monday. I said, "Ok...cool." Then he asked if we had and money for food. I told him we were cool. "I know you *muchachos* are cool, but are you hungry?" he asked laughing. We laughed together and I told him goodbye before I hung up. I heard a horn beep. I looked out the window and then locked the door before shutting it and running to get in Mocha One's Land Cruiser. I gave all the guys a fist bump. "Mocha," I said. "I like your ride, *vato.* This mug is hella tight!" "Thanks, *vato,*" he said. "You know I know about those *vatos.* I'm from Dallas, Texas!" "That's what's up!" I said. We drove for about 45 minutes. Then we pulled into this big ass yard with a house that looked like a mansion. "Look, fellas," he said. "They've already paid Rico for the two hours. All four of us are going to be here.

But if y'all are going to be eating pussy or fucking, I'd ask for the most cash I could possibly get. Shit. If I fuck one of these old white bitches, I'm at least asking for $500. And if I lick her pussy, I'm going to need a couple hundred more." Damn, I'm about to get paid for dancing and fucking. I was thinking. I like this. Then Mocha said, "But whatever we do, we need to be wrapping it up by 11:45 so we can be on the road no later than 12:15." Everyone was cool with Mocha's plan. "Alright then," he said. "Can we get a bark for Midnight Express doing the damn thang?!" Mocha screamed. WOOF, WOOF, WOOF!!" we all barked. "Now, let's go make this money!" Mocha said. We all stepped out of Mocha's tight ass ride and headed towards the big ass house. We rang the doorbell and this older white lady, who looked like Large Marge from that Pee Wee Herman movie, opened the door and said, "Y'all come on in!" in a hella country ass voice. We walked in and the house was incredibly nice. There were winding steps that led upstairs. As she walked up the stairs, she instructed us to follow her. We heard lots of women, but could only see Large Marge. I laughed to myself. We finally made it up to the second floor and she walked us into this big ass bedroom and said, "Hi guys! I'm Irma Jean. Sorry I was so rude at the front door, but I didn't want the birthday girl to show up and see y'all standing outside. She thinks it's an all girls' night and we're playing bingo. Ok, men. You can dress here and if you need me to lotion you up or give you a blowjob, I'm your girl. She was laughing as she said it but I think she was serious. Wow, I thought. She just says what she feels like saying, I guess. I mean if you have a big house like this then you're probably so rich that you can say whatever comes to mind. Large Marge walked out of the room and everyone started getting ready. Mocha handed me a bottle of oil and told me to grease down my whole body. So I did. I was nervous so I asked Mocha and the fellas if they had any tips on what I should do or what I should say. One of the dancers told me that your body and dick say it all, so just act like you're so into them. Another dancer told me to tell them how beautiful and sexy they are and they'll tell me what they need from me "That's when you hit 'em with the bill," Mocha said. We could hear music playing, so we walked downstairs. There were about 50 white women. Most of them were old. And there were a couple who might have been in their 20s. They were screaming and waving money. Mocha sat on the birthday girl's lap. I had three women around me and one of them had bad breath but some big titties and a fat ass. She pulled me away for a second and said, "Can I talk to you?" "Yeah, sexy lady...of course," I said trying not to breathe while she was talking. "Can I see it," she asked. "See what?" I responded trying to play dumb. "Your dick," she said. I looked her dead in the eye and pulled my underwear down. She stared at it and said, "I love uncircumcised and headed straight for my dick with her mouth. I backed up and asked, "How much do you have, beautiful?" I said it as sexy as I could. She pulled out a big, thick wad of cash and handed it to me. I counted it and it was $645. I looked at her and asked, "Where do we go?" She grabbed my hand and I followed her through the kitchen. There were some other ladies already in there. They started egging us on saying, "Go, Mary Sue! You go girl!" We went into the laundry room and I pulled out a condom. But before I could, she was on her knees sucking the hell out of my dick. And it felt good. I let her suck it for a while. Then I put the condom on and fucked the shit out of her pussy. She was screaming so loud. She turned around and asked me to put it in her ass. So I did. I came about 15 minutes later. She showed me where the restroom was and I went and cleaned up. Then I went back out and danced and danced and danced. I made a total of $1,152 cash. I gave Mocha $50 for gas money and the rest was mine. I told Mocha I just made $500. They didn't need to know all I made, I thought to myself. We got back in Mocha's Land Cruiser and headed back to Atlanta. But the clock said 12:40 a.m. Mocha said, "You can take $10 back from that $50 if you want, but I can't take you home until we're done dancing around 3:30 or 4:00." I told him I would just sit at the bar and watch them so I could learn some moves. "Ohhh, you got jokey jokes," Mocha said. "Nah, man. I'm serious," I said. "I might want to start dancing in clubs. Shit. I need money and dancing for women is kinda cool." Mocha nodded and said, "I hear you man. But fucking for big money is even better!" He laughed and we all started barking out WOOF,

WOOF, WOOF!! Then I asked him, "Do you think they'll let me drink?" "Of course, mannn!" he screamed. "You are now officially a part of the Midnight Express! Wait til I tell Rico you were the fuckin' man tonight!" We parked in a pay lot up the street from the club. As we got closer to the club, I realized that it was packed and the line was up the street. As we bypassed the line, I was looking at these dudes. Most of them looked straight. We were all getting whistles and I even heard a couple *"hey, papis."* That made me want to catch a taxi. But I knew if I wanted to make a $1000 dollars in one night, I was going to have to dance, act and watch everything these brothers did so I could be driving in a fat ride and making cold cash, I thought to myself. We walked into the club and Mocha and the other dancers told me they would catch up with me later. There were some Midnight Express already dancing, so I decided to sit at the bar closest to the stage and drink and watch. And that's exactly what I did. I sat, watched and had drink after drink sent to me from guy after guy. All I said was thanks. After my fifth Hennessey and Alize, I realized I was good and drunk. When the guys finished dancing, I went into the dressing room and lay down on a bench until Mocha woke me up and told me it was time to roll. We walked to the car and he dropped me off at the apartment. Mocha's cool, I thought. That *vato* kinda reminded me of some of my homies in Sac. He was cool and not gay. Plus, he was on swole and might be hard to fight, I laughed to myself. I walked in the house and the clock read 5 a.m. I was so tired I just lay right on the living room floor. I felt myself going to sleep thinking about getting a new bed. Right before I fell into a deep sleep, my pager went off and wouldn't shut up. I sat up and grabbed the cordless. I tried to halfway stand up to turn on the light so I could see who was fucking paging me. I turned on the light and hit my knee on the stereo. I screamed. That shit hurt so bad. I was going to call the number and curse them out. Then I looked at the number and I hoped Gustavo was Ok because the area code didn't look familiar. I called the number and a voice said, "Thank you for calling the Four Seasons. How may I direct your call?" I looked down at the pager thinking my dumb ass brother just paged me and didn't put the room number in. So I looked at the third page

I got and it said 1015. "May I have room one thousand and fifteen, please?" I asked. "Haha. Do you mean room 10 15?" the operator asked. What's the fucking difference?" I asked. "Ok. Sure. I'm connecting you now," the operator said. The phone rang three times with no answer. I was getting pissed because I was still drunk and sleepy as fuck! "Hello?" Star said into the receiver. I knew it was her. I could never forget that voice. "Star! What's up, baby?" I asked. "Nothing," she said quietly as she started crying. "What's wrong you?" I asked. She was quiet for a few seconds then said, "Everything's messed up! My whole life is messed up and I don't have anyone to talk to." "Well, I'm glad you called me because I really miss you," I said. "You do?" she asked. "Hell yeah! When can I see you?" I asked. "I'm in Philadelphia right now," she said. "I just packed my stuff and I'm on standby for the 7:30 a.m. flight. I was leaving at noon, but I've got to get out of here." I was fully awake now and asked, "Did someone hurt you?" She said no and that she was Ok. But I knew something was wrong. "Can you meet me at the airport?" she asked. "Yeah," I said. "No problem. I'll jump in the shower and be up there as soon as I can." She gave me the information on her flight and what time she would be landing. That is if she was able to get on the flight. After taking my shower, I walked to the train station and waited there for her. I was still feeling a little drunk. If she asked me where I was to get so wasted, I was going to lie and tell her I got drunk at home.

<u>Chapter 19: Angel's Demons</u>

I couldn't believe we'd been driving for two days in a Ford Focus. We picked the car up at the Kmart on Piedmont Road and had been driving ever since. Thank God we're cute, I thought. We' had been able to ask truck drivers and various men along the way because neither of our *mensa* asses can read a map. Well, I might not have finished high school, but I do have something rich people wish they had and that's street sense. Anyway, once I get my pussy, I will be rich soon enough and all I'll need to do is take care of my kids and keep my mansion clean. I laughed to myself at the thought of it. I looked over at Naomi and told her how beautiful she was and how I was glad that we were friends. But what I really wanted to say was, "You're a pretty dumb bitch that eats like a vacuum and your feet smell like Doritos and piss. I never knew her feet smelled so bad at my cousin Jaime's. But then again, I wasn't that close. I wonder if Tre smelled them. Maybe it was because we'd been in the car for two days and hadn't had a shower and her feet were just extra sweaty. Who knows? I was just glad she was finally driving. She said she used to drive a scooter with her brothers in the Dominican Republic. So, I thought she knew how to drive. But nope. She wasn't a great driver but good enough to let me get some rest and wake my feet up. I laughed to myself? "What's so funny?" she asked in her thick accent. "Oh nothing, *cholita!*" I said. We kept driving and all I could think about is getting my pussy. I always knew I was going to get it one day, but not this soon. I told D that I was going to be out of town for a couple of weeks. Naomi told me that after a couple days, we would be able to walk good enough. I brought the money D gave me to purchase a couple of Greyhound tickets to get us back to Atlanta. Naomi said Tre had given her money for us to stay in a hotel room so we could rest up before are Greyhound ride home. I remember one time I heard this special girl on Santa Monica tell me and some other special girls that she was going to a psychiatrist so she could get her pussy. I asked her why and she said they just don't give anyone pussies. You had to be a real woman and the doctors would pick who they felt who was real or not. "How can a fucking doctor tell me if I'm a woman or not?" I said. "I've always been a woman." I let Naomi drive for another hour. Then we pulled over because both our pagers were going off with the same number. We pulled into a gas station parking lot to use the pay phone. "You can call them, Angel," she said. "I'm going to close my eyes for a minute." I couldn't believe this bitch was tired when I'd done all the driving while she slept. I pulled a calling card out of my pocket and called the number. "What's happeningggg!?" the voice said like a *cholo*. "Hi, I said. "Did someone page Angel?" "*Si*...its Popeye," he said. "Hi, Popeye," I said. "We haven't met *papi*, but Naomi told me nothing but good things about you."

"Reallyyyyy," he said. "Well, don't believe her!" Popeye said laughing. "How far are you away?" I told him we'd made it to Texas, so all we had to do was make it to him in Del Rio. "Angel, you're almost here," he said. "About five to seven more hours I would say. Call me when you get to the gas station in Del Rio...the Shell gas station. There's only one." I said Ok and good bye and told Naomi to take a piss or shit because we were about to hit the road and get to Del Rio as fast as we could. We both used the restroom and bought some vittles then I jumped back in the driver side and we were back on the freeway. "Now, didn't you say Popeye was white?" I asked Naomi. *Si* she said. "Well, he sounds like a *Chicano*, I said. "I told you he was a *gringo,"* She said. "He just thinks he's *Mejicano*. He's not *muchacha*. He's a *wetto*. We drove and drove. It was dark by the time we pulled into the Shell gas station in Del Rio. Popeye had been paging for the last hour of our trip. But I wasn't going to stop until we got there. The closer we got there, the more I was anxious and excited to get my pussy and get back home with Gustavo and Hector. They're my family and I love them so much that when I get my big house they could live with my husband and my kids and me, I thought to myself. I called Popeye's number but there was no answer. I hung up the phone when I saw a low rider mini truck pull up with a white boy that looked like Phil Donahue driving. *"Hola, muchachos!"* he said. "Hi. Are you Popeye?" Naomi screamed, "Yes that's Popeye!" He told us to follow him. We drove a couple blocks to a big, gorgeous house. It looked orange or pink in the dark, but I really couldn't tell. He opened the garage door and waved for me to go around him. So I did and pulled into his garage. He closed the garage door while we were still in the car. I looked at Naomi and said, "I wish I had my gun." She said, "Don't worry, Miss Angel. I have mine." "That's my kinda girl!" I said as we high fived each other. We sat in the car until Popeye came out from the house and waved for us to get out the car. We walked in and it was really nice. It kind of looked like a bigger version of Chad's apartment. I looked around I tried to figure out if he was moving in or moving out because there were brown boxes with tape on them everywhere. "What can I get you ladies to drink?" Popeye asked. We didn't say anything. "Listen, ladies...I'm kind of tired, so why don't you have some wine and tomorrow my *primo* will take you two lovely ladies to Tijuana so you can be complete." He walked out of the room and came right back with a plate of cocaine. "A little something extra for you two driving that long way," he said. "I'll have some," Naomi said. I just stood there getting irritated with every second that went by. "Look, *papi* can we get our money?" I asked. "Of course you can," Popeye said. "I will be right back. He left the room again and I watched Naomi do line after line after line as if she was in a race with herself. About five minutes later, he came back with two paper bags and put one in front of both of us. I quickly opened my bag and started counting. I quickly glanced at Naomi. Her face was still in the plate. "This is only $1000!" I said loud. Then I opened Naomi's bag. "Aren't you going to count it?" I asked as she kept snorting. "There's a $1000 in that one too," Popeye said. "So...where's the rest?" I asked. "The doctor's been paid already," Popeye said. "All you have to do is bring him the thousand and you'll be ready to snip, cut and have a beautiful *pinocha,*" as he started snorting cocaine. "Why did you pay him already?" I asked. "Because he's busy," he said. "And my friend told me that you have to leave a deposit." "Well, what if we hadn't made it here...then what?" I asked. "What do you mean?" Popeye asked. "I mean you gave the doctor our money but how would you get it back if we never showed up with the stuff?" I was so irritated. "In this life, you have to trust certain people," he answered. "And treat people good-the ones whom you trust." I was confused and trying to figure out what he meant. "Look," he said. "You guys came through with the goodies and now I'm coming through for you. You have to trust me because I trusted you. I sat down and thought about what he said, and I figured he was right because we could have easily sold that heroin in Atlanta. I felt a little better, so I asked if could have a glass of wine. "You certainly may, *mi amor,*" he said. I drank the glass of wine and watched Popeye and Naomi make out in the kitchen. I was so grossed out. I knew she was pretty but that pretty bitch hadn't even brushed her teeth. I felt nasty. I asked Popeye if I could take a shower. He showed me to the bathroom and gave me towels. I closed the door and took off my clothes. Then I sat on the toilet so I could finally take a good shit in a clean restroom. Popeye had boxes everywhere, but the house was so clean. I was glad we were staying the night so I could have a good rest before our operation. I stood up and turned on the shower. I saw a shirt sticking out of the hamper, so I decide to push it all the way in. I opened the lid to push the sleeve in and when I did, I saw San Diego Police Department on the sleeve. I jumped back and said, "Is this fool the police?" I threw my clothes back on. I could hear Naomi and Popeye fucking in the room. I ran to Naomi's purse and pulled out her gun and an extra box of bullets. I was confused. I didn't know what to do. Part of me wanted to go upstairs and blast him and another part of me wanted to ask if he was an undercover cop. But why would he be doing cocaine and fucking a special girl? I sat on the table and thought about driving off with the car and the dope. But I couldn't leave Naomi like that. I wanted to call Gustavo so bad. But he was still in New York. And even if he was home, he would be so mad at me. I sat there so confused. I had another glass of wine hoping that it would help me decide what I should do. But, of course it didn't. I heard some footsteps. It was Popeye walking out butt naked. His body was nice and his dick was fat and pink. He walked to the fridge and pulled out some orange juice and started drinking out straight out of the carton. "Are you one time?" I asked him straight up. He turned around and said, "No, my brother Smiley is. Why do you ask?" "No reason," I said. "I just wanted to make sure we weren't going to be in any kind of trouble." "You mean trouble like your cousin Jaime?" he asked. "He's not my cousin," I said annoyed. "He's my brother." Popeye looked at me and said, "Your brother; your cousin...he didn't want to claim you. He told me about you a long time ago. He said you were trash and that you were a prostitute by the time you were nine years old and that you've been running around having sex and giving people AIDS. Is that true?" "Hell no!" I yelled. "I don't have AIDS! And you're lying! Jaime would never say that!" The room got quiet and I just started crying. I couldn't stop. I felt a hand on my back and he said, "I believe you." He rubbed my back and I kept crying. I couldn't believe Jaime would say that about me. How could he, I thought to myself. Then Popeye went to the fridge and said, "This might make you feel better." He opened the freezer and pulled out a box, sat it on the table and opened it up. There was money...lots of money. He pulled out 10 one hundred dollar bills and counted each one out loud. Then he asked, "Now, do you trust me? You know where my money stash is. You could easily steal it while I'm asleep." This time, he wasn't talking with a thick *cholo* accent. "Come take a shower with me and let me enjoy your parts for the last time and you'll have an extra $1000 to buy you some new panties for your *pinocha,*" he said. I looked at the money. Then I looked at him knowing he had just fucked Naomi and kissed her. It made me sick, but I did need money and he was giving it to me. So I grabbed it out of his hand and walked over to the bag of cocaine sitting on the other table and asked if I could have some. Now it was me that was in a race with the lines. I did line after line and stopped counting after the third one. I woke up and the sun was shining on my face from the window. I felt something itching in my ass, so I put my hands down there. It was a condom stuck half way in and half way out. I pulled it out and sat up. My bussy was sore. I stood up and put a towel around me because I didn't want to put on the same dirty clothes I had worn the last three days. Then, I walked down the hall yelling, "Good morning! Good morning, everyone!" Even though my bussy was sore, I was in a good mood. This was the day that I would become all woman and I was ready to go. I walked in the room. Naomi and Popeye had been fucking again. They were both laid out naked on the bed. "Wake up!" I yelled. "It's time to get our pussies!" Popeye stood up with his dick hard and said, "Before you two go, I need someone to handle this and pointed at his dick. Naomi's eyes opened wide and her head was going straight for his dick. I just walked out and said, "I'm cooking breakfast. I walked out of that room as fast as I could. I knew I had messed around with him the night before, but I was so damn high off cocaine, that I really didn't remember too much. I opened his fridge and saw tortillas, chorizo and eggs and thought to myself, this is one Mexican white boy. I fixed breakfast using a whole carton of eggs, all the chorizo and was warmed up the tortillas on the stove. Then I heard the doorbell. I screamed. Popeye and Naomi came walking out. "What did you scream for?" Popeye asked. "It was just the door bell." He went to answer the door as I looked for orange juice because I was hella thirsty. I pulled the orange juice out the fridge and turned around and saw one of the scariest sights I'd ever seen. It was a short man with three chins hanging down towards his titties. He had extra skin hanging there like he had been melted or something. I asked everyone if they wanted a plate and they all said yes. I introduced myself to the man and he told me his name was Smiley. I had never in my life seen a cop with brown teeth and saggy skin everywhere with saggy titties to match before. And I had come in contact with a lot of popo when I was working on Sunset. I made everyone a plate and then decided I needed to take a shower. I wasn't hungry anymore after looking at smiley. He made me sick to my stomach. I told everyone I was going to take a shower, but smiley said, "I don't mean to rush you ladies, but we need to be leaving in the next 15 minutes if we're going to make it over that border today." I ran to the shower fast and threw my still wet hair back into a tight ponytail. I put on a little makeup as quick as I could. Naomi jumped in the shower and threw on her clothes. We grabbed our things and headed toward the kitchen when Naomi asked, "Where's my gun?" as she looked in her purse. I told her I had it and she said, "Don't ever take my shit!" I was stunned and asked, "What do you mean? She narrowed her eyes and said, "Bitch, don't play *stupida,* I never want you to touch my gun or anything else unless I ask you to!" I just looked at her and said, "First of all, bitch; I was protecting us while you were in there fucking Popeye! At least I was watching and making sure nobody broke in or tried to hurt us!" "*To esa puta,*" she said. "You fucked him all night. Your screaming woke me up, so don't act like you're a classy bitch." I looked into her eyes and saw a devil-someone I'd never seen before. She looked so different to me. I couldn't believe this bitch was trying me. I took a breath and opened my purse. I handed her the gun and walked into the kitchen. Popeye was sitting alone eating at the table. I walked up to him and said, "It was nice doing business with you. I hope to see you again soon" "Yes, I hope very soon," he said. "But you need to go now.

Smiley's waiting for you and he doesn't like to be late." I gave him a hug and a kiss and walked out the house not even waiting for Naomi. I jumped in the back seat so I could keep an eye on the bitch in case she tried anything funny. She walked out and opened the passenger side and said, "We're ready!" with a happy tone. Smiley drove off and was asking us if we were excited about the operation. We said yes. He also started telling us how much work it took to find the right doctor for us and that Popeye only wanted the best for us. I couldn't believe it was going to happen! In just a few hours, I was going to be a woman and all it took was us driving some drugs from Atlanta to the border of Texas and Mexico. We drove about 10 minutes. Then Smiley parked the car and we both got out and followed him over the Rio Grande. He had a Dairy Queen bag with him and we carried our purses and the bags that held our clothes. We walked for about 20 minutes until we were close to the Texas border patrol cops and the Mexican cops. Smiley handed the Dairy Queen bag to the American cop and we went right through. There were so many people going to Mexico. They were walking behind us and in front of us. We walked up to a Mexican cop and he was talking to another cop. He just turned his face as if they didn't even see us walk through. I was surprised because people were showing paperwork before us and he just let us pass him. We made it to Mexico and walked for another 15 minutes. Then, we walked up to a pay phone where there was a man in a white van waiting for us. Smiley didn't say nothing to the man. He just gave him a look. Then Smiley looked over at us and said, "You ladies be safe. Here's my pager and my cell phone if you need anything. I really appreciate you both. Good luck with the surgery." We thanked him and both of us gave him a hug. Then he looked at me and said, "If I was your man, I wouldn't care what you had down there because one hole would be good enough for me," It was so sweet for him to say that, I thought. It made my day. I almost gave him a kiss on his lips until I looked at his teeth. So, instead, I decided to blow him a kiss and he caught it. We climbed into the van and took the seats in the very back thinking we were going to be the only people riding. But we were wrong. We stopped five times and were stuffed in the van like pickles in a jar. We rode for what seems like forever. It was dark before we pulled into Tijuana. I knew we would be coming through Tijuana, but it seemed like it would have made more sense to drive to the border from California. I was happy but thought it might have been too late to operate that night. We drove onto a street that had a lot of bars. There were people everywhere that looked like they were having fun. The driver told us, in Spanish, that we were to get off at this stop. So, we grabbed our stuff and got out of the van. We stretched as the van pulled off. Then, another man walked up to us holding a sign with both of our names on it. He told us to follow him. So we did. We walked into a busy bar and followed the man through the kitchen to a back room. The room was all white and had two beds and a waiting chair. There were all kinds of medical equipment sitting on a tray. I looked around. I didn't have a good feeling until two doctors walked in- one white man and the other looked like he was Indian. He was the kind of Indian that worked at Seven-eleven. I was so happy to see them because they said they both did their training in the United States and that they had two more operations after ours. They asked us to take off our clothes and change into hospital robes. The Indian doctor held two cups of water and some pills. He told us to take the medicine. So many things ran through my mind such as how my life was and how it was going to be. I was so happy. The doctors asked which one of us wanted to go first and I said, "I do!" Then I felt bad because Naomi looked like she was ready too. "Would you like to go first," I asked? She looked at me and said in her thick accent, "I've been kind of a bitch today." I knew she was right but said, "No, you haven't!" The white doctor finally said, "Look, sweethearts. We are very busy. Someone please take these pain killers and drink this water so we can get started." I took four pills, drank some water and took off my robe. The doctors had me stand up as they marked my body with a black marker. Suddenly, I felt really sleepy and it was getting harder for me to stand up. The white doctor said, "Ok, we're going to lay you down and start operating. I smiled and nodded. They pulled back the sheets on the bed and I could see straps on all four sides of the bed. They laid me down and I could feel them strapping my arms and feet. I asked why I was being tied up. The Indian doctor laughed and said, "We're not tying you up. This is for your own safety. I smiled and said, "Thank you, doctor." I was almost asleep when I felt them cutting me with the knife or whatever it was. It hurt and I woke all the way up screaming, "Stop! Stop!" But they didn't. Both doctors were cutting me and I could see and feel everything. I just screamed. Then, I heard one of the doctors ask Naomi where the rest of the money was and I could see Naomi handing them some money. "Where is his ID?" the Indian doctor asked I was screaming for them to stop. I was in so much pain. "Help me, Naomi!" I screamed, "Help me!" I opened my eyes and saw Gustavo. I saw him at a beach. The beach had pretty white sands and big light blue waves. The waves were close to us but they didn't touch. We walked closer and closer to each other but I couldn't get close enough to him. "Gustavo! Gustavo!" I screamed. He just smiled and told me everything was going to be Ok and that I was going to find the man of my dreams. He told me that the man was going to marry me and one day, I was going to have kids-lots of kids. "How do you know?" I asked him. But he was quiet and then he just disappeared. I kept walking but now, I was on a cliff looking at big, beautiful waves flowing from the ocean. I remember them being so very high.

Chapter 20: Tequila Sunrise

"Help us somebody!" is what I started screaming as soon as they dropped us off. I couldn't believe this bitch was still alive. But she had to stay alive until we could get past the border so I could grab the kilos of heroin duck taped behind her legs. Those idiots were supposed to get rid of her dick and stitch the kilos in her body and get her over by the border so I could show the Mexican cops that she was a citizen. This was supposed to be Jaime's job; not mine. He knew I didn't fucking have my papers. But I trusted that Popeye wouldn't lie to me and this plan would work out Ok. People surrounded me holding Angel. There was blood everywhere. Again, I screamed for help and told one of the kids I saw to tell a cop to come where we were. A cop came over and I told him she was American and she needed a hospital. About 15 minutes later, an American ambulance came through the border of Tijuana and I showed them her ID. We both got into the ambulance. I told them that I was her sister and that some guys took her and I had found her lying on the street. They stopped asking me questions because they were trying to keep her alive. I didn't really care. I just wanted this ambulance to stop so I could grab the dope and leave. I started screaming and pretending I was so sad while they kept trying to save her. We pulled up to a traffic light and I started wondering if I was going to get a chance to get the heroin from the back of Angel's legs. I wanted to tear it off of her before the ambulance came but I wasn't sure if they were going to try to make me stay. I started getting scared, so I started screaming that my stomach hurt. But that didn't help. They didn't stop trying to keep the *puta* alive. We drove and I heard the ambulance driver say, "We're almost there. My beeper went off and it read 911. I knew that meant Smiley or Popeye were close by. It was so noisy in the ambulance that you couldn't hear anything but these *mensos* telling her she was going to be Ok. I screamed, "She has AIDS!...she told me herself!" The paramedics looked at me but it didn't bother them. They were still trying to save this *puta's* life. I felt the ambulance slowing to a stop as one of the drivers looked in the window and asked the other driver what was going on. I pulled out my gun and said, "Put your hands behind your back now!" Both men looked at me in shock. One of them begged me to hand him the gun. Just as I was going to shoot him, the back doors of the ambulance opened and there were four people with masks on standing there. "Get out of the ambulance!" one of them commanded. We all jumped out and I heard Smiley say, "Get the dope." I got back in and lifted Angel's legs to pull off the duct tape that was wrapped from the back of her thigh to the back of her ankle. I tore the tape from both legs, jumped back out of the ambulance and we all ran towards the car in front of the ambulance. I heard gunshots as I dove into the back seat. Someone got in after me and we were off with our dope. I couldn't wait to see Popeye. I knew he was going to be so proud of me.

Chapter 21: Party's Over
R

We woke up and Rico yelled for me to get up or we were going to miss our plane. I jumped up, washed my face and brushed my teeth while Rico said he was going downstairs to check out. I grabbed both of our bags and double-checked to make sure we weren't leaving anything. Then, I walked down to the elevator and pushed the button to the first floor so I could meet Rico and we could catch a cab to the airport. As soon as I walked into the elevator, I started feeling so sad. I felt so bad that I wanted to cry. The elevator door opened and everyone walked off and new people walked in. I stood there starting to lose my breath and I knew I just needed to rinse some water over my face. I rode the elevator back up and then I finally made it back down to the first floor. The elevator opened and I saw Rico standing there. "Come on, man!" he said. "We're going to miss our plane!" I got off the elevator and headed towards him. But then, I told him I needed to run to the restroom for a second. "No!" he yelled. "You think I'm playing but we're going to miss this plane so come on, now! You can use the restroom at the airport!" For some reason, him yelling at me seemed to calm me down. Rico reached for his bag and we left the building and got into a cab. We were both quiet during the taxi ride to the airport and we slept on the plane. We finally made it back to Atlanta and Mocha was waiting for us outside the airport in this tight ass Land Cruiser truck. I swear I thought everyone in Atlanta had a nice ride. We threw our bags in the trunk and got in. Rico bragged about how good I was to Mocha and Mocha said the same things about my brother. I was happy my brother was going to be making money too. Who would have ever thought our life would finally be great? We arrived at the apartment and Rico asked us how long was our lease. "I think Angel said it was for a year," I said. "Well, whose name is on the lease?" he asked. "To be honest, I'm not sure," I said. "Angel hooked it up." "Well," he said. "Y'all bruthas need to move...ASAP. If I was you, I would save up some money and get an apartment in Midtown so you can be train accessible." "Ok, cool," I said. I gave both Rico and Mocha a fist pound then climbed out of the back seat and walked towards our apartment. Even though I wasn't as sad as I was in New York, I still felt like something wasn't right. I walked into the house and looked around at the apartment. We didn't have any furniture, so if we were going to move it wouldn't be too hard because we didn't have shit to move, I thought. I threw my bag down and looked at the caller ID. We had several missed calls. I couldn't believe Atlanta had caller ID and they didn't even know what I was talking about when I talked to friends in Sac. I paged Angel first because I couldn't wait to tell her about my weekend and to tell her I fucked Rico. I could tell my sister anything and she wouldn't judge me. She was always happy for me. I wish God made more people with a heart and spirit like Angel's. It would be a much better world, I thought. After I paged her, I paged Hector to see where he was. I waited about 10 minutes and then I called Chad. I really liked him. I dialed his number and the phone just rang. Then, his machine came on so I left a sexy message. An hour went by and no one had called back. I was bored. I called Lorena and there was no answer there, either. I decided to page her. My stomach told me it was time to eat, but there was nothing in the fridge. I turned on my *What's the 411?* CD and took a couple hits of some roaches I had and chilled. I dozed off and woke up at 6:30 p.m. Now I was starving and mad that no one had called me back. Plus, I was still bored. I started thinking about Kevin and how much I missed him. But I wanted to have my shit together when I saw him just like he had his shit together. He was going to college and was so smart. He could play basketball, shoot pool *and* shoot craps. Not only that. He could play spades, kiss good, fuck good...I mean, he was the whole package. Then I started thinking about Chad and Rico. They were good men just like Kevin. They were just as cute with dicks just as big- maybe even a little bigger. They both had their shit together and when I was with either of them, I felt wanted. Ok, fuck it, I thought. I'm not waiting any longer. I'm going to page Kevin and I'm not going to bring up Lupita's bitch ass saying she's pregnant by him. I went to my suitcase in our room and pulled out a folder with Kevin's pager number on it. Hector had written it down the last time he called. I would never remember this pager number since he changed the last one and didn't give me this one. I grabbed the phone and paged him. I sat there for 10 minutes and it seemed like no one was going to call back. Then the phone rang. I answered. "Yeah," Kevin said. "Did someone call K Mack?" I started laughing. 'What's so funny, fool?!" he wanted to know. "Oh, I got your fool," I said. "Aye, yo ass can throw hands, but you can't whip *my* ass!" Kevin said back. "You sure about that?" I joked back. Then Kevin said, "So I've talked to your brother and I'm just now talking to you and you've almost been here two months." "Yeah," I said. I've just been trying to get my shit together." He asked if I was in school and I told him I wasn't yet. "Well, what you and your bro doing right now?" he asked. "Nothing," I answered. "I'm home alone. I just got back from New York this morning." "New York?" he asked. "Yup." I wanted to make him jealous. That's the only reason I told him. He told me him and some friends were hitting a couple bars that were poppin' on early Sunday evenings. He invited me to meet him at Peachtree Street train station on the southbound side at 8 o'clock. I looked at the clock. It was almost seven. I hung up the phone. Then I took a shower and shaved. I put on some Jordans that Rico had given me right before we left New York. He said he bought them for me when he'd left Friday to take care of business. I didn't wait for the bus. I started walking on the freeway so I could hurry up and catch the Marta train. I made it to the station and took off my black derby jacket because I'd worked up a sweat even though it was cold outside. The train pulled up and I got on it. I still hadn't heard anything from my brother or Angel. I felt my pager go off. It was Lorena. Now this bitch wants to call me back, I said under my breath. I was just going to have to call her back later. I made it to the Peachtree Center station and hoped I was at the right place. I walked upstairs and stayed on the southbound side. I got to the top of the stairs and saw Kevin standing with three good-looking guys. All of them were tall. I approached and all three of the guys were just staring at me. Kevin hugged me and then the first guy, who had a big, messy afro and a goatee said, "What's up, man? I'm Todd Grey. The next guy said, "And I'm Bilal Triggins."

Bilal was brown skinned with deep waves on the top of his hair. It was faded on the side. He was also the shortest of everyone and appeared to be about my height, which is 5'9. Then, the third guy said, "I'm Caleb Brown." I laughed. "What's so funny?" he asked with his beautiful smile. "My bad," I said. "It's just that I never met anyone with the name of the elementary school I went to before." "Well, you went to a good school," Caleb said jokingly. Caleb was fine as the other two. He was not as dark as Star, but almost the same complexion as Chad. He was so handsome with a low haircut and a nice edge up to frame his white teeth. All three guys had their own style and I could feel they were good people. I looked over at Kevin and he said, "You still a pretty muthafucka," and gave me a tight hug again. I looked over at all three of the guys and they just stared and smiled. Then Caleb said, "Come on. We need to head up to the Pere Garden before the line gets too long." We all headed towards an escalator and all four of them walked on. They turned around and looked at me and told me to get on. I hesitated at first then put my feet on and held on tight. This escalator was like none I'd ever seen before. It looked like it was a mile high. They were staring down at me kind of laughing. They made it up first and walked off and I was so glad I was off. They all came up to me and gave me a group hug when I made it safely off the escalator. These guys were not only good looking with a nice style, they were genuinely nice. We walked and talked as we headed to the club. This part of downtown Atlanta kind of reminded me of New York with its high-rise buildings. "So, how old are you?" Todd asked. "I just turned 18," I said. "Damn!" Bilal said. "You're just as young as Kev," Caleb added. "So, how do you all know each other?" I asked. "We all go to Atlanta A&M," Kevin said. You know...the famous all men's college?" I was paying so much attention to Kevin's friends that I forgot how much I missed him and how good he looked. He was a little bit taller than me with light brown skin and a beautiful full face. He had deep dimples and he had on a beige, leather Polo jacket that looked so nice on him. We walked about six blocks from the train station right into a bar called Water Works. We saw a table and headed straight for it. They were playing house music and it sounded really good. We took off our jackets and Caleb asked us what we were all drinking. We all agreed on Long Islands. We sat there for a while and tried to converse as much as we could, but the music was just so loud. We had two rounds and then Todd said he wanted to go next store to the Pere Garden Bar. So we did. The club was right next door to Water Works. As we walked in, we could see that this bar was packed wall-to-wall packed and they were playing R&B. I told the guys that the next round was on me. I was getting good and drunk, not to mention lots of looks as I walked and pushed my way to the bar. The bartender asked me what I was drinking and I asked him to make me four Long Islands. I turned to the left and saw the back of a head that looked so familiar. And in front of the familiar-looking head, was a good-looking, tall guy that put me in the mind of Al B. Sure! I couldn't stop staring because it was irritating me that I could actually recognize that back of someone s head and not know who it was. I looked down at my pager and realized Lorena or Victor was calling me and Hector had finally paged. Then, Rico paged a couple of times. I grabbed two of the drinks and Bilal met me and grabbed two. We took the drinks back and sat and tried to talk to each other. Then, I realized I had to pee. I told the guys I would be right back. I went to the restroom feeling so happy that I had some gay, male friends that were funny, smart, and attractive and didn't act feminine. I waited in line and watched people play pool as I stood there. I looked back at the bar area and saw the face on the back of the head I recognized earlier. It was Chad. He was at the bar and boy did he look good! The guy hugging on him was the Al B. Sure look alike. I started getting a little mad and I couldn't figure out why. I used the restroom and walked back towards the fellas when I saw Chad walking my way. He was staring right at me and looking like he was trying to figure out if it was me. I wanted to walk right past him, so I turned my face and looked towards the fellas. "Hey!" he yelled. "Hey," I said back. "I know you're not going to act like you don't see me," he said with attitude. "I don't," I said with equal amounts of attitude. "What's wrong with you?" he asked. "Nothing," I said. "Nothing at all." He pressed up against me and said, "I miss you!" I didn't say anything. I couldn't believe I was tripping off Chad when Kevin, the only man I've ever wanted, was in Atlanta where I was now living. "You must be drunk," Chad said. "Actually, I am and I left my drinks with my friends, so I'll talk to you later," I said rudely. "Man, what's your problem?" Chad asked in a serious tone. "Nothing!" I said again with more force. I looked behind Chad and I saw the Al B. Sure looking dude walking up behind him. He whispered something in Chad's ear. "I gotta go," I said again. "My friends are waiting." I tried to brush by him, but he didn't move. So, I said, "Excuse me!" Chad let me pass through and I saw his friend give me a look trying to figure out who I was. I walked back towards the front of the club where all the guys were standing. They were all talking to each other but I noticed a lot of guys looking at all four of them. "I see you're back, beautiful," Caleb said. "If the Mexicans look like you in California, then I'm making sure I apply for law school there." "Man, all you guys are good looking," I said. Everyone said thanks and we toasted our drinks. The music was jamming! They were playing this house song I'd heard in a club back in Oakland with Kevin. I think the name of the song was *Lonely People*. "I say we order one more drink and then order some food and head over to Caleb's loft," Bilal said. "Well, I say we order a pizza at the diva's apartment up in the sky like George and Weezie," Caleb said laughing and looking at Bilal. Kevin went to order a round and I walked with him. We both had a little space at the bar and I asked him why he had been so shady with me in the past year. "I wasn't being shady," Kevin said. "Yes you were," I insisted. "You wouldn't return my pages. Then, you changed your pager number. What happened?" "Nothing happened, Gustavo," he said. "You're lying," I said. "No, I'm not!" Kevin said loudly. "I'm your brother's friend. I've always been your brother's friend and I take friendships seriously. I kind of heard a little about what went down with you, your brother and that other dude." "What?" I was confused. "What fucking other dude?" "Angelo? The drag queen?" he questioned. "You mean Angel?" I asked. "She's not a drag queen. She's a woman." Kevin rolled his eyes and said, "See? See there? The whole gay shit." "I don't understand," I said. The drinks came and we took them over to the guys. I wasn't finished talking to Kevin and it couldn't wait. Can I talk to you outside, please? I asked. I looked at the guys and they could see that I was irritated because they weren't laughing or smiling. They just looked. We walked outside and it was just as loud as it was inside the bar. There were people standing everywhere. I just started walking and he followed. We walked to an empty alley and I asked, "What's wrong with you?" Kevin looked me in the eye and said, "You are! You're what's wrong with me!" "What did I do?" I asked. He said, "I fucking kissed you when we were little and you tell all your fucking girlfriends! I don't see you for a couple years and then you come back to Sacramento living in a foster home or group home or whatever the fuck it was and you call my house and ask to talk to me. Everyone knows I'm straight and I'm homies with your brother but no, you keep sweating me. Then, we go to the same high school and I fuck you every free time I get and guess what? Word gets around and guess who's opened their big ass mouth? You!! So, now I got to deal with rumors that my family's heard and they start having second thoughts of me going to Morehouse-an all men's college, when I have a full scholarship because they think I'm a fag!!! He was screaming. "Well, I'm not a fag! I love women too! This is just something I like doing sometimes, and you're telling people you want a family and that you want kids with me and that you're my soul mate. Don't you know word gets around and people talk?! He was still screaming. "Yeah, you know how to fight good and you look masculine, but everyone in Oak Park knows you're a fag!" I knew my jacket was in the Pere Garden bar, but my wallet was in my pocket and I wasn't about to walk back in there. I felt sober. I felt sad. I turned away and started walking. I didn't know where I was going I just walked. I didn't even know if Kevin was still there or if he just walked away. I didn't know and I didn't look back. I walked until I saw the Garnett train station. I put my Marta card into the machine. The train was already there. I made it to my stop and saw the bus that rode by our apartment, but I didn't get on. I just walked. I couldn't believe what had just happened. I started off thinking about who I had told. I'd only told three people my whole life and that was Lupita, Lorena and Angel. I'd never heard rumors of me and him sleeping together. I just didn't understand why he was so mad at me. I mean Kevin was my good thoughts when days were bad. Now, he hates me. He really hates me. I made it to my apartment. It was cold. So, I turned on the heater. It was dark. And there was no Angel and there was no Hector. I unplugged the phone and grabbed the last roach I had and smoked it. I started thinking of how I fucked up with Rico by not calling him back when he paged me. Then I started to think how I wasn't drinking vodka and seltzer water like he had told me. Then, I started thinking about Chad and the beautiful guy he was with. I started thinking about how my mom would put a rag on my forehead when I didn't feel good and how she always told me she loved me. I thought about Tia Loose and how she just disappeared from the face of the Earth. I felt really bad. I was thinking that maybe I should just kill myself and how I would do it and if it would hurt. I couldn't cry. All I could do was just sit there with my back against the wall and think about what a mess my life had been and would it ever be regular. I woke up the next morning with my neck hurting. I guess it was from sleeping on the floor with no blanket or pillow. I stood up and put on Mary's 411 CD and took a shower. I had a light headache but felt a lot better than I had the night before. I knew Rico was the first person I needed to call. He was the only person that mattered because he was my boss. I plugged the phone back in and it was ringing. "Hello?" I answered "Where the fuck you been!?" Hector screamed. "Where the fuck *you* been? I yelled back. "Look fool, I came home last night to see you and you weren't there," he said. "So, I called Rico and he said he dropped you off when you got home from New York." Yeah, I'm home," I said. "I know that, dumb ass!" Hector said. I wasn't feeling it after the night I'd had and said, "Look, what do you want?" "Our grandma died," Hector said flatly. "Abiguide?" I asked. "Yeah. She passed away. I just said Ok. "Do you care?" he asked. "No," I responded. "I really don't give a fuck." "Well, I don't give a fuck either, but I've been talking to Victor and he thinks we should go to the funeral." "In Sacramento?" I asked. "Yeah! Where else would it be, fool?" Then I asked, "Why would we want to go to Sacramento? We just left there." "I know," Hector said. "I told victor the same thing and he knows we don't fuck with our grandma like that, but he still thinks we should go." "Well, how the fuck are we going to get to a funeral in Sac when the bitch is dead?" I asked. When I said that, we started rolling. We were laughing so hard we couldn't stop. We laughed for like five minutes straight. Finally, Hector told me that Victor was buying our tickets. "The wake is Thursday and the funeral's Friday morning." "Well, let me call Rico to see if we can take the time off," I said. "Yeah," Hector said. "Ask him for me too." "Duh," I said and we hung up. I couldn't believe we were going back to Sacramento so soon. I knew one thing though. I was going to have to go shopping for some funeral clothes, which would probably be something black, since I always saw them wearing that shit in the movies.

Chapter 22: The Funeral

I finished packing my new Jordans and some other stuff I'd bought from Nike Town and Phipps Plaza. I also packed the clothes I'd bought to wear for the funeral. I was going to buy Hector some clothes, but he told me he was good. I still had mixed feelings about going to Abiguide's funeral, but I was going to respect Victor's wishes. Hector called and said him and Star would be picking me up around eight because we were taking the red eye flight so we could be there first thing that Thursday morning. I still couldn't believe I was flying two times in one week. I'd thought about New York a lot and missed it. I was starting to think that maybe, Atlanta wasn't for me. I really hadn't talked to anyone the last couple of days. I was still kind of sad until I went shopping and gave my number out to a couple of cute guys. Rico wanted me back on Saturday night because he was thinking about me working at this club called Guys and Dolls during the week. I was supposed to do my first set that Saturday night. I told Hector and hoped he had booked the tickets for me in time for me to make it back. It was 8:00 p.m. and I was ready to go. I heard the car horn blow, so I picked up my bags and walked to the car. Both of my pagers started going off at the same time, so I hurried and put my bags in the trunk of Star's trunk and got in the back seat putting hands in both pockets to grab each pager. "Hi, Star," I said. "Hi, cutie." "Who's paging you?" my brother asked as both of my pagers were blowing up. I looked at one pager and saw that it was Chad. He had been paging and calling since Monday afternoon. I didn't feel like talking to him. Then I looked at my California pager. It was Lupita. I wondered what that loud mouth nasty bitch wanted. "Damn it!!" I yelled. "What's wrong," Hector asked sounding concerned. "Angel is what's wrong!" I said annoyed. I looked at Star and was hoping she didn't say shit being that the last time I'd seen her she was pissed off at Hector because Angel was a man. But not this time. She asked if Angel was Ok. "I'm not sure," I said. "I haven't heard from her since Thursday right before I went to New York. It's been a week and we haven't gone this long without talking in years. Hell, I talk to her as much as I talk to my brother." The last time I'd saw her was when Tre and Naomi had picked her up to hang out. But before she'd left, she said a guy she knew from Los Angeles was sending for her that Friday or Saturday and that she was going to be in California for a couple of days. "Well, maybe she's having a good time," Star said trying to make me feel better. "Yeah," I said. "But I've called her on both pagers at least a thousand times." The car was quiet. Then Star said, "Well, let's all say a prayer to make sure she's Ok. We said the prayer and that made me feel better. But I was trippin' on how Star was so Ok with Angel all of a sudden when just a month ago, she hated gay people, I thought to myself. We made it to the airport and went to daily parking. We got out of the car and took our luggage out. Underneath mine and Hector's all black luggage was two Louis Vuitton bags. Hector grabbed them and his. I grabbed mine and we started walking towards the airport. As we walked, I was just staring at Star. She was just so damn beautiful. She had on black jeans with black boots and a jean jacket. She was the closest thing to perfect. We walked into the airport and I asked her if she was coming with us. "I am," she said. Is that alright with you?" I smiled and said, "Hell yeah!" We checked our luggage and went to get into line. I felt like everyone in the airport was staring, but most of all; it was black men-old and young. I walked behind Star and Hector as they held hands and kissed every chance they could. Black men seemed annoyed but no one said anything and I'm glad they didn't because we would have had to handle shit, I thought. We got on the airport train and made it to our terminal. From there, we got onto the escalator before walking to D26, so we could board our plane. As we walked, I saw a short girl with a strut I could never forget. She wore a puffy coat with high heels and stretch pants and a long, blonde wig. Hector and Star went to grab a bite to eat at McDonald's and I told them I would be right there. I couldn't take my eyes off this girl. So I followed her. She turned around and looked as if she knew she was being followed. I could only see her face a little because her big glasses almost covered it up. I tried to keep up, but she just walked faster until we couldn't go any further. I saw her go up and talk to a gate agent. I looked up at the sign to see where she was going. It read Dominican Republic. Who would I know that would be going to the Dominican Republic, I thought to myself. I must be going crazy. I turned and went into the airport store to buy some candy for the plane ride. I looked up and saw the girl coming my way. I went and grabbed a magazine to see if I could get a closer look. Maybe she's a celebrity. Maybe it's Madonna, I laughed to myself. I slowly turned around and I could see her lot better under the lights of the store counter. I looked closer and it was Naomi! She looked over at me and immediately started walking out of the store. I threw my candy on the counter and ran to catch her. I grabbed her arm and she turned around and pulled it away. "Get away from me!" she said. I looked closer and said, "Naomi?!" "No!" she said. "It is you!" I said. "No! I am not!" she said back in her thick accent. "What's wrong with you?" I asked. "Leave me alone," she said. Just then, I overheard a man on the intercom say, "We are now boarding seats 40 D to 30 D." She turned around and started walking and I jumped in front of her and asked, what's going on? You're acting weird. Where's Angel?" "I don't know where that bitch is," Naomi said in a mean tone. "She fucked Tre and I don't like bitches that fuck my men!" "Angel did not fuck your man," I said defending my sister. "If you don't leave me alone, I'm going to scream!" Naomi said. "Listen, bitch," I threatened. "I know you know where Angel is and I'll scream you're a short fuckin' man if you don't tell me something you little *hotto*!" "You don't want to fuck with me and I do mean that!" Naomi said. "I don't know where that *puta* is, but if I ever see her she'll be sorry!" "No, bitch!" I hissed. "You'll be sorry if you even look at her crazy!" We must have looked like we were fighting because airport security came over and asked if I was bothering her. She just walked off to get on her plane. I stood there watching as she handed the flight attendant her boarding pass. I was full of anger. I was so mad and I didn't know why. All I knew is that I wanted to beat the shit out of her. Then I heard Hector yelling, "Gustavo! Gustavo! They're boarding! He pulled me by my sleeve and we both ran back to our gate to board our plane. We took our seats and all three of us were sitting next to each other. I had the aisle seat. I told them everything that had just happened. They both listened and were as confused as I was. I mean something didn't feel right and I had no idea how to deal with it. I wasn't going to be Ok until I heard from Angel. We took off and I just wanted to be somewhere by myself. I wanted to be in Atlanta in our apartment living room talking, laughing and sharing men stories with Angel. I wasn't in the mood for Sacramento. I even started to think about seeing if I could get off the plane and go right back to Atlanta. I finally fell asleep and didn't wake up again until I heard the pilot announce that we were in Sacramento. The Sacramento airport was much smaller then Atlanta's airport. We got off the plane and walked down to luggage claim when I spotted Lorena and Sonya Nava. When I looked at Lorena, I saw her eyes get really big. I looked behind me and saw Star and Hector still holding hands. I totally forgot about how Lorena was going to feel seeing Star with us. I knew she was going to ask me why I hadn't prepared her, but I didn't know she was coming until we got to the airport. We walked up and could see that Sonya was as beautiful as ever with her pale skin and dark, curly hair. And she was so skinny but had a booty and nice sized boobs. She honestly looked like a movie star. "Hi, guys!" she said. "I'm so glad to see you!" She hugged us and Hector introduced her to Star. "Well, hello Star!" Sonya said cheerfully. "Are you from Sacramento?" "No," Star said politely. "I came from Atlanta with the guys. That's where I was born and raised." "That's great!" Sonya said in her teacher voice. "I didn't know we had a visitor, but I'm sure glad you came." We all looked at Lorena and she was quiet. She looked like she had gotten taller since the last time I saw her, but she was still pretty. She was like a Mexican Amazon. Most Mexican girls were short. But not Lorena. She was our height and maybe an inch taller. I walked up to hug her and whispered in her ear, "Chill out. I'll tell you what's up later." Then Sonya said, "Star, this is my daughter Lorena." Star raised her eyebrows and said, "My gosh! You look so young to have a grown daughter, Sonya." Sonya smiled and said, "Oh, you're much too kind, Star. She's actually my stepdaughter. But I think of her as my own." Star spoke to Lorena and Lorena quickly said hi back to Star. "Ok, Victor's outside in the truck waiting," Sonya said. "We didn't park because we were running a little late, but I think we will all fit. Lorena. You may have to sit on my lap. Sonya started laughing. I looked over at Lorena and she wasn't laughing at all. I loved Lorena. She was truly my friend. I hugged her as we walked out of the airport. I started to tell her about everything that was going on. Sonya walked behind us talking to Star and Hector. We made it outside the airport and it was still kind of dark outside and very cloudy. But I could see Victor as he got out of the truck to greet us wearing a 49ers sweat shirt and cut off sweats. You could see his dick bouncing around inside his shorts. He was in shape, tall and still handsome. He came up and hugged me and then introduced himself to Star before he hugged her and my brother. I grabbed Lorena's hand and said, "Let's get in the truck. During the ride home, Victor was telling us that he and Sonya were going to cook some chorizo and eggs with papas, tortillas and pancakes. Star told us she'd never had chorizo, but it sounded good. Victor also told us we could take a nap because we would be leaving to go to the wake at around 3 p.m. He also told us that he'd taken time off from his construction company to be with us. Victor had money. He told us he was poor growing up; even picking tomatoes in the fields when he was really young. But his dad came from Mexico and taught them at a young age to get an education...and always have a craft. His craft was building houses and he was good at it. He built his house in

Elk Grove in a month, he said. I remember their house in Oak Park was small but nice. This house though was big and beautiful. As we pulled up to the house, Hector told Victor that he and Star were going to check in at the Holiday Inn on J Street next to Old Sacramento after the wake. "Nonsense," Victor said. "You can stay here," But Hector insisted on getting a room. I started thinking about getting a room myself, but I knew it would hurt Sonya and Victor's feelings. We ate breakfast and Star, Victor and Sonya acted like they were best friends. They were so impressed with everything she knew about religion and even about the real estate market. They talked, ate and drank more coffee. Hector just sat there looking so proud to be with her. I asked Lorena if we could go to her bedroom because I wanted to tell her everything that had gone on since the moment we landed in Atlanta. Plus, I knew she couldn't take much more of Star. We took our coffee upstairs and I told her everything, from Chad to Rico to Naomi and all about New York. She sat there and couldn't believe all that had happened with me and Hector in the last two months. She was curious about New York since I told her how all the Latino men were there. She thinks black men are cute, but she loves her a *cholo*. She loves hardcore Mexican thugs. That's why she loves my brother. He's tough, but he doesn't sell dope or steal. But anyone who knows him understands that he will whip some ass in a minute. I talked and she asked questions. Then, there was a knock at the door and Sonya told us to start getting ready because we would be heading to the wake soon. I was having so much fun with Lorena I almost forgot about having to go to a wake and funeral. I was so full from eating and drinking coffee that I had to take a shit. I went into Lorena's bathroom when I heard the phone ring. I heard Lorena screaming and telling someone I was in Sacramento. Lorena busted into the restroom as I was finishing wiping my ass and just handed me the phone. "I can't grab it. I might have shit on my hands!" I said. Lorena said gross and started laughing. Then, I stood up and Lorena said, "No fucking way!" as she held the phone. I pulled up my pants and asked what she was talking about. "Your dick is as big, if not bigger, than your brother's!" she said screaming and laughing. "You nasty bitch!" I joked.

"Don't be looking at my clit." She laughed so loud. I washed and dried my hands wondering who was on this phone. I grabbed the phone from Lorena and said hello. "I know your big clit ass haven't been in Atlanta for months and have not tried to contact me." I knew exactly who it was. "Hey, Steph!" I said. "Don't 'hey, Steph' me," Stephanie said. "I'm mad at you!" "Why?" I asked. "Because you know I'm here in Atlanta at this all girls' college with no family and no one at my school is from Sac." "No one?" I asked. "No one!" she repeated. "There's girls from the Bay and rich snobs from Southern California, but that's about it. They weren't ready for this thick Sac chic with all this personality down here, *pinche calaweta!*" We both laughed and I promised we would get together when I got back to Atlanta. We hung up the phone and I asked Lorena if she'd told Stephanie I was gay? "Hell no!" she screamed. "I didn't, but rumors get around and you know Stephanie is still good friends with Lupita." I looked at Lorena and told her that Lupita had paged me on the way to the Atlanta airport. "Call that bitch back!" Lorena said. "Should I use my calling card?" I asked. "Because she's going to know you're calling." "No, just call," Lorena said. I dialed Lupita's number and the phone rang. "Hello?" her grandma answered. "May I speak to Lupita?" I asked. I looked over at Lorena and she was listening on her other phone. "Hello?" Lupita answered. "Hey," I said. "Did you page me yesterday?" "G, is this you?" she asked sounding excited." "Yup," I said. "I so miss talking to you!" she said. "Why?" I asked. "What do you mean...why?" she asked trying to act innocent. "You know why, bitch!" I said. "I've been in fucking love with Kevin since we were little! I told you and Lorena all my secrets about me being gay and my first kiss with him and I even told you how we fucked when I turned 14 and we kept fucking and you promised you would never say nothing!" I screamed. I looked over at Lorena and her mouth was wide open. I couldn't stop there. I had to tell this bitch how I felt. "You knew how much I cared about him and I'd told you he's what kept me wanting to live when we were kidnapped. You know everything about me. I never told anyone about all the abortions you had or how you fucking got molested by your tios or how you've had boys over to your house since you were in junior high, if not sooner. But then you turn around and you got pregnant by Kevin! You fucked someone very special in my heart and for that, I will never forgive you bitch!!!!!! You want to run your mouth about Kevin and me? Well tell this-if that really is his baby-I hope you and that bastard baby die bitch! And I mean that!! Then I hung up. Lorena hung up too. "Gustavo, are you Ok?" she asked. "I'm fine!" I said. "You blew that bitch's hair all the way back!" she said. "You fucking told that bitch about herself." Just then, the phone rang. Lorena's eyes got big again as she answered. "Yeah...yeah," she said. "He's right here. Do you want to talk to him?" She asked the person on the phone. "It's Stephanie," Lorena said. "What's up, Steph?" I asked. "Hi again," she said. "What's wrong with you? We just hung up not too long ago and you sounded happy. "I'm cool," I said. "I just had to curse out your nasty bitch friend." "Who?" Stephanie asked. "Lupita," I said. "But I want to change the subject before I take Lorena over there to beat her ass." "She's pregnant," Stephanie said. "Who gives a fuck?!" I said back. Look, Steph...I need to jump in the shower because Sonya's knocking on Lorena's door telling us to get ready for the wake." "Ok, well that's one of the reasons I called back," she said. "I wanted to send my prayers and tell you to be strong but I could wait on the second reason." "Why wait?" I asked. "Well, the only time I hear you this mad is when you're about to fight, so I don't want to piss you off anymore, "Stephanie said. "Tell me...I'm cool," I said. "But make it quick because I have to take a shower and get dressed." "Ok, well you remember my Uncle Earl?" she asked. "Yeah, I remember," I said. "Well, he's in protective custody in San Quentin and his cell is right next to your dad's." I was quiet at first then finally said, "Ok?" "Well, he knows that my uncle knows you and Hector and he's trying to get in touch with you two." "Fuck him." I said. "Ok, I just wanted to let you know," Stephanie said. "Thanks so much, Steph," I said letting her know I wasn't upset with her. "I'll call you as soon as I get back to Atlanta." I hung up the phone and me and Lorena got dressed. Then, we walked outside to Sonya's car while Star and Hector rode with victor. We jumped on the freeway and finally made it to the funeral home on Franklin Boulevard. We parked and saw people coming out. Nobody looked familiar and I was glad. I walked over to Hector and Star. They looked so nice. Star was dressed like a movie star for real. She looked so classy. We all walked in together and saw my grandma lying in the coffin. I stood by the door and watched Hector and Star go look at her body. Lorena stood with me by the door as Victor and Sonya talked to people that were there. I decided to go take a quick look at the bitch. Me and Lorena walked over. She looked peaceful. She actually looked better than I remembered. As I got closer, I noticed she was wearing a necklace with a heart. It looked just like the one my mom had. I used to love opening her gold heart necklace because she had a picture of me and my brother in it when we were in first grade. Lorena put her hand on my back when she saw me getting closer to the casket. I had to know if that was the same necklace my mom used to wear. So, I walked up to her dead body acting like I was going to hug her and Lorena followed me to make sure I was Ok. I put my hands on the necklace and opened up the heart and saw that it held a picture of me and my brother. Lorena whispered in my ear, "What are you doing?" "Block me," I said. And she did. I never moved so quick. I wrapped my hands around her neck and unfastened the necklace and put it in my pocket. I turned around and looked at the people in line waiting to see Abiguide. They were trying to figure out if I was alright. I hugged Lorena and put my face in her chest as she rubbed my back and we walked off. "Suck my titties," she whispered. I started laughing and couldn't stop. We walked out of the funeral fast. As soon as we made it outside we could not stop laughing. I saw Sonya outside talking to a woman and giving me a dirty look. The morning weather had changed from cloudy and cold to a cold and sunny afternoon. Lorena and I stopped laughing. The sun was glaring in my eyes. I looked a little closer to the woman talking to Sonya and I wasn't laughing anymore. It was my Tia Loose and she looked amazing! She wore a grey suit jacket with a matching skirt and a white button up with black pumps. She still had black hair, but it was longer then I remembered it. Her skin was silky and she wasn't as brown as me and Hector anymore. She looked me straight in my eyes and said, "*Mijito*, come here." That was the worst thing she could have ever said. I looked at Lorena and said, "I'm ready to go." I turned my back to her, but it was too late. She knew it was me and her and Sonya were walking towards us. I could see their shadows approaching. I felt her hands or Sonya's touch my shoulder and I freaked out. "Get off me!!" I screamed. "Mijo, what's wrong?" Tia Loose said. "You!" I responded. "This is weird! It's like someone coming back from the dead." I saw Star and Hector walking towards us out the side of my eye and I was glad. "Where's Victor?" he asked. He and Star were still holding hands. "Hector?" Tia Loose said in disbelief. "Hi," Hector said. Then he looked closer and said, "No fucking way." "Yes it's me...your tia." Loose said. "Can I ask you a question?" I asked her. It was so quiet outside all you could hear was the wind and the sound of cars passing the funeral home. "Yes," she said. "Of course you can." I went right in and said, "We haven't heard from you in almost eight or nine years and you call us out the blue and then show up at the wake and just say, 'hi, *mijito?*" "Yes," she said. "I wanted to see my mom and I wanted to talk to you boys so I could explain everything." "Explain what?" I said. "I don't know if right here and right now is the time to talk about it," she responded. "Can we go somewhere to talk? Please?" Then, Victor walked up and saw Loose and said, "I'm glad you could make it!" Sonya said, "Victor, I think Loose wants to talk to the boys in private. Should we go to our house?" Before he answered, I opened my mouth and said, "No...not right now. You have five minutes to tell us where you been." "Why are you being so mean, *mijito*?" Tia Loose said. "Don't call me that! I'm really serious!" I said. "Calm down, Gustavo, please!" Victor said. "No!" I shouted. No, I'm not calming down! I'm 18 years old coming back to Sacramento to see a grandmother that never did shit for us and stayed drunk every time we saw her before we were sent to Mexico to suck dick and eat a fat nasty lady's pussy on a regular basis so what is so fucking important that you feel like you need to pop up from nowhere and call us?" It all came out at once. "And now you want to give us your sob story?" Tia looked at us with tears in her eyes and said, "I'm not proud of not being around, Gustavo! I was 18 myself when I left Sacramento. And I had no idea what or where my life was going. I always thought of you and Hector! I loved you boys. You know I did. But I didn't love myself and I made some bad choices. If you just give me a chance to explain... please! That's all I ask." She was crying hard now. Victor grabbed Loose and said, "Sonya, can you take her in there to see her mother? I'm going to see if I can take the boys over to St. Patrick's Church. I'm sure the priest will let us talk in one of the study rooms." I looked over at Star and she looked confused. Then I looked at Hector and he looked dazed. I just held Lorena's hand and squeezed it tight.

Chapter 23: Loose's Turn

Sonya walked me into the funeral home. I still don't think she remembers that I kicked her younger sister's ass at Millers Park my senior year of high school. She tried to jump in, but my home girl beat her ass. She seems pretty nice now and she might have been nice then. I didn't really know her like that. I just knew her little sister had been calling Chris. If I would have known then what I know now, I'd wish she would have took Chris from me. I walked in and Sonya stood in line with me. I saw some cousins of mine and they told me to come straight up to the casket. I couldn't believe my mom was dead. I started crying and I couldn't stop. She looked beautiful. I still can't believe I hadn't seen her in all these years. I walked up and gave her a kiss as tears dropped on her forehead. I wiped them off. I loved and hated my mom. But I never thought she would die before I could tell her how I felt about my childhood. I guess it doesn't matter now since she's gone. Sonya grabbed my arm and we walked to the door when Victor walked in. "Are you alright?" he asked. I told him I was fine. "Where's the boys?" I asked. "Loose, they're really adamant about speaking to you," he said. "So I talked them into meeting with you for about 20 minutes at the church. I can honestly say that Gustavo has never spoke about his past and what happened to them in Mexico. So he's really emotional seeing you. I would suggest that you get whatever you need to get out fast so he can have the remainder of the day to digest it." I was a little scared because the only time I've talked to anyone about my problems was when I went to see a therapist recently.

I left my rental car at the funeral home and rode with Sonya and Lorena to St. Patrick's Church. We all met in the parking lot. Sonya said she was taking Star with her. I'm assuming she's Hector's girlfriend. We walked into a study room at the church and sat down at a table where they probably have Bible Study. I was a little uncomfortable with Victor and his daughter being there, but that's what Gustavo requested. I wasn't really sure where to begin so I said, "I want to thank you boys for listening to me. I want to start off by saying the last time I saw you two, you were eight or nine year old kids, right?" Hector said, "We were nine." "Ok...nine," I said. "I was your age that last time or maybe a year older and I was dealing with a lot of things in my home life just as you both were. I knew things were bad at your house, but there wasn't much I could do to help you. You know I would fight Thomas in a heartbeat if he touched you boys in front of me and I would try to fight him if he touched your mom as well. I decided to go to Los Angeles to get away. I was looking for something to save me and I thought it was leaving with Chris and starting a new life, with a new career and the man of my dreams, I thought. Shortly after arriving in Los Angeles with Chris, we got an apartment in East L.A. It was trashy but I cleaned it and made the best of it. Chris had a friend named Smiley that told me he had a lot of connections and that I could audition for movies and television shows. And I believed him. Smiley also told me he had connections at Telemundo. Since I could also speak Spanish, I could audition for some novellas. After a month of being there, I was left alone a lot while Chris and Smiley hung out partying it up. One day, he started beating me. He put me in the hospital and I was there for a couple of days. I had no family in L.A. and no friends. I decided to stay quiet and tell the police I was attacked outside my apartment. Shortly after getting out of the hospital, Chris started telling me I was going to need to get a job. And I did. One morning, I woke up and Smiley was there with Chris in the living room and they told me to get dressed like I was going to a club. So I did. I put on a lace dress with high heels and took time to do my makeup. That same day, they took me to a studio in Sherman Oaks, which is a L.A. suburb. It's where they make lots of films, but not the kind most girls grow up to want to be in-at least not the kind of movies that came to my mind when I was dreaming of being famous. I was very scared of Chris because he changed the minute we arrived in Los Angeles. He told me I was going to be making films...adult films. And when I said no, he beat me. He beat me in front of Smiley and the director of the first movie I was in. so from that point on, I made movies...lots of movies. I made them for five years! I didn't see a dime of the first two movies I made. In fact, I didn't see a dime until I met Pete, who's my husband now. I guess I could say he rescued me from Chris. For the last four years, I've been married to a man who has helped me save a lot of the money and get a lot of the royalties I was owed from films I've done. I'm not proud of what I've done with my life. But I can't change the past. I had to stop doing porn five years ago because the CDC was coming down hard on porn stars getting tested for STDs and HIV. So, the company I was working for sent all their adult film stars to have a physical and get checked." I paused and couldn't talk anymore. I couldn't believe I loved these kids so much that I was telling them the truth. It was so hard. I looked over at the boys and they had no expression on their faces. Then I looked at Victor's tall, pretty daughter and she was crying. I stood up and walked to the window for a second to gather my thoughts. Then I walked back to the table and told them that I was diagnosed with HIV. The room was so quiet, you could hear a piece of lint hit the ground. Victor stood up and said, "Well, I was expecting that. He started nervously pacing around the room. "I've spent the last four years in and out the hospital and trying to deal with my illness. But I'm good now. I'm healthy and I'm taking my medication like I'm supposed to. I never stopped thinking about you boys. I love you now as much as I loved you then. It's been hard just dealing with the fact that I was doing adult movies...and to put this disease on top of it made me think I would never want to show my face to any of my family again. But being sick-really sick the last time-I realized I might not be around much longer and I wanted to make peace with you boys because I love you very, very much. I was young and was hurting and made some bad choices in men and in doing porn films. But like I said, I can't take back the past, but I can make sure of my present. Gustavo, I heard you say you were kidnapped and some terrible things happened to you and I'm sorry! I didn't know. I wish I could have protected you, but I'm here now and I can protect, listen and be there for you as long as I'm alive." I looked at Gustavo's beautiful face and his green eyes. They looked so empty. Then I looked over at Hector. He had his head on the table and started to cry louder and louder. I don't remember the last time I've heard a man weep like him. I wondered if he was crying for me or crying because he had some pain he needed to share and make peace with.

Chapter 24: Back in Sac

I decided to rent a room at the Holiday Inn with my brother and Star downtown near Old Sacramento. I just wanted to be alone with my thoughts for a while. I told Lorena, Victor and Sonya that I would stay with them Friday, our last night. I told my Tia Loose I would call her later on. She was staying at a hotel not too far from us. We both checked into our rooms and I hugged my brother real tight before going to my room even though they were on the same floor. His eyes were so puffy and red. I hadn't seen him cry like that since we were in Mexico. I was happy Star came because she was so nurturing with him and very loving. I know he was happy because they were probably going to fuck nonstop. I went to my room and looked out the window of the 14th floor room. I could see all of Old Sacramento. I couldn't stop thinking about my Tia Loose and what she said. I couldn't imagine how she felt having HIV. She hasn't even made her 30th birthday. I laid there for a while and wanted to daydream about a man, but I had no one to daydream about but Rico and I didn't want to fall for him since he was my boss. I couldn't believe Kevin talked to me the way he did. He sounded like he really hated me. I could call or page Chad back, but the way he was looking at that generic Al B. Sure dude looked like more than a fuck to me. I needed to either call someone or go to sleep...or I was going to dwell on not hearing from Angel or what my tia told us about being missing from our lives the last nine years. I kind of wanted to call Lorena. But I knew she'd heard everything we talked about and couldn't be there for Hector like Star was. I want Lorena to move on and find a man that loves her. She's a good person and deserves that. I dozed off. A while later my hotel room phone rang. "Hello?" I answered. *"Mijo,* it's your tia. Did I wake you?" "No, I'm up now...but can you not call me *mijo* or *mijito?"* I asked her. Silence. "Of course I can," Loose said. "Are you and your brother hungry?" I told her I was. "Well, how about your brother?" she asked. "I'm not sure," I said. "I can ask them." "Well," she said. "I'm going to head to your hotel. I should be in the lobby in about 30 minutes." I got dressed and asked Star and my brother if they wanted to go. They said they were going to pass but to bring them a pizza back. I met my tia in the lobby but I was nervous. I mean, when I looked at her, she was still as beautiful as she was when we were growing up. I walked up and gave her a hug. She had on the cutest jeans and a turtleneck and poncho. You could still see her voluptuous shape underneath her poncho. We walked to Round Table Pizza since I suggested going to the one in Old Sacramento. We sat down and ordered our pizza. "What made you move to Atlanta?" she asked. I looked at her and realized that she was being honest and open with me and Hector so I was going to be honest with her. "We moved for lots of reasons," I said. "There's just not one. But if I had to pick the most important one, it would because I wanted to be with my sister and best friend in life besides my brother. "Who is she?" Loose asked. "Angel," I said. "I met her not long after you left to go to Los Angeles." "It's great to have a friend like that," Loose said. "What makes her so special?" "We've been through so much and know so much about each other and she never judges me," I said. "But what I love about her is at the times when things don't look like they could get any better for her or me, she sees happiness. She sees love. She is the most unselfish person with me and with Hector and I truly believe she would give her life for us. I love her so much and she's the only reason I haven't given up-then or now." "She sounds amazing," my tia said. "Where did you meet?" I heard her ask me the question and I felt the truth coming out as I stared at my beautiful aunt. I never talked about Mexico with anyone; not counselors, not my brother, not Victor and not even with Angel. But as much as I tried to pull back, it was going to come out. I had to release this pain and tell her what happened. I knew I could trust her. I could look in her eyes and tell she wanted to know about the last nine years. I took a breath and felt tears running down my face. I looked into my tia's eyes. She grabbed my hands and looked at me and said, "You can tell me. I'm here for you and won't leave you until I leave this Earth." I grabbed a napkin and wiped my face. I took a deep breath because the last thing I wanted to do was freak and pass out. "I'm going to tell you as much as my mind lets me, tia," I said. "When I called her tia, she smiled and said Ok. Then, I told her about how Thomas took us to meet up with Warren and how we passed out in Warren's car. And then we woke up in a room with Angelo, who is now Angel. Then I told her how Tito shitted on my face. "Oh my sweet Jesus," she said. "She paused to make sure I was Ok. "Yes," I said. "I'm going to try to tell you a little more." I took another deep breath and exhaled. After Tito shit on my face I can't remember much other than him hosing us all down and then us all being locked into a big, beautiful bathroom. Tito watched all of us take off our clothes and shower. I remember after we showered, we all went to separate rooms and each room had beautiful beds. We fussed and argued not to be separated, but I think we were all equally terrified of Tito. I woke up the next morning thinking it was a dream until Rosalinda came knocking on the door of the room I was in. She came in so happy and excited telling me today was going to be a great day and we were all having breakfast downstairs. I followed her to the kitchen, which was downstairs of this big house. I walked into the kitchen while Rosalinda was holding my hand. She walked me to the table where Hector and Angelo were sitting. I stared at Angelo and he smiled. And I felt safe because of the first smile Angelo gave me. Then, I looked over at my brother and he looked at me and started crying. I stood up to go over and hug him and felt a sharp pain on my back. I screamed and fell to the floor and looked up and it was Tito again. That's when I realized it wasn't a dream. It was real life. Tito sat me in my chair and

Hector stopped crying and asked me if I was Ok. Hector was shaking as he asked me, but Angelo was calm. He told me it was going to be alright. Rosalinda heard Angelo and said, "Listen to him. He's a smart boy." We all ate our breakfast. That day and several days after were routine. We ate breakfast, lunch and dinner and we would clean outside and do yard work. The house was surrounded by a jungle. Everything, except for the shed we were in, was green. For days, it seemed like we did the same thing over and over. We would try not to do something at one time or another and Tito would be there with that belt beating us. We did most of what we were asked to do. Then one day, we were ordered to take showers together. Normally, we took them by ourselves. We dried off and I was told to put on a dress. I didn't want to, but I knew Tito's face and today he looked extra mad. He walked me to the basement of the house. It was my first time being there. When I walked in, there were two men naked, smoking and drinking something. I wasn't sure what they were drinking but the closer they got to my face, I could smell it and it smelled like Thomas when he would get drunk. They both were white. The kind of white people I had only seen on TV at the time. I know now they had British accents. But then I just knew it was strange talking. I turned around and ran back to Tito as he stood by the door. But as soon as I did, he hit me with the belt and I screamed. I didn't know what to do, so I stood and both men took me over to a bed that was in the cold basement and made me lift up my dress. They both took turns with me...each one penetrating me over and over. "Was that the only time?" she asked as she was trying not to cry. "No," I admitted. "It happened a lot...sometimes with the same guys and sometimes with new men. Some white; some I don't know what they were. I just did what they said and tried to deal with it." We were both quiet and I realized that hearing myself tell her about things that happened to us in Mexico made me so very mad. "What about your brother and Angelo?" she asked. "Did the same thing happen to them?" "There were a couple of times when me and Angelo were in the same room with each other when it happened, but it was mainly me and Hector. I heard that bitch Rosalinda say, 'it cost big money for my sons to do that kind of fun.' She called it fun always asking, '*mijito* did you have fun, *mijo*?' or she'd say, 'time to have fun, *Mijito*. Come in my room for some fun." "Is that why you hated when I called you *mijo*?"my tia asked. "Maybe," I said. "I never knew if it was that or because you and my mom said it. I don't really know. I just know I hate it. And sometimes I hate it more depending on who says it." We sat quietly. The pizza was on the table and I don't remember anyone even bringing it to us. "How long did you live there?" she asked. I told her it was a year. "Did that stuff happen to you the whole time?" she asked. "Yes," I admitted. "Once it started, it didn't stop until they found us." "Who found you?" "The police... lots of police." "I'm so glad the police came," she said while wiping her tears. "I was too. I couldn't believe it at first. I just remember a new man that smelled so bad, had me on my stomach and was about to penetrate me when I heard men speaking in Spanish and in English. I just lay there even when they told me to put my hands up. Then, one of the officers put a gun to my head and pulled me up and started crying. I couldn't understand him because he was speaking in Spanish. But he got on his knees and hugged me. After that, I don't even remember leaving the house. I just remember a ride in back of a truck with several policemen following us until we made it into the city. We told our stories together and separately to the police that were there." "Were they nice to you?" Tia Loose asked." "Yes," I said. "They were very, very nice. We were all scared, but they were patient with all of us." "How long did you stay there?" "Maybe a week...maybe a couple days. I can't really remember. I just remember them letting us all stay in one room with three beds. And they had nurses checking on us constantly." "Can you speak Spanish?" Loose asked. "No," I said. "Not really. Mom tried to teach us but Thomas said we didn't need to learn it. He just wanted us to speak English." "I remember," she said. "So, how did you understand Tito and Rosalinda?" I told her that Rosalinda spoke English and Spanish and when we didn't understand, Angelo would translate. Now that Angelo is Angel, she still translates," I laughed. "What did your mom do when you went back to Sacramento?" Loose asked. "Nothing," I said. "We didn't see her for some years. We only saw Thomas at his trial and that's only when we testified." "Where were you guys living?" Loose asked as she cried. I told her we lived in foster homes, group homes and on and off with Victor. "Did they find your dad guilty?" "He ended up taking a plea. They gave him 20 years for snitching on everyone." "What about Warren?" she asked. "He was sentenced to 50 years." I said. "What about Rosalinda and Tito?" "The police shot them both the day they were rescued," I said. "Good! Those sick bastards!" Loose said. She was shaking mad. "Yeah, the funny thing was that they had been watching Rosalinda because she was growing lots of weed and other drugs at her house," I said. "They had no idea she was selling us kids for sex." We talked and talked so long that the Round Table people told us they were closing and we would have to leave. We boxed the pizza and my tia came to my room. I went and knocked on Hector's door and we spent the rest of the night talking and eating cold pizza. The next morning, I woke up and my tia was in the bed with me. So I woke her up and said, "Tia you have to get dressed because we need to be getting ready for the funeral." She opened her eyes and said, "You're right." Then she covered her mouth and hugged me so tight and said, "I love you so much! Always, always know that! Loose said. "Sorry I covered my mouth, but my breath stinks." We both laughed and she went to her room to get ready. I was dressed and ready to go. I still hadn't gotten a page from Angel. I was starting to think she was locked up and didn't have her pager. Hector knocked on my door and said it was time to go. I grabbed my jacket and we caught the elevator down to the first floor. We got off and walked into the gift shop to get Star. She was buying gum and I knew her mother named her right because she looked just like something straight out of Hollywood. She had her hair up under her hat and wore a black dress and a blazer on looking as beautiful as ever. We walked outside to meet Victor, who picked us up and said Lorena and Sonya were going to meet us at the church. We went to the funeral and there were many people we knew. There were family and friends, but my mother wasn't there. We left the church to go to the burial ground and still no mother. The funeral was over and they were having a potluck at the church. I asked if it would be Ok for Hector and me to drive with my tia and Victor said it was more than Ok. He seemed so happy that my tia and me were talking. We all got in my tia's car and headed towards the church, but I asked if she wouldn't mind driving me somewhere. She said sure and we headed to Oak Park. "Where we going?" Hector asked. We made it to Oak Park and drove around the big park and then up and down 33rd Street. I asked if we could stop at Oak Park Market so I could get some gum. "I have gum," Star said. "Thanks," I said. "But they have a gum I really like." "You're acting weird!" Hector said from the back seat. "I am weird," I said and we all laughed. I jumped out the car and ran inside the store. When I came back out I asked her to make just one more stop and we could head back to the church. We rode down 12th Avenue until we hit Martin Luther King Drive and made a right. We pulled into a liquor store and stopped. I couldn't believe it. God must have been working some miracles because my mom was standing in front of the store with some other crack heads. She had short hair and was wearing dirty, grey sweats with sunglasses. She was just standing there looking straight ahead. "Why are you playing games," Hector asked. I knew by the tone of his voice that he'd recognized are mom. We sat there quietly. Then my tia asked, "Are you going to buy something here?" I looked over at my tia and asked, "Do you want to see your sister?" "Yes! Hell yeah!" she screamed. "Well, there she is!" I said.

Chapter 25: Beloved Sister

I heard what Gustavo said, but it didn't compute until I looked and took my sunglasses off. I couldn't believe that that was my sister. I opened my door and ran over to her screaming, "Belinda! Belinda!!!" I got right in her face and put my hands on her shoulders. "It's me! Your sister Loose!" I repeated myself over and over. "It's me! Look...Loose!" as I pulled my hair back tight so she could see my face. Still nothing. I told her my name over and over and she just walked away. My sister smelled so bad and her face had wrinkles all over. She had aged so much. I followed her and screamed, "Belinda!! It's me! Loose!" she kept walking and I walked right behind her. Then I heard Gustavo say, "Stop! Stop!" But I kept walking. The faster I walked, the faster my sister walked away. I felt someone grab my arm and it was Gustavo telling me to stop. "What's wrong with her?" I asked. "She's a crack head," Gustavo said. "You told me that," I said. "But why doesn't she talk?" "Look, Loose," he said. "She's been like that for years now. I don't think she can talk. She doesn't even know who we are. She just walks and does drugs and sometimes she stands out in the middle of the street. But people are used to it. "She's gone, Loose...a tweeker," he said. "I couldn't take it anymore. I fell to my knees and cried. I couldn't take everything I'd heard and seen since I'd been back in Sacramento. I lay on the ground and just cried. I looked up when I heard Star saying, "It's Ok, sweetie it will be alright. You're going to mess up your dress." Gustavo, Hector and Star all helped me to my feet and were holding me up. They walked me to the car, put me in the back seat and let me cry. I couldn't stop. I couldn't believe I went to Los Angeles and fucked up not only my own life, I also but let my sister and her sons' lives fall apart. I cried and cried. "I'm going to buy her a ginger ale," Star said as she rubbed my back. "I'll get it," Hector said. He brought back the ginger ale and Star handed to me. I took a sip and told them I was sorry for crying. I tried to collect myself and said, "I need a drink!" Then Star said, "You took the words right out of my mouth! Lead the way!" I sat in the back with my head on Hector's shoulders. It just amazed me how normal and intelligent my nephews were. "Where to?" Gustavo asked. I'd seen this nice Mexican restaurant named Ernesto's not too far from our hotel room, I said. So, we found Ernesto's and decided to sit outside next to the outside heaters they had on the patio. When the waitress came, I ordered margaritas. But she asked everyone for ID. Star pulled out a $100 bill and put it in the waitress hands. She just said, "I'll be right back with your margaritas. I opened my purse to give her $100 back. She didn't want to take it, but I made her. "Look," I said. "I have HIV, but I'm not broke." Everyone at the table got quiet and looked at Star. "What's wrong?" I asked. "Oh, you didn't tell Star. I'm sorry. I thought Hector had already told you. Finally, the waitress came back with the margaritas and Gustavo said, "Please bring us four shots of your best tequila." I looked at Star and I sensed sadness in her face and her spirit. "Star," I said as I reached out and touched her hand. "I'm HIV Positive, but I'm not contagious." "I know you're not," Star said in a whispered voice. "So, what's wrong, *mijita*?" I asked. I looked over at Hector and Gustavo. They were looking at me as if they were waiting to see what I was going to say. "Star, you're not HIV Positive...are you?" I asked. "No," she said. "My mom was. She was infected by a gay man who was having sex with women and men." "I'm so sorry to hear that," I said. "Is she alive?" "No," Star said. She passed." "And how are you dealing with it?" I asked. "Are you having any type of counseling?" "No, I'm just trying to move on." she said. "Well, I was infected from having unprotected sex in adult movies. I wasn't being smart in trusting that the film industry had my best interest. But I take responsibility and it's hard...very hard. I have had days where I was so sick I was ready to die. But now, I take my meds. I still have bad days, but every good day like this makes me want to keep fighting. I know we just met, but I see something special in you and I want you to always know you can talk to me. I'm here for all three of you." We drank more and talked more. Star asked me a lot of questions about my HIV status. I knew she didn't know exactly how or why the disease took her mom. "Listen," I said, I want all of you to always use protection until you know 100 percent that your partner is being honest with you." "What if he's gay and you don't know it?" Star asked. "That's a good question, Star, I said. "I think you should start off with asking the person to tell you if they have desires for men and feel them out." "Are you gay?" Star asked Hector. "Hell nah I'm not gay!" he said with an attitude. "You should know that!" "I'm gay," I said. "And you know I'm gay. Does that make me a bad person?" Gustavo asked Star. "You seem like a good guy and I don't want to judge your lifestyle, but at the same time, I was taught in church that homosexual acts are sinful," Star said. "Well, I'm not a sin," Gustavo said. "I've been gay ever since I could remember being alive and I don't try to hurt anybody. I just want love and a family like everyone else." "So, you are gay, sweetie?" I asked my nephew. Everyone started laughing and couldn't stop. "What's so funny?" I asked. "Why did you call me sweetie?" Gustavo asked. "Well, I'm not calling you what I called you growing up. You said you hated it." "Hated what?" Hector asked. *Mijo* or *Mijito,"* I said. "Why don't you like that?" Hector asked. "Long story and I'm feeling too good and buzzed to talk about it," Gustavo said. We all took a sip of our drinks and I looked over at Gustavo and said, "I always knew you were going to be gay," I said. "Who didn't?" Hector said. "When I was about 11, and you both were around three, I was watching you at my mother's house," I said. "Gustavo, you always played with my dolls and treated them so gentle. You would play with them for hours and I was glad because Hector wore my ass out jumping off the couch, table and whatever he could climb on or up. So, it's no surprise to me and I love you and know you were born that way. But just because you were born that way doesn't mean you can't contract the HIV virus. I love you and want to see all three of you live a long, beautiful life." I started to tear up until I looked over at Star and she was barfing everywhere. I jumped up and we both went to the ladies restroom. Star continued to throw up and she didn't let up. She was finally finished 10 minutes later. I looked over her and said, "So much for the condoms. Girl, you're pregnant" "No, I can't be," Star said. "For some reason," I said. "I think you are. I've been pregnant enough to know the signs." I thought you didn't have kids?" Star asked. "I don't," I said. I started thinking about the child Chris made me give it up because he said he didn't know if it was his or one of the porn stars' baby. I didn't tell the boys that part and I won't until I find my son and make peace with him before I die, I thought.

Chapter 26: Cruel World

It's been almost four months and still no sign of Angel. I decided that I'm going to work really hard and make lots of money so I can hire a private investigator to try and find her. I've gone to the Atlanta Police Department and they said if I'm not a blood related relative, then I won't be able to file a missing person claim being that I don't have any information except we were best friends. I couldn't believe I didn't even know her social security number or anything. I mean, how could we be friends and I not write the shit down somewhere, I thought. I was going to have to visit Jaime's faggot ass in jail to see if he could give me any information. I also talked to Tre, Naomi's freak. He'd come over in January saying that Naomi and Angel were going to get their pussies done in Mexico. But I knew that had to be a lie because Angel would never go and do something like that without telling me, I thought. I couldn't get her off my mind. I had a very bad feeling about the whole thing. I looked around for Angel's freak D, but hadn't heard anything from him. And Hector and me moved. I might never run into him again. I started thinking about all the money I'd made between going back and forth to Stella's in New York and also doing private parties up in the Big Apple. I couldn't believe how much I liked the men there. It was unbelievable. Johnny Rodriguez and me get along so good when I'm in New York. He says he loves me, but I know he fucks those rich white men for money because they like his pretty ass. We have the best sex ever! He fucks me every chance we get in his little studio apartment in the Bronx. It's so different in New York when I'm with him. We both do the same thing, except I dance and occasionally let guys fuck me if the money's right-and I do mean right. I'm not letting no trick fuck for less than a $1,000. But most of the rich men that come into Stella's are bottoms that want to be fucked their damn selves. I never thought I would do a party with someone I was dating. But Mr. Johnny Rodriguez knows how to get me to relax. He tells me we're just there for a fantasy and to get that money. Johnny is perfect. He has beautiful brown lips with perfect eyes and eyelashes and a big, uncut dick like mine. He licks every part of my body when we have sex. I'm not sure if I love him yet. I thought I had my mind trained. I was only going to love one man and that was Kevin. But fuck him! Still, I sure do like his homeboys. And they all seem to like me. It's nice having a group of attractive, smart, gay friends like Caleb, Todd and Bilal. They were all at the club the night I decided to dance at Pere Garden. Chad was there too as I was getting naked on the stage and pouring honey all over my body. Rico was proud of me that night because I brought in a lot of money. All I remember is seeing the guys and Chad all in the club with their tongues dangling out of their mouths as I poured the sweet honey and let anyone who was giving me $20 bills lick my body. That same night, I decided to stay a while and chill with the guys after dancing. They asked me so many questions about how and why I danced and. Caleb asked me if I could get him a job. That night, we sat and talked and Chad watched us have fun out the corner of his eyes. He was with that Al B.Sure wanna be and a group of guys I'd never seen. But they were all handsome-every last one of them. A couple of them had tipped me earlier that night and I think that made him mad. He tried to act like it didn't. I don't think Al B. Sure was there when I was stripping earlier, but word gets around when you're the only Mexican stripping at all black clubs. Caleb, Todd, Bilal and I decided to finish our drinks and either go to Waffle House or to eat at the first breakfast place we saw open. We all grabbed our coats and headed for the door. January in Atlanta is cold, but not as cold as New York. But cold is still cold. We walked across the pay parking lot to ride with Caleb when I heard somebody say, "That wetback bitch think she's all that! That nasty slut probably has AIDS. We all heard the voice say it but everyone kept walking. I stopped. It was the Al B. Sure wanna be with a group of guys. "Yeah, bitch! You betta keep walking, Miss Honeyyyy before I tap that ass back to Mexico or wherever the fuck you from," he said. "Come on, dude." Caleb said. "He ain't worth it." "No," Todd said. "That bitch talking to the right ones. This Philly over here, bitches! I could tell Todd was drunk, so I told Bilal and Caleb to take him to the car. I kept walking with the fellas and looking back every second. We all got in Caleb's Lexus. I couldn't believe college students drove cars like this, I thought. Everyone buckled up but me. We pulled off and it was a one-way, so I knew we had to pass the guys that were talking shit. I looked over at the Pere Garden and noticed Chad and his boys coming out the club. They were headed towards the parking lot. We pulled up to the stoplight and it turned green as we were pulling up. I screamed for Caleb to stop. I jumped out of that car and started punching the fuck out of Al B. Sure. I don't even think he hit me back. I knocked that fool on the ground and then started beating his friend's ass. I looked up and there was a crowd around. Chad grabbed me and said, "Calm down! Gustavo, calm down!" I heard Bilal scream, "Get in the car!" But when I looked over at the car, it was empty but looked like it was still running. There were people everywhere. Chad picked me up and walked me away from the crowd. "You Ok, baby?" he asked. "I'm fine," I said. I looked down at my shirt. There was blood all over it, but it wasn't mine. It belonged to one of those punk bitch fags I had just fucked up. Chad started his car and we drove off. I saw the fellas looking like they were wondering who I was leaving with, but we had to get out of there before the police came. "What the fuck just happened?" Chad asked. "That bitch ass fool was talking shit," I said. "So you kicked his ass?" Chad asked. "He's lucky I didn't kill his ass the way he was talking shit." I said. "Why was he even trippin' with me anyways?" "I don't know," Chad answered. "Yes, you do!" I screamed. "He don't even know me!" Then Chad came clean and said, "Alright. I told him I really liked you." The car got quiet. I was surprised at what had just come out of his mouth, being that I hadn't even answered his calls from the night I seen him and that punk bitch together at the Pere Garden. "So, you're not going to say anything?" he asked. "What should I say, Chad?" "I can't get you off my mind," he responded. I think of you all the time and I've never thought day and night about a dude before." "Do you love me?" I asked. "I didn't say all that now, shawty," he said. We drove to his apartment and walked inside. He turned on the music and a Lisa Fisher song was playing. I loved that song. He took off my shirt and then my pants and we headed to the bathroom. Chad took off his clothes and we jumped in the shower. He washed my body and then I got on my knees and tried to put as much of his dick in my mouth as I could. I stroked with one hand and put my tongue in the crack of penis and licked and licked. He pulled me up after I sucked him for a while and carried me to the bed. He laid me down and spread both of my legs open. Then, he lubed his dick and put it in me. I looked down and knew he was not wearing protection. "We need a condom," I said. "I'm good, baby!" he moaned. "I never have unprotected sex. But tonight, I need to feel you. I want to feel you, baby. I promise I'll take it out before I cum." The only person I'd had unprotected sex with was Kevin…and some of those bastards that raped me in Mexico. I tried to stop thinking negative thoughts about the past and enjoy the moment. Suddenly, Chad had my legs in the air and was sucking my toes while he fucked the shit out of me. He was all in me and I screamed and I screamed. It felt so good. Then he told me that he was going to cum. So, I jacked my dick and he pulled out and we both squirted at the same time. I lay back and he got on top of me still rock hard and we kissed and kissed and kissed. I could taste the sweat from his face and I loved it. I've been living with Chad ever since. I moved in that next day after he asked me to. I've been here for about three months. He knows that I'm going to continue to strip. But what he doesn't know is that I fuck Rico from time to time and Johnny Rodriguez every time I'm in New York. Even though I'm gone a lot, I love cooking and making love with Chad. Hector asked me about moving in with Star since she's about to have his baby. But I told him that I would keep the apartment. I could afford it, but I left that raggedy shit as soon as Chad asked me to move in. Hector finally told Star that he was working for Midnight Express and the Koranett Club when he wasn't doing private parties for Rico. He said he liked the Koranett Club because it was just women and men weren't really allowed to come on the men's side even though they sneak over from time to time. He said he would tell the bouncers to get them out of there. I've been talking to my Tia Loose almost every day even though a week has passed and I haven't heard from her. She did know that I was going to New York during the week, but I told Rico I had to be back for this Freaknik everyone keeps talking about in Atlanta. Chad said it's where the black colleges do their Spring Break. Instead of the beach, they come to Atlanta. I'm going to be dancing at Waterworks and Pere Garden with a few other dancers this weekend. I make more money at the hole in the wall clubs then I do at the main gay club where Midnight Express dances at. I loved that club, but there's so many fine ass guys there that seem to like all of the straight dancers in Midnight Express. I have to admit, I'm excited about my niece or nephew being born. I worked out then took a shower and made dinner for Chad. I was going to take my driver's license test in a couple weeks, so I studied and finished cooking at the same time. I also cleaned up the spare room because some of his fraternity brothers, who are also gay, will be in Atlanta kicking it this weekend and are staying with us. As I finished cleaning, I heard the doorbell ring. I went to the peephole and saw a cute, chubby faced girl standing at the door. I opened up the door wearing just my boxers and nothing else thinking she was probably lost or something. "Can I help you?" I asked in my Mr. Rogers voice. "Oh, I'm sorry," she said. "I must have the wrong apartment." "You're pregnant," I said. "How many months?" "I'm due this month," she said. "Congrats, my brother's girlfriend is pregnant too," I said. I looked at the woman and I could tell she had been crying, so I asked if she was Ok. "I'm fine," she said. "I'm just having a bad day." "Who are you looking for?" I asked. "I'm not sure.," she said. "You're not sure?" I asked confused. "Well, I was at my boyfriend's mom's house and she was showing me baby pictures of him when he was little and I saw a piece of mail in the shoebox where the pictures were with an address that I never knew he lived at before. But the date was December 5, 1992. I thought it was strange." "Well, what's the apartment number?" I asked. "Maybe I can help you find it. Let me put some pants on real quick and I will help you." I ran in the room and put on some sweats and my shower shoes and headed outside. "So, what's the apartment number?" I asked again. She told me the number and then I said, "Well, that's this apartment." It still didn't click until I looked at the mail she handed me. It read Chad E. Sparrow. I looked up and my face must have said it all. She walked past me and into the house. Ii didn't grab her because she was good and pregnant. Once inside, she looked around and saw pictures of Chad and his family on his wall. "Why would he have an apartment and not tell me?" she asked. "I'm not sure," I said. I couldn't think straight and I couldn't believe Chad had a girlfriend. "Well, maybe it's the wrong Chad." I said. "No...no that's him on the wall!" she screamed. "We've been together since college! I know who my fiancé is!" Now, who are you?" I didn't know what to say. So I said, "I'll tell him you came by," I said. "What do you mean you'll tell him I came by?!" she yelled. "I'm not leaving!" This was going bad fast but I said, "I think it would be best if you do leave. I'm not trying to be rude, but I don't know you and you're in our place." She looked me up and down and said, "Are you gay?" she asked. "I'm not going to answer that," I said. "You already did," she said as she cried and walked to the door. Her cries grew louder and louder. Then she turned around and said, "I'm not going nowhere!!" as she sat on the step outside. I closed the door and paged Chad 911. "Why the fuck didn't you tell me you had a girlfriend!" I said as soon as the phone rang. "What?!" he asked. "You got some bitch over here saying you're her fiancé." "What? Ahhhh shit!" he screamed. "She's outside and won't leave," I said. "Fuck!! Fuck!! Fuck!!" Chad screamed. "What did you tell her?" "What the fuck are you asking me?" I asked right back. "Did you tell her anything about you and me?" he asked. "I didn't tell her shit because there is no you and me!" I screamed. "But if you think the tears coming down her face say we're fucking, then you're probably right!" "Don't do this to me right now!" Chad pleaded. "I need you! Please don't do this! Chad said hysterically. I listened for a minute then cut him off and said, "Look, what are you going to do?" "I don't know," Chad replied. "I'll give you a suggestion," I said. "Tell her the truth, Chad because she already knows." That night was a mess. She and Chad argued out in the parking lot for about an hour. I sat there watching TV and kind of feeling bad for him. But shit, he made his bed, so he would have to lay in it, I thought. I looked out the window and saw that she'd left and he was walking back up to the apartment. He walked in and his eyes were so swollen that it was obvious that he had been crying. He went straight into the bathroom. I knocked on the door and asked him if I could make him a drink? He said nothing. I tried to open the door but couldn't. I knocked and screamed, "If you don't answer this door, I'm breaking it down!" He unlocked the door and opened it. Then, he just stood there staring in my eyes. I could feel his pain. It felt like it was my pain too. We kissed and kissed and I held his hand and walked him over to the bed. I lit a blunt that I was saving to smoke right before I went to dance that night, but I knew he needed the blunt and me. We both smoked away and then I laid him down as I sucked his dick. I could smell the sweat from his balls from working all day, but it didn't bother me. I actually loved it and wanted to make him cum. I did and then we both fell asleep.

Chapter 27: Mama's Babies

I couldn't believe I was going to have a baby. I was excited, sad, scared and happy all at the same time. I was going to have an abortion at first but Hector told me not to because he wanted me to have his baby. The thing is I don't know if it's his baby. Me and him always used condoms. Rich and I did not. I couldn't believe I was in a situation like this. I changed my home number and my pager number and hadn't been stripping since I realized I was pregnant. I'd been talking on the phone a lot to Hector's Aunt Loose. She's a very wise woman. I had also been talking a lot to Nichelle. She's a great friend and I've told her everything. I even told her I wasn't sure whose baby it is. She just listens and gives me great advice. She said that if it's Rich's baby, then I'm set for life because my child support check will be pretty large. She also said that even though I like Hector, I would probably get tired of him eventually. I asked her why she thought that and she said good dick gets old when there's no money coming in. I decided to talk Hector into going to school to learn a trade. I suggested barber school since he knows how to cut hair well. He starts Atlanta Area Tech in the fall, but is going to continue to strip as much as he can to save for the baby. I'm in love for the first time and it feels good. Who would have ever thought I would have fallen in love with a Mexican guy that's a year younger than me. His ass is smart, funny and I know I'm safe with him. He's no punk by any means. He will fuck someone up for disrespecting me in a minute. I love that about him. I can't believe my stomach's getting big and I'm only five month! I haven't told any of my family, but word gets around quick and I'm sure someone figured it out. I miss my cousin Chad a lot. This time last year, I was hanging out with him and his fraternity brothers at Freaknik.

I was really depressed and he came over and scooped me up and told me I was going to have some fun. Well, I had lots of fun. Guys were trying to get my attention and talk to me everywhere I went. I was so glad I was with my cousin and his boys or I would have been like meat to a dog, I laughed to myself. I was too sleepy to cook dinner, so I decided to order pizza. But I wanted it nice and hot so when Hector woke up and got ready for work he could eat. I usually dropped him off at the club around 10 p.m. But tonight we were going to have to leave early. It's Friday and Freaknik. Those are two things that cause gridlock. I grabbed the yellow pages to get Pizza Hut's number when I heard a knock at the door. Bam! Bam! Bam! I walked over and grabbed my bathrobe. I could hear Hector asking who was at the door. I peeked out the window and saw Akilah's car. I looked again. She was standing at the door. I opened the door and she was crying. "Come in, girl!" I said. "What's wrong?" Through her sobs I could hear her say, "I just left an apartment that Chad's been staying at and I didn't even know about it!" She cried and cried so I walked her over to the couch. I could hear Hector opening the bedroom door. I screamed, "We have company! Put on some clothes, please!" "I'm decent," he said as he walked into the living room. That's when Akilah started screaming. "What the hell, Star?!" she yelled. "Is this some kind of game you're playing with your cousin?!" "I don't understand, Akilah! Girl, what's wrong with you?" I asked very concerned. "Him!" she said pointing at Hector. "Him! Who is that?!"she screamed. I looked over at Hector and he looked just as confused as I was. Please calm down, Akilah." "I can't calm down!" she screamed. She took a breath then said, "I went to look for an address that Chad had on a bill to see why the mail was being sent there. When I arrived, he was over there!" She was pointing Hector. "When was this? I asked. "About an hour ago," Akilah replied. "No, Akilah," I said calmly. "Hector was here." "I'm not crazy, Star," she said. I just saw his ass at my fiancé's apartment-an apartment that I didn't even know he had. When he opened the door, he had on boxers with no shirt and hazel or blue eyes!" I looked over at Hector and said, "Can I please talk to you in the other room?" We walked into the master bedroom and I asked, "What the fuck is going on?" "I don't know," Hector said. "Is she telling me Gustavo's living with Chad?" I asked. "Look," he said. "You need to call your cousin and ask him." "So what...you can't tell me?" I asked. "Star," he said annoyed. "I'm a grown ass man and I don't get into shit like this with family. If it's not concerning or hurting you, then I don't have a problem with it. I grabbed my phone and paged Chad 911. I waited for the phone to ring, but he never called. I was so upset to see Akilah in so much pain. I went back to the living room and tried to comfort her but she was so upset that I thought we should call her family or maybe I should take her to the hospital. An hour went by before she calmed down and said she had spoken with Chad. She said she waited outside until he came home from work. Akilah told me that Chad told her he was always attracted to men and that he'd tried to fight it but couldn't. He said that he loved her and that was never a lie, but he couldn't live a lie about his sexuality and who he was going to choose to love anymore. I listened as she talked and couldn't believe I was having this conversation with the same woman that just years before would take me to the hair salon, shopping and always be so kind to me. My heart hurt for her because I felt helpless and could not give back the same generosity that she had always given me. Akilah stayed for a couple more hours until one of her sisters came and picked her up. We had the news on and there was no way I was going to be able to take Hector to the club with all the Freaknik traffic. The news said that there were two hundred and fifty thousand people in town. We ordered our pizza and decided to stay in and eat and fuck like we usually do. After we had sex, I looked over at him and realized how much I cared about him. I thought about calling Gustavo, but I thought I should wait and talk to him in person. The weekend passed and I was having my first ultrasound. I was excited. We woke up early that morning and I cooked us a quick breakfast. I was ashamed to say I had only been to the doctor's office once and that's when they told me I was pregnant. The doctor told me they also needed to run some blood tests on me and I let them but was scared for the results. My mom died from AIDS and then I met Hector's beautiful Aunt Loose. She's sick and it made me a little nervous about my blood work results. I've learned that AIDS has no pity on anyone. I drove to my doctor's office, which was also my pediatrician. Dr. Brown also reached out to me when my mother passed. She's a very kind doctor. We waited until I was called in and Hector walked in with me. I undressed, put on a robe and we sat and talked about whether the baby was a girl or boy. Dr. Brown came in and we did the ultrasound. "Well, look what we have here!" she said. "We have two heartbeats." I looked at Hector and he looked like he was going to pass out. But I was so glad to know that with Hector being a twin and me having twins, that the baby was his. I started crying. I was so happy! "Well, Mr. Huerta," Dr. Brown said. "Would you like to know the sex of your children?" "Yes!" He said. "It looks like two boys," the doctor said. I was in disbelief but so happy at the same time. The doctor's visit was over and we held hands all the way to the car. I said, "Let's go visit your brother and tell him!" "I don't think that would be a good idea," Hector said. "Why?" I asked. "It just wouldn't," Hector replied. "So, Rico doesn't allow Gustavo to have visitors?" I asked. He was quiet, but I had the address to Chad's new apartment. I wrote it down when Akilah was at the house Friday. I drove towards 75 North and Hector asked where we were going. I told him we were going to see his brother. The closer we got to Chad's apartment; it was obvious that Hector knew where we were going. But he kept quiet and turned up the music. We pulled up to Chad's apartments and he showed me where they lived. We got out of the car and headed up the stairs. I knew they were home because Chad's car and motorcycle were both there. Hector knocked on the door and Gustavo answered the door. He gave us both hugs and welcomed us in. Chad was on the couch playing video games. "Hey cousin," I said. "What's up, beautiful," he replied. "I know there's a lot going on and at some point, we're going to need to discuss a lot about our relationship," I said. "But right now family, I just wanted to let you know I'm having twin boys!!" I screamed. "Are you serious?!" Gustavo screamed. He jumped up and hugged me so tight I could hardly breathe. Then Chad stood up and said, "The boys couldn't have asked for a better mother!" We all sat down and watched the news and talked about how much fun Freaknik was. Gustavo told me that Piedmont Park was so packed on Sunday that you couldn't even see the grass. He also told me that Chad's fraternity was out in the park with Speedos on like they were at the beach. We all laughed and talked and decided to eat at Houston's-my favorite spot. Life was good and I had to accept Chad's lifestyle. It was bad enough that he would have to deal with enough drama from my aunty and Akilah's family. I wasn't going to be against him too. I still never got the whole story on how Gustavo and Chad met, nor did I want to know at this point. I respected Hector for not telling me what I wanted to know about Chad and Gustavo's situation. That was his brother and he loved and respected him with all his heart.

Chapter 28: Cruel Intent

I opened my eyes and looked at Chad while he was sleeping on my chest. I was going to wake him up and tell him to move because I couldn't breathe when all of a sudden, this heat came over me. It felt like I couldn't breathe, but I was still breathing. It felt like I was sweating, but there was no sweat. I didn't know what to make of it. I couldn't ask him to move. All I could do was sit there and stare at him. I looked at his hair and how it was perfectly cut. And I could smell the moisturizer he used on his hair mixed with a little of his sweat. I looked at his big, beautiful, dark arms holding me like I was the only thing that mattered. Then I started crying. But I wasn't sad. I really wasn't sure what I was feeling. I just knew that out of nowhere, something came through my body and gave me a feeling I'd never experienced. "What's up, babe?" Chad asked while he yawned and rubbed his face. "Oh, nothing," I told him. He opened his eyes wide and asked, "You sure you're Ok, babe?" I could smell his morning breath. But today was different. It didn't stink. It smelled like a drug. And I wanted more leaned over and put my tongue all down his throat. Then he put me on my side and sucked my ear as he put his dick inside of me. He took it nice and slow, but I could feel every inch of him inside me. And it felt good. I felt tears running down my face and I guess he could see them.

"What's wrong, baby? Am I hurting you?" he whispered in my ear. "No, babe," I said. "I love you!" I whispered back. "What, baby?" he asked. "Say it again!" as he pushed his dick all the way in me. "I love you...I love you, baby!" I screamed. We fucked and fucked and fucked until I could feel all of him and his cum inside of me. After he came, I went and grabbed a wet rag with some soap on it and wiped his dick and stomach. He just watched me and smiled. Then he started chanting, "Someone's in love...someone's in love. "Stop it!" I screamed as we wrestled in the bed. "What do you want for breakfast?" I asked him. "*Papas con chorizo,* he said in his southern voice. We laughed and then I jumped up and started to cook. I couldn't believe I let Star and Hector talk me into going to hair school this fall at Atlanta Area Tech. Hector's going to be a barber and I'm going to become a beautician. Our plan is to start our own beauty and barber salon. I hadn't told Chad the news that I was going to retire from exotic dancing. But he told me it didn't bother him at first but he didn't think he would be able to deal with it forever. I was going to break the news to him about retiring when Star had my nephews, but I decided to go ahead and tell him. I knew had had been under a lot of stress with Akilah wanting him to pay child support for their new baby girl Paige. She was so cute and so little. I'd only seen her once when Chad's mother brought her over and dropped her off for a couple of hours. Akilah's been making it hard, but Chad told his mom about me. I can tell she doesn't like me. But I know she loves her son, so she will respect his choice, which is me. Sometimes I wonder if it's that we're gay or maybe she thinks at 18 years old, I'm too young to be in a relationship. She's southern as hell, but she's a beautiful older woman. She reminds me of Star. "Baby!?" I yelled. "Yeah, yeah. I'm the man, so what is it?" he bragged while holding my California pager. I know...you love me and you probably want to marry me." He was laughing, but that's what I wanted. I wanted to marry the man I loved, even though I never knew it would be Chad. I always thought it was going to be Kevin. Well, I thought wrong because I loved Chad and I could feel love all through my body. "So what is it?" Chad asked. "What is what?" I asked. I looked down and asked why he was holding my pager. "It's blowing up," he said. I looked down at all the numbers of people that had paged me, but the last one didn't look familiar. It was a Los Angeles area code. It must be my Tia Loose at someone's house. Or maybe she has a new number, I thought. "Ok, I'm taking a shower, Mr. Green Eyes since you ain't sayin' nuthin," Chad said jokingly. "I'm going back to school with Hector," I blurted out. "Good, he said. "So what do you want to major in?" I told him cosmetology. "So you want to be a beautician? He asked jokingly. "Yeah," I said. And that's funny?" "No," he said. "Not really. But I've never heard of you saying anything about hair." "Well, I said. "It hasn't always been a passion of mine, but I want to learn and eventually be a salon owner. What do you think?" "I believe if it makes you happy, and then do it," he said. "Well, I've saved some money up from stripping, so I'm also going to retire my dancing boots…that is if you think I should?" "I would love that!" he said. "Just hold on to your little money and I'll take care of you until you graduate beautician's school. Then I will sit back and let you make all the money!" he kissed me and held me tight. I could feel his dick getting hard again. He picked me up and threw me on the couch. "Wait," I said. "What about breakfast? It's going to get cold!" "This is what we call the Down South Quickie," he said. We finished and my asshole was sore but it was sore because my man was taking what was his, I thought to myself. Yup! I'm the shit! I'm 18. I'm in love and have a man that loves me too. He is my Mighty Mouse. He's not really tall, but strong and long everywhere else, I laughed to myself as I walked into the kitchen and warmed our plates and store bought tortillas' looked over at my pager. It was going off again. I decided to call the number. "Los Angeles County Hospital…how can I help you?" the voice said. My heart raced and I thought my Tia Loose was in the hospital. I hadn't talk to her in about a week and that was unusual. Damn, why didn't I call her? I thought. "What room number?" the voice asked. I looked down at my pager and saw a text that said 308. The phone rang and rang and rang. "Los Angeles County Hospital the voice said again. "Umm, not sure what just happened," I said. "But can I please get room 308?" the phone rang again. I was getting annoyed until I heard the Angel's voice on the line. I knew it! I could hear her voice so clear on the phone. *"Hi, pinche calaweta,"* she said in a low voice. "My God, Bitch!" I screamed. "Where have you been? I've been fucking worried sick about you every day, Angel!" "I'm in the hospital," she said in a whisper. "The hospital? How long have you been there?" I asked. "I'm not sure," she said. Well, are you ok?" I asked. "No," she said. "Is there anyone there with you?" I asked. She said no again. "Alright," I said. "Is there a nurse or anyone I can talk to?" She didn't say anything, but I could tell she was still on the phone. I watched the clock and ten minutes passed. Finally, I heard another voice say, "Hello, this is Nurse Smith. With whom am I speaking?" "This is Gustavo Huerta, Angel's brother," I said. "Well hello," the nurse said. "The hospital has tried to contact Angel's relatives and no one has gotten back with us." "Well, I'm her family and I need to know what happened." "Sir, I'm not allowed to give out that information over the phone," she said. "But I can tell you she's going to be moved to a hospice in a week. Do you know what that is?" "Yes," I screamed. "I'm coming from Atlanta right now." "Can you please hand Angel the phone?" "Yes, no problem," she said. "We'll see you soon. "Angel, can you hear me?" I asked. "Yes," she answered. "I'm on my way!" I said. "I'm coming now." She was quiet but I could hear her sob. It was a light cry-kind of like a dog when he's old and ready to die, but just a little more quiet. "I'm coming, sister," I told her. "I'm coming." I hung up and tried to get my thoughts together before I broke down. I knew I had to be strong and figure out how I was going to get to Los Angeles. Chad walked in the room and asked me what was wrong and I told him the conversation I had with the nurse and Angel. He looked at me and said, "Let's go." "What do you mean?" I asked. "You have to work." "Don't worry," he said. I'll work all that out. Just pack us some bags and food because we're going on a road trip." I knew what he was saying. I just couldn't believe how this man had my back. I ran up to him and gave him a kiss. "Ok, we can do that later," he said. "Let's get ready." So, we got everything together in 45 minutes. Then, I called Hector to tell him what was going on. But he told me Star was having mild contractions. I was happy that my nephews were going to be born, but I had to go get my sister and bring her back to

Atlanta, I thought. Driving that first day, I felt bad for Chad because he wouldn't let me drive without a license. He drove the whole way. We stayed in two different hotels because he was tired and so was I. We had to contain ourselves as much as we could because we made love at both hotels. We tried to make them Southern Quickies. We finally made it and I asked Chad if we could stop at a payphone. I told him I wanted to call my Tia Loose to let her know I was in L.A. She really wanted me to come visit. I just didn't think I would be able to under the circumstances. But I put my change in the pay phone and dialed her number. A man answered the phone. "Hi," I said. "I'm calling for my Tia Loose. Is this Pete?" "The one and only, *vato,*" he said. I laughed and said, "Hello, Pete. I've heard nothing but great things about you from my tia." "Likewise," Pete said in a *vato* kind of way. "Would you like to talk to your tia?" "Yes, please," I said. "How much you going to give me for her, *vato?*" he said. "Hand me that phone, crazy!" I heard my Tia Loose. "Hi, sweetie!" I told her I was sorry for having gone so long without talking to her. "How are you?" I asked. "I'm fine, sweetie. I miss our talks," she said. "I was going to call you tonight and give you some news. We just moved into a big house in Laguna Beach by the ocean and I want all of you to come-even the babies...when they're born, that is," She started laughing. "That's why we haven't talked. I've been busy moving. And even though we had movers, it was still a lot of work. I knew if I called you, I would spill the beans and tell you I moved. Oh well, now you know and now I want my family down here to spend time with their tia." "Well, today's your lucky day," I said. "I'm in Los Angeles right now...me and my boyfriend." "Oh my Goodness!" she screamed. "There is a God!" I told her Angel had called and that she was at L.A County Hospital. "I'm on my way there now," I said. "Ok," my tia said. "I'm getting dressed. What's her last name?" I told her it was Perez and she said she was on her way. She called me mijo again, but I let it slide. I knew she was happy to hear from me. I hung up the phone and went back to the car and gave Chad a kiss. Then, we found the hospital. It kind of looked like shit. We talked to the lady at the front desk and were escorted to the elevator. When we stepped off the elevator, I felt a chill and so did Chad. It was cold and quiet on the floor. The nurse left us at the desk and the woman asked how she could help us. I told the nurse that me and Chad were Angel's adopted brothers and that we had just found out about her condition. It took some time because they said we had to be a relative and show proof in order to go see her. Then, Nurse Smith came out and talked to us. She was an older white woman who kind of looked like Mrs. Kravitz on *Bewitched.* She sat and told me that she was not supposed to give us this much information about a patient. She also told us that someone did a butcher job on her genital area and she had been in a coma for several months. "Is she going to pull through?" I asked. "Like I told you on the phone," Nurse Smith said. "She is going to be sent to a hospice as soon as a room becomes available. Would you like to see her?" I told her I would and she told us to follow her so we could wash our hands and get you a mask. That's when I knew it was serious. I looked at Chad. We walked into room 308. Angel was just lying there asleep. "Should I wake her?" Nurse smith asked. I told her we'd wait. I looked around the room and realized where I was. At that point, I couldn't take it. It took every ounce of my will to keep myself from breaking down. I walked over to her. She looked almost like a skeleton. I leaned over and kissed her forehead and her eyes opened. "Hi, beautiful," I said. "Hi, girl," she said as she smiled. "What happened, sister?" I asked. "Why are you in here?" I was crying all over her and couldn't help it. I never, in a million years, thought I would be at a hospital looking at my sister in a bed near death. "Over there," Angel whispered. I looked where she was pointing. There was a piece of paper on the table. Chad walked over and got it and handed it to me. I looked over at Angel and she told me to read it. I wiped the tears from my eyes and stood up. I looked over at Chad and he had a blank stare. "Read it," Angel said. "Dear G, I'm writing you this letter in case I don't make it to see you again. Naomi, Smiley and a white man named Popeye set me up. The white man talked like he was Mexican, but he's white. I just wanted to tell you how much I loved the way you made me feel. You always told me how pretty and smart I was. I realized in my life that God didn't put many people in my life that really cared about me. But one was enough. And it was you. I also want you to tell your brother that I love him too and even Jaime, if you ever run into him again. I've been wanting to tell you something for a long time. But I couldn't because I never wanted you to be mad at me. But I must tell you now because this is the last chance I'll have. Kevin is no good for you. I've listened to you tell me about him from the first week we met in Mexico. I didn't have a good feeling then and I don't now. He's not for you, so don't waste any more time with him." I stopped because I couldn't read anymore. I handed the letter to Chad. I got on my knees and laid my head on the side of Angel's bed getting as close to her as I could without hurting her. "Would you like me to finish the letter?" Chad asked. "Yes," Angel said. "I know you have big dreams thinking Kevin's going to be the one and you are going to have a great life but he's not the one. Is there one out there for you? Of course there is. You're so beautiful. Not only are you good looking but I know you loved me unconditionally, even when we were in the shed and didn't even know what each other looked like. I know you hated when I would bring up Mexico and what happened to you. But it happened and there's nothing we could do about that or anything else we didn't like in our life. I was sick from what they told me, but the nurses and doctors said I was lucky to live at all with all the blood I'd lost. They also told me I had full blown AIDS. I never tricked without a condom! Never! Maybe I was infected from those perverts in Mexico. Or maybe when I was molested at the foster homes I lived in. It doesn't matter because it's life and it's now. You remember how you always bragged to people about how I stay positive and nothing gets me down? Well, I'm going to tell you why I'm like that. I learned at a very young age to forgive. I had to forgive anyone who trespassed against me. It works. I forgive and let go. I want you to do the same with whoever hurts you- now or in the past. I've already seen Heaven. I was there and then I came back. Heaven was a beautiful, blue ocean with waves so high. I mean really high. You and me were talking and you let me know I was going to be Ok. It was a paradise. I was almost there forever but I fought and I fought because I couldn't say what I needed to say to you. So, I'm saying it now with the hopes that you read this letter. I love you now, then and always. P.S...take care of yourself. P.S.S...I know you love me too. See you in the other world one day. Love your sister, Angel Perez." Chad put the letter on the bed and walked out the room. I sat there and couldn't believe this was happening. This was the worst I'd ever felt in my life. I thought seeing my mom fucked up on drugs was the worst. But it wasn't. This was, and I didn't want to be there. I wanted to go in a closet and hide. I lay on the hospital floor and cried. And then I heard, "Get up, get up," Angel said. I stood up and looked her in the eyes. "Let's be happy," she said. "Please let's be happy." "How?" I wondered aloud. "Girl, you can do it," Angel whispered and we both laughed. I couldn't believe she was still calling me girl and wanting to have fun. I tried my hardest to keep a smile but I couldn't see her on the hospital bed. It got the best of me. Mr. Huerta, you have a visitor," Nurse Smith said as she walked in the room. "I'll be right back, Angel," I said. "Don't you worry. I'm going to change her I.V. and she will be here waiting for you," Nurse Smith said. I walked out the room and could see Chad and Tia Loose down the hall sitting in some chairs. I walked but felt weak. I wished this was a nightmare and would soon be over. My tia asked if I was alright. But she could tell I wasn't. We all sat down and Chad explained to my tia what the nurse had told us and the letter that him and I read. "So, what do we do from here?" Tia Loose asked. We were all quiet and then Chad said, "I'm going to the restroom and then to find a pay phone. I need to make some calls." I gave him a kiss and he walked off. "Is he your first love?" Tia Loose asked. "Yes and no," I said. "No, because I was infatuated with a guy since I was 6 or 7. We had something. I'm not sure what it was. And yes to Chad because I don't ever remember feeling so great about loving someone. I can't explain it but it just hit this week if you can believe it." "I believe it," Loose said. "I was trying to fight my feelings for him and didn't want to feel good about loving someone when I didn't know where the love of my life was." "I don't understand," Tia Loose said. "For the last couple of months I've felt so happy when Chad's around. It's so close to what I feel when I'm around Angel. I tried to fight feeling good about myself around him because I didn't want to share what I have with

Angel with anyone. But then I couldn't fight it. The feelings were there, but they were also feeling that I could only have with a man. I have every feeling in the world when I'm with Chad. He makes me forget all the pain I have. I'm the same way around Angel. She makes me feel Ok about being Gustavo Huerta. I love being around her, I love the fact that she accepts everything fucked up and evil that has been done to us and still smiles." I stared at my tia as she wiped her eyes. Then I said, "I don't know if I can handle this, tia This is too much," I said weeping. She came over to me and wiped my tears with a Kleenex and said, "You have to handle this, Gustavo, my beautiful nephew. You're strong. You're very strong," she said. You've overcome losing your mother to drugs and being at peace with it. I saw it when we were in Sacramento. I know how much you loved my sister and you've made peace with her not being who she used to be. I loved her and I love you." I listened to her and said, "I would give my life for my brother." But Angel and me have something that you couldn't even imagine to understand," I said. "I do understand," my tia said. "What do I do about Angel?" "I'm not sure," Loose said crying. "I think maybe we should pray." We held hands and took turns asking God for the strength and wisdom to help us make it through this time of need. Chad came back with food from Burger King for all of us. We ate and then I walked back to Angel's room. As I walked in, I looked at the numbers 308 on the door and felt pain. Lots of pain. I walked over and had a seat so I could get myself together. I wiped my tears with a napkin and sat in the hospital chair in her room and just stared at her while she slept. Chad came in the room and told me that tia loose needed to ask Angel what she wanted to do with her body when she passed? I couldn't believe I was having a conversation with the man I loved about what to do with the body of the sister I loved when she passed. Chad also told me we needed to write down what she told us she wanted to happen after her death and have her sign it. I was numb. I felt like my body was present but my soul was gone. The next morning, Chad woke me up. He'd slept in the waiting room and I slept in a chair. I talked to Angel and shared stories with her when she was awake. Her eyes popped open when she heard Chad come into the room. He told me my tia was in the waiting area with breakfast. I asked him if he didn't mind getting my toothbrush for me in the car. I stood up to go kiss Angel before I went to brush my teeth and eat. Suddenly, all I heard was a beeping sound that was so loud it hurt my ears. In a matter of seconds, there were nurses in the room. They told me to stand back. Shortly after, they said they'd lost her. I couldn't cry. I couldn't scream. I was so in shock that I just wanted to find a gun and kill myself. I just stood in the room. My tia came in and hugged me but I couldn't hug her back. She let me go and went over and kissed Angel on her forehead. Then I went over and touched her curly, black hair that used to be so thick. Now it was thin and almost straight now. "I love you and I always will," I whispered in her ear. I kissed her for the last time and walked out of the room. I felt like I was floating. I saw doctors and nurses. I heard Tia Loose say something, but all I wanted was a bed. Chad came over and hugged me tight. "We're going to follow Tia Loose to her house," he said. "What about Angel's will?" I asked. "Don't worry," Tia Loose said. "I'm going to take care of all that right now." Chad and I walked to the car and waited for her to come out. Then we drove to her house. I looked out the window and everything was just beautiful. I looked over at Chad. He smiled at me and it looked like even his gold tooth was winking at me. Still, as much as I wanted to be happy, all I wanted was a bed. We arrived at my tia's huge beach house. "This is gorgeous, baby!" Chad said. I looked and tried to speak, but the words would not come out of my mouth. Tia Loose motioned for us to come on in. So we did. I could tell she was excited to be in her big, luxurious house. She wanted to show us around, but I just couldn't. I needed a bed so badly. "Are you boys ready to eat or would you like a drink?" she asked. I tried to be nice and instead just asked if I could lie down. "Of course you can," she said before escorting us to this big room on the second floor of the house. "Ok guys," she said. "Here's your room. She gave us a kiss and told us that if we needed her, she would be downstairs. We closed the door and I walked to the window to see how beautiful the ocean was. I just stared into the blue water hoping that maybe Angel would appear or give me a sign that she was in

Heaven. I couldn't stop thinking about the letter. I opened the envelope that I'd put the letter in, and pulled it out. I turned around and looked at Chad spread out on the huge bed. "I'm going to take a shower," he said. "Do you feel like joining me?" I wanted to go over and kiss him, but I didn't. I told him I would be in the restroom in a minute to join him. He came over and kissed me and then left the room. I unfolded the letter and began to read it again. I read it three times and thought, whoever this white boy named Popeye is, I'm going to find him and kill him. I put the letter back in the envelope and tried to think where I'd heard the name Smiley before. Then I remembered that a lot of *vatos* in Sac have that nickname. I shut the blinds and closed the curtains. I couldn't see a thing except for a crack of light coming out of the restroom where Chad was taking a shower. My first thought was to just get under the covers and stay there until I woke up from this nightmare. But instead, I walked into the restroom because I knew I was musty and needed to wash my ass before I got into my tia's beautiful bed. I took off my clothes and started to head to the shower. Then, I stopped to think why God had spared my life and blessed me with Chad. Why was it that I was alive and didn't have AIDS but instead had the man of my dreams? "Come on, baby," Chad said. "I need you." I walked over and got in the huge shower. Chad took a washcloth and started cleaning me everywhere. After he finished, he pulled me near him and the water just poured on us. I kept my eyes open and just tried to look the best I could with water and shampoo rolling down my face. I stood still while he kissed me around my neck and my ears. Chad turned the water off and said, "Baby, I'm going to dry you off and we're going to lie down." I was quiet and I felt weak. He dried me off, picked me up and carried me to the bed. Then, he tucked me under the covers and went back into the restroom to dry himself off. "You're so strong," I said. He walked back into the room naked and sat on the side of the bed. "Why do you say that?" he asked. "Because you pick me up all the time like I weigh 80 pounds," I said laughing. But the laugh turned into a cry and I couldn't stop I rolled over so he couldn't see my face. He sat on the bed behind me rubbing my back and saying it was going to be Ok. I woke up. The room was pitch black and I wasn't sure where I was. I felt around the bed to see if anyone was lying in the bed with me. My heart started beating fast because I knew I had just woken up from a nightmare. I stood up and felt around the room. I just knew it was mine and Chad's place. I felt around and felt around. I knocked something over while feeling around the room. I found a light switch, so I pushed it up to see the same beautiful room that was in the nightmare I'd just had. I put my back toward the wall and slid down to the floor. I just stared at the bed and wondered how I was going to live the rest of my life without Angel. I woke up to Chad asking me why I was on the floor. I couldn't answer him. "I talked to your brother," he said. I didn't respond to him. "Your brother is a daddy." I looked at him and smiled. "Parker and Seth Huerta," he said. I covered my face and started crying. Chad tried to pull my hands from my face, but I wouldn't let go. "Parker is 6 pounds 3 ounces and Seth is 7 pounds 6 ounces," he said. I told your aunt that we needed to get on the road tomorrow afternoon at the latest. I just listened and didn't say a word. "She suggested that you stay and she would fly you home when you felt a little better. I told her I would talk to you to see how you feel." "I'm leaving with you," I said. "Are you sure?" he asked. "Yes, but I just need to lie down," I said. "I think you should eat something, babe," he suggested. I told him I didn't have an appetite. "Well, I'm going to go eat. Your aunt just cooked," he said. "I'll bring you something in case you get hungry later." "Tell her husband I'm sorry for being rude," I said. "I just don't feel too good right now." Chad told me Pete was in Texas but was driving back that night and would be there with his best friend the next morning. Pete's friend was some guy from Sacramento that my aunt said she thought I knew when I was little. "Will you please call Hector and Star and tell them that I love them and my nephews?" I asked. "I already took care of it," Chad said. "Their anxious for you to get home and meet them." he kissed me on my lips and said he would be back up in a little bit. I woke up to Chad kissing me on my neck. "Where are we?" I asked. "We're still at your Aunt Loose's house," Chad said. I asked what time it was and he said it was around midnight. "Are you in the mood to walk down to the beach?" he asked. "Not really," I said. "Do you mind if I put it in for a minute?" he asked. "Sure," I said. I could hear Chad pouring some lube out of a bottle. And then I felt him rubbing it in my ass. Seconds later, he was in me. "Can I go deeper?" he asked as he lay sideways and made love to me. "Yes, baby...go deeper," I said. "Go deeper baby...please go deeper." I knew he needed a release from everything we'd been through the last couple of days and I knew I needed him to want me. He held me tight as he went deeper in my hole. "Baby, thank you...baby, thank you," Chad said over and over. He was going slowly. But he was all the way in me and he started fucking me harder and harder. "Cum with me baby...cum with me," Chad said. I spit on my hand and grabbed my hard dick that was ready to explode. And then I knew from him holding my body tight with his arms and his legs that he was going to also explode inside of me.

Chapter 29: Chicken's Roost

I woke up again. But this time the curtains were open and I could see the sunrise on top of the ocean. Chad was sitting in a chair close to the window. He was also staring out at the water. "Good morning," I said. "Morning, baby," Chad said. "I hate seeing you so sad. I wanted to say something to make your pain go away but I didn't know what to say." I can't believe she's gone," I said thinking of Angel. "I know," Chad said. "She was supposed to be here so I could tell her about how good you treat me and that Hector has kids," I said. "Why would someone so great have to die so young? Why would someone like her have to be alone almost up to the minute she passed? Why didn't anyone comfort her while she was sick? I just can't understand why my friend; my sister that was a great human being, be left alone to die." "She wasn't," Chad said. "We were there." "But what if we hadn't made it?" I asked. "But we did make it," Chad said. "And I believe it gave her the peace to move on." I stood up, walked over to Chad and said, "Thank you for everything." We took a shower, put our belongings in our luggage and decided to go downstairs and spend an hour with Tia Loose before we left. We opened the door and I looked down the long hallway and just loved how nice her house was in Laguna. I was impressed with Laguna beach and happy for my tia. We walked towards the stairs and I heard some men talking. I couldn't make out what they were saying. I just knew it sounded like lots of men laughing and talking. We made it to the stairs. As one man was walking upstairs, the other two were just standing by the door as if they were about to leave. The man walking up the stairs looked like someone I'd seen on TV. I just couldn't remember who. He saw us and said, "You must be Gustavo." He sounded Mexican. "Yeah, I'm Gustavo," I said. "And this is Chad." "You boys are some good looking men!" he said. Then he put his hands on my shoulder and said, "I'm Pete...your tia's husband." I wanted to push his hand off of me when he touched me. But I didn't. Still, I wasn't sure why I felt that way. We all walked down stairs and three other guys shook our hands. I noticed that one of them looked strange. He had lots of extra skin, but he wasn't fat. My tia came out to where we were standing and asked if everyone had met. "Smiley, I think you met my nephew years ago," she said. I heard the name Smiley and remembered back to childhood when he was fat and looked like Jabba the Hut. I looked around. Everyone was smiling and talking. Then I looked closer and listened to Pete talking and I said, "Popeye. You go by Popeye, right?" "Yes, *vato*," Pete answered smiling. "How did you know his nickname, Gustavo? "My tia asked. "Are you white?" I asked. "White on the outside...*cholo* on the inside," Pete said laughing. "When's the last time you seen Naomi or Angel?" I asked. I looked at his face change. He wasn't smiling anymore. "Sweetie, what's wrong?" Loose asked." "Popeye!!!" I screamed. "Are you Ok, *vato*?" Smiley asked. "No, bitch!" I screamed. "I'm not Ok!" Before I knew it, I was punching the shit out of Smiley. He didn't even have time to punch me back. And then I heard a gun. "Listen, *puto*," Popeye said. "You better calm down!" "Put that gun down, Pete!" Tia Loose said. Chad pulled me off of Smiley, who was on the ground, while the other two guys just stood in shock. "I know you two mutherfuckers killed Angel!" I screamed. "You white bitch!" I watched as my tia tried to push the gun down but couldn't. "Get out of my house," Popeye said.

"You're going to pay for this," I promised. "Stop!" my tia screamed. "Stop it, Gustavo! What's wrong with you?!" "They killed Angel!" I said. "Your husband did it." By now, I was crying uncontrollably. I felt Chad grab the bags and my arm. We walked backwards out of the house and all the way to the car. Chad told me to buckle up and we hauled ass out of there. We drove to the first police station we could find. We went in and told them everything showing them the letter Angel wrote. We were at the station all day and night.

Chapter 30: Searching for Normal

I'd just gotten off the phone with the detectives in Los Angeles who were handling the case. They told me they'd found Popeye and Smiley and the judge refused to set bail for them. I was glad, although I wanted them to come find me so I could kill Popeye myself. I was so glad Lorena's flight was coming in at 1 p.m. because since we'd been back in Atlanta, I hadn't gotten out of bed for anything. Chad said I was in mourning. But I felt like a part of me was dead. I'd only seen my nephews once and that was when they came over after leaving their first doctor's appointment. They were the most beautiful babies I'd ever seen. Seth and Parker were so cute but so pale. They were very light skinned-almost white and Parker had a head full of red hair. I guess sometimes when you mix Mexican and black you just don't know how they're going to come out looking. I knew I needed to get out of this funk for me and my nephews. They deserved to have an uncle that's not so fucked up in the head, I thought. I couldn't believe Hector and me was about to start school. I had to get my shit together. Lorena was going to be here until the following Monday night. I told her I wasn't up for going out and she said it was ok because she really just wanted to spend some time with me. I told Chad he should hang out some with his friends since he'd been making sure I was alright the whole time. He said there hadn't been a dull moment since he met me. He said drama had followed us but it was just a test of our love for each other. He also said that when he met and found out my age, he was not going to let himself fall in love with me. I told him it was too late because I knew he loved me. We decided to have a cookout that Sunday and invite Caleb, Todd and Bilal. Lorena was going to love my friends, I thought. "Baby, are you ready?" Chad asked. We left the house and headed to the Atlanta airport to pick up Lorena. Then we headed back to the house. We talked a little about her flight and asked if she was hungry. She said she was, so we stopped and picked up some barbecue for lunch. I knew Lorena had a million things to ask me since I really hadn't answered any phone calls. But I knew she was going to wait until it was just her and me. We made it back to our place and Chad said he was going to do some running around and would be back shortly. We walked into our apartment and Lorena grabbed my hand and walked me over to the sofa. "I love Chad!" she said. "Me too!" I said. "You would never, in a million years, even know he was gay!" she said. "That's how I like them," I said. We laughed. Suddenly, I was feeling so guilty about being happy and I started to tear up. "I'm sorry, Gustavo," Lorena said. "I know how much Angel meant to you. Can you tell me what happened?" I hadn't talked about Angel's death or how it had happened since we were at the police station. Once we'd left, I'd kept pretty quiet about it. Finally, I wiped my tears and told Lorena everything. When I looked at the time, it was almost 5 p.m. We'd talked for hours. I looked over at Lorena and she was wiping her tears. "Have you spoken with your tia?" she asked. "No," I said. "And I don't think she's called." Chad wanted to call her, but I told him no, not yet." "Do you think she knew about it?" Lorena asked. I told her I wasn't sure. Then she asked me if I was mad at my tia. "To be honest, I really don't give a fuck about her," I said. "I know that's probably fucked up, but guess what? My sister is gone and she's not coming back, so fuck all of them." I hope she didn't know anything about Angel. "If she did know something, why would she come to the hospital?" Lorena asked. I told her I didn't know. Then I changed the subject. "I wonder where Chad is?" I asked. "I want to meet a guy like Chad," Lorena said. "You think there any good guys in Sac?" I told her that there was good and bad guys everywhere. "So are you ready to hear about your good girlfriend Lupita?" Lorena asked.

"That bitch gave up her baby for adoption." "What?!" I screamed. "Yeah, one of my homies went to this club in Old Sac and she was out dancing and having herself good old time," she said. "Well, how does that make her someone who gave up their baby?" I asked. "She told my homeboy she didn't have no kids," Lorena reported. "So, either she gave it up or lost it. But either way, that hoe's out fucking and sucking for free." We both laughed, but mine was a laugh that didn't feel that great. Even though I hated Lupita, she was still one of my best friends growing up, I thought. "I'm not even 19 and I've been through more shit then an 80 year old," I said. "My dad always says you and Hector are special boys and are on this Earth for something great," Lorena said. "Yup," I joked. "Shaking this ass for some dollars." I started laughing. "When you started, you loved stripping. What happened?" Lorena asked. "I love dancing for men and traveling and making money and I didn't want to give it up," I confessed. "But I fell in love and I do love Chad. I couldn't imagine thinking about another man." "Well, you don't have to love the guys you dance for," Lorena said. "Just dance for them right." I kind of agreed but I couldn't even fake it when all I wanted was Chad. "Damn, bitch!" she said. "He has you dick whipped!" I agreed again. "He has me something; something that feels great and safe," I said. "I love Chad." "I know that's right!" Lorena said.

Chapter 31: A Woman's Decisions

I didn't know having twins was going to be so much work. But I sure am glad I had them with a man who helps me out. I heard the phone ring so I picked it up and said hello. "Hi, girl!" Nichelle's country voice said. I knew it was her but I asked if it was her anyway. "Yeah, girl! Who else would it be?" she asked. "You said I'm your only female friend." She started laughing. "Hey, girl," I said. "Where have you been hiding?" "Girrrlll, it's a long story," she said. "I'll have to fill you in when I see you." I asked her when she was coming to Atlanta. "I'm here now!" she said. "I just left this old man's house I came to visit for the weekend. Girl, he has money but his house was nasty and so was his dick. I couldn't do it. I tried but I couldn't. I told Nichelle to come over and she could stay Labor Day weekend with us if she didn't mind being bothered with twin boys. I also told her that Hector was going to be working at the club all weekend making all the money he could possibly make. I was glad Nichelle was coming over and spending some time with me. After I danced for Rich at his bachelor party, I told Nichelle and she was pissed. Nichelle told me she cursed Quincy out for even being a part of that scandalous shit. I believed Nichelle didn't know any of the shit that was going on like those white bitches Meagan, Summer and Debbie did. That shit had to make the Guinness Book of World Records for being the most embarrassing and hateful things in life, I thought. I still don't believe Royalty had any idea about me dancing for my own boyfriend's bachelor party. It pisses me off every time I think about it. And to make things worse, that bitch gave me cocaine and wanted me to finish dancing for those bastards. She better be glad that the cocaine didn't hurt my babies. I was in the living room breast-feeding Parker when I heard the doorbell ring. I walked over to the door with him still attached to my breast. I looked out the peephole and it was Nichelle looking as radiant as ever. I opened the door and she screamed in her southern voice, "Hey, mama!" "Shhh," I whispered. "Hector's asleep. He will be waking up to go to the gym and in about an hour." "Girl," Nichelle said. "You look so good! And damn! You lost all your weight already." She opened up my robe and looked at my body in my granny panties and said, "Bitch, you mean to tell me you had twins and didn't even get a stretch mark? Damn you're lucky. I was only pregnant four months and I have stretch marks all over like I had a fight with Freddie Kruger. "When were you pregnant?" I asked. "Girl, long story!" she said. "Where's the other baby?" she asked. "In the room with Hector, I said. "Well, let me take a look as she pulled the baby blanket away from Parker's head as he was still eating. Nichelle looked up at me and her smile became a look of shock. "Nichelle, what's the matter?" I asked. "Girl, where can I put these bags?" she asked. I pointed to the guest bedroom, which was my room growing up. She walked her bags into the room and walked back out just as soon as she could. "Where's the bar?" she asked. "I don't have one," I said. "But there's vodka in the freezer and champagne in the fridge." "Well, let me make me a stiff drink," she said. I heard our bedroom door open and it was Hector walking out with Seth. He was crying, so I knew he was hungry because he was my quiet baby. I introduced Hector to Nichelle. "Hey, what's up," he said. "Hi, Hector!" Nichelle said. "I've heard so much about you that I feel like I know you!" "Likewise," Hector said. "Baby, Nichelle is going to stay with us this weekend if you don't mind." He said it was cool. "I'm about to throw on my gym clothes and go work out if I can," he said. "Of course, baby. Nichelle can help me while you're gone," I said. Hector put on his gym clothes and drove off. I was so happy he'd passed his driver's license test because I needed him to be able to drive with our babies. I looked over at Nichelle and she poured herself another vodka and cranberry. She looked over at me and asked had Hector left. I told her he had as I laid Seth in his basinet. "Star, why didn't you tell me you had Rich's babies?" she asked. I was quiet and didn't say nothing. "Star," she repeated my name. "I know you're not in denial about this are you?" Still I said nothing. I just sat quietly on the couch. Nichelle walked over to both of the babies in the bassinet and said, "Good Lord! Those *are* Rich's kids!" "Why do you say that?" I asked. "Now girl, I know you're not playing dumb," she said. "Those kids are pale. And one has red hair. Hector is browner than me and I'm black. And Parker looks just like him." "Well, you look Latina or mixed and you said both of your parents are black," I reasoned. "That's true," Nichelle said. She stood there for a minute with her finger on her chin and then took a big sip of her drink and said while screaming and laughing, "You're about to be a rich bitch!" She walked over, sat on the couch and looked me in my eyes and said, "The day I met you, I was just glad that there was another sista with me in Colorado-and a black ass beautiful sister at that. And when I found out your age I thought, damn she's young and has sense enough not to fuck with broke bustas. So I'm telling you that you need a blood test ASAP," with a serious look on her face. "But what if they are Rich's sons?" I asked. "Then what?" Then you stick that bastard for everything he has," she counseled me. I just sat and listened to her. She told me he didn't give a fuck about me, so why should I give a fuck about him. I sat there and thought about how much I loved Hector and how it would hurt him. And then I wondered if I could really live a lie if they weren't Hector's sons, I thought. "If they are Rich's, then you sit back and live off that fat child support check!" she said. I stood up and walked over to the vodka bottle and thought about taking a drink. But Nichelle said, "Girl, it will work out. I promise." "I'm in love with Hector," I said. "He is fine," she said. "But I need a tall, black, rich, big dick man!" "Well, he's not tall," I said. "But he does have a big, black dick," I said. "Are you serious?" Nichelle asked. "Yes," I said. It's long, fat and so brown that when it's soft, it looks as black as my arm." "Damn, girl," she said laughing. "I may need to get me a Mexican. "I love him," I said. "He can fight...he can fuck...he has street sense...he's intelligent...I mean, what else could I ask for?" "He's 18 and strips for a living, girl," she countered. "Not to be an asshole, but don't you think one day he might want some different pussy? I could be wrong but Star, you have two kids and you need to look out for your future." I listened to her and she made lots of sense, so we sat there and weighed the pros and the cons. "Ok, enough talking about me, Nichelle. How have you been?" I asked. "Girl, fucking with Quincy dumb ass ain't easy," she said. "What did he do this time?" I asked. "Well, I was four months pregnant and I caught him at his apartment he has in North Carolina, she said. "He was in the bed with two of those raggedy white girls you met!" she said. "Who?" I screamed. "Debbie and Summer's big titty ass," she said. "Oh no, girl," I said. "I'm sorry to hear that." "Me too," she said. "Well, what happened to the baby?" I asked. She said she miscarried from the stress. "I'm so sorry, Nichelle! Why didn't you call?" She didn't answer. Instead she wanted to just change the subject. "So, what's up for this weekend?" she asked. "Well, we promised Gustavo and my cousin that we would stop by and brings the boys over on Sunday for a cookout," I said. "Would you like to come?" I asked. "Is everyone there going to be gay?" she asked. "I told her I wasn't sure but that it was a possibility. "Good, I love hanging around a bunch of fags," she said sarcastically. Girl, you better be careful with that word," I said. "The fags are crazy in Atlanta." We laughed and sat to talk some more. It was good to finally have a friend other than Hector in my life. Even though my cousin and me are still close, it's taking some time getting used to seeing him in love with a man.

Chapter 32: Gone

Lorena and I just talked and talked until Chad came walking in the door with some red roses for me. "Baby, are these for me?" I asked. "Yes, he said. "And I bought some for Lorena too, but they're in the car with all the groceries I bought for Sunday's cookout." "Oh, I love you, brother-in-law!" Lorena said as she hugged Chad. Lorena and I followed Chad to his car to help bring in the groceries. We finished putting everything away and talked about how fun the cookout was going to be. I walked into the bedroom and rolled a blunt for us to smoke while me and Lorena marinated the meat. I was sitting on the bed when Chad came into the room and said, "I'm glad to see you having a good time with Lorena." "Yeah," I said. "We talked a lot today about everything that's gone on the last month and she just kept saying that I'd been through bad times before and I can overcome anything with faith." "She's telling you the truth, Gustavo," he said. "I know," I said. I just can't think too much about Angel or I start getting frustrated with myself." "Why?" Chad asked. "I mean, if I hadn't gone to New York that weekend with Rico, I could have talked her out of leaving with that skank bitch Naomi," I said. "Well, what if you did stay and she still left," he asked. "She wouldn't have left because she trusted me like I trusted her and she would have listened to me," I said. "Ok, well, we can't change the past, so let's just concentrate on today," he said. I knew he was trying to help and as much as I loved him. I just didn't think he understood the pain I was in," I thought. I finished rolling my blunt and went into the kitchen so we could smoke. "I feel like dancing," Lorena said. Chad and I started laughing at the same time. "What's so funny?" she asked. "I do feel like dancing!" "Well then...let's go dance," Chad said. "Where?" I asked. "Lorena doesn't have a fake ID and you know, since I'm not stripping anymore, Rico might tell them I'm not 21 at any of the clubs we go to." "Why would he do that?" Chad asked. "I don't know if he would," I said. "I'm just saying." "You're high, *pinche calaweta*," Lorena said. I agreed. I was high as a kite. Lorena and I finished up in the kitchen and Chad told us we should take a short nap and wake up at 11 p.m. to get ready for the club. "We're going to start getting ready at 11 tonight?" Lorena asked. "Yeah, is that too early?" Chad asked. "What time do they close?" she asked. "Well, this club is called the Sleazy Queezy and it closes at 6 a.m.," he said. "How come I haven't heard of that club?" I asked. "You have," he said. "You just haven't been. But tonight, we're going to the Marquette Lounge." "Hell yeah," I said. "I've been wanting to go there." Lorena went to our guest bedroom and me and Chad did what we loved to do most...and that was fuck. We made love and then both of us fell asleep. The alarm went off at exactly at 11 p.m. and I jumped up and showered. I let Chad sleep a little longer. I put on my clothes and went into Lorena's room and watched her put on her makeup and curl her hair. "Lorena, you look pretty as hell," I said. "I feel fat," she said. "I think I'm about to start my period." "Gross," I said. "Girl, you wished you had a period!" she joked. We laughed and sat in the living room to wait for my sexy man to finish getting ready. "I'm done, shawties!" he yelled as he walked into the room. "Baby looking good!" I screamed. "Looking dapper, *mi hermano*," Lorena said. We locked up and got in the car drinking Hennessy and Coke. We took the back streets from where we lived to MLK and Ashby. Chad parked next to a McDonald's and the parking lot was packed. Is this a straight club? Lorena asked. "Nah, shawty...this is gay," Chad said. "Really?" she asked. "Because the guys in line look hella straight." We got out of the car and stood in line. Once we walked in, they were jamming Miami bass music! We walked over to the bar and ordered more Hennessy. "I can't believe some of these men are gay!" Lorena screamed. "Their all gay," I said. "Wow!" she said. "I've only been here one day and I'm having the time of my life!" "I'm glad," I said. "What you two talking about?" Chad asked. "Nothing," I said smiling. "I'm glad to see you smiling," he said "I am too," Lorena said. "It's time for you to be happy, G," she added. "You've been through too much shit in your short life." "Short life? Don't be talking down to me just because I ain't 6 feet like you," I said laughing. "No, silly. I mean you're only 18," she laughed. "I'm only 18, but haven't seen nearly as much as you have. You deserve Chad and whatever else God brings to you." We hugged and then I looked over at Chad. He proposed a toast. "In life, you get very few real friends…so if you do, treat them with love and respect." We cheered and all hugged again. Then Lorena wanted to give a toast too. "G, I have known you for almost all of my life and have always been intrigued with who you are as a person and as a brother. I know Angel is looking down as your angel and is proud of you just like I am. This cheers for Angel!" We all cheered but I couldn't take hearing Angel's name anymore. I knew they were trying to be nice but it felt like a knife in my heart. "Look," I said. "I need to dance. So we all walked on the dance floor and shook what our mamas gave us. The next morning, I woke up to Chad getting dressed. "What time is it?" I asked. "10 a.m.," Chad said. "Why are you getting up?" It's Saturday," I asked. I'm going to catch up on some more work at the office and then run by mom's house and take her with me to see my daughter." He leaned over and kissed me and told me he would check on me later to see if Lorena or I needed anything. Then he left. I fell back asleep and when I woke up, it was 3 p.m. I decided to get up and go into Lorena's room to see if she was awake. She wasn't so I pulled back her covers and got in the bed with her. She woke up shortly after I jumped in the bed with her and we talked about how hung over we were. We decided to stay in and watch movies. I told her how I felt guilty for not really giving Rico a notice that I was quitting and I knew at some point, I needed to call him and let him know about Angel if he didn't already know. I also told Lorena how I just stopped calling Johnny Rodriguez and I knew he was pissed with me. I just knew there was no reason to call him if I was in a relationship. I didn't want to hurt his feelings. Johnny seemed like he was really into me. But, maybe I was just another client that paid him with my good ass instead of money. Chad called and we told him we could go get something to eat but were too tired for a club. Plus, we needed to get ready for this Labor Day cookout. We decided to just invite close friends and family even though we had enough food and alcohol to feed an army. We also decided to take Lorena to the park for a little while so she could see the Jazz Festival at Piedmont Park. Chad came home and we went to my favorite chicken wing spot. We came back home and watched movies. We fell asleep shortly after that. The next morning, I woke up and made a quick breakfast and started getting the potato and macaroni salad ready. Lorena woke up and gave me a hand. "Lorena, I wish you lived here," I said. "Maybe I will," she said and I smiled. I was trying to keep a positive attitude as much as I could. But there were times while I was cooking that thoughts of my Tia Loose and Angel came to mind. I tried to cook faster and think of something else. I was excited about seeing the fellas Todd, Caleb and Bilal. I'd juiced them up so much to Lorena that she couldn't wait to meet them. "Lorena," I said. I asked you something yesterday and you ignored my question." "What, Gustavo?" "Are you Ok with seeing Star, Hector and their kids?" She paused and took a swig of the Corona she was sipping on and looked straight at me. Then she said, "Look, I did and do love your brother. But your brother didn't want my baby or me so I must and have moved on." I was quiet and continued to chop celery. "On the plane ride to Atlanta, I thought it might be weird," she said. "And I day dreamed that he wanted me when he saw me. But you know what? After seeing you and Chad, I know God has a good man for me. I just have to be patient." I put down my knife, walked over and gave her a hug. It was 1 p.m. and Caleb and the rest of the fellas were first to come over. I fixed everyone a drink while Lorena talked to the guys about where they were from and how liked going to an all men's college. She also told them how she knew Kevin and had grown up with him. You know Kevin wanted to come, Bilal said. "That's nice," I said from the kitchen. Everyone fell out laughing at my response. Chad was walking in and out the house taking out and bringing in meat. About an hour later, my brother and Star walked in with my nephews. I heard a female's voice that I'd never heard, so I peeked out of the kitchen and saw this tall, beautiful girl with curly hair like Mariah Cary's. Caleb said, "You better work, ma!" I walked out into the living room and the fellas were ranting and raving about how beautiful Star and Nichelle were. I looked over at Lorena. She was quiet. I walked over to her and said asked if she wanted another Corona. "Yeah," she said. I'm going to grab a beer and go help Chad like I should have been doing." "So you are twins!" Nichelle said. "You're cute too. Are those green contacts?" Everyone started laughing. "No, I said. "They're mine. "I dated a guy once and he was a good old country boy until I went over his house and found green, blue and purple contacts along with panties and bras in his drawer." Everyone started laughing again. Even my brother was laughing. I finished up with the sides. Nichelle came in and asked if she could get a taste. "Sure," I said. "Damn, boy!" she said. "This is good! Can you cook Mexican food this good?" "Sure can!" I said. "I've met my new best friend," she joked. "Shit, I thought I could do it all. "Do what all?" Caleb asked Nichelle as he walked into the kitchen. "Well, let's see," she said. "I can cook up some turnip and collard greens and make 'em look like a million dollars with 15 cents and I got good pussy." Everyone fell out on the floor. It was good to see everyone having fun. Hector took the boys into our room and laid them on our bed. "Where's my cousin," Star asked. "He's outside at the grill," I said. She walked into the kitchen and told me how sleep deprived she and my brother were from having to wake up all times of the night with my nephews. It was good to talk to Star because I really liked her for my brother. "Hey, hey, hey," Chad yelled in the living room. He went into the bedroom to see the babies and then came back out. Nichelle took one look at him and said, "Damn! Brothers with gold teeth are gay now too?" She had us laughing again. "Every damn guy in here is fine," she said. "What's the straight men in Atlanta look like, Richard Simmons?" I looked at Chad and even he was laughing at Nichelle's last comment. The phone rang and Chad answered it. "Hey," he said. "I'm about to go meet my fraternity brothers at the gas station because their lost. I will be right back. Everyone make yourselves at home. Gustavo, you might need to help Lorena watch the food on the grill." "The fraternity brothers are gay too?" Nichelle asked. "Lawd, can I please have some vodka on the rocks?" I looked around and saw how much fun everyone was having. I walked into the restroom in the hallway and splashed water on my face before any negative thoughts came to mind. I walked out and headed to the grill and helped Lorena as we talked about Nichelle and Star. "Chad's car is still here," I said. "Yeah, he took his motorcycle," Lorena said. "He looks good on that bike." we took the last of the meat upstairs and told everyone we would be eating in a few minutes. We heard a knock at the door. "I'll get it, Hector yelled. "Gustavo, could you come here?" he asked. I walked to the door at the same time as Star and heard her say, "Hey, Jessie. Come on in." I made it all the way to the door and saw a cop standing with this tall guy. "Jessie, what's up?" Star asked. "Is anyone here related to a Mr. Chad Sparrow?" the cop asked. "I am," me and Star said at the same time. "Mam, how are you related?" the cop asked. "I'm his cousin," she answered. "And you, sir?" "I'm his boyfriend," I said. "Mam, can you step outside?" the cop asked. "I'm sorry to inform you that your cousin has been involved in an accident. "Is he Ok?" Star asked. I heard the tall man that Star called Jessie start crying out loud. Then I read the cops lips as he said, Mam he has passed away." I couldn't believe what he'd just said. I just stood there in disbelief. Seconds later, all I could hear was, *mijito* doesn't live here. And it repeated in my head over and over.

Made in the USA
Charleston, SC
27 April 2013